I0667551

Meltdown

A Paranormal Fantasy
~
{Book Three}

The Forest Immortal Saga

Kristina Schram

Mischief*Maker*Media

Published by Mischief Maker Media (USA)

First printing: September, 2014

Cover Design, Interior, and Technical Expertise: GorKee

Cover Photo: 1) Angry Young Man, from iStockPhoto

Chapter Icon (Ko-gok): Keegan Unzen

ISBN: 978-1-939397-14-0

Visit Kristina Schram on the World Wide Web at:
www.KristinaSchram.com

Acknowledgements

My beta readers have been awesome, as usual: Elizabeth Schram, Heather Duane, Gordon Unzen, Keegan Unzen, and Ian More. You'd think I'd have more ways to say thank you, being a writer and all. But I don't. I'll just say to all of you that without your help, my books would stink. So thanks for keeping me from stinking!

Dan, you know what you do... You support me through thick and thin, you make my heart swoon, you keep me rooted. You do it all and I'd be a lesser person without you. And Mom, you know how hard this road can be, so thanks for listening to my woes and for being a sounding board for my ideas!

Lastly, to all my fans... Like a tree, you help me dig deep—to search for the sustenance that gives life meaning—and at the same time, you help me reach for the sky. Thanks for rooting for me!

To trees
and
those who cherish them...

Keep fighting
to keep them around
and they'll keep fighting
to keep you around.

A little madness in the Spring
Is wholesome even for the King.

~ Emily Dickinson

She turned to the sunlight
And shook her yellow head,
And whispered to her neighbor:
"Winter is dead."

~ A.A. Milne, When We Were Very Young

When the cold rains kept on and killed the spring,
it was as though a young person had died for no reason.
In those days, though, the spring always came finally
but it was frightening that it had nearly failed."

~ Ernest Hemingway, A Moveable Feast

Chapter One

Out Like a Lion

On a cold, dark afternoon in early April, life was about to change for Gabe Hawthorne. Unaware, he lay on his bed petting his cat, Gypsy, while trying to study for a math test. It was hard to concentrate because he couldn't stop shivering in the cold turret. He pulled the quilt tighter around him and reset the heating pad, which had clicked off.

As he turned the page of his notebook, a cold wind whipped about outside the turret, rattling the odd assortment of windows encircling the room. He sat up, making Gypsy meow in annoyance. Had something just tapped on the glass? His heart beat a little harder. Maybe the Dryads had awoken at last...or were the dark ones coming for him?

He quietly slid out of bed and tiptoed up a short stairway to look through the half-moon window that dominated one wall. The sky was wild and gloomy and seemed disinclined to change its mood. March had come in like a lion and had stayed that way, all the way into April.

The tapping noise increased and he squinted up at the little white balls hitting the glass. Ice. Nothing sinister, just sleet. He breathed a sigh of relief and returned to his bed, gathering the quilt around him once more.

It had been a long winter, and it appeared not to be over yet. While Gabe had his reasons for not wanting winter to end—very good reasons—at the same time he felt like he couldn't stand the frigid cold and the snow...*everywhere snow*...for another second. There had to be two feet still on the ground, and although the days had grown longer, it was still too cold for much melting to occur. Maybe the White Witch of Narnia had turned their world into winter forever, because it certainly seemed that way.

Until lately, most of the winter season had been enjoyable for Gabe. Even though Mrs. Morrigan and Mrs. Deacon had managed to get their survey of the forest completed, the snows had started soon after and nothing could be done to the woods until spring. So that was good news.

The holidays had been festive, as well, with Mom making an extra effort this year to be jolly. He and his brothers, Kris and Jer, didn't get nearly the amount of presents for Christmas as they had in the past, but no one seemed to mind. Gabe was grateful just to have a warm home, plenty of good food, and his family around him. They kept him from brooding too much about the impending spring, when the Dryads, along with the dark ones, would awaken.

He had hoped to have figured out how to save the dying forest and defeat Straif by now, but he hadn't. In any spare moments not taken up with basketball and the seemingly endless supply of homework and chores, he spent reading almost all the tree books on the bookshelf in his turret room. While they'd been interesting, they imparted no new knowledge that would move him closer to a resolution.

On top of this failure, everything seemed to be going wrong lately. The furnace in the basement of their old Maine farmhouse was dying a slow, painful death and they didn't have enough money to buy a new one; Jake Morrigan, after being beat out by Gabe for MVP in basketball, had been working extra hard at making Gabe's life hell; and about three weeks ago, Abazi had descended into some weird sort of funk and had yet to come out of it. When challenged, she claimed it was because she was going through an identity crisis. Which might be true, but it was making her cranky and out of sorts and there was nothing Gabe or the others could do to help her. And they were desperate to— if Abazi wasn't happy, nobody in their group was happy. She'd make sure of that.

If it were just Jake and his goons bullying him, Gabe could have handled that. But Jake also kept making comments about how the bank was going to take the Hawthorne's house if Gabe's parents couldn't pay the property taxes coming due. The house was paid off, but the property tax, which amounted to several thousand dollars, was a problem, and Gabe had overheard Mom telling Dad she wasn't sure where they'd find the money. Grandma May and Grandpa Hawthorne were just barely making it themselves, so they couldn't help.

Since finding out about the taxes, Gabe had taken on extra hours at Woodlands General Store to help out, but he didn't make all that much, and now they only had a week left to come up with the money. Plus, they still had the furnace to replace. The fireplaces would provide some warmth, but according to Mom, they wouldn't keep the pipes in the cellar from freezing. And burst pipes meant more money down the drain. Literally.

The furnace not only heated the house, but their water, too, and Gabe wasn't too keen on taking cold showers, especially lately. Normally a warm-blooded sort of person, he'd felt unusually cold all winter. He eventually determined that it had something to do with being a Dryad, and with what had happened last fall when the Freeze had nearly caught him.

After escaping spending the winter as a tree by eating a berry that kept him from transforming, Gabe had tried once a week to see if he could transform again, and one day he was able to turn a finger into a twig. Since then, he'd avoided all attempts at turning. He was thankful he could still do it, but had no intention of having to hibernate all winter, or being stuck with a stick for a finger. Imagine trying to play basketball, fearing your finger might snap off at any second.

Gabe had yet to forgive Oswald for letting him nearly succumb to the Freeze, or for the fact that Gabe's mom still asked about the Dryad two or three times a week. She wouldn't let it go, and that annoyed Gabe to no end. He'd just as soon forget everything to do with Oswald.

But that was hard to do. Lately Gabe had been experiencing this overwhelming desire to open the small, ornate chest that Oswald had reluctantly returned last summer, to don the dark green cloak inside, to prepare himself. But prepare himself for what?

So far he'd successfully avoided the temptation, but only because the last time he'd touched the cloak, it had made him want to turn into a tree. And that would be bad. Not only might doing so make him stay as one, but worse, being a tree made him want to kill things.

"Gabe!" Kris shouted up the stairs, followed by the sound of pounding feet. "Guess what?"

Gabe sighed. So much for studying. "You finally figured out that two plus two is four?"

Kris ducked his head as he entered the turret room, the top of his dark Mohawk just grazing the frame. Jer, the youngest of the three, was right behind him. "It is?" Kris laughed, then rushed over and jumped onto Gabe's bed, nearly falling off the other end. Jer joined him so that the two of them were draped over Gabe's bed along with half of Gabe. He refrained from yelling at them to get off, but only because their body heat was warming him up.

"What do you want?"

"The storm that's blowing through right now is bringing a warm front with it. It's supposed to be in the sixties tomorrow, and the seventies for the rest of the week!"

Gabe struggled to sit up. "Really? Cause if you're messing with me, I'll cut you." He made a slicing motion across his throat.

"Really," Jer confirmed. "I can't wait!" Chin on his hands and blue eyes sparkling, he sighed happily. "Mom says it's unusual to get that warm in April, but I'll take it since she also said it's unusual to be this cold."

Gabe would take it, too. He'd even give it a hug if he could. Finally his purplish skin color could return to its normal, more attractive hue. "How are we going to celebrate?"

Kris rapped his knuckles on the floor. "I wish we could go out to the woods. I'm worried about Hollie. I thought maybe we'd hear from her at least once this winter, but there hasn't been anything. I've been looking." He frowned worriedly. Over the past couple months, Gabe had spotted Kris at least five different times standing by the barn staring forlornly at the line of trees separated from the yard by the Briar Borders.

Gabe had caught himself scanning the woods on occasion, and once or twice, thought he'd spied Wildrr's watermelon pink cap. But Wildrr wasn't a Dryad, he was a fairy. So while it was nice to know he was around, it didn't say anything about how the Dryads were doing. Maybe he should summon the little guy and ask. He'd told Gabe to call and he would come. Though with Gabe's run of bad luck recently, Mom would come in just as Wildrr made his appearance.

"It's been too cold, Kris," he tried to reassure his brother. "I've felt frozen all winter, and I'm not a tree. I imagine they're still sleeping, but when this warm front comes through they'll start to stir." That was his hope anyway.

Kris sat up and crushed a pillow between his hands. "I'd hate to live like that. I don't think I'm the hibernating type."

"Just on weekend mornings," Gabe poked.

Kris smacked him with the pillow. "That's because I stay up late reading."

"Or inventing. He talks to himself as he works, Gabe."

Kris smacked Jer with the pillow. "I do not, goober. And if I did, it would be the words of a genius."

"Or the ravings of a lunatic!" After a bit of a struggle, Gabe pulled the pillow from Kris's grip and clutched it to his chest.

"We could invite Kimber and Abazi over," Jer suggested. "They could help us celebrate." Jer liked Kimber, but having only recently turned thirteen, he was still cautious about inviting her over for himself. He liked having a good excuse.

"Abazi would probably say no," Gabe said. "She's been in the worst mood lately." And the timing of it worried him. After basketball season ended, they'd gone out on two dates. Before that, both of them had been so busy with school and practice and games and work that they could never seem to find the time to get together. Of course, Gabe would have dropped everything to make it work, but Abazi had been more elusive about setting something up. Finally, a month ago they'd gone to a movie, which was great, though he didn't remember much about the movie, being that he was too busy figuring out a suave way to hold Abazi's hand. He never did.

On the next date, which, worriedly enough, was right before Abazi's mood had plummeted, they'd gone out to eat at a little diner in Haliton, the next town over. Gabe had no idea what he'd done wrong—in fact, he thought the date had gone really well. His wavy brown hair had actually behaved, and he'd even worked up the nerve to kiss Abazi. He *thought* that had gone well, too. He'd liked it, anyway. But maybe he'd done something the wrong way. Maybe he'd accidentally bitten her lip, or drooled on her. Both were dishearteningly likely possibilities.

"Kimber knows something about Abazi's bad mood," Jer volunteered, "but she won't talk about it. Said it wasn't her story to tell."

"So there *is* a story to tell," Gabe said, feeling slightly relieved. It hadn't been the kiss!

Kris pushed himself to his feet and ambled over to the bookshelf, behind which lay the hidden door, to peruse Gabe's tree books. "I wonder what the story is?" He pulled out a book and started skimming the pages.

Gabe hugged his pillow. "I wish I knew. Abazi won't talk. I've tried a few times to get her to, but she always changes the subject, usually by calling me an idiot."

"Sounds like Abazi." Kris snapped the book shut with one hand. "I say we go over there tomorrow after school and force her to come outside with us."

"We could light a bonfire and roast hotdogs and marshmallows!" Jer exclaimed, then frowned. "I know we burn wood to heat the house, but should we do it outside where the Dryads can see it? Would that be weird?"

Gabe shrugged. How would he know? It wasn't like he was the spokesperson for all Dryads. "I know that Hollie doesn't burn wood; she burns coal." The Dryads did use dead wood for weapons, but only after asking for permission and giving thanks. The Ko-goks didn't touch dead wood at all since it burned their skin. They'd eaten their own kind, and meat, too, and were now paying the price. "Besides, they're all still sleeping. But maybe the smell will wake them up..." Which would be great. After Gabe's last conversation with Hollie, he'd been really worried about the Dryads not waking up at all.

"Goodbye, Gabriel," she had said to him. *"Enjoy yer rest. Springtime'll come soon enough, and with it, great trouble."*

"Great trouble?"

"Many of us are afraid we'll not wake come buddin' time. Ye'll be on yer own against the Ko-goks."

If that wasn't disturbing, he didn't know what was.

"We could do it if we handled everything ourselves," he went on, warming to the idea. "Mom and Dad have other things to worry about."

The two brothers nodded solemnly. They knew about the impending tax bill because Gabe had told them about it, and had started counting up their savings to help out. "Hot dogs and marshmallows aren't expensive," Jer determined. "So they won't have to pay much."

Kris smacked his palm against the book. "Let's do it! I've been Jonesing for some marshmallows lately. We can do S'mores, and if that doesn't get Abazi to come, then I'm afraid she's a lost cause."

"We already have that huge pile of brush we gathered last fall," Jer said. "That would be perfect for the bonfire."

Gabe nodded. Good food, warmth, drawing Abazi out of her funk, and waking the Dryads...what could go wrong? It sounded like a great idea.

He should've known better.

Chapter Two

The Quickening

"A 'Welcome Spring' bonfire actually sounds like fun," Mom said at supper. "What do you think, Keith?"

Dad didn't answer right away. He looked worn out, as though he'd been up all night, or maybe his meds weren't working properly. The pork chop in Gabe's stomach started to feel like wet cement. Dad had been doing so well lately. *Please don't let there be a setback!*

Dad laid his napkin across his plate. "Sure, why not? Like Jer said, we could burn up that brush pile."

"Well, maybe half of it," Mom replied as she rose from the table with her plate in hand.

"Awww!" all three boys complained at once.

She started the tap water to wash the supper dishes, then turned back to them. "Now don't you *awww* me. You light that pile on fire and we'll have the whole woods up in smoke." That quieted them. "Besides, I want to save the other half for making mulch for the blueberry bushes. If we have extra, we can sell it." She rubbed her forehead wearily, using the back of her wrist, since her hands were dripping bubbles.

Gabe and his brothers pushed out their chairs and began to clear the table. Dad stretched and made to stand up but Gabe got to him first. "You stay sitting. I'll get your dishes. Want dessert?" Dad was still too thin after his surgery. His diabetes had done a number on his kidneys and he'd gotten a transplant. All winter he'd seemed to be getting better, but lately, with the stress from not having money to pay the taxes and the long, hard winter, he seemed tired all the time. Mom, too. She was simply doing too much.

Dad waved his hand. "Nothing for me. I'm stuffed. And I can get my own dishes, Gabe." He grabbed his plate and stood up.

Gabe backed away, a little hurt. He got that his dad wanted to fend for himself, but there was no reason to be so sensitive. Without another word, he and his brothers finished putting the food away and wiping the table and counters, then left their parents to talk as Mom washed up the last of the dishes.

"I'm going to finish studying for my test," he told Kris and Jer in the hallway. "We'll ask Abazi and Kimber tomorrow, and do the bonfire Saturday, which should give us the day to get things ready and fetch everything we'll need from the store. I'll pay."

Gabe worked Saturday and had already decided he'd buy the hotdogs and marshmallows himself; it would be one less bill for his parents. Besides, maybe Dad was in a bad mood because he was anxious about the tax bill and this would help get him out of it. Gabe supposed that sort of worry would make him a bit snotty, too. Actually, he was pretty sure he'd have acted worse about it. But still…he'd only been trying to help.

"I can give you some money," Kris offered. "But it would take away from what I want to give Mom and Dad for the tax bill."

"Don't worry about it. I get a discount, remember?"

"If you're sure…" Kris said uncertainly. "Because you shouldn't have to pay for all of it. We eat a lot of food, you know."

"I'm sure. I want to do it." He did, actually. Paying for the food for their party sort of made him feel like an adult.

"So how do we convince Abazi to come?" Jer asked. "Cause I don't think Kimber will come alone."

"Just leave Abazi to me," Gabe replied with much more confidence than he felt.

Kris sighed forlornly. "I wish Hollie could come."

"I'm not sure bonfires would exactly be her scene. Besides, like I said, maybe the smoke will wake her up."

Kris fell back against the wall. "It *has* to! It's getting late in the season for it, isn't it?" No one answered because no one really knew if it was late or not. "But I think spring is finally here now." He tried to sound positive, but again, who knew what could happen in this strange and wild state.

"You know, Kris." Gabe absently reached up to touch the ceiling. "I think I feel warmer already."

Kris's eyes widened. "Really?"

"Really." And actually, Gabe thought maybe he did. He wasn't sure, since he'd grown used to being cold all the time. But maybe his toes and fingers weren't as stiff as usual, and he thought his ear tips had warmed a little. It was possible. "Now I've really got to study."

"Me, too," Kris groaned, pushing away from the wall.

Jer grinned. "I don't." They took turns attempting to punch his shoulder, but he was too quick. He pulled a yo-yo out of his pocket, then threw it a few times. There'd been a yo-yo show at school in November and since then Jer couldn't be found without his favorite blue Duncan Dragonfly. He'd gotten really good at it, doing tricks like Behind the Back Trapeze and Mach-5. "I'm going to work on my project, though, so that counts." Before they could interrogate him about what his 'project' was, he ran off, laughing and throwing his yo-yo.

Kris watched him go. "What do you think the little turd's up to?"

"No good," Gabe answered. "See you tomorrow. Let's try to get going early so we can ask Kimber and Abazi about the bonfire."

"Better make sure I'm awake, then." There was a moment's silence. "So you're really feeling warmer?"

"I am." And Gabe did feel warmer, for sure this time. He also felt something else, a sort of quickening in his blood, like a rush of adrenaline before a big game. It felt strange, but good.

"Cool." Kris gave Gabe a relieved smile before turning and heading off to his room.

Gabe twisted the skull doorknob and turned on the light, his eyes landing on the flowing female figure carved on the door at the top of the stairs. The woman reminded him of Wildrr's tree friend, the Lady. Gabe had saved her life, or so Wildrr claimed, and now Gabe felt a certain ownership of her. He wondered if he'd meet her again, and rather hoped so. She was *really* gorgeous. And probably very nice, too.

The tapping had stopped inside the turret, replaced by the thud of heavy rain. If this kept up, the snow should melt quickly. Gabe listened to the sound for a while, lulled into a near sleep. After a bit, he roused himself and continued studying. When he felt he'd learned all he was going to learn, he closed his books and shoved them into his backpack. Picking his way around a shirt, a soccer ball, and a wad of socks on the floor, he set the backpack by the door leading downstairs.

He thought about heading to bed. It was after eleven, but he didn't feel the least bit tired. In fact, he felt strangely restless, as though something was stirring under his skin. All he wanted to do at this very moment was race outside and inhale deep breaths of fresh air, let the rain coat his skin, be absorbed into his veins. He wanted to feel alive again. All winter he'd stumbled about in a sort of daze. Only when he'd played basketball or been with Abazi had he truly come alive.

But going outside in all that snow and rain probably wasn't the best idea, and he ended up pacing the floor, wondering what to do with himself. He walked around the turret, pulling off his shoes and jeans as he went. His wanderings took him past his glowing fish tank, a stack of video games, and then, the old chest—the one Oswald had claimed was his, but wasn't, since it supposedly belonged to the King of the Forest Immortal—Gabe.

Gabe bent down, one knee popping, and traced the tree carved on the lid. Just touching the wood made his heart beat harder. Before he could change his mind, he pressed a button on the box and the latch released. With shaking hands he lifted the lid and the spicy scent of crushed pine needles whispered out to greet him.

Swallowing hard, he reached inside and drew out the heavy, dark green cloak he remembered from last time, the one with the white flower embroidered on the back. Gabe pulled the cloak around his shoulders, smelling what he had the first time—apple and sun and sweet air. The cape fit perfectly, as though made for him to be worn at this exact time, on this very day.

He abruptly stood. Donning the cloak hadn't eased his restlessness; in fact, seemed to increase it. He didn't feel like growing, not like last time, but he did feel an overwhelming urgency, stronger than anything he'd ever felt before, to get outside, into the fresh air. He had to go. *Now.*

Fastening the ties on the cloak, he pulled open the bookshelf and shut it behind him before slipping down the wooden pole to the ground below. Once he landed, he unlocked the little door and pulled it open. Not much snow covered this spot, protected as it was by shrubs, and he ducked out into the night air. The throbbing, sweet smell of spring filled his senses and his whole being came alive.

This was more like it!

It was still raining pretty hard, drops hammering the tin roof of the barn like mad woodpeckers. He pulled up his hood, and the sound of rain stopped. But then other sounds began—voices, whispers at first. Someone was nearby. Gabe hurried out into the yard, and feeling himself in grave danger, spun around, searching the yard. A surge of adrenaline roared through him and he sucked in air. The voices were growing louder. He yanked off the hood to hear them better and instantly the strange sounds ceased. He stopped spinning, dizzy now, and waited. Nothing. Drops pelted his face and body, and their coolness felt good on his hot skin. He longed to tear off his cloak, but at the same time felt strangely reluctant to do so. It was his disguise. They wouldn't know it was him.

But who was *they?*

The hard rain was starting to hurt. He pulled the hood back on and the voices returned.

Murderer!

Kill him now!

Kill them all!

Gabe yanked the hood off and the voices ceased, as though he'd thrown a switch. His chest rose and fell and adrenaline surged through his veins. *Adrenaline...cr warming sap?*

Whichever it was, he knew he had to run. He had to escape... The voices. His life. Abazi. Everything in his life was driving him crazy. He had to get away!

His feet began to move and he found himself sprinting down the driveway. He managed to get halfway along it before the cry building up inside him came roaring out. The forceful sound echoed around him, and liking it, he did it again, louder this time. No one would hear him. He was too far away from the house. Well, no one human, anyway. There were others who could hear his call, but he was not afraid of them. If the dark ones came after him, they'd have a battle on their hands. And he would win, against all of them. He knew it.

"They're comin'!" he yelled to the night. "We must flee!"

What was he saying?

There was no answer to that, so he kept running. He leaped into the air and spun around like a whirling dervish. Twenty feet later, he landed on his feet and kept running, feeling immensely powerful. "This is yer King! Our time has come! Gather yerselves and release. We must fly far!"

He raced onto the highway and pelted down the middle of it, feeling light as air. He jumped and spun around, releasing white petals that flew from him like snow. He kept running. Running away from something. Running toward something. He wasn't sure which, just knew that he must keep moving. He ran and he ran, feeling amazing. The freedom! The power! The exhilaration! He didn't want it to end.

And then things changed.

With each step, the cloak grew heavier on his shoulders, pulling him back to the ground. He had to get it off. Undoing the clasp, he clawed the heavy material from his shoulders and it fell to the ground with a muffled thud. The rain battered against him and the cold seeped inside his shirt. He looked down. He was barefoot and wearing only a t-shirt and boxers, and suddenly he was very cold. He began to shiver, staring down at the cloak lying corpse-like in a pile at his feet. He spun around. *What's going on? Why am I here in the rain and dark?*

He picked up the cloak and felt a faint reminiscent spark. He'd put it on, he remembered now, and then everything had gone a bit mad. But how, he wasn't sure. What he did know was that he was freezing, which could be remedied if he just put the cloak back on. But he was afraid to do that. Something happened to him when he was wearing the cloak, something strange.

Turning about, he realized he was on the highway, almost to the stoplights. He was two miles from home, a long walk back. He decided to run, not just because he was cold, but because he was afraid. If *his* sap was starting to run, then the same could be happening for the dark ones. He did not want to be caught in his boxers with only a flimsy wool cape for protection.

He clasped the cloak to his chest and began to run. His feet slapped along the cold pavement like flippers, whap, whap, whap. Up ahead, snow covered the road, which was odd, since it was raining, and he slowed as he neared it.

Not snow. Flower petals.

Thousands of flower petals covered the black surface and he had the strange, frightening feeling he'd been the one to put them there.

He continued running, feeling the slippery softness of the flower petals beneath his bare feet. Something had begun, he realized. A sort of quickening.

The time was upon him…upon the entire Forest Immortal…to awake.

Chapter Three

Not Enough Time

"A bonfire?" Abazi looked skeptical. "Are you sure your people will be okay with that? You are burning your dead, you know." Today she was wearing an aqua-colored, beaded headband that made her black hair look even blacker. The beads were the only color in her outfit, which was a black turtleneck, black tights, and a black miniskirt. Other than the miniskirt, she looked like she was in mourning. She'd been dressing mostly in black for three weeks now.

With only five minutes before classes started, Gabe was still trying to get Abazi to commit to coming over tomorrow night, and she wasn't having it. He rubbed a weary hand over his face. This conversation was going nowhere fast and he was too tired to get into an argument. The restlessness he'd felt for most of the night had dissipated and now he only felt dead tired. Two cups of coffee had yet to break through the fog in his mind, brought about by exhaustion.

After his strange adventure in the cloak, he'd lain awake for hours, mulling over what had happened. Where had those voices come from? And why did wearing the cape bring them out? Why had he felt the need to run? Well, that was an easy one. Likely because the 'other' voices had called him a murderer. But had this guy (who'd proclaimed himself King) really killed someone? Or did they just think he had? And were kings held accountable for committing crimes?

Just as important, how was Gabe 'channeling' King Guy's voice? Perhaps something bad had happened to him and the experience had somehow managed to weave itself into the cape's fabric. This explanation sounded bizarre, and yet, perfectly reasonable to him. Even so, he still hadn't come up with a good answer to any of his other questions, which left him feeling slightly queasy, as though he, himself, were now the target of those 'other' voices.

"That's the idea," he answered Abazi distractedly. "We're hoping to wake them. Remember when I told you what Hollie said about the Dryads not waking up this spring? Well, I'm worried we haven't heard from them yet."

That earned him another dubious glance. "Why do you care? If the Dryads don't wake up, then all your problems are solved." She watched him carefully as she spoke, like a hawk eyes its prey. He didn't like the sensation at all.

"I care because even though the Dryads are a bit weird, I kind of like them. The only one I don't like is Oswald and that's mainly because he doesn't like me." *And because he likes you and I'm worried that the feeling is mutual.* "I'm not sure I trust Dame Hazel, either, but I don't want to see her dead." And then there were Wildrr and his Lady, and Filidh, the strange forest guy, and the odd Wych Elms, not to mention Hollie. He felt protective toward them all.

"Will there be chocolate?" she asked, surprising him.

"Of course. My mom won't go without. Regular food first, then S'mores for dessert."

"Hey, Hawthorne!" Jake Morrigan's snotty voice cut through the air and Gabe swung around to face him. Candi Morrigan's obnoxious son strutted toward them, looking generically expensive, as usual. Well, expensive to Gabe. These days he was lucky to get a new t-shirt. "Now that the snow's melting, my mom's going to be getting work started on clearing the woods. If I even hear you making any trouble for her, I'll bust your head open." He turned to Abazi and flashed his pearly whites at her. "Hey, babe."

One dark eyebrow shot up, a warning signal Gabe knew well. "Did you seriously just call me babe?" Jake's smile faded. "Because that's pretty old school, *babe*."

Jake relaxed, not realizing she was mocking him. He was not the brightest bulb in the bunch. "I knew you'd like a guy who was old-fashioned," he said smugly.

"Wrong answer, *babe*. When I refer to old-fashioned, I'm thinking the 1880s, not the 1980s."

Gabe had yet to figure out why Jake continued to pursue Abazi. She was never nice to him, and in fact, was pretty ruthless with her insults. Maybe he had a mother complex, like that weird guy Oedipus. Abazi and Mrs. Morrigan both could be pretty brutal.

Jake gave a fake laugh. "Well, at least I know how to dress." He eyed Gabe's tattered Levi's and faded plaid button-up shirt. "Talk about the

1980s," he scoffed. "Actually, he looks like a homeless person, or one who's about to be." He gave Gabe a meaningful look.

"Now, now, now," Abazi scolded, shaking her finger at Jake. "There's no need to get nasty."

"I'm just saying that it's obvious some people in this town are losers."

"And you're a big winner?" Gabe took a step forward. The caffeine was starting to kick in and he felt an overwhelming desire to show Jake just how big a loser *he* was.

"At least my parents can pay their tax bills."

Gabe's fists clenched. "Will you shut up about that?"

"What's this, Gabe?" Abazi demanded, her dark eyes flashing.

"They're broke," Jake sneered. "That's why I made the homeless person joke."

Abazi turned on him. "Get lost, Morrigan. Your face is making my eyes hurt."

"They're going to get kicked out of their house!" he said, slowly backing up. Abazi took a threatening step forward and Jake moved faster. "Homeless Hawthornes!" he yelled quickly before slipping into the crowd plodding toward class. Several heads turned Gabe's way.

Ignoring the curious looks, he joined the line of students, not waiting to see if Abazi was following. Because of her bad mood, he hadn't yet told her about the tax situation. And now she would think he was withholding information from her on purpose.

"All right, I'll come to your bonfire," she said, moving up alongside him. "And I'll bring the sodas."

Before his mouth could drop open in astonishment, she disappeared into her first class. Slightly stunned, he dashed into the science room just before the bell rang. Boy, he did not get that girl. But she was coming to the bonfire, and right now, that was all that mattered.

Well, that and maybe the fact that he'd found a flower bud coming out of his ear this morning.

~~~~~~

Most teens only had to deal with pimples and bad hair days and figuring out what to wear day to day. Gabe had to deal with all that *and* spikes coming up through his skin. And now? He had to add flowers springing from his orifices. Great.

Gabe tapped his fingers on the steering wheel as he waited for his brothers in the family's beat-up, Ford pick-up truck. He couldn't wait to graduate and go to college, then get a real job and make some real money. He was tired of being poor. Granted it hadn't been that long, and they weren't really, *truly* poor. He'd known kids back in San Jose who were poor-poor, like Joey Anderson. He'd always claim he'd forgotten his lunch, but Gabe knew it was more likely that there wasn't any food at home and Joey's alcoholic mom either hadn't filled out the free-lunch form or Joey was too proud to accept what he would call charity. That's why Gabe always packed extra and gave Joey half.

Joey was proud, but he wasn't stupid. He knew what Gabe was doing. In exchange, he helped Gabe fix his bike, then Dad's car one time, even the washing machine, whatever he could get his hands on. Joey wasn't one to take handouts, plus he loved tooling around with machines. It was a good system.

Now, for the first time in his sixteen years on this earth, Gabe understood a little of the hardships Joey had gone through and wished he'd done more for his friend. Empathy was a funny thing…it was so much easier to feel it when you'd struggled yourself with the same misfortune.

And Gabe was struggling, but not just with a lack of money. During pre-calc, he'd felt a nearly overwhelming urge to jump out the window. The storm had cleared and the sun had appeared for the first time in weeks. It felt so good on his skin, so alluring, so tempting. He needed more of it. Luckily Mr. Boos, his pre-calc teacher, had called on Gabe, distracting him enough to get his roiling blood back under control.

Thank goodness. Because who knew what else could come out of him? Sap from his mouth? Flowers from his fingers? Branches out of his butt? He snickered. Okay, that last one was kind of funny.

"What are you laughing at?" Kris asked as he climbed into the cab. "Because I didn't actually trip on that curb. It rose up and grabbed my foot." He grinned. "Almost took me down, but I fought back and won the battle to curb my enthusiasm." He gave an amused hoot. "See what I did there?" he demanded, then roared with laughter.

Encouraged by his brother's goofy good cheer, Gabe decided to confide in him. He had to tell someone about what was going on, if only to keep him from going berserker on somebody. "I did something strange last night," he said when Kris's laughter settled into an occasional snort, "and it started something even stranger. Something big."

"You farted and blew out a hole in your bed?"

"Ha, ha. Very funny. Do you want to hear what happened or not?"

Kris nodded eagerly. "Yes, yes, yes!"

"You know that box Hollie took from our barn? And you know Oswald returned it to me, right? So last night I was starting to feel really restless. I couldn't settle, and I was pacing around my room when I saw the box. I opened it, and I put on the cloak that was in there."

"There wasn't anything else in the trunk?" Kris asked, obviously disappointed. "Like a map or the key to another trunk?"

"Not that I saw, but I didn't really look. I put the cloak on and after that, well, things got a little wild."

"Keep talking," Kris prompted, looking almost ghoulish in his anticipation.

"I went outside and began running, and I felt like I could fly. Then these voices started up in my head, calling me a murderer. But when I pulled off the hood, the voices stopped. It was really weird. For some reason, I thought I had to get away. That we all had to get away. So I ran and ran until I got hot and I pulled off the cloak and I realized I was at the stoplights."

"That's a couple miles away!"

"No kidding. And it was raining and I was only in my boxers and a t-shirt. I was freezing, but I couldn't put the cloak back on. I was afraid I'd end up in Canada. So I headed back home and a little ways along, I found all these flower petals, and I'm pretty sure they came from me. And this morning I woke up with a flower growing out of my ear."

Kris swallowed. "That couldn't have been fun to see."

"Well, it wasn't too bad, being that I also have spikes that push through my skin. But still...I'm afraid they'll start coming out at any time. Spikes, flowers, the works."

"Yikes," Kris said sympathetically. "You'd look like a Goth flower child. You know..." He tilted his head to one side. "Sounds to me like you've got spring fever."

Gabe turned to his brother. "Spring fever?" He laughed. "That's exactly it!"

Kris gave a wry smile. "Not so stupid, am I?"

Gabe frowned. "I never said you were stupid."

"Not usually directly, you mostly just imply it."

Gabe felt himself grow warm. "I don't really think you're stupid, Kris. But you can be a bit boneheaded sometimes."

"This from the guy who consistently forgets to rinse the soap off the dishes before putting them in the rack to dry?"

Gabe held up his hands. "Okay, okay! So we're even." He leaned his head back against the seat, relieved. He wasn't going crazy. He had spring fever. He could handle that. The trick was to be aware and catch things before they went too far. He still didn't know what had happened with the cloak, but he'd figure that out later.

"His Highness has arrived," Jer announced, climbing into the truck. "We can now depart."

"That's my line." Kris laughed.

"You wish. So Kimber said she'd come, and she'd bring the fixings to make S'mores."

"Cool," Gabe replied, not just because he wouldn't have to buy all that stuff, but because he really liked Kimber. She was the opposite of Abazi—sweet, kind, full of goodwill, and she never, ever teased him. At least not like Abazi did. He really did admire Kimber. She might have cerebral palsy, but she was one of the toughest people he'd ever met. She didn't let her CP keep her from doing things, and she never complained. Like Gunga Din, she was a better man than he was...

"Tell Jer what happened," Kris urged.

On the drive home, Gabe related the incidences of last night. This time he added more detail, like about what the voices had said. "Wow," Jer breathed when he was done. "That is wickedly wacked."

"Wickedly?" Kris repeated. "It's just wicked."

Jer sighed. "I know. But in this case wickedly sounds better. And besides I was doing a play on words, since it's actually wiggedy wack."

"So that's your educated opinion on what happened to me?" Gabe asked dryly. He'd hoped for a little better from Jer. Usually he had some keen insights; he was pretty smart for a thirteen-year-old.

"No. I think the guy who had the cloak before you killed someone. Him and his gang, or family, maybe. He was accused of murder and he fled. They all did."

"But do you think he really did kill someone?" Gabe asked faintly as they pulled up alongside the barn. Had he actually worn a murderer's cloak? Did that kind of thing rub off on a person? He was already worried enough about what turning into a tree did to him.

"Beats me. Did it feel like he'd done it?"

Gabe thought about it. "I don't remember feeling guilty, just a little anxious. I wasn't even all that scared, actually. But then, if he was a sociopath, he wouldn't have felt remorse."

"Did he *feel* like a sociopath?" Kris wanted to know as he followed Jer out the door. Gabe met them on the other side of the truck and they headed toward the house, the sun gloriously hot on the top of his head.

"I have no idea. I'm not sure what a sociopath would feel like. He felt strong and sure of himself. I could tell he was a leader."

"A leader like that cult guy, Jim Jones, who made his followers drink poisoned Kool-Aid?" Jer questioned.

Leave it to Jer to know something so morbid and obscure. He and Kimber might look alike, with their blond hair and blue eyes, but Jer was not sweet like Kimber. Not at all. "No. I don't think so. But again, I don't know for sure."

They dropped their bags near the door. "Hey, boys," Mom greeted distractedly. She was wearing a blue apron dusted with flour and her brown hair was tucked back in a messy bun. Today she was making blueberry bread for the store, using blueberries they'd picked and frozen last summer. They'd harvested so many blueberries that Gabe thought he'd end up turning blue himself. Luckily Grandpa May, who had owned the farm before dying from a heart attack, had left two chest freezers down in the cellar. "How was school?"

"Fine," they all replied.

"The bonfire is on," Kris informed her, moving on to more interesting topics. "Abazi and Kimber are coming and bringing drinks and the S'mores stuff."

"They don't have to do that," Mom said halfheartedly. She didn't like taking from other people; she typically was the one who shared her bounty. Unfortunately, these days, there was very little bounty to share.

"They wanted to do it," Gabe said hurriedly. "Said they wouldn't come if they couldn't bring something."

Jer looked at him funny, but went along with it. "Yeah, that's right. They insisted."

She sighed and rubbed her forehead with the back of her hand, leaving behind a trail of flour. "Well, I guess I should just be grateful, hm?" She didn't sound grateful. Her eyes were distant, almost bitter.

"Where's Dad?" Gabe asked, hoping to lure her back from wherever her thoughts had taken her.

"Oh, he's doing something on the computer." She tossed her head in the direction of the second floor. Last fall Dad had taken over Gabe's old bedroom, turning it into an office of sorts.

"Did he find work?" Kris asked eagerly.

Mom's eyes narrowed. "Not that I know of. Why?"

"Well, because I think working would make him happy," Kris improvised. None of the brothers was going to mention the impending tax situation. Not if they didn't want to stir up a hornet's nest, with Mom as the queen bee. The *killer* queen bee.

Her stance softened. "Yes, it would. But he's looking for one, which is a good thing. And he's keeping his skills sharp. It's only a matter of time."

Time we don't have. "Are you going to do the bonfire with us?" Gabe asked.

She shrugged. "We might. This weather change really is lovely. Heartening, actually. I just hope the snow doesn't melt too quickly."

Jer paused in reaching for an apple. "Why?"

"It can cause flooding problems. The stream out back can flood and cause a big mess in the yard and cellar, which we do *not* need right now."

"Is there anything we can do?" Kris asked. "Like put down sand-bags?"

She laughed as she took a couple loaves out of the oven, and the smell of blueberry and cinnamon filled the warm room. "I'm not sure that'll be necessary. But maybe you can go down in the cellar after homework is done and find the sump pump."

Kris rubbed his hands together excitedly. "Gladly!"

"You do know what one is, don't you?" Mom asked dryly.

"Does he need to?" Jer asked around a mouthful of apple. "Just the name alone is enough to get him all worked up."

"I know what a sump pump is! Grandpa May showed it to me during our last visit. It should be working because he and I checked it out, oiled it up, made a few adjustments."

Mom groaned. "Don't tell me you tried to *improve* it?"

Kris grinned. "Let's just say it's going to pump sump like nobody's business."

She sighed. "No more tinkering. Just make sure it's working, all right? Maybe check its back-up battery, too."

"I'm on it."

"I can see you're pumped up about it," she joked, and they all groaned. "Hey! That was a good one. Now give me your lunch bags and go do your homework. I'm a busy lady."

They deposited their lunch bags on the counter and went their separate ways. Jer and Kris ran upstairs to their rooms, discussing the sump pump and various strange uses for it, like draining the tub when needed, or as an emergency toilet emptier.

Gabe headed up to his turret room, his heavy backpack over one shoulder. He was grateful to have such a cool room, but still had to wonder why a turret was necessary on a Maine farmhouse. Who did his ancestors feel they needed protection from?

Murderer!

The voice rang out in his mind, clear as though the accuser were standing in the room with him. He spun around. Could it be? Could the murderer have lived in this room? Was it truly a sanctuary, or was it a prison?

Gabe let loose a yawn. The lack of sleep and all that running from yesterday were hitting him hard. Maybe he'd take a quick nap before starting work on his English paper. He dropped his backpack on the floor and fell onto his bed, almost asleep before his head hit the pillow.

The roar of voices drifted through the house and up the stairs. "Give him to us! He's ours!" Gabe peered out a window, down into the front yard. A crowd of people had gathered and they looked angry. Gabe could actually feel their fury vibrating the air all around him.

He had to get away.

"He's up there!" someone in the crowd pointed at the turret. At that same moment, the sound of splintering wood signaled the defeat of the downstairs door. Not long after that Gabe heard footsteps on the stairs, the sound of marching soldiers.

He raced to the bookshelf and pulled it open. Quick as a firefighter, he slid down the wooden pole and was out the tiny door that led outside.

"There he is!" a woman screeched, pointing a gnarled finger at him. "After him!"

Gabe turned away from the yard, where many still lingered, and headed toward the woods beyond the hedge. No wait, not that way. He turned about and dashed toward the section of woods near the ocean. He ran and ran, with the mob right behind him, screaming and cursing him.

When he reached the cliff that overlooked the bright blue sea, he skidded to a stop. There was nowhere else to go. Nowhere to run. He was trapped.

They were all trapped.

"No!" he cried and sat up straight. Gasping for air, he looked around. He was in his room, his fish tank still bubbled peacefully, his backpack was on the floor where he'd left it. Then his eyes landed on the cloak he'd spread out over a chair to dry.

The cloak. It had started this. Maybe it was time to get rid of it. Maybe, just maybe, he should give it back to Oswald.

The thought made him smile. Yeah, that sounded like a great idea.

Chapter Four

Burning the Stick
at Both Ends

On Saturday, Gabe finished his shift at the store, then hurried home. Jer and Kris had been tasked with preparing the bonfire and Gabe was excited to see what it looked like. It hadn't been all fun and games, he soon found out, since Mom had them using the chipper most of the time to make wood chips.

Gabe stuck the hotdogs in the fridge, set the buns and chips on the counter, then quickly changed his clothes and joined his brothers. Both were covered with sawdust and the white chips coating their hair made Kris look as blond as Jer. But they seemed to be in a good mood, laughing and joking as they hauled the bags of woodchips to the barn.

Gabe was admiring the pile of brush when they returned. It was about six feet high and just as wide—big, but not insanely so. Truth be told, he wouldn't have minded it getting out of control and burning down a few trees in the woods.

On second thought, as much as he hated Straif, he couldn't imagine burning him alive.

He burned Isis alive.

But he didn't own up to it.

Which was odd since Straif struck Gabe as the type who would have been proud about doing something so heinous.

"That looks really awesome," he said to his brothers when they joined him.

"It is," Jer replied proudly. "And we made enough woodchips to fill a silo, so we have plenty to sell this spring. Oh, yeah, we're awesome!" He did a little "awesome" jig.

"Cool. I suppose the girls will be here soon. Should we try to light it?"

"The rain didn't help," Kris said, "but the wind last night and this morning dried out the wood quite a bit."

Gabe remembered waking up once and hearing the windows rattle, then falling back to sleep. Luckily the wind had died down now, so it would be safer to burn. He squatted. "I see you already have a bunch of newspaper at the bottom. So all we need is a lighter."

Kris pulled a long blue one from his pocket. "Like this?" He flicked it on and waved it about like a sparkler. "I get to light it."

"I want to do it!" Jer protested.

"Fine. You do half, I'll do the other half."

"And I don't exist?" Gabe said in a bland voice, not wanting to let on that he really wanted to light the fire, too.

"All right, a third. I'll start here and stop here." Kris pointed.

A minute or so later they'd all had their turn and now waited with bated breath to see if the fire would take. There was some hissing and popping as flame met moisture, but slowly, the kindling started to catch. Smoke slipped into the sky, filling the air with a pleasant apple smell. Most of the branches had come from the apple trees they'd pruned in the fall. Gabe inhaled, and all at once felt frightened. What were they doing? How could they burn his people?

And then, just as quickly, the feeling dissipated. *It's just dead wood*, he told himself. Besides, they'd *had* to prune the apple trees. They had some disease that needed to be cut out. Plus there were numerous branches shooting straight up that sucked energy from the tree without producing any fruit. So they were not sadists, nor were they roasting anything or anyone alive.

Gabe was letting himself be mesmerized by the beauty and destructiveness of fire when he heard someone shouting. "Hey, you pyros! You could've waited!"

Speaking of beauty and destructiveness… Gabe stood up from his crouching position and smiled at Abazi glaring at them through Mrs. Wistman's backseat window. "You came."

Kimber and Abazi slid out of the car and approached the bonfire as Kimber's mom drove closer to the house. "What are you smiling about?" Abazi snapped as she neared him, dressed, as usual, in black. She looked like a cross between a ninja and a wraith, and Gabe found the look oddly alluring.

"I was just thinking about how you're like fire," he answered, surprised at his daring. But then again, ever since wearing the cloak he'd felt different. Braver, stronger, *wilder*. Add that to the intoxicating smell of spring in the air and a person was bound to take some chances, live a little.

Her eyes narrowed. "Because I like to burn people?"

He laughed. "That, too." He decided not to explain himself. Whatever he said would likely be misinterpreted. And face it, there was quite a lot of room for misinterpretation.

"Hey, Kimber," he said over Abazi's head. "Glad you could come."

She smiled at him, her blue eyes full of bonhomie as she held up a homemade shopping bag. "I brought everything."

Jer hurried forward and took the bag from her, then opened it and peered inside. "Sweet! You got the graham crackers that are already in squares. I hate trying to break the rectangles in half. I end up crushing most of them with my manly strength."

"Me, too!" Kimber giggled and held up her curled fingers.

Jer frowned. "I'd do it for you, you know."

She shook her head. "If I can't break my own crackers in half, then that would make me pretty pathetic. But still…if they're already done for me, why go looking for trouble?"

There was a whoosh and Gabe turned to see the fire really take hold, billows of smoke rising into the air. He felt his mood soar along with the smoke. Things were going to get better from here on out. He could feel it.

"You can probably see the smoke from downtown," Abazi commented. "It's like a mushroom cloud."

"Nice fire!" Hands full, Kimber's mom waved with her elbow and they waved back, then she went in the house with the rest of the drinks and food.

"I think we're going to have to let it die down before we roast anything," Kris said as he took turns poking at the roaring fire with a long stick and leaping back out of the way of the flames.

"Did you have to make it so big?" Abazi complained. "I'm hungry!"

"It's only five o'clock," Gabe said. "When do you normally eat?"

"I didn't eat lunch," she grumbled.

Gabe groaned inwardly. "Don't tell me you're on another stupid diet?"

"So what if I am? I don't have your insane metabolism. I tried on a pair of pants yesterday and they didn't fit. I'm getting fat."

"If you're fat," Kris snorted, "then I must be a whale. Besides, I think you look fantastic." If he hadn't said the compliment so casually, Gabe would've had to punch his brother in the mouth. But Kris wasn't really paying all that much attention; his interest was the fire and keeping it under control.

Abazi's face contorted into several expressions—disbelief, belief, happiness, annoyance. "I could still stand to lose a few pounds."

"You lose a few pounds and you'll blow away," Gabe finally found his voice. This was ridiculous. Abazi was gorgeous exactly how she was. "Besides, you're only sixteen. It's natural for you to gain weight. People grow all the way into their twenties, you know."

She'd smiled at the first sentence, but the second one brought out her frown again. Gabe had a feeling he needed to learn when to stop talking. "I'm almost seventeen," was her only response.

Kimber took her arm. "Can't you just tell them?"

Abazi shook her head mutinously. "It's none of their business."

"It *is* their business," Kimber said firmly. "They're our friends." Abazi's lips pressed together—she was obviously not happy—but she didn't stop Kimber from speaking. "Abazi has a birthday a week from today, on Saturday."

"Happy early birthday!" Kris cried. "We need to have a party."

"No party!" Abazi practically shouted.

"Abazi's mother," Kimber explained, "died on Abazi's birthday."

"Oh." Kris looked mortified. "Sorry, Abazi. I didn't know."

Abazi's bad mood finally made sense to Gabe. The anniversary of her mother's death was approaching. Of course she'd feel like crap. The strange part was that Gabe had the distinct feeling that Abazi hadn't liked her mother all that much. So was she in mourning? Or was she mad that a person she didn't like had ruined her birthday forever?

"I'm sorry, Abazi," Gabe said softly. "That really sucks."

"It would if I cared," she snapped. "But I don't, so I'm fine. Can we get some food around here? If I'm going to be fat, I might as well be the best fat person I can be."

Gabe bit down on his lower lip. He wanted to tell Abazi to cut the melodrama, but how could he? She'd lost her mother, and the anniversary of her death was on Abazi's birthday, for cripe's sake. "Sure. Jer and I will go get it."

"I'll help," Kimber volunteered.

She, Jer, and Gabe left Kris and Abazi to tend the fire. Kris looked a little nervous to be left with two such volatile partners to manage, but it couldn't be helped. Gabe grabbed the wheelbarrow they'd used to haul brush and pushed it toward the house.

They met Kimber's mother on her way to her car. She was a tiny woman, full of energy and good will. Even though Kimber didn't play

basketball, Mrs. Wistman came to all the games and helped sell conces-
sions. Basketball wasn't exactly her sport, she explained, but she liked
helping out. "I hope I brought enough food," she said as she opened
her van door. "You boys grow each time I see you! And Gabe! What
size are those feet of yours?"

Gabe blushed. "I'm a fourteen now."

"Goodness, they're almost as long as I am tall!" She wasn't far off.
She was even shorter than Kimber. "I'm off to do inventory. You kids
have fun." She pulled herself into the van. "Try not to burn down the
woods, and keep an eye on my sweet, sweet angel!"

With that, she was off down the driveway, her head bopping from
side to side to the beat of the latest pop hit. Kimber smiled. She was
one of the rare teens who seemed unembarrassed by a parent. "Oh, to
have half her energy," she sighed.

"I think we could probably light a city on her energy," Jer laughed.
Over the winter, he'd helped out at the store Mrs. Wistman owned—
Shirt Yourself, a t-shirt and gift shop next door to Woodlands—so he
knew what he was talking about.

They were about to head inside when Mom and Dad pushed open
the door. Gabe ran down the steps and grabbed the handles of the
wheelbarrow. "You can put all that in here."

Mom had a cooler, where she'd put the drinks, and Dad had the
metal, two-pronged marshmallow sticks and the grocery bag Gabe had
brought home. "I'll get the rest," Mom said, hurrying back up the
steps. Kimber and Jer followed her, leaving Dad and Gabe alone.

A couple quiet seconds passed. "I wonder when she'll stop treating
me like an invalid?" Dad complained, dropping the words into the
waiting silence like a bomb. Gabe shrugged uncomfortably and mumbled something that could have been interpreted as anything. He didn't
want to say the wrong thing and make the situation worse, or get his
dad mad at him again.

"I know I'm not fully recovered," he went on, "but I'm not helpless,
either."

Gabe thought maybe Mom was just noticing how tired Dad was
looking lately. He'd been doing so well, but now he looked like someone had dragged him through a puddle, squeezed out the water, and
hung him up to dry. "Oh, she's probably just worried because we don't
have the money to pay the taxes—" As soon as Gabe said the words,
he wished them back. This is why he usually mumbled his re-
sponses...no chance of anything being misconstrued, or even heard if
he was lucky.

Dad looked over at him. "And how do you know about that?"

"Oh, um, well, I just happened to hear you guys talking about it in the kitchen. I was coming down for a sandwich."

"Do your brothers know?" He paused. "No, wait. Silly question."

"Are we going to get kicked out? Cause I have money saved up. And so do Kris and Jer. Maybe if we all pitched in?"

Dad shook his head. "Don't worry about it, Gabe. It will all work out in the end. It always does."

Gabe wasn't so sure about that, especially since Dad didn't look particularly convinced by his own words. That wasn't like him at all and it scared Gabe. He quickly changed the subject. "You're joining us for hotdogs and marshmallows, aren't you?"

"Can pigs fly?"

"Um, no."

"Really?" Dad laughed. "Yeah, we'll join you for a little while. I can still put away the hotdogs with the best of them." Jer, Kimber, and Mom came out at that moment and Gabe started pushing the wheelbarrow over to the picnic table Kris and Jer had dragged out from the barn.

It wasn't long before Abazi let go of some of her sulk and joined in the fun. Dad kept teasing her and before long, she was going right back at him. Gabe was glad to see them looking happy. It seemed like forever since they'd been able to kick back and just have fun and not worry about anything.

After an hour or so, Mom and Dad went inside, leaving them to finish off the marshmallows. Everyone had a chair, spread around the dying bonfire. Strange to think how something so big at one time was now so small, and by the time the night was over would only be ash and bits of charcoal. Gabe shivered. It was a creepy analogy for life. One day there'd be nothing more to any of them, and that was one of the many scary things about death…leaving nothing behind to be remembered for.

"Anyone want more marshmallows?" He held up the bag. "Four left."

"I couldn't eat another bite," Kimber groaned.

"I'll take 'em." Kris held up his hand. Gabe tossed him the bag and Kris popped all four into his mouth at once. Then he started pushing the marshmallows back out and making retching sounds.

"Gross!" Abazi laughed. "You look like you're turning inside out."

After several pulsations, he sucked the gooey white mass back in, chewed twice, and swallowed. "Ewww!" Kimber pointed. "How did you do that?"

"It's a talent," Kris replied, nonchalantly examining his fingernails. "I do so many things so well."

Everyone was laughing now and Gabe felt almost buoyant. Spring was here…a new beginning. Life was good.

"Hey, Hawthorne!"

Gabe turned around and his good mood dissipated. Jake Morrigan was strutting down the driveway, looking as though he owned the place. Granted, if Mom and Dad couldn't pay their taxes, he soon might.

"What are you doing here, Jake?" Abazi was on her feet, fists on her hips. She looked furious.

His expression went from smug to surprised. He hadn't expected that sort of fury from her. "Thought I'd join the party." He sounded not completely sober and Gabe guessed he'd probably been drinking. There wasn't much to do in Ranger on a Saturday night. Though he wondered where the rest of Jake's posse was. He never traveled alone if he could help it.

"You aren't welcome here," Abazi growled.

"Is that so? Well, maybe someone should let my uncle know that there's a fire burning without a permit. I'll bet you don't have a permit, do you, Hawthorne?" He turned to Gabe. "Probably can't afford one." He snickered appreciatively.

"You're just making that up, Jake," Gabe sneered. Or tried to. Unfortunately, a fire permit sounded exactly like something they would have needed and Jake's uncle was the chief of police.

Jake pulled out his phone and aimed it at the fire, making sure Gabe was in the picture. "There. Got proof now."

Gabe leaped forward. "Give me that!"

Jake pulled the phone to his chest. "Don't think so. Someone's gotta make sure you don't burn down the whole town."

Gabe's skin started to feel itchy. Any minute now the thorns would come, and if they came, maybe he'd turn into a tree, and if he turned into a tree… Well, that never worked out satisfactorily. He breathed in and out, trying to relax. "Listen, Jake. You can stay. Have some marshmallows." Too late he remembered there weren't any left.

"If that scumbag is staying," Abazi spat. "I'm leaving."

Jake's expression was hurt at first, then angry. "At least I know how to handle my liquor!"

Gabe had no idea what Jake was referring to, but judging by Abazi's face, it wasn't nice. "Take it back, Jake," he warned and took a step forward, trying to look as tall and muscular as he could.

"No way. I've been looking for a reason to grind your face into the ground, Hawthorne, and I think I just found it." Jake slipped his phone into his jacket pocket, then took the coat off, setting it on the picnic table. It promptly fell to the ground, but Jake didn't notice as he stalked toward Gabe. "Let's go."

The prickling sensation grew. Oh, crap. Oh, crap! He could *not* turn into a tree right now. "We don't need to fight, Jake." He held up his hands in a conciliatory gesture, then quickly lowered them. The thorns especially liked coming out of his hands.

"Wuss," Jake jeered. "Afraid to get your butt kicked in front of your little friends?"

"My parents are inside. They'll kill me if they catch me fighting."

"*I'll* kill you," Jake growled, "if you don't put your hands up and fight."

"Back off, Jake." Kris stepped between them. "You don't know what you're getting into with Gabe." Oh, Kris. Talk about adding fuel to the fire.

"Oh, yeah?" Jake wobbled a little as he moved closer. With him came the yeasty smell of beer. "What's he going to do? Cry on me?"

"He could slice your throat without taking a step," Kimber said coolly. Everyone, including Jake, looked at her in surprise. "Kris isn't kidding, Jake. You think San Jose is some nice little town? Gabe had to learn young how to fight, and he does it well. He could kill you without even thinking about it."

Jake's slightly unfocused eyes looked a little worried, but that wasn't enough to stop his mouth from running. "Maybe he looks tough to little girls, but when it comes to fighting a real man," he pointed awkwardly at his chest—his thumbs sort of went in different directions— "he's weak. You're all weak," he slurred. "Especially you." He spun around and pointed at Abazi. "All your kind is weak. Your mom couldn't control herself and ended up dead and your dad does whatever my mom tells him to do. *Weak.*"

One second Abazi was standing there staring at Jake, the next she was flying through the air with a guttural cry. She slammed into him, knocking him to the ground. Then she was on top of him and swinging both fists wildly at his face. Jake could barely hold her off. "You stupid, idiotic caveman!" she sobbed. "You and your family are all parasites. Worthless parasites!"

Gabe raced over and plucked her off Jake. He set her down, still swinging, and put out his hand to help Jake up. "Come on. Before she jumps you again."

"Get away from me, you freak!" Jake screamed.

"Just calm down, Jake," Gabe said, approaching the sniveling boy.

Jake clumsily pushed himself to his feet. "I told you to stay away from me!" He took a wild swing, his knuckles connecting against Gabe's cheekbone, below his right eye. Gabe's head barely moved and Jake stared at him in surprise. "You're all a bunch of freaks!" He pointed his finger at all of them. "I'm telling on you and the town will see that you're pushed out. They'll make you go away, *Hawthorne*. Forever!" With a ghoulish half-laugh, half-sob, he turned and stumbled down the driveway.

"Jake!" Gabe called. "Please don't say anything!"

"Shut up!" Jake shouted. Then he stopped for a moment and turned around, slowly, as though on a rusty spindle. "You know, I really can't stand the sound of your whiny voice, Hawthorne. You think you can have her, but you can't. I'll win her back, just you see!" With that, he turned and jerkily ran off.

Gabe could only stare after him in disbelief. Jake was going to tell Chief Mara about the bonfire and his parents would have to pay a fine, which they couldn't afford. But could Jake really get the whole town to come after them? Probably not. But his mom, Candi Morrigan, could. That woman was like a modern-day, female version of Attila the Hun.

"We should go after him," Kris said. "Make sure he keeps his mouth shut."

Gabe sighed. "We'll only make things worse."

Kris smacked his palm with his fist. "Just let me punch him once. I owe him for all the elbows he threw at me in practice."

"Just leave him. He's drunk. He'll pass out somewhere and sleep it off." Then Gabe realized what he was saying. "On second thought, if he drove here…"

Abazi looked sick. "He's a jerk, but I don't want him killing himself, or an innocent bystander."

The group raced down the driveway. Jake's red Ferrari wasn't there, which was odd. They hadn't been that far behind him and he was drunk. No way could he have gotten to his car, started it up, and driven away without being seen or heard. "I'm going to get the truck," Gabe called. "Look for his footprints in the snow. See if he headed into the woods."

Fifteen minutes later, Gabe had driven all the way into town and back, but there was no sign of Jake. He drove the road going the other direction before it dead-ended a half mile down, but Jake was nowhere.

When Gabe returned, he found everyone halfway down the driveway, congregated into a group. He pulled up and stopped, cranking down the window. "I didn't see him anywhere. Maybe he called a friend and they came and got him at the main road. It's the only answer for how he disappeared so quickly."

"It's not the only answer," Jer said ominously, glancing at the woods around them.

"But they're still sleeping," Gabe replied uncertainly. "Aren't they?"

"If they weren't, we'd have heard from Hollie by now," Kris said. "I know we would."

Gabe stared at the woods, straining his ears, his tree senses. But he heard nothing and felt nothing. The forest was dead and empty.

And yet he was quite certain it wasn't.

Chapter Five

Like It's Alive

While Gabe parked the truck, the others did what they could to put out the bonfire. Luckily, being mostly small branches, it had already burned itself down to coals. They started with buckets of snow and piled it on. Then, after the fire stopped steaming, they shoveled everything into the wheelbarrow and hauled it to the edge of the woods where they dumped it on a pile of snow. Then they covered it with more snow. When there was no sign that a fire had ever burned in the front yard, they headed indoors to warm their cold-swollen hands and figure out what to do next. Mom and Dad were watching a movie in the TV room, so after making up some hot chocolate and a bowl of popcorn, they headed up to Gabe's room for privacy.

As they sipped the hot chocolate, Gabe filled the girls in on the incident with the cloak. He didn't want to talk about Jake yet, about what might happen if he told on them. "Kris thinks I have spring fever," he concluded, then took a handful of popcorn—what was left. Most of it had disappeared while he'd been talking.

"But what about those voices?" Abazi wondered aloud. "Where did they come from?"

"The cloak, of course," Jer answered. The 'of course' might have come across as snotty, but the awed look on Jer's face nullified that. "It's magic, Gabe. Like in Harry Potter!"

"But it doesn't make me invisible like his does, although that would be awesome. It does, however, make me feel like I can do anything."

"So you have an *invincibility* cloak?" Abazi smirked and Gabe was glad to see it. She was returning to her old self and her dumb puns. He desperately wanted to ask her about what Jake had said, about her mom, but he sensed that now was not the time.

"Can I try it on?" Jer begged, clasping his hands together.

"Not on your life," Gabe answered.

"Why not?"

"Because it would probably kill you."

"Why would feeling invincible kill me?"

"I don't know. Maybe you'll think you can fly and jump out a window or something. I could do that and save myself, but you'd go splat."

Jer looked sulky. "I wouldn't jump out a window. I'm not that stupid."

"I know that, but the cloak doesn't."

Kimber shuddered. "You make it sound like it's alive, Gabe."

"Maybe it is," he replied grimly.

Kris had been strangely quiet; normally he'd already have the cloak on by now. Gabe glanced at him, but his brother was looking up at the tree etched into the half-moon window. "So what do you think we should do, Kris?" he asked, more to see if his brother was paying attention to their conversation than wanting his opinion.

"What? Oh, um, sure. Whatever you say."

Gabe's eyebrows went up. Kris was never one to hold back his thoughts on a subject. "So we can shave your head and paint flowers on it?"

"Hm? Oh, yep. Right."

"Kris!" Abazi hit him with a pillow. "Where are you?"

Kris grabbed the pillow off the floor and hugged it to himself. "I'm right here," he said grumpily. "Just thinking."

The room went silent after that. It seemed that everyone except Kimber was brooding about something and Gabe had a feeling that didn't bode well. Kimber took turns studying each of them and when she reached Gabe, he could only shrug. He thought maybe Abazi was dwelling on what Jake had said, Jer wanted to try on the cloak and was plotting ways to do it, Gabe was thinking about Abazi, among many other things, and Kris was thinking about…well, Gabe didn't have a clue about that.

He cleared his throat. "So what do we do if Jake rats on us?"

Abazi roused herself. "Oh, let him. What harm can it do? At worst, they'll fine you. You pay the fine and everything will be fine." She gave them a queasy smile. "Crap. Even my puns are awful today."

"Your puns are always awful," Gabe said. "But that's besides the point. What's going on with you?" He might as well try to find out now, when there were witnesses in case she tried to kill him.

Abazi glared at him. "You wouldn't understand."

"I know it's something about your mom and her dying on your birthday. But there's more, isn't there? Something to do with what Jake said."

"You expect me to share that with you when you've kept things from me?"

He pulled back. "What things? I just told you about the cloak. I didn't tell you earlier because I didn't have time."

"I'm talking about your parents' tax situation. About the fact that you might get kicked out. Then you'd have to move and I'd never see you again!" Her eyelids blinked rapidly as she fought back tears. "So I'm not saying another word about my mother."

"Abazi!" Gabe started, but she pushed up from the bed.

"I'm outta here. Let's go, Kimber," she ordered, when Kimber didn't move.

"I'm sure Gabe was going to tell us," Kimber replied calmly.

"I was…" he started.

"*Kimber*," Abazi said again, her tone dark, then she turned and headed down the stairs.

Kimber sighed and awkwardly pushed herself out of a beanbag chair. "I'll see you guys Monday."

"We'll walk you home," Jer volunteered.

"Just stay back a little way. And not you," she nodded at Gabe. "Give her some space. This is not a good time of year for her. It never has been. Her mom died when Abazi was eight."

Eight. Yikes. "What happened to her?"

Kimber was about to answer when Abazi's voice carried up the stairs. "*Kimber!*"

"I'd better go. Don't put the cloak on anymore, Gabe. And maybe you should hide it."

He nodded absently. "Yeah, sure."

His brothers followed after Kimber, returning twenty minutes later, winded from running. Gabe had spent the time watching his fish swim around and around, flitting here and there without a care in the world. He envied them.

"Did she tell you anything?" he asked as soon as Jer's blond head came through the doorway.

Jer shook his head. "No time. Abazi was practically running the whole time. Poor Kimber could barely keep up." He looked angry about that, and Gabe couldn't blame him. Abazi was acting like a real snot.

Kris plopped himself onto the beanbag chair Kimber had recently vacated. "Still warm!" He snuggled into it. "So what are we going to do about Jake?"

"Abazi might be right," said Gabe. "Just let it go. I know it will involve a fine, but what can we do?"

"It's weird that he didn't drive his car," Jer remarked.

"That is weird," Kris agreed. "And he left his phone behind. Remember? He put it in his jacket pocket and his jacket is probably still by the picnic table."

Jer popped up. "I'll go get it!" He returned a couple minutes later, holding the jacket in one hand and the phone in the other.

Kris grinned. "Yes! We can delete the picture!"

Gabe smiled, feeling positive for the first time in over an hour. "Do it, Jer. Then wipe your fingerprints off."

"What do we do with it now?" Jer asked as he deleted the photo, then rubbed at the phone with his shirt to eliminate his prints.

"I'll bring his phone and jacket to the Lost and Found at school."

"Good idea," said Kris with a stretch, followed by a yawn. "I'm tired."

"It's only nine-thirty," Gabe pointed out.

"All that fresh air," Kris spoke through another yawn.

Jer joined in, stretching and yawning dramatically. "Yeah, we were outside all day. Time to turn in."

Gabe realized that he was tired, too. His spring fever high seemed to have worn off and the effects of too little sleep for two nights in a row (he'd had weird dreams last night) and getting up early to work were taking a toll. "Yeah, all right. I'm feeling a bit whipped myself."

After his brothers left, Gabe meant to get up and brush his teeth and put his retainer in, but he was so tired that he passed out right on his bed. Which was probably just as well. There was too much to think about and right now thinking wasn't going to help anything.

~~~~~~~

The next morning was bright and sunny, and didn't match Gabe's mood at all. When he woke up, the first thing he spotted was Jake's jacket, bringing back all his worries about the idiot telling on them. Then, at breakfast, Mom and Dad looked exhausted and Kris was sullen, complaining that Jer had slipped out to the barn and was probably working on the trebuchet they were building together, *without him*.

Their family was falling apart.

"What happened to you?" Mom asked Gabe when she looked up from sliding a muffin tin into the oven.

"I didn't sleep well."

"No, I mean your eye." She pointed.

Kris looked worried when he finally took in Gabe's appearance. "Dude!"

Gabe turned and peered at himself in the old mirror above the phone. His mottled reflection showed a large bruise under his eye. "Oh, um, snowball fight. I think one of them had some ice in it." He turned away. "So Jer's missing, hm?" he asked, hoping to steer the conversation away from his eye. It must have happened when Jake had hit him, which was strange since he hadn't felt any pain.

"If he *is* in the barn like Kris thinks, he got up awfully early." Mom stretched her arms above her head. "I was here at 6:30 baking."

Kris and Gabe glanced at each other. "Oh, well, maybe he's still in bed and I didn't see him," Kris said quickly.

Seconds later, they slurped up the last of the milk in their cereal bowls and sprinted upstairs. Jer's door was slightly open and Kris pushed on it. "You'd better be in here, dork, cause Mom and Dad are looking for you." It was a white lie designed to get Jer to betray himself, but nothing in the room moved.

Gabe flicked on the light. Jer's bed was empty. "Where is he?" he asked worriedly as they searched the rest of the room. "His bed isn't even very messy, like he didn't sleep in it."

Kris glanced up at him from his position on the floor—he was searching under Jer's bed. "Maybe he didn't."

"Then what did he do— Oh, *no.*"

Kris nodded. "The cloak."

They raced back downstairs, past a startled Dad, who spilled his tea as they pounded by. "Where's the fire?" he called, but neither brother answered. They had to get to Gabe's room. They had to know for sure.

Up in the turret, they searched everywhere, but the cloak was nowhere to be found. "No, no, no!" Gabe groaned, his head between his hands. "He's dead. I know it. I woke up feeling something was wrong, now I know what it was."

"You don't know that," Kris said calmly. "Call Abazi and tell her what's up, then meet me in the barn. There's still a lot of snow left, so we might be able to follow his footprints."

"I don't want to call Abazi!" The very thought made Gabe nauseous. She was mad at him and there was nothing he could say to change that, and he hated it.

"Just do it. Jer's missing and we can't tell Mom and Dad. Not yet, anyway. We need people to help search. We need Abazi and Kimber."

Gabe let loose an aggravated groan. "All right. But if it comes to it, I want it known that I'm doing this under protest."

"Duly noted," Kris replied, pretending to write it down.

They headed back to the kitchen. Dad was gone and Mom was washing dishes. "Find Jer?" she asked over her shoulder.

"Oh, he's pulling one of his hiding tricks on us," Kris said casually. "I'm going to the barn to look for him." He pulled on a light jacket. "See you out there, Gabe."

"Yeah, sure." He grabbed the phone and took it into the hallway. With a shaking finger, he punched in Abazi's number. He was relieved when the phone went to the answering machine. Abazi's dad, Mozi, told them to leave a number and an "amusing" message. "Hey, Abazi. It's Gabe. Jer took my invincibility cloak and now we're going looking for him. You and Kimber want to join us?" It was vague enough to keep Mr. Wanibagw from asking too many questions if he heard it, but hopefully with enough detail to get her to come.

Mom was finishing up with the dishes when he returned. "You have plans today?" she asked tiredly.

He blinked guiltily. "We're just looking for Jer. You know he's really good at hiding."

"Hmmm. All right."

"Do you need us to do something?"

"No. Go enjoy the day. May not be many more like this."

He studied her face. She looked like she'd given up. "You mean, the weather?"

She glanced at him. "Hm? Oh, yeah. Sure. This spring weather may not last. It's only April, after all."

"April is supposed to be full of flowers, isn't it?"

"That's rain showers. But here in Maine we can get snow in April." She wiped her hands on a faded dishtowel that really needed to be replaced. Gabe could see a few holes where the material had worn through. "Now go on. Seize the day." She tried to smile, but it failed to make it to her eyes.

"Okay. But you'll let me know, right? If I can help?"

It was her turn to study him, though a little suspiciously. "Yeah, I'll let you know. Now go!" She snapped the towel at him.

He grabbed his jacket and hurried out the door, torn between wanting to help her and needing to find the missing Jer. But since Mom wanted him to go and Gabe knew the effects of the cloak, finding Jer was the priority.

He met Kris in the barn. "Are the others coming?"

"I don't know. I left a message."

"Search upstairs. I'll look around down here."

A couple minutes later Gabe found Kris outside, scanning the yard. "You found nothing, I take it."

"No." Kris kicked at a mound of snow. "Hollie would find him. She said she—"

"Hey, losers," a voice called from the woods. They spun toward the line of trees that separated them from their neighbors. Abazi was marching toward them, looking like yesterday had never happened, followed by a puffing Kimber. "So you lost your brother, huh?" She stopped in front of them, panting. "Hence the name, *losers*. See?" She seemed surprisingly chipper this morning.

"You made good time."

She shrugged. "My dad was lecturing me on how I need to be more involved in tribal activities. I heard the message and used it as an excuse to escape." She looked at them, her heavy breathing slowly subsiding. "So why the panic?"

"We think Jer took the cloak," Gabe replied. "It's missing."

"What?" Kimber gasped, joining them. Her flushed face quickly lost all its color. "No!" Gabe stared at her in surprise. "I think that cloak has powers," she explained. "Strong powers. I felt it the first time you took it out of the trunk, Gabe. And now Jer has it!"

"We don't know that for sure," Gabe tried to reassure her.

"Um, duh." Abazi rolled her eyes. "I think if the cloak is missing and so is Jer, that we can safely assume he has it. Question is, where did it take him?"

Gabe swallowed hard, remembering how the cloak had made him feel like he could run forever. "I was hoping you could track him," he said to her. "You and Kimber are really good at that."

"I'm not so bad myself," Kris interjected. "Mozi taught me some stuff." Over the winter, Kris had worked a few times at the store when Abazi went to visit family and Mozi needed to re-stock shelves. Gabe could always hear them chatting, but never knew what about. Never really cared, actually. Now he wished he'd joined in.

"Okay, where do we start, then?"

Kris indicated the yard. "We're still surrounded by snow, so I say we go where his tracks lead."

"What if he took the driveway?"

"Then we're screwed, and so is he."

Gabe ran an agitated hand over his face. "He could be anywhere."

"Over here!" Kimber called, pointing at the back yard. There was a trail out to the wood crib, tramped down from going back and forth to fill up the wood boxes. Grandpa May had built a chute for sliding wood into the house from the outside. Another trail had been packed down that led into the woods—a safe area, according to their mother—for collecting more dead wood. The snow had been so deep this year that they'd stuck to the trails. But where Kimber was heading, a set of tracks led off the trail, toward the ocean.

Gabe felt sick. Jer had gone that way? That was bad news. Where the woods ended, there was a bit of land, and then a rocky cliff overlooking the ocean. A trail led down the cliff to the water, but it was treacherous and you had to take it slow. Knowing the cloak's power, slow was not what Jer would be doing.

"Come on!" he cried, and then took off. Kris bent over and Kimber jumped onto his back. There was no way she'd make it through this stuff. The snow was thick as wet cement and just as heavy. Gabe was only wearing sneakers, not considering they'd be tromping through the snow, and within minutes his shoes and socks were soaked.

"This is my fault," he muttered to himself. "I should have hid it."

"It's not your fault, idiot," Abazi said behind him. She was breathing hard as she pushed through the snow. "You couldn't have known."

"You see, that's the problem," he argued through clenched teeth. "I did know. I knew he wanted to wear it, and instead of saying I was worried that he would get hurt, I treated him like he was two. I *know* Jer. I know how he thinks. This is my fault."

"Okay," Abazi conceded, a little too readily in Gabe's opinion. "So you screwed up."

Gabe gulped. "Right. I did."

"Do you feel better?"

"Not in the least."

"So taking the blame for someone else's actions doesn't do you any good." She was silent for a few moments, then said, "We can only do what we can *now*."

"Um, yeah," he panted. "Right." He wasn't sure what she was talking about, other than pointing out the obvious, but she was talking to him, so he didn't push his luck and argue like he wanted to.

The trees started to thin at this point and he focused on getting to the cliff. He had to find Jer. He had to reach him in time!

He broke through the line of trees, with Abazi right behind him, sprinting as fast as they could. But what they saw straight ahead made them freeze in their tracks. Jer was standing at the cliff's edge, arms upraised as though praying to the heavens. The cloak flapped in the wind blowing off the ocean and he looked like some sort of prophet. At any moment, he could slip and fall, or the buffeting wind could throw him off balance.

"Jer!" Kimber cried as she slid off Kris's back. "Watch out!"

Jer jerked around, his eyes wide, his face pale. He started to wobble. His arms flailed, and then he was falling backwards…off the cliff.

Chapter Six

We Are Invincible

Gabe didn't even think. His arm shot out, transforming into a branch as it flew through the air. He caught Jer around the waist and pulled hard. When his brother was far enough away from the cliff, Gabe set him down and let his branch arm change back to normal. Then he ran to him.

"Are you all right?" Kimber cried, hobbling after Gabe. "Jer!"

He didn't answer as he turned to face them. Silently, he raised his arms into the air once more and Gabe realized with a sinking feeling that his brother was not yet out of danger. "Ye'll not have us!" he cried. "We shall overcome! We're immortal. We are *invincible*!" Jer glared at them triumphantly and everyone slowed way down.

Gabe held up a placating hand. "It's just us, Jer. Your brothers and your friends. It's the cloak. You have to take it off."

Jer responded by wrapping the cloak more tightly around his frame and taking another step backward. "Ye'll have to catch me. Catch us. *All* of us!"

This time Gabe didn't wait for his brother to fall. His twig fingers caught the back of Jer's cloak and whipped it off, smoothly as a magician. Jer spun around. "Hey!" he shouted angrily, and then, "What the heck?" Glancing behind him, he skittered away from the cliff's edge. "What am I doing here?" He looked frightened and exhausted.

In three swift steps, Gabe was at Jer's side. "Here, put this on." He gave Jer his jacket. Kimber wrapped an arm around Jer's shivering torso and led him away from the ocean's grasping fingers. The wind off the ocean was icy cold, but Gabe no longer felt it. He'd been strangely incited by Jer's odd words, and his blood was running hot. The desire to pull the cloak around his shoulders was strong, but Gabe resisted. *Now is not the time*, he told himself, which was worrisome, since it implied that a time was coming when it would be what he had to do.

"When did you leave the house?" he asked

Jer blinked. "I don't know. Late last night, I think. You were asleep. I was just going to try the cloak on in your room, then you stirred a little. So I sat down to wait, and I think I must have fallen asleep. When I awoke, it was really early, before the sun was up. I didn't want you to catch me, so I took the cloak and went down the pole. I hid out in the barn, and it took me a while to build up the courage to put it on. I kept remembering what Kimber had said about it being alive. But in the end, I just couldn't resist." He looked ready to cry.

"Well, now you know why I didn't want you to wear it."

Jer stifled a sob. "I-I didn't get it until I put it on. And then, well, it was like I was a different person. There were voices in my head telling me to run. To get everyone away. And that's what I did. Well, *I* ran, anyway. I couldn't get everyone away because no one was there." He sounded spooked.

Kimber shushed him. "You're all right now, just don't do that again."

"I won't!" Jer cried vehemently. But even as he said this, he couldn't seem to take his eyes off the cloak. Gabe tightened his grip. This time he'd be sure to hide it. Luckily the turret had several built-in cupboards with hidden doors, perfect for concealing precious treasure. There was no way he could give the cloak to Oswald now.

"Come on. Let's head back to the house. Mom's worried."

"Okay," Jer said quietly. "I *am* hungry."

The group turned to go, but Gabe hung back. He looked out over the vast ocean and wondered about what was on the other side. Britain would be the first stop, then Europe. It was quite a ways to travel, even by plane. But a long time ago people had done it by boat. Had his cloak wearer escaped his pursuers by ship? Was he a murderer fleeing for his life?

"Come on, Immortal." Abazi tugged at his arm and he swung around, surprised. The others were already way ahead, Kimber bouncing up and down on Kris's back as Jer scurried to keep up.

"Immortal," he repeated. "Strange that Jer used that word, too."

"Yes, but no one is immortal. Not even the Dryads of the Forest *Immortal*. Look at what's happening to the trees, what happened to Isis."

"I'm not so sure. We have kids and they carry on our genetics. That's a sort of immortality."

She gave him an odd look. "That's what I'm afraid of."

"That you carry your ancestors' genes?"

"No, just my mother's. The rest I don't mind too much."

Before he could ask her another question, she spun away and ran to catch up with the others. He watched her go for a few seconds, wondering what her mother had done to make Abazi so angry. Because that's what he saw in her eyes when she said the word, *mother*. There was such fury in them that one would think Abazi hated her. So what had happened?

Gabe was determined to find out.

~~~~~~

When he entered the yard he was surprised to see several vehicles parked outside. His surprise quickly turned to fear when he noticed one was a police cruiser. The cops must be here because Jake had told them about the bonfire. He quickly joined the others who were standing back, staring at the cars.

"Mrs. Morrigan is here, too." Kris pointed at the distinctive pink Hummer she drove everywhere.

Gabe stepped forward, feeling sick. "I'll take the blame. They'll have to fine me."

"They won't fine you, martyr," Abazi sighed irritably. "Your parents are in charge of you and it's their property." She paused. "Are you really that short of money?"

Gabe's cheeks went red. "It's because there's so much property here. Mom didn't expect the taxes would be so much and Dad's medical bills just keep coming in."

Abazi's expression was surprisingly contrite. "Yeah, all right. I get it. But I wish you'd told me."

"I wanted to, but you haven't exactly been in the best mood lately and I didn't want to make it worse."

She glanced up at him. "I'm not made of glass."

"No, more like things that go *boom*." He took a deep breath and headed up the front porch steps. When he opened the door, the sound of voices flew out at him.

"If you know something, Ayla," Mrs. Morrigan yelled, "then you'd better start talking!"

The screen door slammed behind Gabe and Mrs. Morrigan went silent as all heads swiveled toward him. There was Mr. Morrigan, who, with his sleek blond hair, shiny loafers, and perfect clothes, reminded Gabe of a mannequin. Next to him stood Mrs. Morrigan, eyes bright and cheeks flushed, wearing her typical outfit, tight pink clothes and a *lot* of cleavage. Mrs. Morrigan's brother, the Chief of Police, Carl Mara, leaned against the refrigerator. He was the polar opposite of his sister—pot-bellied, with half his shirt hanging out and his navy blue tie askew. He wore large, brown-framed glasses that flattered no one, and had greased and slicked his dark brown hair over an expanding bald spot. An oversized, cheesy mustache, currently housing a piece of egg, seemed an obvious attempt to compensate for the lack of hair on his head.

"There he is!" Mrs. Morrigan pointed accusingly at Gabe. He froze where he was.

"Uh, what's going on?" he asked, deciding to play dumb. He was only a minor, after all. They couldn't do much to him, could they?

"Jakie didn't come home last night! What did you do to him?"

"Me?" His hand touched his chest. "I didn't do anything."

"He was here last night, wasn't he?" Mr. Morrigan stepped forward.

Mom turned to Gabe, confused. "Gabe?"

Mr. Morrigan came closer. He had a wide smile on his face, inviting confidences. "You're not in trouble, son, we just want to know where he is."

"He did come here last night," Gabe admitted. "But he left. We went looking for him because, well, he didn't seem to be in the best, um, health. But we didn't find him or his car or anything."

"Why didn't you say anything to us?" Mom demanded.

"Because it wasn't a big deal. He was mad at me because I won MVP and he thought he'd cause some trouble. He was alone, though, and there were five of us so he backed off and left."

"Liar," Mrs. Morrigan breathed. "Why would Jakie be jealous of you? He's the most popular boy in school." She gave a laugh, like her son being jealous of *anyone* was absurd. "Besides, your parents are broke, you live in the middle of these stupid woods, and you're nothing but white trash."

"Now, now, Candace," Mr. Morrigan soothed, though his smile had slipped a little. "Let's not go jumping to conclusions or saying things we might later regret."

Her pink lips pursed into a tight ball. "I'm just saying that Jakie wouldn't have done what this boy is saying." She eyed him more closely. "He stole things last fall. Remember I told you about that? Yes, we got everything back, but still, he's a thief." Gabe was about to defend himself when she leaned closer. He could smell her strong perfume, likely expensive, but awful. The gold necklace she always wore was lodged in her cleavage, very possibly permanently. "What's that on your face? Is that a black eye?" She looked almost avid at the possibility. "You two had a fight, didn't you?"

"Is that true, boy?" the chief finally found his voice.

"No. Jake swung at me."

"Did you swing back?" The chief had a greasy smile, like he'd just got done eating a bucketful of fried chicken. "It's what boys do. Fight."

"I didn't touch him, Chief Mara. I was raised to never take advantage of those weaker than me, and at that time, Jake was weaker than me. I told you he wasn't himself."

"And just why exactly was he not *himself*?" His fat fingers curled into quotation marks.

"Now you don't have to answer that, son," Mr. Morrigan interrupted, looking uncomfortable. "It's circumstantial, anyway."

"Oh, that's all right," Gabe said, smiling directly into Mr. Morrigan's cool gray eyes. "I think Jake had a few too many drinks. He was drunk. There were five of us there, and we all saw it."

"How dare you?" Mrs. Morrigan screeched. "We'll sue you for libel!" She swung around and pointed at the porch. "*All* of you!"

"Slander," Mr. Morrigan corrected. "And you can bet your, um, behinds we will."

Mom stepped forward, looking unexpectedly menacing. "Oh, yeah? Well, if I hear one word about Gabe or any of my family having anything to do with Jake's disappearance, I'll sue you for slander and libel and negligence and whatever else I can think of!"

"And how are you going to pay your lawyers?" Mrs. Morrigan sneered.

"With the money that we win," Mom answered back, looking ready to pounce on Mrs. Morrigan and beat the snot right out of her.

"All of you can leave my house right now," Dad boomed and Gabe stared at him in surprise, "before I throw you out!"

"Now s-see here!" Chief Mara stuttered. "I'm an officer of the law."

"And you're trespassing," Dad reminded him. "You have no cause to suspect Gabe of anything, so move along and go find that kid. He's not here!"

Mrs. Morrigan shook a shiny pink claw at Dad, making the numerous gold bracelets on her skinny wrist dance skittishly. "You'll regret this, Keith. Just as I'm sure you regret not marrying me!"

Mr. Morrigan grabbed her arm and pulled her away, not looking at all pleased with that little exchange. "You'll be hearing from us soon," he threatened, then pushed past Gabe and out the door.

"He didn't do anything, you old biddy!" Gabe heard Abazi shouting at Mrs. Morrigan. "So leave him alone!" Despite the seriousness of the situation, he couldn't help grinning.

Chief Mara glanced out the door, then wiped his hand across his mouth as he returned his gaze to Gabe. "Just don't plan on going nowhere, you hear?"

Gabe nodded, then couldn't resist asking, "Should I still go to school?"

"What?" He pushed up his glasses with his middle finger. "Oh, yeah. You can do that." He stomped out, missing Gabe's smirk.

Mom didn't miss it. "So when were you planning to tell us that Jake had stopped by? And that your black eye was from him, not a snowball?"

"Right after we found Jer?"

"You found Jer?" She looked past Gabe to see the others staring through the screen. "Jerome! Where in heaven's name were you?"

"I just took a walk, Mom. It's so nice out I didn't want to miss any of it."

"Oh, well, that's okay, then. But next time tell someone, all right?" She ruffled his hair, then turned to Gabe. "Let's hear it. The whole thing."

He relayed the story as best he could remember it. Abazi looked a little uncomfortable when he reached the part where she'd tackled Jake, but Mom only smiled and gave her a thumbs-up. Luckily his parents were already quite aware that Jake hated him. He hadn't even had to tell them. Mom had caught the end of their first practice when Jake kept harassing him and afterwards had asked, "What has that kid got against you?" When she heard it was Mrs. Morrigan's son, she muttered, "History really does repeat itself." Apparently she'd suffered the same problem with Mrs. Morrigan.

"Hmmm," she replied when he was done. He'd even explained how they had covered up all evidence of the bonfire— "I'll pretend I didn't hear that," she'd remarked dryly. The others had backed him up throughout his story, with Abazi being the most vociferous. "So you're sure that's everything?" Mom persisted. He nodded. "All right, then, we should be fine. You have several witnesses, so that helps. Just keep your nose clean this week."

"Shouldn't we join the search?" Kris asked. "We can scout out the woods, look for his tracks."

Mom visibly shuddered. "Just stick to the yard and road."

"But you know people disappear in those woods all the time," Kris persisted. "The same thing might have happened to Jake. You don't have to go," he continued hurriedly. "We'll do it."

"We will?" Gabe wasn't so sure about that.

"I'm going into those woods," Kris said determinedly.

"We'll stay in a group, Mrs. Hawthorne," Abazi spoke up. "Right, boys?"

They all, except for Gabe, chorused, "Right!"

Mom didn't look too happy. "All right. You can go in the woods. Even though Jake's a spoiled little brat, I don't want anything happening to him. And this will look good that you're searching for him."

"We'll get our stuff," Kris said, then rushed off before Gabe could stop him.

It looked like they were going into the woods.

Chapter Seven

Trying to Muddy the Trail

Like all the other times when they headed into the woods, they took no chances, loading up with the weapons they kept stored in the barn. Jer had organized sections for each person, depending on their skill. Abazi was excellent with the tomahawk, Kris was great with a staff, Kimber used the bata—a short stick that worked as a cudgel—with stunning, and because of her spasms, unpredictable ferocity, and Jer had been working on handling the willow whip. Gabe wore a bata at his waist, as did everyone, but kept his hands free in case he needed to transform.

The whole time they were getting ready, Kris was antsy, practically bouncing up and down in his effort to get them to hurry.

"What is with you?" Abazi demanded when he told her to get the lead out.

"Time's a wastin'," he replied shortly, twirling his staff like a baton.

She studied him as she strapped on her tomahawk, then grabbed a staff for herself. "She's going to be all right," she said finally.

Kris shrugged. "I don't know what you're talking about."

"Yes, you do, and don't try to deny it. You're worried about Hollie."

"Okay, fine. Maybe I am. She said she had ways to avoid the Freeze. But she also told me that there's a price to pay if you do it wrong. What if something went wrong and now she's dead? I mean, what other alternative is there? Spring has sprung, and I haven't heard from her!"

"We haven't heard from any of them," Abazi pointed out. "It was a long winter and it's really only the beginning of April. Maybe they don't wake up for another week or two. We don't even see leaves around here until late April, early May."

Kris swung his staff in a wide arc, nearly cracking Jer on the head. "Hey, watch it!"

"Sorry," Kris mumbled. "I just want to get going."

"I'm ready," Gabe announced. "Everyone else?"

Everyone said yes, and Kris practically ran out the barn doors, taking the lead. Gabe let him. He wanted time to think, to process what had happened to Jer and what Kris had said about Hollie. He was worried about her, too. If he was feeling the flow of sap, shouldn't she be feeling it, as well? And he couldn't stop thinking about what the cloak had done to Jer. He'd only had enough time to throw it under his bed and hope nobody else found it and tried it on—like Mom. Or Dad. Then again, it might be good for Dad's health.

Or maybe not. With the cloak on, Jer had been about to jump off a cliff. Maybe that's what had happened to the man being chased—he leaped to his death. Though from his words, he didn't exactly strike Gabe as the suicidal type, and there had been others with him, too. Had they followed him like lemmings, racing toward their death? It was too gruesome to contemplate. In fact, Gabe didn't want to contemplate any of it. It was all too weird. He just wanted to be like everyone else in his family. Somewhat normal. That's all he was asking for.

Fat chance that he'd get it.

"Tracks!" Kris pointed at the overgrown hedge, which had finally lost the last of its blanket of snow. For the longest time the Briar Borders had resembled a glacier. Now the eight-foot tall hedge was green, and green meant it was possible to get through, if you knew how. Gabe knew how, but Jake didn't and wouldn't be able to get past the prickly mass.

Unless he'd been taken.

"Two sets," Jer clarified, staring at the snow-covered ground. "One looks like sneakers, size ten, I'd guess." Jake was a size ten, which Gabe shouldn't know, but did. For some reason, Jake found Gabe's bigger feet a threat to his manhood and was always comparing his feet to Gabe's, as if he were trying to catch up. Like having size fourteens was a great thing. Gabe had a hard enough time finding shoes in that size, much less ones they could afford. Both he and Kris had to get new shoes recently and afterwards Mom had actually *prayed* that their feet were done growing.

"The other?" he asked, joining the group huddled around the prints.

"Small," Kris replied. "But not Hollie's, unless she's wearing shoes now." Hollie pretty much went barefoot all the time. Her feet were long and narrow, almost like a chicken's. These tracks were oval-shaped and smooth, giving no indication of what, or who, had made them. "We must have missed them last time because it was getting dark out."

Gabe started to follow the trail and found himself at the driveway where the woods formed a tunnel over the drive. He headed into the woods, stopped when he saw the tracks loop around towards the hedge, and headed back out. Was it possible someone had grabbed Jake, pulled him into the woods to hide him while Gabe and the others searched, then dragged him toward the hedge? Well, of course it was possible. But is that what had happened?

Gabe peered closer at the trail. Whoever had made the tracks had doubled back and taken Jake through the hedge rather than just head further into the woods. It was almost as if they'd been trying to 'muddy' the trail. "Any ideas about who might have taken him?" he asked the others, thoroughly stuck.

"I'm not sure these are Ko-gok prints," Kris replied.

"Oswald, then? Or Filidh?"

"My money is on that Filidh," Jer spoke up. "From what you said, he sounds kind of shifty. I can see him holding Jake for ransom, maybe thinking we want him and would pay to get him back."

"I'd pay the man to *keep* the jerk," Abazi growled.

"It's a risky thing to do," Gabe said. "It brings too much attention to the woods and I don't think any of the forest dwellers want that attention."

Abazi fingered her tomahawk. "Well, it isn't doing us any good talking. Gabe?" She indicated the hedge.

He stepped forward, feeling a little nervous. Would the vines still listen to him? "Open up!" he cried, sounding satisfyingly warrior-like, and the twigs began to slither apart before the 'p' in up had even made its way out of his mouth. He grinned. That had been easy. Then his grin slipped away as a chilling thought occurred to him. What if this was a trap, with Jake as the bait? He shivered, then pulled back his shoulders determinedly. Trap or not, they had to go forward. They had to find Jake before Straif did.

Kris slipped through, followed by Jer and Kimber, and Gabe gestured for Abazi to go ahead of him. He wanted to make sure the hedge behaved and didn't close on someone while they were in the middle of it. When everyone was through, the vines and twigs reunited, forming a barrier solid as a rock.

The trail continued on the other side, with no attempt made to hide it. The going was slow in the high, slushy snow that filled the clearing between the hedge and the woods. Spring had come, but that didn't mean winter had gone. After only ten or so yards, Kris had pulled Kimber up on his back, so he was probably really feeling the strain. But he didn't show it, joking with her as they bounced along. Gabe made a mental note to carry her back.

When they reached the woods, everyone stopped and caught their breath before plunging into the darkness within. Not for the first time Gabe thought how eerie it was to enter a woods that seemingly held no living creatures beyond trees and moss. No tracks, other than the ones they were following, marred the white expanse of snow that seemed to stretch on forever. Only the sound of their breathing filled the heavy air around them. There should have been birds, squirrels, *some*thing. But there was nothing. Most of the living had either fled or been eaten by the dark ones.

The footsteps suddenly disappeared, and about ten feet afterwards, so did the snow. Kris stopped in his tracks, slowing dropping Kimber and reaching for his weapons. Soon they were ready for battle, spinning in circles, nervous. Something strange was going on. How could the footsteps just disappear? Gabe looked up, ready for an attack from above, but all he saw were the smooth gray torsos of the beech trees. Nothing more.

He waited, and at last he heard a familiar sound. Running water. Shambolic Stream must lie ahead of them. He crept toward it, followed by the others, and within seconds, was gazing at the black snake twisting and turning through the white woods. In several areas the snow had retracted, as though melted, sometimes going twenty feet beyond the banks of the stream.

"The stream changed course," Jer was the first to figure out. "See." He pointed. "It really does move around."

"I wonder if it does that on its own," Kris asked. "Or does someone tell it to move?"

"I imagine someone tells it," Gabe answered, and finally got why a moving stream was useful. "It not only throws people off, getting them lost, it can hide evidence someone has been this way."

"But who tells it to do that?"

"I don't know, but it's a good sign, right? That someone here is awake."

"It could just be that fairy of yours," Abazi pointed out. "The one that wanted to kill you. What was his name?"

"Wildrr." Gabe hadn't told the others he'd saved the Lady, just that she was okay and that Wildrr was no longer on the warpath. He didn't want Abazi accusing him of being a glory-hog again.

"Right. He wouldn't have hibernated. Neither would that weird guy…Filet, was it?"

"Filidh," Gabe provided absently, thinking hard. "Whoever it was is likely the one who kidnapped Jake." He pointed at the melted patch of ground. "One jump and the footprints are gone."

"One really big jump, with Jake in tow," Kris argued. "And the footsteps must pick up again somewhere."

"Kris is right." Kimber started walking toward the stream. "We'll have to search on the other side."

They followed after her, spreading out along the rushing brook. After an hour of searching on both sides and quite a ways up and down the stream, they met back at where the tracks disappeared.

"Any sign of anything?" Gabe asked hopefully. He'd seen nothing, heard nothing, felt nothing. The woods were dead.

"It's like they disappeared into the sky," Jer said woefully.

Gabe's heart started beating a little harder. *Into the sky…* Could it be? "Maybe the trees grabbed them."

Five heads tilted upward, scanning the trees. "Well, if they did," Abazi said after a moment, "they're long gone."

"But don't you see? The trees had to be awake to do that!"

Kris frowned. "You think? Because they look pretty dead to me." His voice sounded dull, almost defeated.

Gabe stared around him at the seemingly lifeless place. "Not completely."

"Why don't you try calling to them?" Kimber suggested.

"Using what? My cell phone?"

Her blue eyes regarded him with infinite patience. "Use your voice, Gabe. Maybe you can wake them. If you're truly the King of the Forest Immortal, they will listen and they'll do their best to respond."

Oh, crap. She really meant it. And the worst part was that maybe she was right. He closed his eyes for a moment, then opened them. This was probably going to be pretty humiliating. His lips parted. "Trees!" he hissed. "Wake up!"

"You have to do it louder than that," Kris said, irritated. "A mouse wouldn't hear you."

"Fine." Gabe closed his eyes, cleared his throat, and let loose. "Trees! This is your King! Waaaaake uuuuuup!"

When he opened his eyes, he was surprised to see his brothers and Abazi and Kimber kneeling on the ground, hands over their ears. He didn't think he'd been *that* loud. And besides, nothing had happened in response, not even a twig so much as wiggled.

Kris pulled his hands away. "Holy crap, Gabe. A little warning would've been nice."

"You told me I needed to be louder. So I was louder."

"That was loud enough to trigger an avalanche on the mountain. Cripes." Kris shook his head. "I think you blew my eardrums."

"Well, apparently it wasn't loud enough." He indicated the trees. "Nothing."

Abazi stood and brushed off her knees. "Well, I'm stumped." She laughed. "Get it? Stumped?" She looked around at them. "Oh, come on! That was funny." Kris gave her a feeble smile. "Oh, great. A sympathy smile."

"Let's go get lunch," Gabe suggested. He was hungry, and he wanted to keep Abazi's good mood alive.

"We can eat at my house," Kimber offered. "My mom says I owe you guys some meals." She said it casually, but Gabe had the feeling there was more behind the offer. Like charity. He didn't like charity. Well, unless he was the one offering it. Besides, Kimber's mom was a small business owner with pitiful health insurance, and from what Abazi had told him, Kimber's treatments were expensive, so money was tight for them, too. Strange, but in San Jose, he'd never have thought like that.

"Thanks, but we eat a lot more than you, Kimber. Your mom wouldn't know what hit her. We have leftovers from yesterday. We'll eat those."

She didn't respond for a moment, as though she was weighing what he'd said. "All right," she finally agreed. "But one of these days I want to make supper for your family. It's what people do. Take turns."

"Sure. Cool. Make spaghetti. It's cheap and it goes a long way. Otherwise you're going to need to take out a second mortgage." He wasn't kidding, and kind of felt guilty about how much he and his brothers ate. They couldn't help it, though. Growing five inches in a year was enough to drive a runway model to eat.

She laughed. "All right. Spaghetti it is. I can make it, too, which helps."

"Speaking of food," Kris said. "Let's get going. I'm really starving now." He motioned for Kimber to climb up on his back and when she was set in place, he took off. A hungry Kris was a desperate Kris.

Gabe followed after them, more slowly. He'd hoped things would be different in the woods now that it was so warm. Heck, he would even have welcomed seeing a dark one. But he hadn't glimpsed so much as a shadow. The woods still slept.

He stopped and held out his hands, palms upward. "Help me," he called out in a low voice. "Show me what I need to do." He waited, then tried again. "*Please!* I need to know how to save you!"

"*Read the book,*" a voice whispered in his ear. He looked around. The others were a ways ahead of him, hurrying to keep up with Kris, and gave no sign of hearing anything. And there was no sign of anyone nearby who could have whispered in his ear. "*The book knows,*" the voice came again, weak, as though half asleep. Or dying.

And he thought he recognized the voice, but couldn't place it. He ran around all the trees within twenty yards, searching. "Hello?" he half-whispered, not daring to call too loudly. "Are you there?"

"Gabe! What are you doing? Come on!" It was Abazi, beckoning to him from behind a pale birch tree. "Hurry up. My feet are freezing and I have a paper I need to finish."

"I-I'm coming," he pushed out. "Just thought I heard something." It wasn't a lie. He truly had thought he'd heard something. No, he *did* hear something, a voice telling him about a book. But what did it mean? Was he really supposed to find a book that would tell him what to do? And if so, where was it?

Then he realized where. In his room. On the bookshelf full of hundreds of books.

He'd never find it in time.

Chapter Eight

Blood of Men

The brothers escorted Kimber and Abazi home. Kris was unusually morose during the walk; sometimes he got into these weird funks. They never lasted long, but while they were going on, he was a pain to be around. When they reached Kimber's house, they decided to split up. Everyone seemed to be in agreement that a little time apart, pretending things were normal by doing homework or laundry or whatever, was what everyone needed right now.

After lunch, Gabe spent a couple hours working on his paper. This showed a tremendous amount of control on his part, being that all he wanted to do was pull out every single book on his bookshelf and read through it, hoping to find the 'answer' as the voice had promised.

As his paper was printing, Gabe thought about Jake's whereabouts. What could have happened to him? Had someone from the woods really taken him? If so, who? And why? His best guesses were the ones they'd already produced: Filidh and Wildrr, since all the tree spirits still seemed to be asleep. If Gabe were to choose between the two, he'd pick Filidh. Wildrr was pretty small to be forcing someone as big as Jake to come with him. But he did have those magic panpipes, Gabe remembered, which could make Jake go anywhere Wildrr wanted him to. But why? Filidh, on the other hand, had the size advantage, but again, seemed to lack motive. Was he working for someone else, maybe?

Gabe sighed and stapled his paper together. It was just as likely that Jake was holed up somewhere, licking his wounds and plotting. So it was up to Gabe and his brothers to track the jerk down and make him tell the truth about what happened.

When his paper was safely stowed in his backpack, Gabe headed for the bookshelf and scanned the packed shelves. He'd pretty much taken out all the books at one time or another. He hadn't read them all, not even close, but he'd skimmed a fair number. And none of them had seemed to offer any particular wisdom about saving a bunch of tree spirits.

His eyes hit the end of the shelf and had whipped around to start the next one down, when they suddenly backtracked. A book with an orange spine caught his attention, probably because it was one he had avoided. It was called *Poems and The Spring of Joy*, and since Gabe tended to find poems either boring or incomprehensible, he mostly avoided them. Limericks were more his style. *There's a place in France where the naked ladies dance…*that sort of stuff. Vulgar, but quite entertaining.

He pulled the book off the shelf and was surprised to find its cover was real wood. He carefully opened the dusty book, which smelled of hot attics and musty paper. Perusing the contents, he saw it was published in 1929 and written by a Mary Webb. He'd never heard of her. At the table of contents, he scanned the titles, finding a number of them rather intriguing: *Green Rain, Fairy-Led, In Dark Weather*.

When he found one called *The Wood*, he decided to read it, and was surprised at how good it was. When he was done with that poem, he flipped through a bunch of pages and stopped at *A Hawthorn Berry*. A shiver whipped through him, cold and thrilling. *Could this be it?* He read the poem aloud, his lips moving slightly.

How sweet a thought,
How strange a deed,
To house such glory in a seed —
A berry, shining rufously,
Like scarlet coral in the sea!
A berry, rounder than a ring,
So round, it harbours everything;
So red, that all the blood of men
Could never paint it so again.
And, as I hold it in my hand,
A fragrance steals across the land:
Rich, on the wintry heaven, I see
A white, immortal hawthorn-tree.

He read it twice more, all the while thinking, "Wow. Wow!" He'd never connected to poetry before, but this poem really caught him, as though written for him. *About* him. *A white, immortal hawthorn-tree?* That *was* him! The line, "So red, that all the blood of men could never paint it so again," appealed to his morbid side and he quickly memorized it. He flipped a few more pages along, stopping at a poem called *The Door.*

I heard humanity, through all the years,
Wailing, and beating on a dark, vast door
With urgent hands and eyes blinded by tears.
Will none come forth to them for evermore?
Like children at their father's door, who wait,
Crying 'Let us in!' on some bright birthday morn,
Quite sure of joy, they grow disconsolate,
Left in the cold unanswered and forlorn.
Forgetting even their toys in their alarms,
They only long to climb on father's bed
And cry their terrors out in father's arms.
And maybe, all the while, their father's dead.

It was weird, but Gabe felt that way all the time lately. The poem was macabre and maybe a bit dramatic, but perfect. This Mary Webb had captured his feelings completely. Who was she? Was there some connection to her and the cloak? He hurried over to the computer and googled her. Someone must know about her. Walter de la Mare, a poet his English teacher had mentioned only last week, had written the *Forward* for her book.

After reading all he could about Mary Webb, Gabe decided she likely had nothing to do with the cloak itself. She had been born in England, and later developed some sort of thyroid disease that made her eyes and throat bulge like a frog. Her husband supposedly cheated on her, and she died pretty young by today's standards—age 46. One well-known author wrote a parody that mocked Webb's work, calling it overblown. Gabe didn't see her poems that way, but then, maybe the critic didn't understand what it was like to be physically different, as he and Mrs. Webb did. Maybe she didn't get what it was like to have darkness all around you, to struggle to see the light.

But even if Mary Webb had nothing to do with the cape, maybe someone who did had read her work and found a connection to their own dilemma. There still might be a message somewhere in one of her poems, something that would show him the way. He resolved to read the entire book. But not tonight. He was too tired and he'd miss something, he was certain.

Tomorrow. He'd read it tomorrow for sure.

~~~~~~

Gabe hated Mondays. And this Monday was starting like most others…crappy. The truck took forever to start and they were nearly late to school. And then, when he was hurrying to his locker, one of Jake's friends tripped him, sending him sprawling to the floor. It hurt, but the worst pain was inflicted on his ego as kids laughed at him. When he stood up, he was hoping he'd see Jake sneering at him, but there was no sign of him. And his friend wasn't laughing. No, his friend looked mean and angry…and slightly scared.

But Gabe didn't have time to think about that; the bell was going to ring any moment. He picked up his bag, dialed his combo, grabbed a few books, and sprinted to class. In each of his classes, he got the same reaction: people staring at him and pointing. Whispering. Strange looks. He and Abazi didn't share any classes in the morning, so he wasn't able to get her take on what was going on. A quick pit stop in the bathroom showed no boogers, hair okay, zipper up, no thorns or flowers. So what was the deal?

He found out at lunch. Abazi rushed toward him, grabbed his elbow, and steered him to their usual table. It was empty. "I tried to catch you in the hallway before classes, but I didn't see you!" She seemed unusually ruffled.

"I was running late. The truck wouldn't start. It floods so easily."

She pulled a newspaper out of her backpack. "This is bad." She slapped it down on the table in front of him. "Really bad."

Gabe stared at her, his stomach rumbling. He was feeling both hungry and queasy. He grabbed the paper and scanned the front-page headlines.

Local Emergency Prompts Early Release of The Ranger Rag

Followed by:

Ranger Boy Goes Missing
Local Family Under Suspicion

Ranger, Maine – Jake Morrigan, son of Candi Morrigan, owner of Ranger Real Estate, and Dick Morrigan of Morrigan & Halston, LLC, has officially been declared missing after he disappeared from the May Farm. This is no April Fool's Joke, folks. Jake was last seen by Gabriel Hawthorne and his friends. Allegedly, a fight ensued between Hawthorne and Morrigan, leaving Hawthorne with a black eye and Jake missing. It is assumed that he ran off and hid in the nearby woods.

Jake Morrigan is a popular star athlete at Ranger High. He plays soccer, basketball, and baseball, leading his teams to several victories. He narrowly missed out on Team MVP in basketball to Hawthorne, which may have been a reason for the fight between them. It was also possible they were fighting over a girl.

This reporter sat down with Candi Morrigan, the boy's mother, for an exclusive interview. As many of you know, Mrs. Morrigan is the epitome of femininity, but when it comes to her children, she's a wildcat. "I want my boy back!" she told *The Ranger Rag*. "If I have to tear down those woods with my own two hands to find him, I'll do it." Mrs. Morrigan is a prominent local citizen, leading the fight to clear the forest near May Farm. Her goal is to bring Ranger into the 21st century by building condos, an exclusive theater, and offering upscale services people are used to having in these modern times. This writer wholeheartedly agrees that decent cell phone coverage would be a nice change! "Those Hawthornes," she added, with a tear in her eye, "know something about what happened to my Jakie, and I won't rest until I find out what it is!"

Jake Morrigan is not the first Rangerite to go missing. The best-known case is that of Bruce Holt, a local who disappeared twenty years ago. The belief was that he went missing around the May Farm, prompting speculation about the Mays and Hawthornes and their role in his disappearance. No charges were ever filed, but it's obvious to this reporter that something strange is going on over in that part of town.

Chief of Police, Carl Mara, is conducting the investigation. He is asking people to keep an eye out, but to not go in the woods on their own. "Pair up," was his advice, sage advice, in this reporter's opinion, knowing what happened to Bruce Holt and many other poor souls over the years. He told *The Rag* that he had two or three leads he was following up on as we speak. If anyone knows anything, please contact his office ASAP!

We wish the Morrigan family the best of luck in finding their beloved son, and as always, Rangerites: Keep us informed!

Gabe knew he should know better, but he couldn't believe Ronald Pruspin had actually written this story. It was so full of innuendo and libel that Gabe could have a pig defend him in court and win. But Ronald would get away with it because Gabe and his family didn't even have the money to feed a pig, much less hire it as a lawyer.

He dropped the paper on the table and buried his face in his hands. This was bad. Really bad. "Can you believe they implied the fight was about a girl?" Abazi cried. "*I'm* that girl!"

Gabe looked up. "*That's* what you got out of the story?"

"Well, no." She looked slightly chagrined. "I'm totally p.o.ed that they're implying your family had something to do with Bruce Holt's disappearance and now Jake's. That's totally bogus crap. And typical Ronald Pruspin. He's such a weasel!"

"I agree. But what can we do? We're screwed. *I'm* screwed."

Abazi reached out, hesitantly, and placed her hand on his arm. It was warm and made his skin tingle. He froze, fearing so much as a tic would make her take it back. "We'll fight this. We'll find Jake and return him safe and sound to his loathsome mumsie. All right?"

He turned and looked at her, barely daring to breathe. "All right."

"You don't sound like you mean it."

"Probably because I don't. We don't have the money to sue him and Jake isn't the first person to disappear in those woods. Something happened to him and there's a good chance it was not something good. Even if the dark ones didn't get him, the forest is treacherous and it's still cold out, even with the warm front that's moved in. He could very well have passed out in the snow and frozen to death."

"Then explain the footsteps," she implored, squeezing his arm.

He glanced down at her hand, feeling a little dizzy. "I don't know what happened there. Maybe a giant bird grabbed him."

"Or a tree. Come on, Gabe! Don't make me be the optimist here. It doesn't suit me."

He couldn't help it. He looked into her eyes and grinned. She was fighting for him! She was *touching* him! "You look really gorgeous when you're full of righteous indignation."

She pulled her hand away and he silently cursed his clumsiness. "Yeah, well, I have good reason to be indignant," she muttered, turning away, "especially when it comes to Ronald Pruspin and Candi Morrigan." She opened up her backpack and pulled out her lunch bag. "And you can bet Mrs. Deacon would be in on this, too," she went on, her anger rising again, "if she weren't staying with her sick sister."

"I was wondering what had happened to her. She hasn't been in the store for weeks."

"Her sister needed intestinal surgery—apparently she had a blockage. Probably from having to listen to the Deacon's daily lectures on doing your duty and thinking she was saying doodie and pushed too hard." She snickered appreciatively. "Anyway, I think not having her here to back Candida up has made the witch desperate."

Gabe grinned. "Candida. Now that's an appropriately gross name."

Abazi laughed loudly, causing others to look at her. She didn't even notice, which is something Gabe liked about her. She marched to the beat of a different drummer, and that drummer was Animal from *The*

Muppet Show. "One of my best. Now eat something. We're going to need our strength for the days ahead."

He nodded. "I have that feeling, too. That things are changing. That something is about to happen."

She pulled out a sandwich, then turned to him, her expression deadly serious. "That's because we're going to make it happen. And woe be to those who get in our way."

Chapter Nine

Bag It

Abazi was quiet for the rest of lunch and Gabe didn't much feel like talking either. Every word, every look, every whisper seemed accusatory. No wonder the other students were treating him strangely. They thought he was a murderer. At the very least, a kidnapper.

The second half of the day went much the same as the first. Gabe decided to keep his head down and do his work. But his relief at escaping school turned to anxiety when he and his brothers pulled up next to the barn. An empty police cruiser was parked in front of the house.

He jumped out of the truck and slammed the door behind him, not waiting for his brothers. He had to know what was going on. He heard his mom yelling as soon as he stepped onto the porch. He pulled open the door and stepped inside, followed by his brothers, both breathing hard from racing after him. Police Chief Mara was there, along with his deputy, Officer White. Officer White looked a little sheepish. His son was on the basketball team and was friends with Gabe.

"You took out a search warrant? Really, Carl?" Mom cried. "You couldn't have just asked? We have nothing to hide. Besides, you know there are witnesses that back up Gabe's story?"

"I know. But being as they're his friends or family members, I have to follow up on things."

"Being that your sister is behind this, you mean…"

"It's just a formality, Ayla," Chief Mara mumbled, looking nervous. He glanced at the door as if expecting someone. When Gabe heard a car door slam outside, he knew who it was. The Morrigans.

Mom went to the door, slammed it shut, and locked it on Mrs. Morrigan's screeching protests. "She's not coming in here." She folded her arms and waited for the chief to protest. He looked very badly as if he wanted to, but he knew he had no legal leg to stand on. Candi Morrigan wasn't an official, nor was her husband, and so neither were allowed to come in if not invited.

There was a banging on the door and Gabe jumped. He felt awful, all tingly and hot, as though he'd actually done something wrong. But he hadn't! He was being persecuted for something he hadn't done. They had no right!

"But Gabe didn't do anything!" Kris put Gabe's thoughts into words. "He's innocent!"

"Yeah!" Jer echoed.

Mom held up her hands. "Which means we have nothing to hide. Get on with it, Carl. Do what you have to do."

"I want to see the boy's room," he said, nodding at Gabe. "He's our main person of interest."

"Don't you mean suspect?"

"I mean, person, Ayla," he grumbled. "Stop putting words in my mouth."

"Come on," Gabe said. "I'll show you the way." He retrieved his key from around his neck and headed down the long hall to the turret. He heard the officers' boots clumping behind him and the sound reminded him of Edgar Allen Poe's *The Tell-Tale Heart*. Lately it seemed as though everything happening to him related back to a poem or a story, as though life was trying to tell him something.

He opened the first door, pounded up the steps, then opened the second. Once in his room, he turned on the overhead light.

"Hoo wee!" Officer White breathed when he left the stairwell. "This is some place you got here, Gabe."

"No fraternizing, White!" Chief Mara huffed. "Just do your job." He nodded at Gabe. "You stand here by the door and don't touch anything."

Gabe did as he was told, spotting his brothers and Mom and Dad on the stairs behind him. His brothers looked thrilled; Mom and Dad, worried sick.

The officers made their search, though what they were looking for eluded Gabe. A smoking gun? A bloody knife? Jake himself? Whatever it was, it didn't look as though they were finding it. After fifteen minutes of searching, looking under the bed—Gabe was glad he'd moved the cape to a hidden nook—rooting through Gabe's drawers, and kicking his clothes around, Chief Mara grunted, "Nothing here."

Gabe would have sighed with relief, but that's when he saw it. Jake's hoodie. Sitting right on the chair where Jer had left it. Despite his willing them not to, his eyes widened and his breathing sped up. He shifted his gaze over to the window, trying desperately to calm down. He couldn't make them suspicious. It was just a sweatshirt. Lots of kids had them. They had no way of knowing it was Jake's.

"Let me through!" a voice cried behind him and he spun around. Ah, crap. Candi Morrigan had somehow gotten into the house. What had she done? Picked the lock? Climbed through a window? Whatever it was, she was trespassing, but that wouldn't matter, not if she found the hoodie. Gabe didn't know what to do. Should he go sit on it? Grab it and put it on? But it was too late to do anything. She pushed her way past his family and elbowed Gabe aside.

"Candi!" Chief Mara whined, just like a little brother would do. "You're compromising a potential crime scene. Get out of here!"

"I'm not leaving until you find proof this boy did something to my son." She pointed accusingly at Gabe. "He's never liked Jakie. Not from day one."

"He's never liked me!" Gabe cried, too late realizing how that sounded. "Well, he started it, not me."

Dad came to stand beside him. "I think you've spent enough time here, Chief. And with Candi here, this has turned into a spectacle. You find anything now and it won't matter because any lawyer will argue that she planted it." Gabe turned and stared at his dad. Wow. That was the perfect thing to say.

"How dare you, Keith!" Mrs. Morrigan cried. "My son has gone missing…" She took a moment to suppress a sob that seemed just a little bit fake. "And all I want is some answers." She spun around, her eyes taking in the room. Gabe's insides froze. She was going to see it. It was right there, plain as day. But she turned away to face Gabe. "Where is he? What have you done with him?"

"Nothing!" Gabe protested, his eyes unintentionally flicking toward the hoodie. "He was looking for a fight. I defended myself. That's it."

Her eyes narrowed and she slowly turned around. "Aha!" She strode over to the chair. Grabbing Jake's hoodie, she raised it triumphantly into the air. "This is Jake's!"

"Is it?" Chief Mara demanded of Gabe.

Gabe nodded. "He left it here. We brought it inside so it wouldn't get ruined." He wasn't going to say the real reason, that they wanted his phone to destroy evidence.

"I think he was up in this room!" Mrs. Morrigan cried. "And you did something to him!"

Dad stepped forward. He looked angry, the hollow in his cheek throbbing. "That boy did not come in this house, and if you make one more unfounded accusation, Candi, I'm calling my best friend out in San Jose, who happens to be a very good lawyer, and I'll start proceedings to sue you for all your worth."

Mom looked at him in admiration. "Well said, Keith. I second that."

Chief Mara stepped between them. "Now there's no need for that." He held out his hand for the sweatshirt. "Give it to me, Candi. We can't use it for evidence, but we'll use it for the dogs."

Candi looked at him in dismay. "You're kidding me, right? You're going to listen to them?"

"Keith's right, Candi. You tampered with the scene by coming here."

Her lower lip sticking out, she handed the sweatshirt to him. He turned and gave it to Officer White. "Bag it and put in a call to Blaine Johnson. We're going to need him and his dogs for tracking."

Gabe might not like Chief Mara, but he wasn't as incompetent as he looked. Unfortunately, bringing in the dogs meant they planned to go into the woods. "We found tracks," he blurted out. The sooner they found Jake, the sooner this would be over. "They lead into the woods, then they disappear. I can show you where they are."

Chief Mara studied him through the thick lenses of his glasses. "Why don't you do that, son. We won't be able to do much today, but it will help to know where he might have gone."

Gabe nodded and his family headed back down the stairs, followed by the chief and Officer White, leaving Gabe alone with Candi. Before he could leave, she grabbed his arm and pulled him back. He could feel her nails biting into his skin like an eagle's talons, and wished he were wearing a long-sleeved shirt.

"You're not going to get away with this, so you might as well just give up now." The heavy, cloying scent of her perfume and the bubblegum she was chewing made his mouth and nose water. Fear cantered down his spine like a racehorse, though he wasn't sure why he felt so afraid of her at that moment. It wasn't like she was going to kill him.

Right?

"I promise you, Mrs. Morrigan," he tried to say as calmly as he could, but his voice squeaked a little. "I didn't do anything to Jake. I know you don't want to hear this, but he was mad and he'd been drinking. He wanted a fight."

"Jakie doesn't drink!" Her false eyelashes batted indignantly. "How dare you lie about him!"

Gabe had a feeling she was right, that he wasn't going to win this, but he tried again. "Do you know where his car is? I thought he would've driven it over, but he hadn't."

Her blue eyes scrunched up and she leaned in close, so close he could see the fine blond down on her cheeks and tiny veins covering the tip of her nose. "It's at home."

"But why? Why didn't he drive it over to my house?"

"You're trying to pin something on him, young man, and I'm not falling for it. Jakie is a saint. You're jealous and have been since you moved here. Jakie told me so."

"I'm not jealous of Jake, and never have been. He's jealous of me! But I'll give him one thing. At least he wasn't stupid enough to drive while he'd been drinking."

Her lips pursed together. "I will ruin you and your family and drive you out of this town. Do you hear me, Gabe Hawthorne? I...will...ruin...you." Each stressed word was like a thorn in his chest.

"Leave my family out of this! Just leave us alone! Stay away from us and stay away from our woods!"

She smiled suddenly, a sickeningly triumphant one. "*Your* woods? Au contraire, my friend. When I get done, there won't be any woods. But in the meantime, I've started proceedings to take ownership of the forest. And when your parents can't pay their taxes, we'll have your land, too. I'll own it all, and I'll be the first to light the match to burn it all down."

"Jake's in those woods," Gabe growled, his heart thumping painfully in his chest. "You'll end up burning him, too."

Her smile stayed firmly in place. "I have good reason to believe he's holed up somewhere safe. I'll deny it, of course." Her breath, hot, moist, and sweet, fanned his cheek. "So I win, Gabe. Might as well face it. This family is broken."

"Never, Candi," a voice came from the stairs. Gabe was surprised to see his dad emerge from the stairwell. "We'll bend, but we won't break. Now get out of my house before I throw you out a window."

Her eyes flickered and she gave a shaky laugh as she pulled back from Gabe. "You and whose army? You're weaker than a baby, Keith. Too bad. You used to be so manly."

Gabe took a threatening step toward her. His skin felt prickly and hot and he knew the thorns were on their way, but he didn't care. His eyes bored into hers and she must have seen something dangerous in them because she took a wobbly step back. "We're his army, Mrs. Morrigan. Now you heard my dad. Get out. Before we help you."

"Fine!" She pushed past Dad. "But I will win. Don't you doubt that."

Her heels clattered down the stairs and Gabe briefly wished she'd fall and break her neck. Then he quickly took it back. That made him no better than Straif. But it did help him understand Straif a little better. Anger made you ugly; it made you do ugly things. He had to control his or be controlled by it.

A few deep breaths later, he felt his dad's hand on his arm. "Don't let her get to you, Gabe. She always had a big mouth."

"Thanks for coming to my rescue."

Dad gave him a strange look. "Oh, I don't think you needed my help."

Gabe wondered about that look, but his dad turned to go before he could figure out what it meant. "They're waiting for you," he called over his back. Then he turned around and looked Gabe in the eye. "My advice is not to say anything more than you need to. All right?"

"All right."

"And you don't know anything more about Jake? Nothing happened that you're afraid to tell us? Cause you can tell us. We won't be mad."

"I told you everything that happened. Ask Kris and Jer. Kimber, too. She can't lie."

Dad held up his hands. "I believe you. Just checking. It's normal to keep things back in a situation like this. But you can tell us. *Anything*, Gabe," he stressed. "We're behind you one hundred percent."

Gabe felt his eyes tear up. "Thanks, Dad. There's one thing. Candi just told me that Jake's holed up with a friend."

"Do you believe that?"

"If he's holed up anywhere, it's not with a friend."

Dad looked grim, but not surprised. He turned to lead the way down the stairs, his step heavy. Gabe remembered the end of the poem, *The Door*, and shuddered.

> *They only long to climb on father's bed*
> *And cry their terrors out in father's arms.*
> *And maybe, all the while, their father's dead.*

He couldn't stand it if all this led to his father getting sick again. He had to protect his dad, keep him safe. Even if that meant not telling him anything more about what was going on, or about what *The Ranger Rag* had implied, or how kids were treating him in school. It would be too much of a burden on him, and the stress might lead to his death.

From here on out, Gabe was on his own.

Chapter Ten

Eyes Screamed

Everyone but Gabe's parents was waiting for him out on the porch. Dad headed to the bathroom to take some insulin—he'd had problems with people reporting him for drug use, so he avoided injecting in front of others, especially people like Candi Morrigan.

Gabe seized the opportunity to talk to his mom. "Keep Dad here. The snow's still deep out in the woods and it will be too much for him."

She nodded. "I was thinking that, but I have no idea how I'm going to keep him here without making him feel worse than he already does. He needs to feel useful." She looked worried and tired and Gabe hated that all this stuff was happening. Hated that he couldn't just take all his parents' worries away.

"Mrs. Morrigan said she's started proceedings to take ownership of the woods. Maybe Dad could find something on the Internet that will stop her. Any information will be useful, actually. I'm not sure how she can just take the property and get away with it."

"I don't think she can, not legally, but I'm sure Dick's found some sort of loophole. It's his specialty," she added bitterly.

"Mrs. Morrigan also implied that Jake might be with one of his friends, or holed up somewhere. I'm not sure if that's the truth, but it wouldn't hurt looking into."

Mom looked more hopeful. "I'll talk to Mozi and get Dad to check out the property thing. Maybe his lawyer friend, Scott, will know something about property law."

Dad came out of the bathroom at that moment. "Ready to go?"

"Gabe just told me Candi is trying to take ownership of the forest."

"What?"

"Do you think Scott would know anything about how to stop her?"

"I can call him."

"Good. I'll talk to Mozi about Jake. He might know something we don't about Jake's friends or some place he might go." Even though Gabe was sure someone in the forest had taken Jake, he couldn't get the image out of his mind of Jake hiding out at the old mill. It was the perfect hideout, after all. Maybe they'd go check it out after school tomorrow.

"I'll call Scott after we get back."

"You'd better do it now, Dad," Gabe said, feeling weird to be telling his dad what to do. "She said she'll take our land, too, when we don't pay our taxes."

Mom stared at him. "How do you know about that?"

"I didn't mean to, but I heard you and Dad talking about it."

She heaved a big sigh. "That's all I need. You guys worrying, too."

"I'm not worried," Gabe lied. "We can fight this. We can come up with something before it's too late."

"That only happens on TV or in books, Gabe. This is real life and in real life, the good guys don't always win."

"Well, I think in this case, we'll win. What good does it do us to think otherwise? We can't just give up!"

Mom smiled. "Well, I didn't think I'd ever hear those words coming out of your mouth, Mr. Pessimist."

"I'm not letting them kick us out of our house. I'm not leaving this place!"

"Or *those* words." Dad laughed. "All right. We'll stay and do our homework. Just be careful out there, Gabe, and remember what I said. Don't offer any unnecessary information."

"I won't," Gabe promised, and he absolutely meant it at the time.

"Are you coming, Hawthorne?" Chief Mara called through the door.

"Just getting my jacket," Gabe yelled back, grabbing his off its hook. "Good luck," he wished his parents, and standing side by side, they both gave him an identical look of pride mixed with sadness.

"Be safe," Mom replied.

Mrs. Morrigan had changed into pink boots with furry tops and was standing by her pink Hummer talking on the phone. The signal, when it did come in at the farm, wasn't strong, so she kept banging the phone against her palm in an attempt to get rid of the static. Mr. Morrigan was gone. Apparently he'd decided that being a lawyer and getting involved in Candi's housebreaking schemes wasn't a good mix.

"I don't care what you have to do, Dick, just get those papers through!" She glanced up and saw Gabe. "He's here. I've got to go. Do your job and we'll be fine." She clicked off the phone.

A wet droplet hit Gabe's nose and he glanced up. The sky was darkening, bringing rain, and it was getting late. They'd better hurry before the trail melted away or couldn't be seen in the dark. The difficult part would be getting through the hedge. There was no help for it, they were going to have to take the extra time and go around.

"It's this way," he said and took the lead. Without looking back, he led the group down the driveway and past the hedge. They tromped through the dark woods, skirted the hedge, then entered the meadow. Gabe briefly wondered why he hadn't just done this in the past, then answered his own question—because he wanted to avoid the woods as much as possible, for as long as possible. The hedge helped him do that. In fact, he thought maybe that's why it was there. To keep him out of the woods. Not in a malevolent way, but in a protective way. Mom had said it had seemingly sprung up overnight after he'd been taken. Maybe it was put there to make sure he wasn't taken again, or didn't wander off into danger.

The question was, who had put it there? Dame Hazel? The Rogues? Faeth? Who?

The idea that the hedge was there to protect him made him feel strangely better. Someone out there was looking after him and this gave him a renewed confidence. "This way," he directed as they crossed the meadow.

He could see the faint line of footprints leading to the woods and he headed toward the forest at an angle so that when they met up with the trail, they were once more nearly at the line of trees. As they neared the woods, it suddenly occurred to him why whoever had taken Jake had backtracked out of that part of the woods by the road. That way led to Bittersweet territory, where the voracious vines, that liked taking over trees and eventually killing them, ruled. Which suggested a tree spirit might be the one responsible for the kidnapping. He still wasn't ruling out Filidh, though. The Bittersweet seemed capable of going after anything. Maybe it, too, was going mad from the sickness.

He stopped at the edge of the woods. "Are you sure you want to go in?"

Chief Mara looked at him suspiciously. "Why not?"

"Yeah, why not?" Mrs. Morrigan demanded. "Do you have something to hide?"

"I just mean that the woods don't have the best reputation."

Chief Mara visibly gulped. He might be an idiot, but he wasn't stupid. "It is getting dark, with the rain coming."

"Nonsense!" Mrs. Morrigan cried. "I've been in these woods. There's nothing in there that this little puppy won't stop." She pulled a pistol from the inside pocket of her jacket. "You have one, too, Carl. Better get it out."

He blanched. "Put that away, Candi! We don't need to be accidentally shooting someone."

She sneered at him, but she slipped the gun back into her pocket. "Well, don't blame me if someone gets mauled by a hungry bear. And it won't be me, Carl. I can outrun you, you know. Always could." Mrs. Morrigan, Gabe thought absently, was a strange mix between girlie girl, tough tomboy, and evil villainess. It was a powerful combination, and it made him nervous.

"Let's go, then. It'll be dark soon and the trail has already melted quite a bit." The trail was still noticeable, but in a few days would likely be gone.

"Why are there so many footprints alongside the trail?" Officer White asked what the chief hadn't thought to question.

"We came out looking for Jake yesterday." Gabe indicated his brothers. "Our friends came, too."

"Are you kidding me?" Mrs. Morrigan cried. "Talk about messing with crime scenes."

"We just followed a trail of footprints, Mrs. Morrigan," Gabe said politely. "We were looking for your son."

"I think you were trying to plant evidence. These could be *your* footprints we're following."

"Jake's a size ten, right?"

She shrugged. "I think so."

"Jer's an eight. I'm a fourteen now, and Kris went up to a thirteen last month, pretty much the same day he turned fifteen. Abazi and Kimber's feet are too small."

"Then what's this odd print next to his?" She sounded suddenly unsure.

"I have no idea. It's not a sneaker print, that's for sure."

Chief Mara leaned over and studied the prints. "Take pictures!" he ordered Officer White. "Use your phone since that's all we have right now."

Officer White pulled out his cell phone and took several shots from various angles, using his body to shield the phone from the spotty rain. When he was done, he had a strange look on his face, as though he'd seen something he just as soon wished he hadn't.

"We'd better get going," Gabe said and moved forward. Like all the other times, the moment he stepped into the woods, he felt its strangeness. But this time, something was different. Something had changed. Something big. He kept moving, all the while trying to track what was different.

Twenty minutes later they reached the spot where the trail ended abruptly. Chief Mara stopped, then looked up, as though expecting Jake to be above him. Gabe had done the same, but he'd had good reason to believe Jake actually *could* be above him.

"What the he—, um, heck. What the heck?" Hands on his ample hips, he looked all around, perplexed. "Where did it go? It was just here!"

"Maybe he backtracked," Jer said. "It's an old trick."

Gabe nodded, wondering why they hadn't thought of that before. He peered down at the footprints, but really couldn't decide if they were clean, or had been stepped on in reverse. Too much melting had occurred. But if Jake had backtracked, where had he gone? Mrs. Morrigan's words about Jake holing up somewhere safe came back to him. Was this all some trick to give her leverage to have the woods destroyed?

"Are you saying my Jakie pulled a trick on us?" Mrs. Morrigan demanded, going on the attack.

Jer shrugged. "I'm not saying anything, really, but if the shoe fits..."

Kris laughed. "Good one, Jer."

"Thanks!"

"It's not funny!" Mrs. Morrigan roared, her fingers clenched into fists. "My son is missing and you accuse him of tricking us!"

Gabe shook his head, not understanding why she was continuing with this farce if she believed Jake was safe. Unless... Well, unless she'd put him up to it. The thought was less surprising than it should have been. Mrs. Morrigan was a schemer and it was very likely that this was one of her schemes. Send Jake over to Gabe's house, have him start a fight, then make him disappear. She could have her wish granted in two ways...get Gabe's family into trouble and rally the townsfolk behind her in her quest to clear the woods. They'd be happy to cut it down if doing so kept their kids safe.

"Are you sure Jake isn't holed up with one of his friends, safe and sound?" he poked. "I mean, that's what you implied to me up in my room, right?"

She glared at him. "I never said any such thing. He is *not* with any of his friends." She spun around, her eyes frantic. It was strange. Before, she had practically told him Jake was safe, but now she looked genuinely frightened. "If I have to, I'll burn this woods down to find him!" She shook her fist at the trees.

The wind stirred suddenly, making the trees sway. At least, Gabe thought it was the wind making them move. He glanced back at his brothers. They were looking up, and he followed their gaze, his stomach flipping over when he saw what they were staring at. The treetops were thrashing about as though caught in a tornado, and yet there wasn't much more than a small breeze, one that barely moved the hair on Gabe's head.

A moan echoed through the woods and everyone froze. It sounded like someone in pain. "What was that?" Mrs. Morrigan cried.

"Just the wind in the trees," Chief Mara growled, though he didn't look too convinced. "Rain's coming. I say we head back."

No one argued.

The group started running back to the edge of the woods. Twigs flew through the air, pelting Gabe's cheek. He grabbed one out of mid-air and trapped it in his hand. Then he kept running.

More groans filled the air around them. "Go!" Gabe cried. "Get to the meadow."

Kris and Jer were already far ahead, but Gabe didn't dare leave the others behind. He didn't know what was happening in the woods, but he wasn't about to leave them alone in it. Was the forest waking up? If so, it sounded like a painful process.

He stayed on alert as he ran, hoping to spot a Dryad, or some sign that things had returned to normal. Or as normal as things can be in the Forest Immortal. As he passed by tree trunks, strange images popped out at him from the wood. Mouths were opened in pain, branch hands stretched out to him, eyes screamed. He shuddered, not knowing what it meant—if this was normal or not—and kept running.

At one point he felt he was being shadowed, as though someone were running alongside him, just out of sight. He strained his eyes, hoping for confirmation that the Dryads were alive and awake. But nothing solidified. No one waved and gave him a thumbs-up. No, all he had was a sensation, a feeling. But it wasn't a good one. In fact, he felt on-the-verge-of- throwing-up uneasy.

The group finally broke through the tree line and ran another fifty yards before stopping. Chief Mara's face was beet red and he looked like he was about to have a heart attack. He leaned over and grasped his knees, wheezing and gasping for air.

"Are we quitting the search?" Mrs. Morrigan demanded when she'd regained her breath. "We can't just give up!"

"We'll come back when we get the dogs," her brother told her, though it took him a while to get the words out.

"But the rain will wash away all the evidence," she argued petulantly.

"Not for a good tracker. And besides, the trail ended. Jake must have backtracked." He studied his sister with a skeptical expression. "Are you sure he isn't just having one of his tantrums?"

"How dare you?" she gasped theatrically. "You know Jakie!"

"Yes, I do," Chief Mara replied dryly and Gabe revised some of his opinion concerning the chief. He might be related to Mrs. Morrigan and he might not be the nicest guy on the planet, but he was proving himself to be no dummy. Plus, he didn't seem to be all that beholden to his sister. He had a mind of his own. "That's why I asked."

"You really seemed convinced he was okay," Gabe needled.

Mrs. Morrigan's eyes widened, then she gave a twisted smile. "I only told you that Jakie was safe because I thought I could catch your reaction—you know, disbelief or guilt."

He looked at her politely. "Did you catch anything?"

The smiled twisted further, then she swung away from him. "Who do I need to call to get those dogs, Carl? There were two sets of footprints on that trail. Why were there *two* sets?" She sounded genuinely confused.

"I don't know why there were two sets, and I'll do the calling, Candi. Just leave it to me."

"And have you screw it up?"

He stared at her blandly through his rain-spotted glasses. "I'm starting to think young Hawthorne isn't just blowing hot air. If you know where Jake is, Candi, you'd best say now."

She gazed at him levelly. "I don't know where he is, Carl. Now do your job, or I'll call someone in who can." She spun toward the road and started marching toward it. They followed after her, though Gabe's mind was spinning a hundred miles per hour. Was Jake really safe, or had something gone wrong? Maybe Mrs. Morrigan had planned this out, but something, or someone, had gotten in the way. Maybe the forest had made things go wrong.

By the time they reached the driveway, the rain was coming down hard and everyone was sopping wet. Mrs. Morrigan hopped into her Hummer and roared away without so much as a goodbye. Officer White tossed them a salute before climbing into the police cruiser, but Chief Mara surprised Gabe by following him up onto the porch.

"What happened in those woods today?" he asked. He'd taken off his hat and was wiping the rain off the brim.

"I don't know. It got pretty windy, didn't it?"

The chief's eyes narrowed skeptically. "I didn't ask for a weather report, Hawthorne. I want to know what I'm in for when I bring those dogs in there. I've heard things about those woods. We all have. I don't want to be losing any more folks…or dogs."

Gabe took a deep breath. He couldn't tell the chief the truth, but he could warn him off. "All I can tell you is that it wouldn't be a bad thing to believe what you've heard. Stick close together and don't go too far in. It's really easy to get lost."

The chief replaced his hat. "You talk as though from experience."

"Our cat got lost in there." It wasn't a lie, but it wasn't exactly the truth, either.

"If you were Jake, where would you hide out?"

Gabe started feeling nervous. "Not in those woods, that's for sure. If he did backtrack, he could easily have taken the road into town or to a friend's house. What I don't get is why he didn't drive his car over. He'd been drinking, but that doesn't mean he wouldn't drive. People do dumb things when they drink." Gabe was talking too much, but he couldn't help himself. "I just thought that seemed strange."

Chief Mara studied Gabe for several long seconds. "You think of anything else, any of you—" he pointed his finger at Gabe's brothers. "You let me know. Right away. Call the office. I'll get the message."

Gabe swallowed and nodded. "You won't put off getting the dogs, will you?"

"Officer White is making the call now. Get inside now and dry off." He turned to go, then swung back around. "And stay out of those woods. I don't always like agreeing with my sister, in fact, I despise it, but those woods are dangerous. I wouldn't mind seeing them go myself."

With that, he clattered down the steps and into the waiting cruiser. The car took off with a lurch and the brothers watched it drive away.

After the cruiser disappeared, Kris broke the silence. "The woods were waking up, weren't they?"

Gabe nodded. "I think so."

"They didn't sound too good."

"No, they didn't."

Kris looked a little sick. "You think Hollie will be like that?"

"I don't think we can afford to think anything else."

"You think they'll turn against us?" Jer asked, his blue eyes wide.

"I think we'd better get ourselves ready for the possibility."

Gabe unfurled his fist and looked down at the twig in his hand. A black sooty powder clung to the little branch, like it had been singed in a fire. The Forest Immortal was waking up…but maybe it would be better for everyone if it had remained sleeping.

Chapter Eleven

The Team's Mascot

Abazi's first words after he told her about what had happened yesterday were far from comforting. "Why didn't you hide the hoodie?" she demanded as she furiously spooned strawberry yogurt into her mouth. "Now they have evidence!"

"We wanted to erase the photos on his phone. After that, we forgot about it. But I told you, the chief says the evidence is tainted now because Mrs. Morrigan entered the scene."

"That might be what he told you, but that doesn't mean it's the truth."

"You think he lied to me?"

"Well, no. I don't exactly like the chief, but he's not all bad," she admitted grudgingly. "He just might not know proper procedure. I'm not sure dealing with crime scenes is something he has a lot of experience with."

"They're going to bring in the dogs."

Abazi was quiet for a moment, considering this. "Do you really think the woods are waking up?"

"Something strange was going on in there, I know that. It's past time, anyway. They should be waking up. But…well, not like this. I think. I don't know." He ran his hands through his hair, making it stand up on end. He really needed a haircut, but he wasn't going to get one. He didn't have the money, and his mom would just give him a buzz cut. If she used the scissors, he always ended up looking like he was wearing a mushroom on his head.

"Do you think we're ready?" she asked, scraping out the last of the yogurt and sticking it in her mouth.

"I don't think we have a choice." He paused. "But we could meet after school, in the barn. Do a refresher course."

"We'll be there."

"Good. My parents are also looking into some things, too."

"And that is…" she asked suspiciously, pulling her black jacket closer around her.

"Nothing to do with you, Big Ego," he teased. "Mrs. Morrigan made it sound like Jake was safe and sound, but then, when we were searching, she acted nervous, like she wasn't sure that was true anymore."

"Weird. Did they find anything?"

"Not yet. My mom called your dad and he's looking into things on his end. He hadn't heard anything, but someone else might have. As my mom put it, Mrs. Morrigan has a voice like a foghorn." Abazi smiled in agreement. "And my dad is researching about Mrs. Morrigan taking the land. If she can do that. He has a lawyer friend. Unfortunately, he's out of the country until the end of the week."

"Well, that's something, I guess. Taxes are due Friday, though, right?"

"Yeah. Grandpa's talking about mortgaging his boat, but guess who stopped that?"

"Candi Craphead?"

"Got it in one. She delayed the process anyway. She's either friends with the bank president, or has something on him."

"Oh, she has something on him, all right. Rumor has it that they're *well-acquainted*, if you catch my drift."

Gabe rubbed his aching forehead. He was spending a lot of energy lately trying not to let his thorns or flowers pop out at random times and the constant vigilance was exhausting him. "I don't know what to do. I wish I had more money. We don't need all that much, but we've been strapped for cash since my dad got sick. Grandma May and Grandpa Hawthorne, too."

"We'll figure something out," Abazi said, placing her hand on his arm. This was the second time in two days she'd done that. He almost thought losing their house might be worth it. "Leave it to me."

"Are you hiding your tremendous wealth, Abazi Wanibagw?"

She smiled and withdrew her hand to dig inside her lunch bag. She pulled out an apple and took a big bite. "I'm really a multi-billionaire. It's all those casino dollars."

He grinned and took a swig of water. "Thanks for your help. It's good to see you're feeling better."

She shrugged and he regretted bringing up her earlier bad mood. But she surprised him. "I've decided that there are more important things to worry about than my stupid birthday and my stupid mom."

He didn't push anymore and they finished their lunch in a companionable silence. When the bell rang, she stood up. "See you at the barn. Be ready. I'm in the mood for a fight."

He smiled. "Me, too."

The rest of the day was long. People were still staring at him, pointing and whispering. Even the teachers treated him strangely. He almost couldn't blame them. Jake was one of them, Gabe wasn't. Who were they going to believe? The stranger? No, and he probably wouldn't, either.

To the accompaniment of the windshield wipers, he told his brothers the plan on the ride home. "Oh, goodie!" Jer rubbed his hands together with a mischievous gleam in his eyes. "My outrageously ingenious scheme is finally complete," he said in the voice of an evil cartoon villain, "so at last I can unveil it!"

"What is it?" Kris demanded.

"You'll see," Jer replied, enigmatically.

Kris was fidgety the rest of the ride home, his knees jiggling up and down, making it nearly impossible for Gabe to shift. "Jer, just tell him before we all die!" Gabe shouted at one point, but Jer refused with a stubborn shake of his head.

They made it safely home, just barely, and Gabe was relieved to park the truck and follow his brothers into the house. Mom was putting away dry dishes when they clomped noisily into the house.

"Shoes off!" she cried.

"But we're going out to the barn as soon as we get a snack," Kris told her.

"You have your homework done?"

"Finished it in school."

She looked at Jer and Gabe. "I've got some reading to do," Gabe admitted. "But I'll do it at bedtime." It was the truth. They'd taken all their big tests last week and he'd finished up his paper for English. His classes were all starting new units so he didn't have anything big on the agenda. Besides, he really wanted to read more of Mary Webb's work.

"I'm done," Jer said, grabbing a banana. "In fact, I could've done it in my sleep," he bragged.

"All right," she sighed, not bothering to push. "But I don't want to see any bad grades when I check them on the computer."

"You won't," Kris promised, making himself a sandwich. "Just face it, Mom. You've raised three geniuses."

She snorted. "Three geniuses who don't know how to hang up a towel or clean a toilet."

"I said we're geniuses, not angels."

"You've got that right." She turned to Gabe, a special meaning in her eyes. "How was school?"

"Fine," he lied. "No problem. Hear anything from Mozi?" He had to know if she'd heard about the newspaper article, basically accusing them of being mass murderers.

"He's got his gossip network going, but nothing has come in yet."

He stifled a sigh of relief. "Well, I'm not worried," he assured her. He was, of course, but he couldn't stand seeing how sick she looked. Like everything was crashing down on her at once. He'd been worried about his dad, but Mom wasn't getting any younger and all these prob-lems were taking a toll on her. "We'll figure things out."

She regarded him steadily. "You've changed, Gabe. For the better," she rushed to add. "Good for you."

"Yeah, he's started changing his underwear more than once a month," Kris joked and everyone had a good laugh at Gabe's expense. But he didn't care. He changed his underwear every day, so it wasn't the truth, but the joke had lightened the mood and when Kris threw him a wink, Gabe knew he'd done it on purpose. He nodded back, grateful.

"All right. Ready, guys?"

"What are you doing in the barn?" Mom asked.

"Just some training stuff. You know, like we've been doing." Mom was under the impression that they were working out to get better at sports. She probably would have shut down the operation if she knew they were working on their skills to fight evil dark ones. "Where's Dad?"

"In his office. He's been very secretive up there, keeping the door closed. That's not like him." Gabe wondered if she was worried Dad was secretly napping. It wouldn't be the first time. Sometimes Dad just couldn't keep his eyes open, but he didn't want Mom to know and worry.

"Oh. Okay. Well, maybe he's up to secret agent stuff."

"I wish." She smiled. "All right. Go. Have fun."

"I'll be there in a minute," Jer said, then ran upstairs.

"What do you think he's up to?" Kris asked as they crossed the yard to the barn, hurrying in the heavy rain.

"The usual. Trouble," Gabe half-joked.

The inside of the barn was dry and smelled of hay and dust. Gabe in-haled deeply. Over the winter, whenever he felt out of sorts, he'd come to the barn to work out. He and his brothers had installed a bar for doing pull-ups and had set up their dad's old weights, left behind at Grandpa Hawthorne's house. There was a tomahawk block in one corner, surrounded by hay bales donated by Kimber's mom. They'd put the block together not long after their last adventure with the dark ones, following Mom's instructions. It worked really well and everyone was getting quite good at throwing. Grandpa had given them a thick rope he didn't need and they'd hung it from a rafter to use for climbing. The barn had turned from a disused, sorry old building to a major training center. Gabe felt quite proud of it. They all did.

The sound of car doors outside the barn signaled the arrival of Abazi and Kimber. Abazi had gotten her driver's license back in February, taking her test on one of the rare nice days they'd gotten this winter. She didn't like driving and made no secret of it, avoiding it whenever she could. Worse, it always made her cranky. Unfortunately, it was raining pretty hard and Mrs. Wistman was likely working, so Abazi probably felt forced into driving, for Kimber's sake anyway.

They appeared in the doorway, shaking out there jackets and pushing back hoods. Gabe watched Abazi carefully, but she looked no crankier than usual.

"Where's Jer?" Kimber asked.

"Right here!" he cried from behind her.

"All right. Let's see it." Kris took a step toward Jer, holding out his hand.

"Patience, grasshopper," Jer said. "All in good time."

By this point, Gabe was curious, too. "Just show us, Jer. Kris will be useless until he sees what you're scheming."

"I'm not scheming anything. But I do have something to show you. All of you." He ran to an open space in the middle of the barn. "Prepare to be amazed."

From behind his back he produced a round object with a flourish. The size of a large moon pie, it appeared to be made from wood. Jer flicked his wrist and the thick disc whipped out on a four-foot long string, then snapped back to Jer's hand, lightning quick. He turned to a post and flicked again. The disc smacked the post, then returned, all in a second. Jer spun around and smacked another post.

When he was done, Jer turned to face them. "Ta dah!"

Kimber started to clap. "That's a neat trick, Jer!"

He frowned. "It's not a trick. This is a bandalore. That's yo-yo to you amateurs. I figured since this is a larger version and made from wood, I'd use the old word for it."

Kimber laughed. "I stand corrected."

Jer smiled sheepishly. "Sorry, but I've been working really hard on it."

"We all know you're good with the yo-yo," Kris said irritably. "I thought you had something cool to show us. You know, your project. You've been working on it long enough."

Jer sighed. "Don't you get it, Kris? This is made of wood. The Ko-goks don't like the touch of wood. I'll be four feet away, so I can hit them without getting hit." He paused. "Well, at least when they're in their human form."

The genius of Jer's idea finally hit Gabe's brain. "Not bad, Jer."

Kris laughed. "Don't gush, Gabe. It's an awesome idea, Jer. Can I see it?" He held out his hand, and Jer reluctantly placed the oversized yo-yo, or bandalore, as he called it, into it. Kris moved away from every-one and flicked it out. He wasn't nearly as good as Jer, but he was able to get it to come back. Gabe already knew from playing with Jer's regu-lar yo-yo that this wasn't his forte, so he didn't even ask to try. He was more likely to hit himself in the head than do any damage to a dark one.

"The jury is out on whether or not the yo-yo was once used as a weapon," Jer said as Kris tried another throw. "It may very well be possible that I'm the first."

"How'd you make it?" Gabe asked.

"Grandpa helped me. He has a special tool that he uses for making repairs to his boat that shaped the wood. We used wood from a dead alder tree, which you said was protective, right, Gabe?" Gabe nodded. That had been months ago and only in passing. Jer never forgot any-thing. His memory was both impressive and annoying.

Abazi held out her hand. "Let me try." Kris handed it over and Abazi made a few attempts. She, like Gabe, didn't really have the knack for it. "Hm. I think I'll stick to the tomahawk."

Gabe thought this might be a good time to reveal his new weapon, since he couldn't always be relying on turning into a tree. He ran over to the worktable and pulled out a short, solid stick, used for throwing, with a thick bulb on one end for gripping and a notch on the other. Then he grabbed a longer stick with a slightly pointy end and slipped it into the notch. His weapon wasn't as nice looking as Jer's bandalore, but he'd made it himself using wood carving tools he'd gotten for his birthday a few years ago, so he was pretty proud of it.

He held it aloft. "Behold! The atlatl!"

"The what-a-little?" Kris repeated with a laugh.

"At-lattle," Gabe pronounced slowly. "It's an ancient spear thrower. But I'm not throwing spears, just pointy sticks. You know, using wood, like Jer. Hit the Ko-goks with their kryptonite." Gabe went to stand by the barn door. "Get back. I don't want to hit anyone." Then he took aim at a post twenty feet away. When everyone had cleared the area, he let loose and the stick flew through the air, smacking against the post with a satisfyingly hard thud. He was grateful he'd actually hit the post in front of Abazi. He didn't always.

Kris nodded appreciatively. "That's a lot of power. I feel like an underachiever. All I came up with was this." He ran to another part of the barn and pulled out a piece of wood about a foot long and two inches in diameter; attached to it was a rope. He turned to face a post, then swung the end of the rope over his head like a lasso, releasing it after a few revolutions. The wood piece flew through the air and wrapped around the post, followed by the rope, so that the post was effectively tied up. "It's like bolas," he explained, "only with wood. A special gift for the dark dorks."

"Whoa!" Jer cried. "That was awesome."

Kris smiled smugly. "Great minds think alike, Jer."

"It seems you boys have been busy," Abazi mused. "But you weren't the only ones." She ran to the center of the barn and executed a perfect front handspring.

"How did you do that?" Jer asked enviously. "I'm still trying to get cartwheels down."

"I took gymnastics when I was a kid. I was rusty so I had to practice a bit. I can do a back handspring, too. And I can do flips without using my hands."

"No hands?" Gabe was impressed. Once in a great while he was blessed with a dream where he could flip like an Olympic gymnast. It was the most wonderful, freeing sensation he'd ever experienced. It also made him feel very powerful. "I'd like to see that."

She gave him a saucy grin, then performed a perfect front sumi. "Like Superwoman, yeah?"

"Definitely," Gabe agreed and they smiled at each other. Then, sensing the others were watching, Abazi looked away. But it was a nice moment and Gabe would savor it later, when he was alone and no one could see the goofy look on his face.

As he was turning his head, he caught Kimber's expression. She looked crushed, her eyes brimming with tears. Before he was sure of what he'd seen, she turned away and wiped at her face. When she turned back, the tears were gone, but she still looked upset.

Kris and Jer went up to Abazi and demanded she show them how to do flips while Gabe sidled up to Kimber. "Hey."

"Hey," she greeted, pulling back her shoulders as though nothing had happened.

"Everything all right?"

She shrugged, biting her lip. "I'm the only one who can't do anything special, and I'm getting sick of it. I'm always a burden to you guys. You have to carry me around like some sort of useless sack of oats. I hold you back."

Gabe didn't know what to say. Kimber was usually so upbeat and handled her cerebral palsy with a lot more courage than he ever could. "I don't agree. You're very good at tracking."

"Yeah, maybe. But I can't even walk that long before I get tired. You know, I try not to let it get me down, but it's hard, especially knowing my dad left because of it."

"He did that? What an idiot!" Gabe's fists curled up. People could be so stupid. "When my dad was diagnosed with diabetes, my Grandpa Hawthorne did everything he could to learn about it and help my dad. After the transplant surgery, he used up all his money to help pay our bills. Real parents make sacrifices for their kids *and* don't think of them as sacrifices. Sounds to me like your dad was never cut out to be a parent, or even a human being."

"Oh, I don't really blame him. My parents were very young when they had me. It's just that sometimes I wish I were different. That I could run and jump, or even just make my hands do what I want them to do."

Gabe wished desperately that he could say the right thing, but nothing came to mind. He was stuck handing her a worthless platitude. "Well, I bet there's something you can do really well that none of us can do. Just keep thinking, Kimber. Don't give up. We want you with us. We *need* you with us. You're very levelheaded, and you keep us from losing heart."

She gave him a weak smile. "Are you saying I'm the team's mascot?"

His cheeks went hot. "What? No! You're more than that. Much more."

She shook her head sadly. "Thanks, Gabe. That's nice of you to say, but I know the truth. I'm in the way. I shouldn't even be here now."

Before he could argue, she left him to join Kris and Jer as they watched Abazi do a front walkover. Kimber's expression as she clapped for her friend was envious, and Gabe couldn't blame her one bit. He just hoped she would get over her funk, find her thing that would make her feel part of the group. Because he liked having Kimber around. He'd meant it when he said they needed her for her level head. But he supposed nobody wanted to be known for having a level head. They wanted to be known for their awesome ninja moves.

They spent the next couple hours practicing their tricks and trying out each other's. Gabe's cartwheels were openly mocked, with Abazi telling him he looked like a giraffe with hiccups. Kris's weren't much better, but Jer quickly improved and had moved on to round-offs. Abazi declared him a natural. They then focused on hand-to-hand combat, which, true to her word, Abazi relished. Kimber sat out, claiming she felt tired. Gabe knew the truth, but didn't say anything.

Gabe had Kris in a headlock when Dad appeared at the barn door to announce that dinner would be ready in fifteen minutes. "You girls can stay if you like."

Abazi looked tempted. She liked food, especially Mom's. She claimed her dad couldn't cook his way out of a plastic takeout bag. Luckily Kimber's mom brought meals over a few times a week and they all ate together.

But Kimber demurred. "Thank you, Mr. Hawthorne, but I think I need to head home. I'm not feeling myself today." She smiled at him, but Gabe could see she was holding back tears. Poor Kimber. He knew what it felt like to be the odd man out. But at least—most of the time—he could hide that part of himself. She couldn't.

Abazi looked disappointed and was about to say something when Gabe intervened. "Okay, then," he said heartily. "We'll see you both tomorrow."

Abazi opened her mouth, closed it, opened it again, then closed it grumpily. "Yeah, sure. Tomorrow."

She and Kimber raced out to the car and Gabe saw that it was really pouring now. As he and his dad and brothers hurried to the house, he noticed how much the snow had gone down. By the time the rain stopped and Chief Mara could get the dogs out, there wouldn't be any trail left for them to follow.

Dinner was strangely quiet that night. Everyone seemed more tired than usual, even Kris and Jer. *Probably the fresh air*, Gabe told himself, even knowing it was likely more than that. It was hard to be energetic when your parents resembled death warmed over. Dad looked like he hadn't slept in a week, and Mom was heading that way. Gabe hated that they had to worry about paying taxes and now about Gabe's role in Jake's disappearance. It just wasn't fair.

But there wasn't anything he could do about it. Tax day was only days away, and they weren't any closer to coming up with the funds. Soon they'd be out of money and out of a home. Grandpa Hawthorne didn't have the room to take them in, and *no way* was Gabe going to go live with Grandma May.

Chapter Twelve

Gollum of Doom

Speaking of Grandma May, Gabe started thinking about her that night as he lay in bed reading for his English class. Gabe was actually enjoying the poems Mrs. B. had assigned them, feeling a new appreciation for poetry after reading all of Mary Webb's work. In a funny coincidence, he was studying the work of the poet who'd written the introduction for Mrs. Webb's book—Walter de la Mare. The poem was called *The Listeners* and it was really eerie, which Gabe both liked and didn't. Eerie was interesting, but it also stirred the imagination and when his imagination was stirred, Gabe couldn't help but think of things that go bump in the night. And since he didn't want to think about that sort of thing, he let his mind drift to Grandma May.

Ever since that day last October when they'd given her the deed to the house, they had only seen her a few times. Some weeks back she'd found a couple of their staffs in the woods and had returned them, setting them on the porch without coming in. She rarely came over to visit Mom anymore, sticking to her little house in the woods. According to Mom, Grandma's arthritis was acting up, but Gabe had the feeling she was either hiding out for some strange reason or up to something. Probably both.

Of course, maybe she didn't want to leave her house for fear that if she did, Mrs. Morrigan would take it over and kick Grandma May out. Gabe could imagine Mrs. Morrigan doing exactly that, claiming that possession is 9/10ths of the law. She wanted Grandma's house to complete her evil scheme and Grandma May wasn't having it.

After hashing the Grandma topic over and coming up with nothing useful, he had no choice but to return to his poem. It was still raining out, the tap-tap-tapping filling the room around him, making him think of fingertips on the windows, knocking to come in.

And then he heard it…another kind of tapping, coasting along just under the sound of rain. The words from *The Listener* came back to him.

Is there anybody there?' said the Traveller,
Knocking on the moonlit door;

And then:

Never the least stir made the listeners…

Gabe felt as though he was one of the listeners and no way was he going to answer that knock. Someone was trying to get into the turret. He was tempted to stick his head under his pillow and hope whoever was there would just go away.

But then a thought occurred to him. What if it was Jake? What if he had escaped from whomever had taken him into the woods and needed Gabe's help? Or it could be Hollie. Gabe stifled a groan and pushed himself off the bed. Heading toward the bookshelf, the trunk caught his eye and he stopped. For some strange reason, he felt an overwhelming desire to put on the cloak, to give him courage, and maybe some of its apparent mojo would rub off, too.

He hurried over to his hiding place and pulled out the cloak. Before he could think more on it, he flung it around his shoulders and breathed in deeply. A moment later, the magic began and he already felt stronger. *Invincible.*

He unhooked the bookshelf and pulled it away from the wall. It creaked as it swung on its hinges, revealing a gaping black hole. But he was not afraid of it. He was Gabriel, King of the Forest Immortal. He was not afraid of anything, certainly not some puny noises.

He jumped onto the pole and slid down, barely feeling the wood burning his palms as he flew downward. He landed with a thud, took two strides, and unlocked the door. Without waiting to listen, maybe get some idea of who was out there, he flung open the door. As soon as it was open, several *somethings* pushed past him and shimmied up the pole. They murmured and hissed as they raced upward, leaving him behind…and alone.

Intruders! Gabe jumped onto the pole and pulled himself up as fast as he could go. He had to stop the attackers before they reached his family!

But when he pulled himself into his room, he was surprised to find a crowd of hooded figures milling about, touching things, whispering to each other, twitching. "Hey! What are you guys doing here?"

A familiar figure strode toward him. "We've come. At last. When do we go? When?"

Despite his cloak, Gabe felt a frisson of fear run down his back. "What are you talking about, Oswald? What's wrong with you?"

Oswald's dark eyes danced about, never settling on Gabe's face. He wore his typical green cloak and tan pants with leather boots up to his knees. His reddish-brown hair was curly as always, but there was something different about him, something Gabe couldn't quite put his finger on. "I told ye we're here. Now lead us to safety. It's time."

"Time for what?"

Oswald's gaze finally met Gabe's and Gabe felt his stomach sink. The Dryad's eyes looked strange, odd and shifty, and the whites had turned a strange yellowish color. "Time to leave this place."

"Where are you going?"

"Away! Ye know this, Gabriel! So why are ye askin' me such questions? Ye began this, and ye must finish it."

Gabe started feeling even weirder. That, combined with the energy from his cape, made him want to do what Oswald was suggesting. He pushed the urge away. "I can't leave this place. It's my home."

"None of us want to leave. But we do want to live, so leave we must."

The strong smell of wet wool filled the air, along with something more sinister—a sickly sweet smell, like fruit begun to rot. "Oswald, you're acting really strangely. All of you are. Are you sure you're all right?"

Oswald's strange eyes focused on Gabe. "I don't understand ye."

Gabe spoke slowly, wondering what about what he'd said didn't make sense. "You and the Rogues are acting weird. Last fall you would never have come to me for help. You would never have asked me to lead you. What happened? Did Straif get to you?"

Oswald's forehead wrinkled. "Straif? Who's he?"

Gabe ran a hand through his hair. "When did you wake up?" he tried a different tack.

Oswald shrugged, his eyes returning to their hummingbird-like flight. "I don't remember. I feel as though I never slept."

"I think you need to take the Rogues and return to your hideout. Hang out there for a few days until you can adjust to being awake."

"Some did not awake," Oswald replied in a dead voice.

Gabe felt his throat tighten. "What do you mean? Who?"

"I cannot recall their names."

"Hollie? Did Hollie wake up?" Gabe glanced around, suddenly realizing that he didn't see Hollie anywhere. "Where is she, Oswald? Where's Hollie?"

"Not here. Gone," Oswald pushed out, the words an effort for him. Had he done something to her?

Gabe didn't know what to do, and the tightening sensation spread to his chest. Something was very wrong. The Rogues were all acting loopy and Oswald had no idea where Hollie was. Oswald seemed to always know where Hollie was, or at least would do whatever he could to find out. So she was either still asleep, or lost somewhere, or, well, Gabe didn't want to conjecture any further than that.

"What about Dame Hazel?"

"Dame who?"

"Dame Hazel. You know…your leader?"

"Ye're me leader, Gabriel. Ye're the King of the Forest Immortal." He said this perfectly seriously and that worried Gabe more than anything.

"No, I'm not. You are, Oswald. You're in charge of the Rogues, and you're more of a king than I'll ever be."

Oswald swung his head back toward Gabe. He'd been watching the fish swim in the glowing fish tank, as were several other Rogues. The hypnotic movement seemed to calm them. He reached out and grabbed a handful of Gabe's cloak, and for a moment Gabe thought Oswald was going to pull Gabe toward him, but he only fingered the cloak's material respectfully. "Ye wear the cloak. It's yers. The hawthorn cloak. It's not an oak on the back. Not an oak," he whispered again.

"I'll give it to you."

Oswald shook his head furiously and Gabe noticed how white the scars over his eye and along his jaw seemed. Then he realized why. Dark spots, like smudged coal, dotted the Dryad's face and neck. He wondered what they were, then thought maybe the marks had come from the coal used for their fires. "No, it's not mine! I know that now. It's yers and ye must lead us."

Gabe was growing twitchy himself. "Where?"

"To safety."

But Gabe had no idea where safety was. He just knew that the Rogues couldn't stay here, not with Mom and Dad and the police snooping around. His mind whirled, trying to determine what he should do. One option was to bring them back to their hideout, but he quickly dismissed that idea. In their current addlepated state, he had to keep them away from Straif.

For now he'd let them sleep in the barn. That should work. He could only hope that if he told them to stay there, they would. Otherwise, he might wake up to find them driving his truck or eating breakfast at their dinner table. He couldn't do that to his parents. Tomorrow he'd figure out where to put them. Mom and Dad didn't go in the barn much, but with the warmer weather he wouldn't put it past either of them to wander in there looking for some tool or whatnot.

"You can stay in our barn for the night," he said to Oswald. "You'll be safe there."

"We must leave here."

"We will," Gabe answered, improvising. "Soon."

Oswald stared at Gabe, his unsettling eyes making Gabe nervous. "Do not leave it too late. Last time it nearly led to our undoing."

Gabe wished he knew what Oswald was referring to, though he couldn't quite connect it to anything that had happened between them. It was almost as if whatever it was, it had happened in a past not their own.

A group of Rogues started pushing each other, fighting over one of Gabe's pillows. He rushed over to them. "Hey, knock it off." They stopped immediately, turning to stare at him. He held out his hand and they both handed the pillow over to him. "Thank you. Now head back down the pole and wait for me outside. All of you."

Without another word, the jumpy band left the room, disappearing into the darkness. Soon only Gabe and Oswald were left. "Ye won't leave us behind?" Oswald asked quietly. He looked a little more like his usual self, proud and regal. He should be wearing the cloak, not Gabe.

"Never," Gabe promised. "I'll not abandon ye." He stopped himself. Had he just said 'ye'? He was pretty sure he had. It seemed the strange Dryad dialect was rubbing off on him.

Oswald nodded. "I trust ye."

You didn't used to, Gabe wanted to say. But he kept those thoughts to himself. "Come on. You'll be safe in the barn. It's..." he almost said, *it's made from dead wood*, but if Oswald didn't remember Straif, there was no reason to get him worried. "It's a good shelter," he finished lamely.

Oswald bowed. "Lead the way."

Gabe slid down the pole and Oswald followed after him. He made sure the small door didn't lock behind him, then, after searching through the steady rain for any lights in the house, he led the group across the yard and into the barn. They followed him up to the loft, quickly finding hay bales to sit on.

"I need you to stay here in this building," he said in a slow, clear voice. They all stared at him politely and he was reminded of *The Listeners*. It was not a pleasant image. "You'll need to stay quiet and hidden until I come and get you. All right?"

They nodded in unison, like robots. It was rather eerie seeing these warriors, once independent and fierce, acceding to him like children. He hadn't liked Oswald's bossy behavior before, but it was better than this odd docility.

"We understand, King Gabriel," Oswald acknowledged him out loud. "And we'll do as ye wish."

"Thank you, Oswald. Will you need food? Something to eat?"

Oswald shook his head. "We're not hungry."

But Gabe thought they had to be. They looked like they were starving, their cheekbones sharp and eyes sunken. "Okay. But I can get you something if you need it."

"We need only to escape, Gabriel, and then we shall begin again."

Gabe felt a shiver crawl up his back, a tiny Gollum of doom. "Sure. Okay. I'll see you tomorrow then. I'll check on you in the morning."

"As ye wish."

"Good night," he called, but no one answered back. They were all sitting perfectly still, gone were the twitches he'd seen in the turret. As he turned to go, he realized he preferred the twitches.

Once back in his room, he pulled off his cloak and returned it to its hiding place. He was feeling more and more twitchy himself and didn't want to end up running to Quebec, as nice as that sounded. After undressing, he spent time restoring his things to their regular places. The Rogues had touched everything, often leaving things wherever they happened to lose interest. He wondered what was wrong with them...why they were acting this way. *Maybe it's a trick*, his mind conjectured. Maybe. But if so, what was the goal of it? They'd had him trapped in his room. If they'd meant to do something to him, wouldn't they have done it then, when he was alone and unable to escape?

Gabe closed his poetry book and stuck it in his backpack. What was going on with the Rogues? Was their illness the result of Straif and the dark ones devouring the young of the forest? It was an unnatural act, for sure, and it threatened the whole balance of the woods. Normally, if a tree got a fatal disease, it would die, but a part of it would always continue on in its offspring. But if there were no young, there would be no more trees, and hence, no more Dryads. Straif had started something big. Or had he? He'd once claimed to Gabe that a crime had been done to them, and that he was only reacting to it. If that was true, what was the crime?

Gabe thought back to Oswald's change of face. Before, he would never have called Gabe King. Now he was acting more like a follower than a leader. Gabe didn't like that. He didn't know what had caused the change, but he was determined to find out, whether it was the illness or a trick. He was also determined to find Hollie. Tomorrow was an early release day at school. They could go to the Rogues' hideout and track her down. It was time. It was beyond time, really, and Gabe just hoped it wasn't too late.

After setting out his clothes for the next day, Gabe laid down on his bed. His eyes closed and he reviewed everything that had happened up to this point, reworking some points, questioning others.

When he was done, he knew what to do with the Rogues. It was a temporary solution, but it should work. The trick was to get them to go along, because he had a feeling none of them would want to go where he was thinking of taking them.

Chapter Thirteen

In Each Other's Arms

The next morning it was still raining. Gabe stared out the window at the gloomy day and ate the egg and cheese sandwich Jer had made. He hadn't had a chance to tell his brothers about the Rogues and he was aching to. If only Mom would clear out. Dad was still upstairs sleeping, but Mom, who'd never been a morning person, had decided that when Dad had gotten sick she had to be the one to make sure they got off to school, and it made her surly. The fact that the furnace was emitting weird noises did nothing for her grumpy mood.

"Gabe, go check it out," she said after one particularly loud screech. "Bang on it a few times if you have to."

She looked tired and at the end of her rope and Gabe did as he was asked without a word, shoving the rest of the sandwich in his mouth as he headed downstairs. "Come on," he said to his brothers. "You can help."

"I'm eating," Jer complained. Gabe gave him a look. "Oh, yeah. Sure."

Mom frowned at this sudden show of brotherly love, but didn't say anything. She'd taken up drinking coffee to stay awake during the day and it wasn't nice to her stomach.

Gabe made his way down the dark stairs to the cellar. He found the string for the bulb and pulled it. A dim light flickered on, doing little to push back the shadows. Gabe hated it down here, especially after last summer when a dark one had tried to get at him through the wood chute.

Followed by his brothers, he headed over to the ancient furnace, seemingly held together by duct tape and prayers. It was making a piercing noise and a part of him was afraid it was going to explode right there. There was a loud clang, then the furnace exhaled wheezily. No more sounds came out of it after that and Gabe looked at his brothers worriedly.

"That didn't sound good."

Kris shook his head. "Not at all." He bent over. "There's no flame right now. We'll have to wait to see if it kicks back on."

"What was that?" Mom yelled down the stairs.

"I don't know," Gabe shouted back. "We're going to wait and see if the flame comes back on. It should kick in soon."

"All right. I'd better look up some furnace repair people just in case."

"Should we tell Dad?" Jer asked.

"No," she replied firmly. "Let him sleep." She shut the door on them, leaving them in the gloomy light. The only sound was the sump pump, which, despite the tinkering (Kris would say, *because of*), was doing its job adequately. So far, no water in the cellar.

"So why did you want us to come down?" Jer asked. He'd brought his sandwich and took another bite of it. He was a slow eater and made no apologies for it. Gabe preferred the gulp and swallow method. Chewing, he liked to say, was for sissies. "And who is choking for?" Mom always quipped back. "Not me," he claimed, though that wasn't exactly true. Sometimes he ate so fast he'd overdo and end up gagging. But he couldn't help it. He was always hungry.

"I had visitors last night."

"What?" Kris cried. "Why didn't you get us?"

"And who was it?" Jer added, which was probably the more relevant question.

"It was Oswald and the Rogues, and I didn't get you for two good reasons. One, there were a ton of them and they were acting weird. Two, it was late and I didn't want to risk waking Mom and Dad."

"But still!" Kris grimaced. "We weren't that far away."

"I'm sorry, but there was something wrong with them. I couldn't leave them alone."

"But Hollie was there, too, then!" Kris hooted excitedly. "How was she?"

Gabe winced. He hadn't wanted to answer that question, at least not so soon. "Actually, she wasn't there. Oswald said something about not all of them waking up. When I asked about Hollie, he couldn't say whether she had or not. In fact, it was like he didn't know her. He didn't remember Straif or Dame Hazel, either. And he—they all did, come to think of it—had these dark smudges on his cheeks and—" Gabe paused. "Just like that twig I caught out in the woods when we were with Chief Mara. I think maybe they have some sort of sickness."

"We could look it up," Jer suggested. Kris only stood there hunched over, scowling. "I'll go get a tree book."

"There's a good one on my shelf. It's got a bright green cover. It's hard to miss."

"I'll be right back."

When Jer was gone, Gabe turned to Kris. "We don't know anything at this stage. Hollie could be hiding out. Oswald was acting really weird, so maybe she and the others who weren't sick ran away from them and hid out."

"Maybe," Kris reluctantly agreed.

"Hollie's smart, Kris, and she can take care of herself. Besides, she knows Dame Hazel. She might have gone to her."

"Then we need to find them!" Kris kicked at the dirt floor, sending up a little puff of dust. "We need to go into those woods and find them!"

"I agree," Gabe replied.

Kris looked shocked. "You do?"

"I do. We have a half day today. We'll go when we get home."

Kris's eyes narrowed. "Why did you change your mind? You hate those woods."

"I don't hate the woods, not exactly," Gabe admitted. "I'm just...well, you know." He didn't meet Kris's eyes because he didn't want to see the derision in them. Kris wouldn't have been scared of the woods. "But anyway, we have to find them, because we're running out of time."

Jer's footsteps pounded down the stairs. "Mom said it's late and we have to get going. I'll skim the book at recess, all right?"

"Okay. We're going into the woods when we get home. You tell Kimber, and I'll tell Abazi. Get your homework done in school, all right?" His brothers nodded. That's what they usually did anyway.

"So what happened to the Rogues?" Kris asked as they headed toward the stairs.

"They're in the barn," Gabe whispered. "I put them there last night and this morning, when I went out to check on them, they were all sleeping."

"The barn?" Kris echoed, and stopped on the stairs to face Gabe. "They can't stay there. Mom will find them. She finds *everything*."

"I know."

"So what are we going to do with them?"

"I'm moving them tonight."

Jer's eyes widened. "Tonight? When it's dark?"

"What choice do I have? Besides, Oswald thinks I'm taking them somewhere. He kept saying that I was to lead them."

"That's really weird, coming from Oswald," Jer noted. "He wouldn't follow you out of a burning building."

"I know, right? So that's why I'm worried. I woke him up and told him to stay put. I promised we'd move out when it got dark."

"We're coming with you," Kris said.

"I can't risk it," Gabe argued. "What if Mom checks on you? Plus, it's crappy weather. I have the cloak, which will help me, but it's just going to be cold and wet for you guys."

"We'll use pillows in our beds, just like you're going to do, and wear raincoats. Not hard, Gabe."

Gabe was secretly relieved; he'd done his duty and tried to keep them from going. They wouldn't listen. Not his fault. "All right, but don't say I didn't warn you."

His brothers nodded solemnly, then their faces broke into satisfied smiles as they started up the stairs. Mom was on the phone. "Any change?" she mouthed.

Gabe shook his head. "It hasn't started back up yet."

She sighed. "Well, I'll have Grandpa Hawthorne look at it, then we'll see if we need to do more." She tensed. "Right now?" she spoke into the phone. "That would be perfect. Thanks, Jim. You're a life saver." She waved at them to get going. They grabbed their backpacks and headed out the door, full of nervous excitement.

~~~~~~

Abazi asked a lot of questions about Oswald, which annoyed Gabe, but eventually she agreed to meet them after school to go search for Hollie and Dame Hazel and any other Rogues they could find. Like Jer and Kris, she looked excited at the prospect.

"Aren't you nervous about going back into the woods?" he'd asked.

She shook her head, then laughed. "Okay, maybe a little. But I've got spring fever, and I have to do something or go nuts."

Gabe felt the same way. His spring fever had been manageable these last couple days, probably because the rain had a way of dampening everything, even a person's spirits. But now that they had a mission, he could feel the fever surging up inside him again.

They agreed to gather at the barn, fully armed and ready to go.

Mom met them at the door with a grim expression on her face. Her arms were crossed and she looked tired and cold. "The furnace died, so I need you guys to fill up the wood box in the cellar."

"But we were going for a hike," Gabe said, instantly regretting the words.

Her eyebrows lifted—a bad sign. "Oh, really? So you're okay with freezing pipes, no water, no heat?"

"Um, no. I just, well…" He stopped talking. He wasn't going to win this one, not even close.

"Can we go after we fill the wood box?" Kris asked. "We'll even fill the smaller ones in each room. Right, guys?"

Gabe nodded and Mom relaxed. "I suppose."

"Are we going to get a new furnace?" Jer asked. "Won't that cost a lot of money?"

"We're looking into our options. Grandpa knows someone who might be able to get us a good deal."

"But what about the taxes?" Gabe knew this would really cut into any money they might have used to pay the tax bill.

"We can't let the pipes freeze, and we can't put it off. If we get a cold snap, which is entirely possible, they'll burst, and that would cost us even more money."

"But it's April," Gabe argued. "Could it really get that cold again?"

"It's Maine, so, yes, it could. We could get snow in May."

Jer shivered. "Weird."

"Yep, but that's our reality now." She took a deep breath. "Why don't you get started? It should only take about half an hour if you all work together."

"Do you want us to light the fires in the fireplaces?" Kris asked.

"That would be nice." She headed toward the stairs leading up to the second floor. "I'm going to check on your dad. He forgot to eat lunch."

When she was gone, the brothers divvied up the tasks. Each would light a fire, then take turns hauling wood. Working together, it took them about half an hour, as Mom had predicted. As they hauled wood into the house, they kept an eye out for Kimber and Abazi, but there was no sign of them.

"Kimber said she could come, right?" Gabe asked Jer on the porch before heading inside.

"She thought she could. She doesn't have therapy today so she's free. She didn't seem all that excited, though." He frowned, not understanding what that was about. Gabe knew, but he wasn't saying. He'd been hoping Kimber had moved on by now.

"Hm. They should be here by now. Let's get our snacks. Make it snappy. We have a lot of ground to cover before supper."

Dad was eating lunch when they came in. As was typical lately, he looked tired. Stubble dotted his chin and jaw line and his hair—what was left of it—stood straight up. "Hey, boys," he greeted, holding up a glass of milk to them. "You have a free afternoon. Lucky you."

"We all finished our homework in school," Gabe rushed to say. "So it really is a free one."

Dad nodded vaguely. "Good plan."

"So what are you up to this afternoon?"

"Oh, this and that."

"Sounds good!" Kris said heartily as he scooped peanuts into a plastic baggie. "What are you doing?"

Dad half-shrugged. "Oh, nothing exciting. You guys are obviously in a hurry."

Gabe deliberately slowed down. "We were planning a hike up into the mountains with Abazi and Kimber."

"Well, don't let me hold you up. I've got things to do myself."

"Just don't *over*do, Dad," Gabe said gently.

Dad frowned, then gave a shaky laugh. "Don't worry about me. I've been under-doing for too long."

Kris patted him on the back. "Good to see you're getting back in the saddle."

Gabe glared at Kris. "But don't get overtired. You know that isn't good for you."

"But neither is moping around feeling sorry for myself. I'm tired of being useless! You all treat me like a sick child, especially your mother. I'm not a child, and I'm not sick!"

Gabe looked up to see his mom standing frozen on the stairs, her expression stricken. She swallowed hard, straightened her shoulders, and strode into the kitchen, as though she hadn't heard a thing. "Wear rain gear, boys. And be careful. It will be slick on those rocks."

"Yes, Mom," the three boys chorused.

"Fires all started?"

"Yep."

"I'd better go check on them, add some more wood." Gabe noticed she was wearing another sweater and her arms were wrapped tightly around her torso. "Be home in time for supper. I don't want to worry." Then she was across the room, heading for her office.

"Okay," Gabe called after her. "We will." She didn't answer, and Gabe's stomach roiled. What he really should be doing is finding ways to make money to pay that tax bill. He had things he could sell. There was stuff in the barn. He should be spending time on that, not on some silly goose chase looking for a Dryad who was probably safe and sound in her cave. She had a home. Soon he and his family wouldn't.

"Ready, guys?" he said to his brothers. "See you in a while, Dad," he added quietly. Dad gave him a distracted wave and Gabe wondered if he realized Mom had heard him.

Hurrying across the lawn, Gabe spotted Abazi's car on the far side of the barn. Maybe they'd gone into the barn out of the rain to wait for the others to show. When he found them, he'd explain to everyone that he couldn't waste his time on this hike right now. He needed to make money, and *now*.

"Where are they?" Kris asked as they stepped inside the barn.

"Shhh!" Jer hissed and pointed up at the loft.

Gabe's eyes widened. Had they gone upstairs? Abazi! She just had to stick her nose where it didn't belong. He raced up the steps, then stopped short at the top. Abazi and Oswald were clasped in each other's arms dancing while the Rogues clapped and Kimber sang a song.

Seeing Gabe, Abazi jerked back from Oswald, her eyes sparking angrily.

Gabe didn't wait for an explanation. He spun around and raced back down the stairs.

Chapter Fourteen

Rabbit in a Snare

Gabe didn't make it far before tripping and sprawling onto the wet grass just outside the barn. Stupid feet! Before he could get up, Abazi pounced on him, sitting on his back and refusing to move.

"Let me up!" he growled. "I'm getting wet."

"That wasn't what it looked like," she said, not moving.

"Oh, and what did it look like?"

"When Kimber and I arrived, we saw you hauling wood so we decided to wait in the barn until you finished. We heard strange noises upstairs and I remembered what you said about the Rogues. So we snuck up there to take a peek and it was weird, Gabe, like looking at a bunch of zombies. Oswald was pacing back and forth, practically wearing a groove in the floorboards, and he saw us, so we had no choice but to go up there. That's when he grabbed me and started whirling me around the floor. He kept saying, 'Now ye're mine forevermore.' It was creepy." She shuddered dramatically, but Gabe wasn't buying it.

"And you couldn't just pull away?"

"He wouldn't let me go. I felt like he was drowning, and I was his life raft. He's very strong, you know, and he smelled woody. Like when you cut into wood, you can smell it pretty strongly."

"Can you get off me now? I'm soaked." Truth was, it was hard to be mad at Abazi when she was straddling him. And he wanted to stay mad at her.

"Do you accept what I'm saying as the truth?"

He remembered how angry she'd looked when he appeared, as though he'd interrupted something she didn't want interrupted. "Sure, yeah. Whatever. Now get off me." When she didn't move, he did a push-up, tilted sideways, and bucked her off. "I'll be right back. I need to change." His pants were sopping wet, which made a good excuse. Mainly, though, he needed some time to get his thoughts straight.

When he was on his feet, he saw the others standing in the barn doorway, peering out. Oswald was with them. Gabe thought he would look triumphant, having won Abazi, but he only looked lost and confused. Gabe didn't like it. Oswald was not the type of person who was ever lost, or confused.

Mom and Dad weren't around when he climbed the stairs to the turret. Once in his room, he changed his pants, pulled off his hoodie, and strode purposefully over to the nook where he'd hidden the cloak. He knew he shouldn't put it on, shouldn't risk it, but like before, when the Rogues had shown up, he couldn't resist its allure. He needed to wear the cloak. He felt like he had no choice.

Before he knew it, the cape was falling around his shoulders like a protective shield. It felt good…warm and secure and powerful. He could do anything, be anyone, when he wore the cloak. More importantly, in this cape, Oswald was merely a speed bump along the way. Bothersome, but not threatening.

Back outside, he hurried to the barn. Everyone was gathered on the bottom floor, including the Rogues and Oswald. "We'd better get going," he said as he entered, having decided that it was best to get the search over with now. He'd find a way to earn money tomorrow. Besides, he didn't want to leave Abazi with Oswald in the barn, or let Kris go alone into the forest. Bad could only come of it.

"We're comin' with ye," Oswald said. "We, um, we need to check on things." For a moment Gabe thought Oswald was being vague to hide something from him, but then he realized the Dryad wasn't sure what he had to check on. Just that he did.

"You can't be seen."

"They can go out that little door at the back of the barn." Kris pointed at it.

It probably wasn't a bad idea, having the Rogues come along. Leaving them here would expose them to being found. Besides, who knew what they might get up to left to their own devices? No, it was probably best to keep them close at hand, at least until tonight when he could take them where he wanted them to go.

"All right. You can come. But we have to stick together and watch for Ko-goks. All right?"

The Rogues looked confused. "Ko-goks?" Oswald repeated. "What are those?"

"Bad guys," Kris answered.

Oswald's forehead creased. "But why? We all get along in the woods. We have to. It's how we survive."

Abazi, who was standing by him, placed her hand on his arm. "Things are different now, Oswald. But we're here to protect you. All right?"

He smiled warmly at her, his eyes full of light and fondness, maybe something more. "We'll follow ye anywhere."

Gabe had to fight to control his desire to push Oswald through a wall. He had no right to say things like that to Gabe's girlfriend!

His stomach soured, and he turned away. Who said Abazi was his girlfriend? It wasn't like they were even hanging out together all that much. Ever since their kiss Abazi had kept a distance between them, making sure they were never alone together, almost as if she had no interest in continuing things between them.

His fingers tightened into fists and his whole body shook with anger and fear. He was losing her! He couldn't lose her!

When Gabe looked at her again, he saw that she was staring at him. There was a message in her eyes, but he couldn't read it, not through the haze of fury that had overtaken him. But he couldn't let on that he was bothered. He didn't need thorns and flowers popping out every-where. He shook his head, pulled in a deep breath, and strode over to the small door.

"Let's go," he said tersely, then stepped outside, into the rain.

Gabe led the group, glad that he hadn't forgotten the way, glad that the rain was letting up a bit. He needed to stay in command. It was the only way to control his feelings, especially when he glanced back to see Abazi helping Oswald along, her arm supporting him. It was enough to drive a person mad, but he forged on. The cape helped in this, its power coursing through his limbs, and he was able to lead them on-ward without feeling the least bit fatigued. He started wondering if he could wear the cloak all the time.

Climbing the cliff bordering the Rogue's hideout was easier this time, thanks to the cloak, and Gabe was able to lift Kimber using his tree arms. Oswald watched Gabe doing this, his shifty eyes wide with fasci-nation. He looked like someone who'd never seen anything so strange and wondrous. If Abazi wasn't being so solicitous toward him Gabe might have felt sorry for the guy.

Before long they were in the rocky ravine that was home to the Rogues. Looking around at all the massive, moss-covered boulders, the clear stream and the gnarled roots, Gabe was reminded of his meeting here with Filidh, the strange creature man who was determined to take back the place as his own.

They followed a path along the stream, which had been narrow and low last fall, but now ran with the intensity of a mighty river. It had widened by four feet on either side, and had flooded several of the nearby caves. Gabe's throat tightened. He couldn't remember if Hollie's cave was close to the water, or farther back. He didn't even want to imagine what they'd find if the stream had flooded her cave.

Feeling more of an urgency, he led the group across the slippery stone bridge that spanned the pool where he and Oswald had fought, the waterfall thundering above them like an angry Thor. When they reached the other side, they climbed stone stairs to the top of the cliff, where they could see the waterfall emptying into the pool. At this point, Gabe couldn't remember which direction to take.

"Can you lead us to Hollie's cave?" he asked Oswald.

Oswald's forehead, wet from the rain, wrinkled. "Hollie?"

Kris stepped forward. "You've forgotten Hollie?"

"Is she an oak?"

"No. She's not one of yours. She's a—"

"I do not know of a Hollie," Oswald interrupted, his eyes darting around the ravine as though he were afraid of the place. "I don't want to be here. I don't think this is a good place."

"It's your hideout," Jer explained. "We came here one time looking for you. Don't you remember?"

"We fell in the water, right here." Gabe indicated the pool, which seemed twice as big as it had when he and Oswald had fought. "You must remember that."

"He's got himself the rot," a voice called from the other side of the waterfall. Standing opposite them was Filidh, his head cocked to one side. He looked his usual self—bizarre—with his bottle cap and button-adorned leather hat, his robe jacket, and his gnarled fingers gripping a staff adorned with dangling bones. "It be hardest on the oaks."

"Who are you?" Kris demanded, brandishing his staff. "Don't make me take you out, old man!"

"Calm down, whippersnapper!" Filidh cried, his nose and chin, which curved toward each other like the letter C, nearly touching. "Yer brother kens Filidh, don't ye, Gabriel?" Filidh's little eyes glittered mischievously.

"Yes, I do," Gabe answered. "I see you've weathered the winter just fine."

"Better than most round here." Gabe didn't like the sound of that.

"So what's the rot, and what can we do about it?"

Filidh's eyes were almost lost in the folds of his damp olive-striped skin as he squinted at Gabe. "There's a price for information like that, sure enough. Willin' to pay it?"

"If it's good information, and doesn't involve giving up my first-born, then yes."

"Ye ken what Filidh wants and it's nothing to do with babes. Got no use for the likes of that."

"You want the ravine." It wasn't exactly a secret. "But it's not mine to give."

"Then I'll be movin' on." Filidh turned to go.

"Wait!" Gabe couldn't just let the only person who had any answers walk away. He might not fully trust Filidh, but he didn't seem entirely without scruples. "Where can I find you? If I can work something out with the Rogues, that is."

"Filidh be everywhere. Ye only have to think of me and here I be."

Gabe wasn't so sure about that. "Can you at least tell me how long they've got?"

Filidh snorted. "Ye ken time means nothing to Filidh."

"I know that. But toss me a bone on this," Gabe begged, hoping the forest man wouldn't take him literally.

Filidh tilted his head to the right, then to the left. "Two settings? Give or take?"

"What're two settings?" Kris demanded.

"Two days," Jer answered. "Two settings of the sun, right?"

Filidh cackled. "Now there's a bright one. Rare these days, especially with yer sort."

Jer grinned. "Told you guys I was brilliant."

"If you were truly brilliant," Gabe muttered, "you'd know how to stop the rot and then I wouldn't have to sell my soul to the old guy."

"Filidh heard that," Filidh growled, cocking his head. "Now don't tarry, King. Ye're the answer, but ye don't ken how to put it into play. Only Filidh kens that."

"Super. I call you if I need you." Filidh nodded, then there was a sharp crack and he was gone.

"Who was that?" Oswald demanded, staggering a little as he approached Gabe. He looked dizzy and out of sorts, worse than yesterday. "What did he want?"

"He, um, well, he says he knows how to cure you."

"Cure me?" Oswald looked insulted. "There's nothing wrong with me."

"He thinks you have the rot."

Oswald recoiled. "The rot? I've nothing of the sort. No. No way. Absolutely not." He shook his head over and over as if by doing so he could make what Gabe was saying untrue.

"You've been acting very strangely, Oswald. Not like yourself at all. Do you know what the rot does?"

Oswald's eyes narrowed as he tried to concentrate. "It don't sound pleasant, whatever it is. Luckily I don't have it."

"Filidh said he'll tell me how to cure you," Gabe forged on, "if you hand the ravine over to him."

"This place?" Gabe nodded. "And it's *our* ravine?"

Gabe was tempted to lie and say no. "I'm not sure you own it, but it's where you and your Rogues hide out."

"Well, then, of course we must keep it."

Gabe bit down on a frustrated sigh and wiped the rain from his eyes. This was going nowhere fast. "I thought you didn't like the place anymore. You just said it wasn't a good place."

"I've changed me mind. And…and I have to check on something." He'd mentioned that before and Gabe wondered what it was he was supposed to check on.

"But if you did have the rot, or maybe some of your band had it, wouldn't you want to cure it? Would you be willing to give this up to help yourselves?"

Oswald stared at Gabe, uncomprehending. "I don't have the rot, nor do any of me Rogues, so why bother askin' such foolish questions?"

"Let's go find Hollie," Gabe said suddenly. Oswald was obviously in denial. That, or the disease was making it impossible for him to think straight. Either way, he needed help. And if Filidh was telling the truth, Gabe had very little time to give it to him. Two settings of the sun was Friday. Tax day.

"Is this Hollie friend or foe?" Oswald asked, having already forgotten that they'd spoken of her only a few minutes earlier.

"Friend. One of your best."

"Funny that I remember nothing of her."

"Yes, that *is* funny, isn't it?"

"Hey, Gabe!" Kris called. "I think this is the path to Hollie's cave." While Oswald and Gabe had been talking, Kris had gone on ahead, scouting out the trail. "I remember walking along the stream for a bit, then heading back that way." He pointed toward the woods. "Come on!"

"We're coming," Gabe called back, and the group followed after Kris.

"Here…this way!" Kris called excitedly after a few minutes of walking. "I remember carrying your sorry behind past this rock, Gabe."

A few moments later they were gathered outside the opening of Hollie's cave. Gabe was relieved to see it appeared perfectly dry and untouched by the wrath of the stream. She had chosen her abode wisely, staying far back from the water.

Not waiting, Kris wiggled his tall frame into the narrow opening. "Hurry up," he called back. Gabe followed after his brother, wondering what they'd do for light once inside. He'd forgotten that his flashlight needed new batteries.

When he felt the sides of the entrance tunnel fall away, he knew he'd made it into the larger, open area of the cave. Luckily Kris had remembered to take care of his supplies. A zipper sounded and he pulled out his flashlight. A round glow soon appeared on the cave wall in front of them.

There was a noise from behind Gabe and he turned to see Abazi enter. "Is she here?" she barked and her voice echoed back at her.

"We haven't had time to look," he answered shortly.

"Well, hurry up. Oswald is growing crazier by the second. He wanted to dance with me again, so I escaped in here. So that was Filidh, huh?" She rushed the question out before Gabe could comment on the dance-obsessed Oswald. "He looks sane and reliable...*not.*"

"He may be crazy," Gabe replied, "but I'll bet he's right about Oswald having the rot, whatever that is. If only we could track down Hollie or Dame Hazel and ask them about it. I'm not sure what to do."

"Well, start by helping me look," Kris said. "We have to be sure Hollie isn't here."

In silence they searched the cave. It was a mess, with pieces of coal thrown about, trinkets scattered all over the floor, and several bright red berries gathered like pools of blood in various spots throughout the cave. This was definitely not how it had been the last time they'd visited. Hollie kept a neat home. Gabe tested the coals and found them ice cold. If she'd had a fire in here, it hadn't been for some time.

"She's not here," he finally determined, *dead or unconscious.* "But it looks like something was. Maybe a wild animal?" He didn't buy it, but he hoped Kris would. "We should probably get back outside. We shouldn't have left Jer and Kimber alone on Rogue duty."

"Kimber's singing to them," Abazi told him. "They seem to like it. Keeps them calm, anyway. But yeah, we probably should get out there."

"Is it a good sign that Hollie's not here?" Kris whispered to Gabe as they crawled toward the exit.

Gabe didn't know. "I think it means she doesn't have the rot."

Gabe's knee trod on something soft. He picked it up and peered at it closely. "Kris, shine your light here."

The pale light focused on Gabe's hand, spotlighting the object sitting in it. It was a shoe. A bright blue sneaker, to be exact. Size ten.

Exactly the same size that Jake Morrigan wore.

Chapter Fifteen

Bodies They Stumbled Across

"Hold up, Abazi," Gabe whispered in a tight voice. "We have a problem."

She backed up. "What is it?" Then she saw the shoe. "Do you need me to tie your laces for you? Just put it back on and let's get out of here. This place is giving me the creeps."

"It's not mine," he hissed.

"Well, then, whose is it?"

"I'll give you three guesses."

"It's Jake's," Kris interrupted. "And it was here in Hollie's cave. If he hurt her I'm going to kill him!"

"Pull it back a notch, Tiger," Abazi ordered. "I'd have to think it would be the other way around. She's a Dryad, remember? And if she's acting anything like Oswald, she's a bigger danger to Jake than he is to her."

"But he was drunk."

"So we were supposed to think," Gabe said. "It might all have been an act."

"Maybe," Kris conceded. "But he's a lot bigger than Hollie, you know."

"But Hollie isn't alone out here. She has other Dryads to help her out."

"Not if they didn't wake up or are sick like the Rogues. Jake is a jerk," Kris persisted. "He wouldn't think twice about hurting her. The guy *pinches* people under the basket. Who does that?"

Gabe sucked in a deep breath of the stale cave air. He needed to think. He needed to clear his head. But it was so dark in the cave and so close. "Hollie's tough. She'll be okay," he said, and could only hope he was right. Jake was known for his dirty play—grabbing uniforms to hold people down when rebounding, trash talk, thrown elbows—but all the local referees knew his family so he got away with a lot. But Hollie could handle him. He had to believe that, and he had to make Kris believe that.

"I'm going to leave the shoe here for now, and we'll continue our search for Hollie. But remember, worse comes to worst, she could always change into a tree."

"And be stuck that way forever," Kris grumbled.

"We can't think that way."

"What about the dogs?" Kris pointed out. "They'll track Jake's scent here from the shoe and find Hollie's cave."

"That's a risk we'll have to take because we can't have them trace it to us. I'm a suspect, Kris. They'll think I did something to him."

Kris groaned in frustration. "Fine." He knocked the shoe off Gabe's hand. "Let's get going."

Outside in the open air, they blinked in the light. All the way through the tunnel they had heard Kimber singing. She had a sweet voice, light and ethereal. The Rogues were all sitting around her, staring at her raptly. Jer looked uncomfortable, sticking close to Kimber and watching the Rogues closely for any sudden movements.

"It's about time," he muttered when he saw Gabe. "They won't let her stop."

"We need to move on," Gabe called out as he stood up and shook out his cape. "Hollie's not here." He snapped his fingers at Oswald. "Hey! Is there anything you need to check on while we're here?"

Oswald's unfocused eyes shifted over to Gabe. "Who're ye?" he demanded, his expression suspicious and distrustful.

"I'm Gabriel." He spun around, glad he'd worn the cape. "See?"

Oswald's expression didn't alter much, but he stood. "So ye are. I'm still waitin' for ye to lead us away. Why's it takin' ye so long?"

"Tonight," Gabe promised. "We'll go tonight." He didn't want to think about what Oswald would do when Gabe brought him to the next place, but it was the only solution he could come up with right now. Oswald was not himself, nor were the other Rogues, and Gabe had to put them somewhere to keep them safe from the Ko-goks until he could track down Dame Hazel and Hollie—if they were awake— and find the answer to solving the rot.

He looked over at Kris, who was rooting around in his backpack. "Ready?"

Kris shook his head. "Give me a sec. I have an idea." He pulled out a piece of paper and proceeded to scribble something on it, hunching over to keep it from getting wet.

"What are you doing?" Jer asked.

"Writing a note to Hollie."

"Don't put our names or any other identifying information on it," Gabe said. "In case the cops find the cave. Which they might."

"Why?" Jer asked.

"Because we found Jake's shoe in there," Gabe whispered.

Jer's eyes widened. "That doesn't sound good."

"That's what we thought."

Kris disappeared back inside the cave. Half a minute later, he returned, looking, if not happy, a little more in control. "I'm ready."

Gabe stepped forward, then stopped. The problem was, he didn't know where else to look. He only knew this area vaguely from their last visit.

"Are there more caves we could search?" he asked Oswald.

"I think so," he answered. "Yes! Most definitely. That was what I was going to check on. I'm sure of it." He didn't look sure at all, but if it kept him calm, Gabe was all for it.

"Lead the way," Gabe told him, and on Oswald's command, the Rogues spread out. "Let's split up," he told Kris and the others. "Make sure they don't get themselves into trouble."

Gabe made sure he got Oswald, since he didn't want Abazi and the Dryad ending up alone together in a dark cave. Just thinking about it made his skin prickle, but he sucked in a deep breath and pushed the feeling away. He had to stay cool and in charge, which wasn't easy wearing the cloak. It seemed to work as a catalyst, not a calming agent.

The search led Gabe and Oswald in and out of countless fascinating caves. All were different, showcasing the bits and pieces of the individual Rogues who had occupied them. When they encountered flooded caves, Oswald seemed determined to go inside them anyway, but Gabe held him back. "I'll use my tree arm to check." He wasn't sure what he was checking for and while his twiggy fingers groped about, he could only hope it wasn't bodies they stumbled across.

Eventually the ravine ended, along with the caves. Oswald whistled long and loud and the Rogues soon assembled, with Gabe's brothers and Abazi and Kimber in tow. Kimber was starting to look worn out and Gabe nodded at Kris. Jer caught the gesture and scowled. "I can do it!" he mouthed. But Gabe didn't think he could. The way was rocky and slippery. It would simply be too dangerous for the both of them.

"Later," Gabe mouthed back. Jer's lips curled into a pout and his eyes grew fierce. Gabe turned away. He didn't have time to deal with Jer's sulks today.

"The Dark Domain," Oswald said when everyone had gathered near. "We must head there."

"What's the Dark Domain?" Gabe asked, not liking the sound of it one bit, especially under the circumstances. But even under normal ones, who would want to go anywhere near a place called the Dark Domain?

"Um, their dwelling. The dark ones."

Gabe remembered now. The Dark Domain must be where Dorn and his goons had taken Gabe when they'd kidnapped him last summer. "Why do you want us to go there?"

"Because that is where we must go."

"Is that where Hollie and Dame Hazel are?"

"It's where we must go," Oswald repeated stubbornly.

Gabe decided not to pursue the matter. Oswald obviously had no straight answers, or this was a trap. "How long will it take to get there?"

"As long as it takes," Oswald answered sharply, as though Gabe's question was idiotic.

Gabe glanced at his watch. It was already close to four. They had two hours, more or less, to get where they were going, talk to Dame Hazel or Hollie, hopefully both, and get back home. He didn't want Mom to worry about them.

"All right. Show us the way."

The trip to the Dark Domain took nearly an hour. The majority of the way was strewn with rocks and when they left the mountainside, the trees grew thick, as did the snow. The smell of spring was in the air, but beyond the sound of dripping, the woods remained quiet and still. The silence gave Gabe the creeps. He had hoped the forest was coming alive, but most of it, it seemed, still slept. Occasionally Gabe thought he heard noises, but when he stopped to listen, there was nothing.

During their trek, they crossed what had once been a road. Gabe figured it eventually turned into the main road into town—the one that passed May Farm and Grandma May's driveway—but had been allowed to grow over, likely to keep people out of the forest. Gabe wondered who had made that happen, and how much they knew about the dark ones.

Oswald stopped suddenly and Gabe realized they were close to the Dark Domain. The way had lightened and the trees grew less thick here. Gabe hurried up to where Oswald had kneeled, head cocked to one side, listening.

"What is it?" Something was wrong. He could feel it.

Oswald didn't answer for a moment, his eyes far away. Then they sharpened and turned on Gabe. "Someone's in the field."

"Stay here," Gabe told him. "Keep everyone back and safe. Can you do that?" Oswald stared blankly at him. "Don't let anyone go into the clearing," Gabe clarified.

Oswald slowly nodded, the movement making the water droplets coating his eyelashes quiver. "No clearing."

Gabe glanced at him worriedly, but Oswald's focus had returned to the field, his expression unreadable and far away. He seemed to be going downhill fast. Maybe Gabe should summon Filidh right now and make a deal. Maybe he should—

"Do you see them?" Kris kneeled down on the other side of Gabe.

Gabe couldn't see much of anything yet. Like last time, a fog hung over the place, not as thick as before, but enough to obscure things. "No. We should probably check things out before we go any further. Come on." He turned around. "Jer, you stay here with the girls. Kris and I are going to scout out the clearing."

He was rewarded with a glare. "I want to come, too."

"Just do as I say, Jer," Gabe growled.

To prevent further arguments, he rose and headed toward the line of trees separating the clearing from the woods. Kris followed after him. Never being the lightest of foot, Gabe was grateful for the snow to disguise the sound of his footsteps. Because now, despite the fog, he could see that the meadow was filled with thousands of black, spiky trees and countless dark ones. Those in 'human' form looked like zombies, loping along through the fog in a sort of spastic shuffle, moaning and groaning. Sometimes a tree would turn into a dark one, and sometimes a dark one would turn into a tree, but never seemingly intentionally. Every few seconds, one of them would crack his branches together, but in quick succession, as though on speed. The ominous clacking was scary enough, but the jittery crashing effect of it was worse. The Ko-goks were out of control, and that made them even scarier to Gabe. In addition to being mean, they were desperate and unpredictable. And this time there was no tree wall surrounding the clearing to keep others out, almost as though Straif wanted them to come in.

"Holy crap," Kris breathed. "It's like a Goth festival gone bad."

"It looks like something's wrong with them."

"Maybe they have the same sickness as the Rogues."

"Maybe."

"They're acting like zombies."

"Yeah, but they're not looking for brains."

"They're looking for your blood."

Gabe grimaced. "Exactly."

"What if Hollie's in there?" Kris asked in a small voice. "What if they caught her and Dame Hazel?"

"Hollie's too smart for that," Gabe replied, though he had a feeling even Sherlock Holmes' intelligence wouldn't save him from the Ko-goks.

"So what do we do now?"

"We head home the long way. If we're late, we'll just tell Mom we got lost. She'll be mad for a bit, but also relieved we're okay."

Kris's head cocked to one side. "Do you hear that?"

"I hear it," Abazi said from behind them. "And stop leaving me out of things. Girls can be heroes, too, or haven't you heard this is the 21st century?"

"Someone needs to watch out for Kimber," Gabe snapped. It wasn't like he was trying to be a Neanderthal misogynist, and besides, he hadn't forgotten that Abazi had danced with Oswald and seemed to like it.

"Then why can't it be you?"

"Because I'm the one wearing the cloak," he answered mulishly.

"So you're buying into this whole king thing?"

"No. But I can turn into a tree if I need to and you can't."

"And what about him?" She tossed her head toward Kris. "Why does he get to be up here and I don't?"

"Because he followed me, that's why."

Abazi scowled. "Nice answer. You always do that, try to make it look like nothing's your fault."

Gabe ran a frustrated hand over his damp face, his palm scraping against the stubble on his jaw and chin. "Listen to me. I didn't ask for any of this, but right now I'm the only one who's truly involved in this. I'm supposed to be a leader. They're counting on me, and if I screw up, I'd rather be the one to pay for it. Not you!"

Abazi took a startled step backward. "All right, Hoss. Take it easy."

Gabe was surprised. Abazi usually didn't back down. "I will, but only if you stop acting like I want to be the hero. I don't."

"Yes, well, heroes usually don't have thorns sticking out of their faces."

"What?" His hand flew up to his chin. What he had thought was stubble was actually the beginning of thorns...and they had grown half an inch in only a few seconds.

"I wouldn't normally think this way, but I vote that we get out of here," Kris said, looking at Gabe in fascination. "Who knows what the Rogues will do if they see the dark ones."

"But Oswald doesn't even remember who Straif is," Gabe argued, between taking deep breaths. He needed to make the thorns go away.

"That's my point," Kris said. "He doesn't remember the danger."

"Well, I'm not arguing with you. We'll backtrack."

"I'm still hearing that strange noise," Abazi said. She held up her hand to stop Gabe's next words. "I'm not being a jerk. I really do hear something strange. I don't think it's Ko-gok. I think it might be human. And he's crying."

"Jake!" Kris said excitedly. "It must be him!"

This was going from bad to worse. "But how the heck do we get to him," Gabe asked, "especially in this fog? And he's likely to be surrounded by guards, too."

"I have an idea." Kris smiled. "Jer and Kimber, come here." He waved them over. When they reached the group, Kris said, "Now listen up."

When Kris was done outlining his idea, Gabe told him it sounded like suicide for the others and homicide for him. "Then again," he added, "I don't think we have any choice. We can't just leave Jake here."

The plan was for Abazi, Kris, and Jer to act as distracters while Gabe used his tree arms to pluck Jake out from wherever they were keeping him. Kimber was to take the Rogues and start leading them home by staying in the woods and skirting the clearing.

"Do you really think the Rogues will go along with that?" Gabe asked.

Kris nodded. "Just have Kimber sing. She'll be like the Pied Piper of the Forest Immortal."

Kimber beamed. "I can do it, Gabe. I know I can." Gabe wasn't so sure, but again, what choice did they have? They couldn't leave Jake here with the Ko-goks, they'd eat him. In fact, it was surprising they hadn't already. Just to shut him up.

"I believe in you, Kimber." And he did. Besides, she needed this. She needed to feel useful. He couldn't take this away from her.

Jer didn't look too happy. "You can't go alone, Kimber."

Her eyes flashed. "Why not?"

"What if the Ko-goks come? How will you get away?"

She shrugged. "I'm sure the Rogues will look after me."

"The Rogues can barely look after themselves," Jer argued. As if to prove his point, a Rogue wandered by, wearing a mound of moss balanced on his head.

"Then you should go with her," Gabe said. "Kris and Abazi can be the sitting ducks."

"But I'll miss out on the fighting!"

"Not if the Ko-goks see you. You'll be doing plenty of fighting then."

Jer's lips turned downward into their familiar stubborn pout. "You're just saying that because Abazi's right. You want to be the hero and nobody else."

"So *you* want to rescue Jake?"

"I could."

"Then be my guest." Gabe indicated the field. "Find your way through that."

Jer turned to study the clearing, filled with a jungle of thorny trees, ghost-like in the fog. Any attempt on his part was sure to end badly, Gabe knew. It'd be like fighting your way through a briar patch. If Jer was lucky, he'd end up like Brer Rabbit, but Jer hadn't been born and bred in a briar patch, and it certainly wasn't the place he loved best. So very probably, Jer wouldn't make it out alive.

Jer was likely thinking the same thing because he said, albeit grudgingly, "Someone has to look after Kimber. Might as well be me." Kimber gave Jer a dirty look, which he didn't notice.

"Good. Get Kimber and the Rogues home safely. I know you don't think that's an important job, Jer, but it is."

Jer didn't look convinced, but he didn't say anything more, which Gabe mistakenly interpreted as capitulation. "Ready, Kimber?"

She nodded, then started singing. The drooping Rogues suddenly perked up and marched toward her. She and Jer began walking along the edge of the woods and the Rogues followed after them like sheep.

When they had disappeared, Kris and Abazi pulled out their weapons. "We're ready whenever you are."

"Get away, you freak!" a frightened voice screamed. "Get away from me!"

"Go!" Gabe yelled to Kris and Abazi, and they took off through the woods, circling the clearing for some ways before entering, bellowing loudly as they ran. The Ko-goks nearby jerked toward them, then froze as though uncertain what to do with the intruders.

Now was the time. Gabe raced out of the woods and through the maze of thorny trees. The dark ones, distracted by Kris and Abazi, barely seemed to notice him as he sprinted by. And then, suddenly, a cry went up, "It's Gabriel!" and they all seemed to see him at once. Branches flung out, catching his arms and shoulders, ripping his clothes and slicing into his skin. The pain was terrible, but he kept running.

It didn't take long for him to realize that the Ko-goks, both in human and tree form, were unusually slow, and he was able to avoid the branches more easily now. Soon he was past the worst of the trees and was nearly to an opening at the center of the clearing. Jake had to be there.

With a mighty roar, Gabe gave in to the power of the cloak, to the power of his tree spirit. Through sheer control, he managed to do as Straif had once done, transforming himself halfway, so that he was neither human nor tree, yet both at once. Maybe if he kept himself part human, he wouldn't kill anyone.

His half-tree eyes made out dark shadows rushing at him from the fog, trying to take him out, but his tree arms tossed them backward like fingers flicking peas. He headed toward a glow in the center of the meadow—Jake. It had to be him. His aura was not very bright, but certainly brighter than the dark ones gathered around him. Gabe's vision sharpened, and this time, he knew for sure it was Jake. He was staring at Gabe, his eyes filled with horror.

"Get away from me!"

Gabe ignored this and advanced toward Jake like a steamroller, taking out Ko-goks along the way. Just as he was about to reach out and grab the boy, a bright glow dashed past him, heading toward Jake. Gabe tried to adjust his vision by squinting, but he couldn't bring the glow into focus, not in this fog. Abazi? Kris? Before he could react, the glow had grabbed Jake and hauled him away from the tree.

"Close in *now*!" a dark figure screamed, and Gabe recognized Straif's voice. This was a trap. They had used Jake as a lure and now Gabe and the glow and possibly Kris and Abazi were all caught, as neatly as a hare in a snare.

There would be no Brer Rabbit escape for them.

Chapter Sixteen

Aurelia of the Beech

Despite the snow, Jer and Kimber were making good progress, until they heard the shouting. Jer turned around to see a horde of dark ones rush Gabe from all sides, surrounding him. "Go, Kimber! Take the Rogues and go!"

But it was too late. Jer's shouting had made her stop singing, and the moment she stopped singing, the Rogues stopped following her. As one, they turned toward the clearing. Then, as if pulled by a string, they began marching toward it.

"Don't go in there!" Jer grabbed at their arms, but they easily shook him off. "They'll kill you."

Not one of them responded with so much as a head turn. They continued trekking toward the clearing as mindlessly as the Borg. Jer had no idea what they were going to do once they reached it. Let themselves be captured? Fight? What?

"Stay here, Kimber," he told her. "I'm going after them."

"Jerome Hawthorne, stop treating me like I'm six!"

"I'm not!" he replied, shocked at the tone of her voice. "I just want you to be safe."

"You're treating me like a child, like you feel your brothers do to you, and frankly, I'm tired of it." She hobbled toward him, looking determined. "I can fight, just like you can. I might not be as fast or strong, but I'm smart. I'm going in there, whether you like it or not. So either get out of my way, or follow me."

Jer stared at her, stunned. "I don't treat you like a child," was all he could get out. *Do I?* Did he? *Never!* This situation wasn't at all like what Kris and Gabe put him through on a daily basis. He was looking after Kimber. She had CP and could get hurt. That's all there was to it. He was *not* patronizing her. He was the good guy in this!

He had no time to ponder the unfairness of Kimber's attack because she had turned her back on him and was hurrying after the Rogues. "Wait up!" But she didn't. She must be very angry with him. Well, she had no right to be. He was the one who should be angry, not her.

He soon passed her by, seething, and caught up to the Rogues. They were heading straight toward the mass of dark ones surrounding Gabe. Jer pulled out his bandalore and gave it a few practice throws. He hoped it worked, never having been able to test it out on a willing Ko-gok.

Well, no time like the present.

Gabe was going ballistic, swinging his tree arms left and right and the light fog billowed around him like a live creature. The Ko-goks attacked with equal abandon, having no seeming plan but to take Gabe down. Some started climbing his elongated torso and Gabe roared angrily as he swiped them off. But soon they would overrun him. There were just too many of them.

"Charge!" Oswald cried, running into the melee. Jer ran, too, spotting Kris and Abazi attacking the dark ones from the opposite side. Kris was throwing his stick on a rope, relying on the touch of wood to clear the way, and Abazi was swinging her tomahawk as she flipped through the air. The problem was, while the dark ones didn't like the touch of wood, it didn't seem to affect them the way it once had, very likely because of their illness.

Soon the dark ones covered Gabe, making it nearly impossible to see him beneath their writhing figures. The smell of decay and rancid blood soured the air and the Ko-goks' screeches made it hard to think. Everywhere were dark ones and tree limbs and howls. The chaos was maddening, as was the smell. Jer felt like vomiting and tried not to breathe through his nose. This wasn't as glorious as he'd imagined, but he had wanted to fight, so he wasn't going to turn tail and run now. Besides, Gabe needed him.

He raced toward his brother, throwing his bandalore at the dark ones trying to cut him off. If he smacked them on the head, it made some impact. Anywhere else, the effect was negligible. It was time to get out his willow whip. He'd been carrying one around for ages, and was great with it in the barn, but had yet to use it in battle.

The first time he cracked the willow branch, he hit nothing but air. The second time he was more successful, clearing three Ko-goks off Gabe's torso in one swipe. Getting his rhythm down, Jer cracked the whip again and again, knocking dark one after dark one off Gabe.

Then the Rogues started getting in the way and Jer had to stop, which was just as well since his arm felt like it was about to fall off.

But what he had done was enough for Gabe to begin moving his limbs again. He started swinging them and the dark ones went flying through the air, exhaling screeches. When they landed, Jer and the others pounced on them. The touch of wood was regaining its effect and all Jer had to do was hold his willow whip to the dark ones' faces and it was enough for them to fling him off and go running to the woods. It was rather surreal trying to hold down these wiggling, skeletal, zombie Dryads, revolting, too, as they were the source of the rancid smell, like they were rotting on the inside.

But Jer was determined not to let the horror get to him. He wouldn't! Even though with every passing moment, he wanted to cut and run, he stayed to fight.

And then it happened.

"Watch out, Jer!" a voice cried out behind him, and he spun around. But the warning came too late. A dark one leaped on him and he fell backward. His head hit something hard sticking out of the muddy snow and his head spun once, twice, before everything went dark.

Next thing he knew he was being dragged along the ground. He struggled to free himself, but the effort sent waves of nausea through his body. Whoever had him—he couldn't see very well through his hazy vision—re-tightened their grip and continued dragging him through the chaos of running dark ones and fighting Rogues.

"Stop!" he managed to push out through rubbery lips. "Let me go."

A voice responded, but he couldn't make out what it had said…his ears were ringing and the noise was overwhelming, almost painful. Moments later, the world grew dark and shadowy, and quieter somehow, than on the battlefield.

"Take care of him, please. I'll be back soon." This time Jer heard everything clear as a bell. His savior dropped his feet, then he felt himself rising upward, into the air, shadows flashing by. Before he could react, he was straddling the branch of a tree and clinging to its trunk. The tree began to sway slightly, back and forth, and he had the distinct impression that he was being rocked like a baby in its mother's arms, which felt rather nice, easing the pain in his head a little.

Jer understood immediately what was wrong with him. He had a concussion. Kris had gotten one when he was eleven, tripping over his own feet while dribbling the ball up the court. He'd used his head and a wall to stop, knocking him out. It was only for a few seconds, but for about a minute after that, he didn't remember anything—not lying there, not talking to the coach, nothing. He thought he'd hit the wall, then gotten right back on his feet. It didn't occur to him that the coach would have had to teleport across the gym to reach his side so quickly.

At the time Jer hadn't really quite understood what had happened to Kris and perhaps hadn't been entirely sympathetic. But now he got it. A concussion was rather scary, not to mention painful. When his head had hit the rock, he'd actually felt his brain slide and collide with the back of his head—same thing that Kris had described. Now it ached inside his skull and he felt sick to his stomach. He groaned, feeling like he might throw up.

"Shhh," he heard the wind whisper to him. "It'll be all right, young one."

Jer blinked and looked around, his vision still blurry, but he couldn't see anyone, not a human or a Dryad. "Hello? Who's there?" His voice was loud and echoing in his ears and he winced. Even in the dark woods, the light seemed too bright and he closed his eyes.

"Stay still now."

Not a hallucination, then. Aural hallucinations, Jer knew, came from inside your head and this was coming from outside. "Who are you?" he pushed out through stiff lips.

"I'm Aurelia of the Beech, and ye're Jerome of the Hawthorn. Gently now, Anscom." Jer felt twig-like fingers touch the crown of his head, growing to cover the area like a net. Each tip lightly massaged his skull, loosening the pain, relaxing him. Jer felt as though the tree was sending healing vibes throughout his entire head; his brain stopped hurting, his muscles went limp, and the nausea subsided. He didn't want the treatment to end, but eventually it did. Slowly, he opened his eyes to see the retreating black branches of a pale white tree. It was a birch. He also saw that he was high up in another, different, tree and he gripped the trunk more tightly, his hot cheek pressing against its cool gray bark.

"Ye're all right now, little Jerome?" Aurelia asked him. He wasn't sure where her voice was coming from, but he could feel its vibrations through her smooth bark.

"I think so," he replied in wonder. "Thank you. And thank you to Anscom, too." But the birch was gone, heading toward the battlefield. Jer suddenly remembered what had happened, and more importantly, why. "I have to go, Aurelia. My brothers and friends are down there."

"It'll soon be over," she soothed. "Stay here for a moment longer. Be sure yer head is clear. You'll need it later, when things grow worse."

"Worse?" How could things be worse than that nightmare happening down in the field?

"While we Dryads have awakened, little one, we're weak. We're not entirely ourselves, the Beech, and most are worse off than us. We need yer brother, Yggdrasil, whom ye know as Gabriel, King of the Forest Immortal. We need his help and he needs yers."

"My help?" Jer snorted. "He doesn't want my help. He still thinks I'm a little kid."

"Then prove to him that ye're not. Put aside childish thoughts and deeds. Ye can only show ye're worthy through action."

"I was trying to fight. I was trying not to be…scared."

"Tis not childish to be scared. In fact, it's foolish not to be. What ye cannot do is let yer own personal wishes and desires supersede the greater good. Yer brother's not perfect, but he's the one we need. Help him, and ye'll help all of us survive."

"I try to help him, but he won't let me." Jer could hear the childish-ness in his voice, but he didn't care. Gabe never treated him like a man, but Jer was thirteen now. Old enough to fight, old enough to look after Kimber. He remembered belatedly that she didn't want to be looked after, and he certainly wasn't doing that now anyway. He hoped she was all right. Was it patronizing to worry about her?

"Tryin' is only practicin'," Aurelia said. "Now it is time for doin'."

"Easy for you to say," Jer mumbled. "You don't have to deal with my brother."

The tree trunk shook in his arms and he realized Aurelia was laughing at him. "Ye think ye're the only one with siblings?"

"Well, no. But I'm pretty sure no one's siblings are as bad as Gabe."

"Yer self-pity'll get ye nowhere, young one, merely dig ye deeper into sorrow."

Jer didn't like how Aurelia kept calling him young one. It was like no one could see him as the man he was. "Speaking of siblings, I should probably go help them."

"They're comin' now. I'll set ye down. Be prepared to run. My trees'll set a path for ye. Get yer people to follow, and we'll guide ye to safety."

That sounded more like it. "All right, and thanks, Aurelia. For fixing my head."

"I merely held ye in me arms, young Jerome, while Anscom healed ye."

"But you kept me safe."

"Return the favor and keep yer brother safe."

"Yes, all right," Jer reluctantly agreed. He didn't need someone to tell him to keep Gabe safe. The problem was Gabe not allowing Jer to do it. He let go of the trunk and Aurelia used another branch to lower him to the ground. When he turned to face her, he gave her a salute. She might be a bit of a lecturer, kind of like his mom, but she had done him a big favor. "Be safe yourself," he told her. "And I'll try to do what you said." He knew he'd said 'try' again, but right now that's all he could give her.

"It'll be hard," she confided, her voice carrying down to him. "It always is, coming-of-age."

His eyes teared up, and he nodded. "You've got that right."

"But it'll come. Trust me on that."

He bowed. "Goodbye, Aurelia." Then he flashed her a grin. "For now."

He could almost see her smile in return as her trunk bent in acknowledgement. "For now."

As her words faded away, there was a tremendous roar and he turned to see a horde of green cloaks racing toward him. Behind them—a ways back—came the dark ones. Jer caught sight of human clothes and then whoever wore them was lost in the crowd.

"This way!" He beckoned the crowd toward him. He turned around and before him, as Aurelia promised, a pathway parted like the Red Sea, one tree after another stepping back as though making room for royalty. *Amazing.*

He pelted down the trail and when he glanced back to be sure everyone was following, he felt a surge of power. They were following *him.* *He* was their leader! So this was what it was like to be in charge. He could grow to like this feeling very much.

Behind the green cloaks, the dark ones flowed into the woods like a malignant river. Soon they would be overcome by Ko-gok sludge. He had to do something, or they'd be trapped in the very path that was supposed to lead them to safety. An idea came to him, but in putting it into play, he was going to have to do something he didn't want to do…give up his leadership role. It was a big sacrifice, but if he didn't do something soon, they could all die.

"Keep running along this path," he told the Rogues behind him. "And don't stop for anything!" Then he clapped them on the back as they ran by. The path was narrow, and he had to stand aside as the Rogues passed him, some limping, most staggering. He kept an eye out for his brothers and Abazi and Kimber, and at last spotted Kris's Mohawk bobbing up and down toward the end of the pack. He pushed his way back to him. Kris was supporting Gabe, who was leaning hard on his brother. He looked awful, his face scratched and bleeding, one eye swollen shut, the same one Jake had blackened, his hair matted with twigs and mud.

"What happened to him?" Jer shouted as he ran alongside them.

"No time to explain," Kris gasped. "We have to get out of here."

"What about Jake?"

"We couldn't help him," Abazi answered shortly. "We didn't get there in time."

A violent screech echoed through the woods and Jer glanced back. Oswald and a few Rogues were fighting off the dark ones, but they were outnumbered ten to one. He swallowed hard, hoping to dislodge the lump in his throat.

"Go on," he told the others. "I've got something to do."

"Oh no you don't!" Kris growled. "You can help me with Gabe. He's pretty beat up."

"It won't take more than a few seconds, I promise."

"Don't argue with Kris, Jer!" Gabe cried out in a choked voice, startling Jer. "Just run, you idiot!"

Jer felt a fury boil up inside him. There it was again...Gabe ordering him around like he was a child.

Then he remembered what Aurelia had said. *It'll be hard...it always is, this coming-of-age.* She was certainly right about that. He drew in a deep breath. "I'll be all right," he said in his most grown-up voice. "I know someone who can help us. Go. Please!"

Gabe stared at him through his one good eye, considering. A drop of blood trickled down his dusty cheek. "Thirty seconds, Jer. If you don't come, we're coming back for you."

Jer looked at his brother in surprise. "That's all I need. Thirty seconds."

Gabe nodded and the others kept going. Kimber glanced back at Jer over her shoulder, but said nothing.

The Rogues holding off the dark ones were tiring. Soon the Ko-goks would break through the thin line and chase the others down. It was now or never. "Aurelia!" Jer shouted upward through cupped hands. "Tell the Beeches to close the path behind us. Cut the dark ones off!"

It was a good idea, but could they do it? Aurelia had said the Beeches were weak. Maybe they'd used up all their energy creating the path. Maybe they had nothing left.

A Rogue fell with a cry and Jer raced to her side. He pulled her to her feet and pushed her down the path. "Go!" She stumbled off as Jer pulled his bow off his back and notched an arrow. He let it loose, then pulled another and another. His wood-tipped arrows hit the dark ones dead center on their foreheads, sending them flying.

But more came in their place. A dark one rushed at him and Jer shakily reached for another arrow. Just as it launched himself, a loud groan filled the air, growing louder with each second. Jer smacked the leaping Ko-gok on the head with the arrow and he fell to the ground, howling in pain. The groan grew painfully loud and Jer covered his ears and watched in astonishment as a line of trees lifted their roots out of the ground and moved into the path. One of them stepped on a dark one and it shrieked in pain, before wriggling out and crawling away.

"Run!" Jer told Oswald, pushing him along. "The path is closing. We have to get ahead of the trees or we'll get trapped with the dark ones."

Oswald gazed at him dazedly. "Who're ye?"

"I'm a friend," Jer said as calmly as he could, despite his growing fear. Oswald looked unhinged. When the Dryad only stared at him, Jer frantically searched his mind for the right thing to say. "The Beeches are helping us. Aurelia of the Beech. You know the Beeches?" *Please know the Beeches.*

"Aurelia?" Oswald said wonderingly. "She's here?"

Thank goodness Oswald knew Aurelia. Not only that, but he seemed impressed with the knowledge that she was close by. "She's asking her kind to close off the path. But we only have a short time to get away. She wants to help you."

"Aurelia wants to help *me*?" He sounded amazed.

Jer pushed him again. "Absolutely. So don't screw this up. Just run that way!" Jer pointed along the path. "And fast! Show her how fast you can run!" He was talking to Oswald like he was a little kid, but it couldn't be helped. The guy was acting like one. Jer wondered if Gabe sometimes did that to him when he was being obstinate or purposely obtuse. Probably.

Oswald nodded seriously. "I can run fast!" He took off, and after a second, the remaining Rogues followed after him.

A few dark ones slipped through the tightening wall of trees and Jer swung his arrow at them. "Stay back! You don't want to feel the sting of my wrath!"

The Ko-goks didn't respond to his threat, not until a Beech stepped in front of them with a resounding thud, separating Jer from the writhing mass. It was time to get out of Dodge. Jer took off, his feet flying over the ground like swooping hawks. The path closed behind him as he raced after the others, and he could only hope that he hadn't left it too late.

He glanced back, anxious to see if the dark ones had made it past the Beech. A few of them had. His stomach gurgled and he ran faster. The Beeches were closing ranks swifter and swifter behind him, threatening to overtake him and crush him between their massive trunks. He looked back one more time and that's when he noticed something one of the Ko-goks had clasped in one bloody hand, something Jer knew he had to take away from him, or it would be all over for the Forest Immortal.

He stopped running and turned to face the three dark ones racing after him. He moved to nock his arrow just as a dark one opened its hideous mouth and screamed at him like a crazed baboon. Jer's whole body went cold at the sound of the awful shriek, but he didn't back down.

He could not back down, not even if it meant his death.

Chaptɛr Sɛvɛntɛɛn

ⴷ Nightmarɛ

"Where's Jer?" Gabe croaked. He felt awful, like a Mack truck had hit him, then had backed up and hit him again. "We told him thirty seconds. It's been longer than that, right?" He wasn't exactly sure. He felt weird. Being part tree had really taken it out of him. All those Ko-goks crawling up his trunk, clinging to his branches, pounding on him, probably hadn't helped, either. But he hadn't killed any innocent bystanders, so he counted himself lucky. Even luckier, Kris and Abazi had come along in time to save his hide. Unfortunately, not in time to save Jake. Someone, or something, had gotten to him first. But who? And was it friend or foe?

Once Jake was gone, they'd only just managed to escape into the woods, with Jer urging them to follow him. The whole scenario seemed so fantastical, like they were in a movie. He wished he could hit the stop button and make it all go away.

"I haven't seen him," Kimber replied worriedly. "I keep looking, but he hasn't shown up."

"We need to go back," Gabe told the others. "He's going to get himself creamed. I knew we shouldn't have left him, but he said he had help, didn't he?"

"He...did...say...that," Kris acknowledged, his words coming out like bullets, and Gabe realized that his brother was bearing most of his weight. He needed to snap out of this strange funk he was in.

Hopefully the powers of his cape would kick in soon. But then he realized it was no longer around his shoulders. "My cloak! Where's my cloak?"

"One of the Ko-goks tore it off you," Abazi panted. She was carrying some of his weight, too, and it was wearing her down. Gabe had to get his act together. He couldn't keep leaning on her like this. "It fell on the ground."

"We have to go back for it."

"We can't go back there," Kris said, and that's when Gabe really started to worry. Kris never backed down from a fight or a challenge.

"Stop. Right now. Just stop!" he yelled, and at last they did. He pulled his arms off their shoulders and slumped to his knees. "I need that cloak. We have to go back."

A few errant Rogues trotted past them, followed by Oswald. He looked perplexed, they all did. "Where are we goin'?" he asked, stopping by their group. "What's happenin'?"

"We're going someplace safe," Kimber soothed him, laying a hand on his arm.

"Someplace safe," Oswald repeated. "Is there such a thing?"

"There is," she assured him. "Just keep following the path, okay?"

A branch swung down from one of the trees and lightly prodded Oswald forward. "Goooo…" a voice came from above them. "Go, nowwww…"

"Who's that?" he cried, but no answer came, only the insistent branch pushing him on.

"We have to go back for Jer," Kimber called into the air.

"Who are you?" Gabe shouted. "Where's Jer?"

"Too late. Goooo…"

Gabe glanced back at the path. There was no one behind them now, only the trees steadily shutting down the space, blocking the way back to the clearing. Jer was nowhere to be seen. "We can't. My brother's in there!"

"Goooo!" the voice boomed, and Gabe realized it was coming from one of the trees, or maybe all of them, speaking in a collective voice.

"Not without my brother. I knew I shouldn't have listened to him. He's just a kid. I shouldn't have left him alone." And he needed that cape.

But there was no going back. The Beeches began to move toward them and more branches descended, pushing them forward. "Goooo!" When Gabe tried to dig in his heels, literally, one branch grabbed him around the waist and lifted him off the ground. Soon he was skimming along. He tried to pry the branch off, but he couldn't budge it.

There was nothing he could do. He didn't have the strength to break loose, and judging by the others' struggles, neither did anyone else. It was as though they were all under a spell.

He was passed along to another tree branch, then another, until the process blurred and his mind darkened and went blank. He was leaving his brother to die. He was abandoning him, and he could do nothing about it. "My brother," he moaned. "I have to help him."

But the trees did not listen, leaving Jer to his fate.

~~~~~~

When Gabe awoke, he found himself in the slushy, snow-filled meadow near the Briar Borders, surrounded by countless bodies. He sat up, feeling hazy and sick. Was he looking at a slaughter field?

"You're awake."

Gabe turned. "Abazi!" He was surprised by the passion in his voice, as was Abazi, judging by the startled expression on her face. "You're okay!"

She rubbed her forehead. "Um, yeah, I'm okay. I guess. I was more worried about you. You're not yourself."

"No," he conceded. "I'm not." Then he remembered. "Is Jer here? Did he make it?"

Abazi shook her head, her eyes grim. "I haven't seen him. I just woke up."

Gabe crawled over to her and collapsed by her side. Even that small effort had exhausted him. "I killed him, didn't I? I left him there to die."

"No, you didn't!" she shouted, startling Gabe. "It wasn't your fault."

"I should've fought them. I should've done something."

"We all should have, but none of us did. I don't think we could have. I think those trees took us, maybe put us to sleep for a bit."

"You felt it, too?"

"Like I was in a dream?"

"Yeah, though that was more like a nightmare."

"Let's not be dramatic, Immortal."

Gabe decided to ignore her comment, being that she was the drama queen of Ranger. "We need to go back, to get Jer."

"I agree, but I'm not sure if we'll be able to."

Gabe pushed himself to his feet, wobbled, then, when he'd steadied himself, he held his hand out to Abazi. She took it and he barely managed to help her to her feet. It wasn't entirely weakness. The feel of her small hand in his was like sunshine after ten days of rain.

"Thanks," she said, and for once, it wasn't grudgingly given.

Gabe hobbled over to Kris and prodded him with his foot. "Wake up. We're going back for Jer."

Kris groaned and rolled over. "Just ten more minutes."

"Wake up, Kris! You're not in your bed."

Kris sat up, immediately on alert. "What just happened?"

"We were transported here by trees. I think they did something to knock us out, to make it easier to move us."

"Awesome," Kris acknowledged. "But weird. Do you think that's what happened in the woods? When Jake's footsteps disappeared?"

"Maybe. But I can't figure out why, or whether someone was helping him or hurting him."

Kris stiffly pushed himself to his feet and looked around. "Where's Kimber?"

Gabe felt a chill as he scanned the meadow. The Rogues were starting to stir, some sitting up, others standing and stretching. They looked as bewildered and afraid as he felt. "Kimber?" he called, then louder and more frantic. "*Kimber!*"

There was no answer. "Let's spread out," Kris said. They fanned out, searching and yelling Kimber's name, but she wasn't anywhere to be seen.

"Now we have two people missing," Gabe groaned. He felt like he was losing his mind. He needed help. He needed…he needed his cloak. It would clear his mind, give him strength. He couldn't be a leader without it.

"Mellow out, Gabe," Abazi said. "We'll find them."

"I need my cloak. It will help. It will," he repeated helplessly.

"First things first. We find Jer and Kimber, then we figure out what to do with them." She indicated the Rogues, who were wandering around aimlessly.

"The Ko-goks have gotten them, I just know it." Gabe felt so tired now. He'd give anything to be able to just lie down and go to sleep.

"What's that?" Kris pointed at the woods. "Over there!"

"Kimber!" Abazi cried in relief, showing she'd been just as worried as Gabe, probably more. She and Kris took off running, and Gabe, reviving a little, joined them, soon catching up.

Kimber spotted them and hobbled toward them, moving as fast as her braces would allow. "I couldn't find him!" she sobbed. "I tried. They let me look, but he wasn't anywhere."

"They?" Kris echoed. "Who are *they*?"

"We're going in," Gabe assured her, ignoring Kris. "We'll find him."

She shook her head. "You can't. The dark ones…they're coming. I heard them."

"They're *still* coming?"

"They're like starving animals, Gabe," Kimber tried to explain. "You can't stop them. They have no fear anymore."

"It doesn't matter. We're going in. I have to save Jer."

He was about to step into the woods when he heard the ominous sound of footsteps. "They're coming!" He drew out his bata and prepared to fight. The footsteps grew closer and closer, but Gabe could see nothing in the dark woods. Where were they? Should he go on the attack, or wait for them to come to him? "Show yourself!" he cried. "Show yourself, or I'm coming in after you!"

A figure appeared. "It's just me!"

"Jer!" Kimber cried, her eyes lighting up. "You're okay!"

"No time for greetings," he told her, grabbing her arm and swinging her around. "There are a few dark ones who made it through and they're after me. Come on!"

Gabe stared at his brother, feeling a rising anger. He wasn't sure what it was about, but he couldn't stop himself. "You said *thirty* seconds!"

"Yeah, well, I had something to do," Jer replied, "and now I've done it, so we can go. We have to get going! Now!"

"What did you do?" Gabe demanded, refusing to budge.

Jer's eyes shifted and Gabe had the feeling his brother was hiding something from him. "I took care of things, and now we should get out of here...before they come." He was breathing hard and he looked jittery, like the Rogues.

"What could *you* do? You're just a kid!"

"But I—"

"And now my cloak is lost!" Gabe cried, feeling a rising panic flood his body. "I should've stayed behind. I could've gotten it back!" His knees felt weak, his head throbbed. "You said thirty seconds! I've lost my cloak because of you!"

Jer took a step away, his eyes tearing up, and Gabe noticed his brother was bleeding from a gash by his right temple. "You were worried about your precious cloak?" he whispered. "Did you care at all about what happened to me?"

"Well, yes, of course! But I need my cloak. I *need* it, Jer."

"I don't think that cloak's good for you, Gabe," Jer answered in a shaking voice. "It's turning you into a real jerk."

"I'm not being a jerk! You're the jerk for making us all worried. We could be home by now, safe and...and..." Gabe couldn't finish the sentence. He was too tired, his mind too muddled to form any coherent thoughts. Darkness skirted the edge of his consciousness, inviting him in.

Abazi took his arm. "Let's get you home, Gabe. If the dark ones are coming, hopefully they won't go any farther than the Briar Borders. We'll put the Rogues back in the barn and get you into bed. You really don't look good."

Gabe really didn't feel good, but he needed to get his cloak. "I'm okay."

"No, you're not, and you're not going after that cloak. We'll look for it later. Right now you need to lie down."

Gabe wanted to argue, he wanted to fight, but he couldn't. He was drained. "All right. Fine. Take me home."

He turned to go, his eyes taking in Jer's quivering lower lip, his trembling fingers. Then he turned his back on him. Jer had lost his cloak. He had ruined everything. He was just going to have to live with that.

"We need a story," Kris said. "For what happened to you. To all of us. We look like we've been in a war."

"We have been," Jer answered shortly.

"We'll just say Gabe got dizzy and fell into a ravine," Abazi suggested. "We went after him and got a few scratches ourselves. The story is that Gabe is getting the flu, that's why he got dizzy. Sound good?"

Gabe thought it did. Good enough, anyway. "Yeah, sure," he croaked. Then he remembered something. His hand flew up to his chin and he released a sigh of relief. The thorns were gone.

Kris and Abazi helped Gabe back to the house, the going slow and exhausting. The Rogues followed, but only when Kimber started singing to them. Her voice soothed Gabe, too, and he managed to push down the rising tide of hysteria building up inside him. Kimber and Jer led the Rogues into the barn while Kris and Abazi stored their weapons, then Kris placed the padlock on the main doors with the hope that the Dryads would stay put for now. Rogue Rogues would not be good. Besides, it would also keep out the dark ones if they came looking.

Mom, of course, freaked out when she saw Gabe. "What happened to you?" she cried. "You look like you fell down a well."

She helped him to a kitchen chair and immediately began her inspection, her eyes filled with concern. Abazi took it upon herself to answer, and Gabe was grateful. He wasn't up to speaking. "He said he was feeling dizzy, Mrs. Hawthorne, then, not long after that, he slipped and fell into a ravine. We went in after him, which is why we look a little worse for wear, too."

Mom had fetched some wet paper towels and was now sponging off his scratches. "Kris, go get my first-aid kit." She looked him over, then Jer. "You two are going to need it, too, I see."

"I think Gabe is coming down with something," Abazi went on, determined to get the whole story out. "Maybe the flu."

Mom focused on her. "Are you okay? And Kimber?" She glanced at Kimber, who, fortunately, was unscathed. Mrs. Wistman would never let her daughter do anything again if she looked anything like what Gabe imagined he looked like.

"Just a couple bruises," Abazi promised.

"I think we'd better get you to bed," Mom said. "You do look like you're coming down with something."

Kris returned with the first-aid kit and with Dad, who looked worried. "You shouldn't be by me," he told him. "I'm sick." And he thought he actually might be. It would explain his feeling so horrid.

Mom's face went pale. "He's right, Keith. We can't risk you getting this. He looks awful."

Dad's lips pursed, and for a moment Gabe thought he was going to refuse. "What happened?" he asked instead.

"He got dizzy and fell into a ravine. They were hiking," she added.

"I'll help him upstairs, then I'll scram."

"I can walk," Gabe croaked. "Please, Dad. If I got you sick—" he had to stop for a moment to swallow the tears in his throat— "I'd never forgive myself."

Dad blinked a few times. "You couldn't blame yourself for that, Gabe," he replied in a cracked voice. "I might already have it in my system anyway."

"I'll get him upstairs," Kris volunteered, then practically pulled Gabe out of his chair. "Come on, big bro. Let's go."

"I'll call later," Abazi said, watching them cross the kitchen floor. "Feel better, Gabe," she ordered.

Gabe didn't respond. He couldn't. Just putting one foot in front of the other was agonizing. Once in his room, his brothers helped undress him and get him into his PJs. Mom cleaned up his scratches, took his temp—102, so he really was sick—and then put an icepack on his swollen eye.

She ordered his brothers to get themselves cleaned up so she could put her homemade salve on their cuts. When they were gone, she tucked Gabe in, kissed him on the forehead, then headed downstairs with a promise to check on him later.

Right before Gabe fell into an exhausted sleep, several thoughts fired off in his brain. All that effort and nothing good had come of it was the first one. They didn't find any Rogues, or Hollie and Dame Hazel. They'd failed to rescue Jake, and Gabe had lost his cloak. Now he was sick and there were Rogues trapped inside his barn with no one to look after them or move them to a safer place like he'd planned.

Then he remembered something that felt worse than all that—Abazi and Oswald dancing together. Pretty much everything else dissolved into a blur, but that image remained clear in his mind.

He'd been betrayed by the girl he loved, and that hurt worse than all his cuts and bruises.

Chapter Eighteen

The Fever

"I think Gabe has the rot," Kris announced as he pulled on a clean t-shirt. He and Jer were in Kris's bedroom; Jer was sitting on the bed next to Little Joe, his blond hair, freshly washed and slicked back. He looked as though something were bothering him—his feet were tapping the floor, his fidgety fingers either locking and unlocking or rubbing his temples. Kris supposed it was the way Gabe had treated him, like it was Jer's fault the cloak had gone missing.

"The rot?" Jer gasped, looking up with wide eyes. "Do you really think he has it?"

"He's acting just like Oswald and the Rogues. All spacey and weak and weird."

"You might be right," Jer acknowledged. "What are we going to do?"

"Maybe we can track down Filidh. Didn't he say he knew how to treat the rot?"

"He did. But he also said it would cost the ravine. Gabe can't give him that. It isn't his to give, and it's the Rogue's hideout."

Kris ran his hand back and forth over his Mohawk, sending water spraying. "The Rogues won't need a hideout if they all die."

"True." Jer thought for a moment. "So how do you think we could find Filidh?"

"We have to get Gabe to call him. That's what Filidh said."

"Gabe *is* pretty out of it," Jer nodded in agreement, "so we might be able to get him to say Filidh's name without realizing what it's for."

"He just has to think it, if I remember correctly." Something caught Kris's eye and he leaned forward to peer at the purplish lump peeking out from Jer's blond hair. "Dude, what happened?"

Jer's hand flew up to the bump on the back of his head. "Oh, this? I fell when I was fighting the Ko-goks."

"Fighting? But I thought you and Kimber were leading the Rogues away. I didn't even see you out there. I was too busy going after Gabe. Well, now that I think of it, I saw the Rogues, but they're kinda hard to miss."

"Kimber and I were trying to lead them away," Jer explained, "but then Kimber got startled and stopped singing, and that was all it took. They heard the fighting and ran off. Kimber and I followed them, not sure what else to do, and we sort of got pulled into the battle. I used my bandalore, and it worked fairly well. I also tried out the willow whip, and that was awesome. I knocked a ton of dark ones off Gabe."

"That was you?" Kris was impressed. "You probably saved his life. Abazi and I couldn't even get close to him for the longest time."

Jer's pale pinks flushed. "Yeah, well, it's a good weapon. And I think the bandalore would've worked better if the dark ones weren't so out of it. They barely seemed to notice it touching them. How'd your weapon work?"

Kris heaved a sigh of disappointment, then bent down to tie his black high tops. "I didn't get to use it much. Not enough space. I suppose one of the dark ones got you?"

"I think so. I fell backwards and hit my head. Someone dragged me into the woods and then—and this is where it gets a little weird—one of the trees picked me up. Her name's Aurelia, and she's a beech tree. She asked a birch to heal me, then she told her friends to make a path so I could lead us to safety."

"So she's a Dryad?"

"Yeah. But she stayed as a tree." *Is this what had happened to Hollie?* Kris wondered. *Is she still in tree form, somewhere out there in the woods?*

"Did she actually *talk* to you as a tree?"

"A little. She was nice."

Kris had the distinct impression that Jer was leaving something out. "Is that why you went back? To talk to this Aurelia?"

Jer grew engrossed in petting Little Joe. "Something like that."

Now Kris knew for sure his little brother was omitting some important detail. The trick was to get it out of him without coming on too strong. "I'm surprised the Ko-goks chasing you didn't come after us, too."

"There were only a few left and from the looks of them, they weren't feeling so hot. They probably gave up after a bit."

"That's probably what happened," Kris said, though he didn't really mean it. Something strange was going on with Jer. His story didn't add up. When he'd first re-appeared after going missing, he'd made it sound like the Ko-goks were still coming after them, that they had to keep running. And now here he was saying they'd likely given up, like they hadn't been a threat after all. So what had really happened during that time Jer was gone? It looked like it was up to Kris to find out what it was. It was time to try the old, *I'll share with you, then you share with me* trick. "I have something to tell you."

Jer looked up, his expression curious, and Kris noted with satisfaction that his brother was taking the bait. "What?"

"When I came up to get the first-aid kit, I decided to let Dad know about Gabe. So, being in a hurry, I opened his office door without knocking and when he heard it, Dad immediately minimized the screen he was working on."

"So?"

Kris tried to be patient. "People never do things like that unless they're up to something."

"Well, unless you know what he's up to, it's useless information."

"But what would he want to hide from me?" Come to think of it, Dad had been acting distant for days now, even a bit secretive.

"Maybe he was looking up old girlfriends on Facebook," Jer suggested with a smirk.

"Yeah, right. Dad didn't have any old girlfriends. Mom was his first, and last."

"Well, then, girls who wanted to be his girlfriend… Or maybe he was just doing research on our tax situation, trying to find a loophole or something."

Kris thought this over. "Maybe," he conceded. "I doubt the girlfriend angle, but I can go for the tax one. Still, it seems like a strange thing to hide. Maybe he's been experiencing some new symptoms and was researching them," he said, half to himself. He heard Jer gasp. "Or maybe not."

"So what happened with Jake?" Jer asked quickly, desperate to change the subject. "Was that him with the Ko-goks?"

"Maybe," Kris answered truthfully. "It was weird. One second I saw him, or what I thought was him, and the next, there was this dark blur of movement and he was gone."

"So maybe it wasn't really him. Maybe the dark ones were trying to lure us in with a decoy."

"If they were, they'd have to have known about Jake in the first place, and that really sounded like him."

"True. So if he was there, what happened to him? Who has him now?"

"Remember when Gabe was at Grandma May's house and he thought there was someone there but he didn't see anything definite? Maybe that same person grabbed Jake."

"But what's he going to do with him?"

"That, my friend, is the big question."

"Big and disturbing," Jer said quietly.

"Definitely disturbing." There was a knock on the door. "Come in," Kris called, but the door was already opening. "Hey, Mom."

"Hey." She stepped inside, jar of salve in hand. "Any injuries I need to know about?"

"Jer hit his head." Jer glared at him and Kris wondered why. It was a perfectly normal thing to say.

"I'm fine," he snapped.

Mom didn't believe him, which was likely the reason for the glare. Jer obviously didn't want her knowing about his head. "Are you all right?" She delicately pushed Jer's hair aside to get a better look. "Any nausea or headache?" Jer shook his head. "Dizziness? Did you feel like your brain moved when you hit? Or do you remember a 'waking up' sensation?"

"It was just a bang on the head," Jer insisted. "The spot where I hit is a bit sore, but my head is fine and I don't feel dizzy or sick to my stomach. It's not like what happened to Kris."

She breathed a sigh of relief. "That's good news. For once," she added. "Just keep an eye on it. If you start to feel funny or different, let me know. Sometimes it can take a while for the symptoms of head injuries to manifest themselves."

"Yes, Mom," Jer dutifully replied. Kris noted that his brother seemed to be avoiding Mom's eyes, and this behavior, of course, made him suspicious. What had happened out there in the woods? Who was this Aurelia and why had she helped Jer?

"So were you boys just out on a hike, or was something else going on?" Mom asked casually.

Kris thought fast. "Still looking for Jake. If he is hiding out and we found him, then we could get Mrs. Morrigan off our backs. And maybe the bad publicity with him tricking us would stop her from trying to take our land."

"Gabe told you about all that?"

"He thought we should know. And he's right."

"Well, Dad's lawyer friend advised us that the best thing was to come up with the tax money. He wanted to help us, but unfortunately he's out of the country, plus he's going through a divorce right now and all his assets are tied up."

"He didn't have any other ideas?"

"Fraid not. I talked to Mozi about places where Jake might be hiding, but word is that all his friends really don't know where he is. The Chief checked all the usual places, and today he's checking any unusual ones, like the old mill. Once it stops raining, which is supposed to be tomorrow, he'll bring in Blaine Johnson and his dogs. He's a fantastic tracker." She sighed and rubbed her forehead. "You're right, though. If we could find him, that would solve a lot of our problems."

Mom handed him the jar of salve. "Put this on your scratches. You guys look like you've been in a cat fight and the last thing we need is for people to start speculating."

"It's not like they're going to heal overnight," Jer pointed out, dipping his finger in the jar. He had a small scratch on his chin and that angry slash over his eye. Kris didn't remember him having that big wound before he'd left them for his 'thirty' seconds. So how had he gotten it?

Another mystery to solve.

Kris had a few deeper cuts on his left jaw, and they looked more like a lion had gotten to him than a cat. He helped himself to the salve and smoothed it on, not for himself, but for his mom's sake. He wouldn't have minded keeping them looking just the way they did—awesome.

"But they won't look nearly as bad as they do now," she said, which was exactly what Kris was afraid of. She took the jar from him and screwed the cap back on. "No more going out for today, okay? It's supper in a few minutes anyway, and I'd like you to check all the fireplaces." Kris had forgotten that the furnace had gone out. Come to think of it, it was a little chilly in his room. He grabbed a sweatshirt and pulled it on.

They both nodded and she left them, looking more worn out than when Dad had gotten sick. "That reminds me," Kris said, after the door closed, "did you read that tree book from Gabe's room?"

"Most of it. It talked about different tree diseases, but not what you can do about them. I'll do some research on the Internet tonight."

"Good idea. So what do you think we should do about the Rogues?"

"Keep them in the barn. At least then we know where they are."

"So did that Aurelia tell you anything useful?" Kris pounced. "Anything about how to save them?"

Jer gave a quick shake of his head. "She just said they're weak, not themselves."

"Nothing else?"

"Nothing." This time Jer met Kris's eyes full on, and in them was a message. But try as he might, Kris couldn't read it. Jer blinked and stood up. "You do the fireplaces. I'm going to help Mom with supper."

He left Kris wondering what was going on inside his little brother's head and how he was going to get it out.

~~~~~~

Supper was a morose affair. Mom and Dad were obviously worried about Gabe. Kris had the feeling they sensed there was more wrong with him than a virus. After clean-up was done, Kris volunteered to bring some water up to Gabe. Mom was convinced he wasn't getting enough liquids in him.

The phone rang and Kris grabbed it before going up. "Hello?"

"How's Gabe doing?" Abazi greeted. "Any better?"

"Not really. He has a fever."

"It isn't the flu, is it? It's something tree-related. I just know it."

"That's what I thought," Kris answered.

"Is there anything we can do for him?"

"Jer's going to look up some stuff on the Internet," he said vaguely, since Mom and Dad were still finishing up the dishes, murmuring to each other in low voices. "See what he can find for, um, *remedies*—" this word in a whisper "—if there are any."

"I'll come over after school tomorrow, bring his homework."

"Sounds good. I'm taking him some water now. I'll tell him you called."

"Yeah, do that." There was silence and Kris was about to say goodbye when Abazi started speaking again. "It was a crazy day," she said, and Kris was a little surprised. Abazi wasn't one to linger.

"Yeah, it was."

"I'm, well, I'm sorry we didn't find Hollie, and, annoyingly enough, that we couldn't save Jake. Somebody got him, though. We can only hope it was someone good."

"You saw that, too?"

"I see everything," she said drily. "Unfortunately, it wasn't much more than a blur."

"That's what I saw. I told Jer it reminded me of Gabe's visit to Grandma May's house this fall. Remember the visitor she had?"

"Oh, yeah! Do you think they're one and the same?"

"It's possible. I could try asking Grandma about it, but I doubt she'd say anything."

"I doubt it, too." Another pause, but this time Kris knew enough to wait it out. "So what do you think Jer was up to?"

Kris glanced at his brother, who was putting more wood in the woodstove. "I'm not sure. I'm trying to get it out of him."

"I knew you'd notice," she said, and Kris felt his ego expand a little.

"I'll call you if anything changes," he said.

"Do that. And Kris…"

"Yeah?"

"Hollie isn't my favorite person in the world—too bossy—and don't you dare say that's the kettle calling the pot black." Kris didn't. "And I'm not sure I trust her… But anyway, she's what I would call a survivor."

"She is. But what I don't get is why she hasn't let us know she's okay."

"Maybe that Dame Hazel is keeping her from us. That's one nutty broad."

"Maybe." But Kris didn't believe that. If Hollie had wanted to find him, she would have found him. Something must have gone wrong. Something bad. He shivered. "Good night, Abazi. I'll see you at school tomorrow."

"Sure. See you then."

Kris hung up and headed to the turret. He didn't bother knocking. Gabe was on his bed, but he wasn't sleeping. He was sitting up, part of him in the shadow of the platform overhanging a third of his bed, mumbling to himself.

"Gabe!"

"Who are you?" Gabe demanded, looking furious and ready to fight.

Kris took a step back. "Whoa, Gabe! It's me, Kris. Your brother."

"I don't have any brothers."

There was a creak on the step behind Kris and he glanced back. "You know me, don't you, Gabe?" Jer asked in a quiet voice.

"Thief!" Gabe pointed at Jer, and Jer shrunk back.

"It's the fever," Kris explained. "It's messing with his head."

Gabe's eyes widened and he glanced wildly about the room. "I must take them. Now!"

"Take who?" Kris asked gently.

Gabe looked a little confused. "Um, the others. Ye know, the, um others."

"Do you mean the Rogues?" Jer asked in a shaky voice.

"Who're they?"

"The others."

"Yes, then. Yes. The Rogues. I must take them somewhere."

"Where, Gabe?" Kris asked.

"I don't know." He leaned forward eagerly. "But I do!"

"You mean, you don't remember what the place is called?" Jer questioned.

Now Kris could see that Gabe's eyes were glazed with fever and excitement. "Yes. That's it exactly."

"What's your guess?" Kris turned to Jer.

"I have no idea."

Kris faced Gabe. "We can help you take them where they need to go."

Gabe shook his head. "Not safe. There are…shadows out there. Ghosts and darkness."

"We'll bring weapons. We can't let you go alone, Gabe."

"We can't let him go at all," Jer whispered. "He's sick, and he said 'ye.' That's not normal."

"We can't leave the Rogues in the barn," Kris pointed out. "Mom'll find them. You know she will. And if she doesn't, Chief Mara might. He'll be getting the tracking dogs out there soon, probably tomorrow, and they'll smell the Rogues. And when that happens, we're all screwed."

Jer took a deep breath. "You're right. I'll do the research before we go. Maybe I'll find something. I have to," he said under his breath, though Kris caught it and wondered what Jer meant, beyond the obvious. Then louder, "Stay with him, otherwise he'll go out on his own."

"I will. Go do your research. Tell Mom I'm keeping an eye on Gabe, making sure he drinks his water."

Jer turned to go, then turned back. "What if I can't find anything?"

"Then we pray. It's all we have left." Jer's eyes welled up, then he fled down the stairs.

Kris pulled up a chair by Gabe's bed and settled in to keep vigil over his brother, all the while wondering what was going on with his other one.

Chapter Nineteen

Death March

Jer's Internet search wasn't very fruitful. He'd left no stone unturned, clicking on everything related to tree disease, tree health, treatments and the like, but nothing useful had come up. He'd learned that tannin, produced naturally by trees, fights disease, but unless he could come up with a way to produce it, the knowledge was useless.

He dreaded what this meant.

Mom had come in at ten to say goodnight. She said Kris was watching Gabe, who was now sleeping. Jer wondered if Gabe truly was asleep or just pretending, but if Mom believed it, that was all that mattered. They needed her to be sleeping peacefully when they snuck out of the house.

At half past ten, Jer quit for the night. After checking on Mom and Dad—both were snoring—he headed for the kitchen. He fed the woodstove, made up a snack for him and Kris, then grabbed their coats and his backpack.

Gabe truly was sleeping, as was Kris. Jer dropped their stuff on the floor, then went to check on Gabe. He stared at his brother for several long seconds, wondering what he should do, what he *could* do for him. He looked strange, then Jer realized that what he'd thought were shadows were actually thorns. Gabe was sprouting thorns, and in the dim light of the lamp, he looked like Straif.

Jer shuddered and went over to Kris. "Wake up."

Kris sprang into a defensive stance. "Bring it!"

"Um, do you want a sandwich?"

Kris relaxed and grinned as he took the plate. "Sorry. I was dreaming about being chased by fat trolls."

"Usually you just roll over and ask for another ten minutes."

"I know. That was pretty awesome, wasn't it?"

"Other than the part where you almost killed your brother."

Kris laughed and took a bite of his sandwich. "Peanut butter and banana. Not bad."

"I thought we'd need the protein. I brought our stuff, too." He indicated the coats.

"Smart move."

"I think we should get Gabe to call up Filidh."

"I already tried. He just stared at me, then shook his head. I thought maybe putting the name in his mind would be enough, but the old guy didn't show. I'll keep working on him, but for now, it's back to our original plan—move the Rogues."

"Do you really think they'll follow us?"

Kris chewed thoughtfully. "I don't know. Maybe. Too bad we don't have Kimber here. They'd follow her."

Jer wasn't sure that was a bad thing, not after what she'd said to him. She thought he'd treated her like a child when he was only trying to protect her. "You could do opera man. They might like that."

Kris laughed. "Or they might run screaming into the night."

Gabe started to stir. "Me cloak," he mumbled, half sitting up. "Where's me cloak?"

"It's not good for you," Jer said angrily. "You know that. Remember what it did to me?"

But Gabe wasn't listening. "It's time. I must lead me people to safety."

"We're going right now," Kris assured him. "We'll take them."

"They'll only follow me." Gabe pushed himself upright, swinging his legs over the side of the bed. Jer now noticed the other dark spots on his brother's skin, splotches that made him look like he had the bubonic plague.

"Let us try," Jer said quickly. His brother shouldn't even be sitting up. He looked horrible.

Gabe struggled to his feet. "No. Me. It has to be me."

Kris caught him before he fell over. "Dude, you can hardly walk and your eye's swollen shut."

"They'll only follow me," Gabe repeated hoarsely.

"I guess we'll carry him if we have to," Jer said.

"He weighs a ton!" Kris protested.

"I can take his feet."

"Those weigh half a ton in themselves!" Jer shrugged helplessly. "All right," Kris groaned, "but I don't like it." Jer didn't reply.

They set about getting Gabe dressed warmly, then pulled on their own jackets and Jer strapped on his backpack. Gabe nearly fell off the pole on his ride down, but Kris caught him at the bottom, likely saving him from a sprained ankle, or two.

When they stepped outside into the night air, Jer was happy to see it had finally stopped raining. The yard was filled with puddles, water dripped from the roof, and droplets coated the shrubs surrounding the little secret door. The glow from the barn's outdoor light revealed that a lot of snow had melted since yesterday. Jer remembered Shambolic Stream and how fast it had been flowing a few days ago. It was likely roaring now. Mom had told them at supper that the ground was still frozen, so the water had nowhere to go until it warmed up a little more. That meant flooding. Lots of it.

Which made Jer wonder where they were actually going tonight. Hopefully someplace dry. He was already feeling the damp cold. Gabe was going to get a chill if they weren't careful.

After Jer gathered a few weapons in the barn, Kris helped Gabe make his way up to the loft, while Jer warily led the way with his flashlight. At the top of the stairs, they paused and Jer shined the light into the open area. When he saw the lumps spread around, he breathed a sigh of relief. The Rogues hadn't done a runner.

"It's time," Gabe spoke into the quiet air.

One by one the forms began to stir. The process was slow, like old people getting out of bed, but finally everyone was on their feet. Jer flashed the light into all the corners, making sure they weren't missing anyone.

Strangely, no one spoke, not even Oswald. The beam caught his face and he winced in the bright light. His eyes seemed darker than usual, almost black, and the moldy spots coloring his skin had grown. He looked worse than Gabe, but then, he'd been sicker longer. Like zombies they shuffled after Jer and his brothers, putting up no protest, asking not a single question. At the very least, Oswald would have challenged Gabe for some reason or another, if only to stir up trouble. But he didn't say a word.

With the help of Kris, Gabe led the way, with Jer and his flashlight right by his side. The night outside the barn light's arc was dark and still, almost too still, and it made Jer nervous. They cut through the path that passed by Kimber and Abazi's houses, both dark, and Jer thought about turning off his flashlight, but was worried some of the Rogues might get disoriented and wander off. Nothing happened, other than a few snorts from Kimber's horses, and they continued on their way.

The dirt drive was squishy and mud was starting to build up, making the going hard. After what seemed like a long time, they finally reached the road into town. With each step, Jer's sense of where they were going grew stronger, and when they made the turn onto an old dirt road, his guess was confirmed.

They were heading to Wolka Mill. Even though the Ko-goks would not come to this place—it was a form of banishment for them—it still felt as though Jer and his brothers were forcing the Rogues on a death march, delivering dying prisoners to their grave. That's what the mill seemed like…a massive grave. But it was the only place to put them.

Crossing the river was scary. The water ran only about a foot below the bridge, and was packed with chunks of ice that clanged loudly against the metal before slipping underneath. *What if the bridge gets washed away?* Jer wondered. *How will we get to the Rogues?* The area surrounding the mill was all wetland, meaning no coming or going from that way. The only other way in would be to come via boat, and they didn't have a boat.

The old iron bridge creaked and groaned as they crossed it and Jer felt a nearly overwhelming desire to turn around and run back the way they'd come. His light hit on the rust spots blighting the span work of the bridge and he had a bad feeling that it was only a matter of time before something gave. Once it did, the whole bridge would be swept away, along with anything, or anyone, on it. Jer shuddered and picked up his pace.

When the last of the Rogues stepped off the bridge, Jer expected it to give right then, but it held, and they continued on toward the mill. Now that he knew where they were going, he took the lead, pointing out potholes and kicking aside cans and bottles to clear the way. The Rogues were so out of it, they wouldn't be able to avoid these potential pitfalls.

The door to the mill remained unlocked and he entered easily. Once inside, the sounds of the river muted and they could hear each other again without shouting. "This way," Jer motioned to the Rogues and led them to the driest room he could find. It was the farthest one from the river and had the most intact windows.

The Rogues filed into the room and sat down without so much as a peep. Jer studied them worriedly. They were dying, he was certain, and there was nothing he could do about it. He felt as helpless as he had when they'd first found out about dad's ailing kidneys. There was nothing he could do to fix this for them and suddenly that really pissed him off.

It wasn't fair! They'd done nothing to deserve this. *Nothing!*

Gabe sunk to his knees and stayed there for several moments. "This is merely a stopover," he said finally. "We're on our way, but ye must wait here until I come for ye once more."

Jer stared at his brother, wondering if he was going crazy. He certainly looked crazy. His hair stuck up all over the place and his skin was turning a sooty black. His good eye in the beam of the flashlight was feverish and his cheeks, in between the black patches, had bright spots of color.

"This is it?" Oswald spoke at last.

"No," Gabe corrected him. "Ye need to hide out here until I come for ye. I *will* come for ye." Jer didn't like how Gabe kept saying ye. It was creepy.

"Ye will?" Oswald sounded doubtful. "Did ye last time?"

Last time?

"Of course I did. I came for ye and we were safe. I'll keep ye safe."

Gabe didn't look like he could keep a caterpillar safe, much less a roomful of people. The uncertain expression on Oswald's face indicated he felt the same way, but he said no more. Jer wasn't sure if that was a good thing or not. Would Oswald stay here, or would he leave, taking the Rogues with him?

"Rest and regain yer strength," Gabe went on. "The war's not yet over. We'll need to fight before we're free. Remember that."

No one answered and Kris helped Gabe to his feet. Kris glanced over at Jer, an eyebrow raised in question. Like Jer, Kris wasn't so certain this was a good idea. But what choice did they have?

Feeling like he was being smothered, Jer turned and hurried out of the room and Gabe and Kris followed after him. The Rogues stayed where they were.

Near the bridge, Kris shouted something to Jer and he turned back to stand beside them. "I need to rest," Kris panted. "Gabe can hardly walk."

"When you catch your breath, we'll both take him."

"Yeah, all right, but it's going to be a long walk back."

Jer was nodding his agreement when something on the bridge caught his eye. Movement. He grabbed Kris's arm and pointed, and Kris stiffened. He'd seen it, too, which meant something really was there, not just a trick of the light or Jer's imagination.

"Should we run back to the mill?" Jer yelled in Kris's ear.

"I think we're going to have to stand our ground. We won't make it far with Gabe."

Jer didn't want to stick around, but again, they had no choice. It seemed lately that everything was out of his control, as though he'd fallen into the roaring river and was getting swept along. He didn't like this feeling one bit.

In the dark it was hard to tell how many of them there were. Jer could only ready his bandalore and wait for the attack.

"Who's there?" Kris shouted, unable to take it any longer. "There are three of us and only two of you." Jer squinted. Kris was right. There were only two figures. At least, that they could see.

One of the figures broke from the bridge and raced directly at them. Jer drew back his arm and prepared to strike. "What are you guys doing here?" their attacker shouted.

Jer's shoulders sank in relief. "Abazi! It's us. Kris and Jer and Gabe."

"No duh," she snorted as she reached them. "Come on, Kimber. It's safe." She turned back to them. "Kimber's staying over at my house. We saw your light go by."

Jer cursed his inability to see in the dark. "What were you doing up so late?"

"Telling ghost stories starring Straif, what else?"

"Hey, guys," Kimber greeted breathlessly. Jer noticed she avoided looking at him.

"So you still haven't answered my question. Gabe, why are you out here? You're sick. You should be in bed."

"He kept saying he had to move the Rogues," Kris answered. "He thought they wouldn't follow me and Jer."

"I don't get why they had to be moved. They were fine in the barn "

"Not if Chief Mara brings those dogs to the house. How would we explain a bunch of sick kids in our barn?"

Abazi wrapped her arms around her body and looked around. "But it's awful out here."

"Do you have any other ideas?"

"No. But that doesn't mean I like this. Oswald's sick, too. They all are. They could die out here."

Gabe groaned and slid to the ground. Kris lunged forward and caught him. "Crap! He passed out. Help me carry him, Jer. We've got to get him home." Jer nodded and tucked his bandalore back in his pocket.

Abazi reached out and touched Gabe's forehead, then looked up at Kris. "He feels like he's on fire."

Jer stared at his brother and a sick feeling overwhelmed him. If he didn't do something, his brother was going to die. He pulled off his backpack and reached inside.

"Here." He held out his offering. "Put this on him."

"What?" Kris cried. "You have his cloak? Why didn't you give it to him earlier?"

Tears stung Jer's eyelids and he blinked rapidly. "Because he was treating me like a little kid and I was mad and he seemed to care more about his stupid cloak than me."

"He was already getting sick by that point, Jer," Abazi said. "He wasn't thinking clearly."

Jer swallowed. "I get that now, but, well, there's something else."

"What is it, Jer?" Kimber asked softly, when he didn't go on.

"It wasn't all being mad at Gabe that kept me from giving him the cloak." Though it was a lot of it. "That cloak changes a person. When you're wearing it, it makes you feel like nothing can harm you. I'm afraid it will make Gabe do something stupid. Like I almost did…"

Kris yanked the cloak out of Jer's hand and wrapped it around Gabe's shoulders. "You just better hope it isn't too late, you idiot." He grabbed Gabe under the armpits. "Get his legs." Abazi and Jer each took one and they hefted Gabe, inanimate as deadwood and twice as heavy, into the air. As they started across the bridge, Jer felt fear squeeze his heart.

His selfishness and his wounded ego might have cost his brother his life. Kris was right. He was an idiot. And now he might be a murderer, as well.

Chapter Twenty

The Ugly Truth

Kris awoke to sunlight streaming in through his window. He was still dead tired, but that was to be expected after their late night and lugging Gabe over the river and through the woods. Gabe hadn't woken up the entire time and Kris worried that the cloak had come too late for him. Kimber stayed behind at Abazi's house, but Abazi insisted on helping carry Gabe the rest of the way home. Once there, she made sure Kris and Jer got him out of his wet clothes and into warm, dry PJs. Then she told Kris and Jer to go to bed; that she'd sit with Gabe for a while. Kris wasn't so sure about that, but she insisted, so he could only hope she didn't fall asleep for Mom to find in the morning.

He rubbed his eyes and groaned. It seemed awfully bright for half past six, his normal waking time for school. He rolled over. Ten o'clock! He leaped out of bed, the floor chilly on his bare feet, and raced downstairs. There he found Mom pulling a fresh batch of blueberry muffins from the oven.

"I'm late!" he cried. "I'm sorry. I must have slept through my alarm, and you yelling at me and—" He stopped, seeing her smile. "Wait. I don't remember you yelling at me to get up now or you'll drag me out of bed by my ear."

"That's because I didn't. School was canceled."

Kris's shoulders sagged with relief. "Phew! I don't particularly love school, but I hate missing it. Too much homework." He went to a cupboard and pulled down a box of cereal. "Why was it canceled?"

"Flooding," Jer answered, coming down the stairs and into the kitchen. He was already dressed. "A couple major roads are blocked, along with a ton of smaller ones. All those streams, I guess."

"How do you know that?"

"I was on the Internet this morning when Mom told me, so I went to the local news station. Apparently the flooding is happening all over Maine."

"That's the danger of snow melting too fast," Mom explained as she pulled out another tin of muffins. "And all that rain on top of it. But at least the rain has stopped."

"But won't the sun cause more melting?" Kris asked.

"It will, but hopefully not as fast." No rain, Kris realized, meant the dogs would be out today. That was both a good thing and a bad thing. Good because maybe they'd find Jake. Bad because maybe they'd also find dark ones.

"Have you checked on Gabe?" Kris asked, trying to sound casual.

"I did. He's doing much better," Mom replied, smiling.

Jer's eyes lit up. "He is?"

She laughed. "Nice to see you were concerned. Yes, his fever has broken."

"He didn't look too strange or anything?"

Mom gave Kris a funny look. "No stranger than usual."

Both Kris and Jer grinned. The cloak had done its job. Hopefully, anyway. Kris was glad Gabe was doing better. Still, he was a little worried about what Jer had said about the cloak. Maybe Jer had just been trying to excuse his behavior, but maybe there was also something to what he'd said. At any rate, Kris now knew what he'd been hiding yesterday—the magic cloak. A Ko-gok must have had it and Jer had wrestled it back, earning a wound as a result. Kris was impressed.

"I'm going to get dressed," he said, slurping up the last of his milk. "Then I'll check on Gabe for you, Mom. See if he needs anything."

"Why don't you do that later?" she said as she wrapped up a muffin. "I'd rather he slept. You can put more wood in the boxes and by the fireplaces, then check on him after lunch."

"All right," Kris replied, though he really wanted to go right now.

Jer followed Kris up the stairs to his bedroom. "I checked on him when I woke up," he said, "but I couldn't see much in the dark and I didn't want to wake him. I made sure that he was alive, though, and that Abazi was gone. Then I did some more research on tree diseases."

"When did you get up?"

"6:30. I actually hear my alarm when it goes off."

"Bully for you. Did you find anything?" Kris pulled on a holey t-shirt with the words *Engineer This!* on it, and an old pair of jeans.

"Nothing new. I'm really worried about the Rogues. I'm glad Gabe is doing better, but I wish it wasn't the cloak making it happen. I don't trust it."

Kris bent over to tie his shoes. So Jer really was worried about the cloak. "How come?"

"I think that's pretty obvious, Kris," he responded snidely. "I almost jumped off a cliff while wearing it."

"All right, then I guess we keep looking, and we can ask Abazi and Kimber if they know anything. They're country girls. They should know something about helping trees."

"And if something went wrong for Hollie," Jer added softly, "well, then maybe this would help her, too."

Kris froze, his finger caught in a shoelace. "You think so?"

Jer shrugged. "I can only hope so, like what we did with Dad. We just kept hoping."

"Do you think Dad's going to be all right now?"

"I don't know. He seems awfully tired lately."

"Maybe he's just worried."

"Maybe."

"He has a lot to worry about, Jer," Kris persisted. "With his illness, and not having a job, and the property taxes, and now Gabe getting sick and this whole Jake thing."

"Yeah, that's a lot of stuff." Jer still didn't sound too convinced.

"But it's hard not to think the worst, isn't it?"

Jer nodded vigorously. "Exactly." He seemed relieved to have the truth out in the open. "Especially if he was researching symptoms. But we can't let him see that we're worried, or that we know, okay? Cause that will just make it worse for him."

"Agreed." Kris finished tying his shoelaces and headed for the stairs. "Let's go take care of the wood, then maybe do some more research. I could look through those books on Gabe's shelf. Maybe there's something in one of those."

Once in motion, Kris realized he was glad for the physical labor. It gave him something to focus on other than strange diseases and missing people. He and Jer were coming inside when the phone rang. Kris grabbed it. "Hello?"

"When are you guys going to get your own cell phones?" Abazi asked.

"When we are no longer destitute," he replied in a low voice, glancing over at his mom taking yet another tin of muffins out of the oven. She didn't seem to hear him.

"I suppose. So how's he doing? When I left he seemed a little better. I think the cloak's working. Your little brother's a dingbat, by the way. What if this disease has a permanent effect on Gabe?"

"He's really sorry about that. He was mad, and then he was worried."

Listening in, Jer frowned. "Is she talking about me?" he mouthed.

Kris turned his back on his brother. "All right," Abazi said. "I guess I can understand being mad and doing stupid things. Not that I ever do things like that."

"Of course not."

"Because I'm a saint."

"Because you're a saint," Kris acknowledged with a smile.

"Exactly. So I have news."

"Good news, I hope?"

"The exact opposite. Good thing we don't have school today because this is big."

"How big?"

"Ko-gok big."

Kris's heart started beating a little harder. "What happened?"

"I'll tell you when we get there. We're going to eat lunch, then come over." Abazi hung up the phone and a moment later, Kris did, too. He glanced up at the clock. It was already noon. No wonder he was starving. One bowl of cereal just didn't cut it these days.

"She hates me, doesn't she?" Jer whispered. "Her and Kimber?"

Kris sighed. "Not everything is about you, Jer." He wasn't sure if he wanted Jer to be let off the hook so easily, but seeing his miserable expression, he relented. He pulled his brother down the hallway to the turret, out of earshot. "She said she understood about being mad and doing stupid things."

"Did Kimber say that, too?"

"I don't know. Why?"

Jer shrugged. "Just wondering if she felt the same way as Abazi."

"Maybe. But at least Abazi doesn't hate your guts. You can be grateful for that."

"Do you think Gabe will hate me?"

"I think if Gabe has the strength to be pissed off at you, then you should count yourself lucky."

That shut Jer up and it was quiet as they headed back to the kitchen to fix lunch. Mom and Dad joined them, then Dad hurried off when he was done, his skin tight with stress. Jer threw Kris a significant glance. Yes, there was definitely something wrong with Dad, and he was definitely up to something.

After cleaning up, they climbed the stairs to check on Gabe. Kris headed straight for the bed and kneeled down next to his brother. He definitely looked better than yesterday, his face clear of black marks and thorns. His cloak was half off, as though Mom had tried to pull it out from under him, but couldn't quite get it free. Gabe's eyes twitched and every few seconds, his whole body jerked, but he stayed asleep.

Kris wasn't sure if that was a good sign or not. He placed his finger to his lips and motioned toward the bookshelf. Jer followed him over.

Silently they began to peruse the titles, hoping to spot the right book, something like, *How to Cure Dryads of Hideous Diseases* or *How to Protect Dryads From Themselves and Their Stubborn Defiance of Nature's Laws.*

Kris pulled out a book that was likely the next best thing, *Tree Diseases.* Jer was already reading one. Mirroring each other, they both sat on the floor and began to read. But Kris couldn't focus. His mind kept returning to his last meeting with Hollie. The impertinent tilt of her nose, her stunning green eyes, her awesome smile. He missed her, but he didn't know what to do about finding her. Perhaps he should go out on his own, without the others, without Gabe—who seemed to be a target for the Ko-goks, and who might have his own agenda. Maybe on his own Kris could actually make some progress.

The idea settled him and he was able to get a little reading in before Abazi and Kimber announced their arrival with a "Knock, knock." Abazi entered the room carrying a tray, followed by Kimber. "Your mom sent this up. She said if Gabe was awake we're supposed to make him eat."

"She must really be worried. She gave him muffins meant for the store."

"She said we could have one, too."

"Then the world is coming to an end," Jer joked, glancing eagerly at Kimber. She didn't smile and Kris wondered what was going on there. Usually Kimber was Jer's number one fan, giggling at the stupidest of his jokes. Jer must have done something idiotic, and that's why he was so worried about Kimber hating him, too.

"He's still sleeping," Kris said.

"Yeah, I got that from the snoring," Abazi retorted. "But he looks better, doesn't he?"

"Definitely." He held up his book. "We've been doing some reading on tree diseases, but we haven't found anything useful yet. You guys know how to treat sick trees?"

"Most people just cut them down," Abazi replied. "Though I don't think that solves our problem."

"If the disease is treatable," Kimber said, "there are sprays you can use to kill the fungus or bacteria—whatever's causing the problem."

"That's just it," Jer said tentatively. "We don't know what's causing the problem."

Abazi set the tray down on Gabe's desk. "That old guy said it was the rot, so I'm guessing a fungus is among us."

"But chemical sprays could really harm the human, couldn't they?" Jer asked.

"We could try something natural," Kimber answered, still avoiding his eye. In fact, she seemed to be addressing all her comments to Kris.

"I suppose. Anyone got anything at home?"

"We might have something in the barn," Jer suggested.

"Or we could get Gabe to summon that old dude, Filidh, and be done with this," Kris said.

"If Gabe was hesitant to do it, it was likely for a good reason," Abazi argued, which was unusual. Abazi seemed to revel in arguing *against* Gabe.

"Maybe Gabe was already sick by that point and not thinking clearly."

"True," she acknowledged. "But we won't know for sure until he wakes up."

"*If* he wakes up," Kris said under his breath, but they all heard him and for a few moments it was eerily silent in the room. "So what was it you were going to tell us?" he asked Abazi. She came and sat down by them, and Kimber joined her, seating herself next to Kris. She really *was* mad at Jer.

"Freddie's Fish Market was broken into and a ton of fish were stolen. Then Mr. Gray reported ten of his pigs missing."

"Missing?" Kris echoed. "How do ten pigs go missing?"

"That's the mystery. There weren't any sounds, no blood, nothing."

"Ko-goks," Kris breathed, remembering what Abazi had said on the phone earlier.

"Right. It's the only good explanation. But it means that they're getting desperate. They've never come into town before."

"Do you think they'll go after people?" Jer asked, looking worried, his eyes slipping toward Kimber. She noticed and her typically kind eyes went hard.

"It's possible," Abazi replied. "Hopefully the flooding will keep people inside. And when we go out, we should be sure to have a weapon on us at all times." She stretched and yawned. "I really need a nap."

"Have you heard anything more about Jake?" Kris asked. He couldn't get the image of Jake surrounded by screaming Ko-goks out of his mind.

"Candi came into the store yesterday evening. I was watching the counter while Dad brought in supplies from the back so I had to deal with the witch. I have to say, she didn't look very good. She's usually so prissy about her appearance, but her hair was a mess and she looked like she hadn't slept for a while. She was with Jen, who was trying to convince her mom to let her go out with 'Uncle Mara' the next day to search for Jake. Candi didn't want her to go, but to give Skanky Pants her due, she kept trying. Fortunately Candi is more stubborn and didn't give in. Can you imagine that airhead prancing about the woods? Might as well just paint a target on her back that says, *I'm Easy Prey*, on it. Or just, *I'm Easy.*"

"Jen isn't all that bad," Kimber scolded. "You just don't like her because she has the hots for Gabe."

Abazi's cheeks went red. "I don't like her because she's a tart! And what's your problem lately, Miss Moody? You're questioning everything I say, which isn't like you, and you're acting like a big grump."

"And you haven't been?" Kimber shot back, surprising Kris, and probably everybody else, too. "I get that it's the anniversary of your mom's death coming up, but why does that mean we all have to suffer for it? And I'm questioning everything you say because I'm tired of you treating me like a little kid you hang out with on sufferance."

Abazi's eyes widened. "Excuse me? Are you saying mourning my mom's death is stupid?"

"No. I'm saying, getting mad at your mom every year because she died is stupid."

"You don't know anything!" Abazi yelled. "You have no idea!"

"Probably not, because you never tell me. I'm a big girl, Abazi. Whatever it is, I can take it. Just tell me!" Kimber looked entirely unlike herself. Her cheeks were pink and her little chin jutted outward as though she were girding herself for battle. Kris rather liked this new Kimber, as long as she didn't turn Kimberzilla on *him*.

"Fine! You really want to know the ugly truth? Well, here it is! My mother was a drunk. Yeah, that's right. Apparently she'd been drinking and decided to run to the store to pick up ice cream. On the way back, she hit a tree. So yeah, real cool. A drunk Indian. I'm a joke, don't you see? Everyone in town knows it's only a matter of time before I become a drunk, too. That's what Indians do, isn't it?"

Kimber's eyes teared up. "Oh, Abazi. I'm so sorry."

Abazi bit her lip. "Yeah, well, that isn't even the worst part. I wanted chocolate ice cream, but we only had vanilla. So she went to get some for me. I killed my mom, all because I wanted stupid chocolate ice cream."

"That's not your fault!" Kris cried, feeling horrible for her, and understanding now why she hated driving so much.

Abazi abruptly stood. "I have to go." She backed away from them, toward the stairs. "Now that you know my dirty secret, you'll hate me."

"Don't go." The creaking voice came from Gabe's bed. "Please... Abazi. Don't go."

Gabe was awake.

Chapter Twenty-One

Not Like the Ring

Gabe's head hurt really badly, and he had to blink numerous times so that he could focus on the people sitting by his bookshelf. What were they doing, and why were they doing it in his room? He blinked a few times and his vision cleared, at least in one eye, to see Kris, Jer, Abazi, and Kimber in the midst of what appeared to be an intense conversation.

"Fine!" Abazi shouted. "You really want to know the ugly truth?" And that's when Gabe learned why Abazi had been so touchy lately, or maybe why she'd been so touchy half her life. But when she pushed herself to her feet to leave, Gabe found his voice.

"Don't go," he pleaded. "Please...Abazi. Don't go."

"Gabe?" Abazi turned to stare at him. "You're awake."

"I'm awake because I heard someone yelling," he replied, deciding at that moment to pretend he'd heard nothing of what Abazi had said. At some point he was going to have to deal with it, but now was not the time. He had a feeling events had been happening without his awareness, events crucial to the fate of the Forest Immortal, and he needed to know what they were. "Now, could someone please tell me why you're all in my room?"

Abazi swallowed. "You were dying, idiot. That's why. We didn't want to leave you alone."

"Dying?" Surely she was exaggerating. "What happened to me?" He didn't remember much after the battle with the Ko-goks.

"We think you had the same illness as the Rogues," Kris explained. "Or maybe you got something from the dark ones when you were battling them. We're not sure. But your skin started turning black and your thorns came out and you passed out. You looked like you had porcupine plague."

A cold trickle of dread slid down Gabe's spine. "Did Mom and Dad see all that?"

"Nope. Luckily the weird stuff didn't happen until late at night. They knew you were sick, had a fever and all that, but I told them to get some sleep and I'd watch over you."

Gabe looked at his brother, feeling a little weird. "Really? You watched over me?"

"Of course I did. Why wouldn't I?" Kris seemed genuinely confused.

Gabe suddenly felt like crying. He was so weak and too many things were happening at once. "No reason. It's just, well, that was cool of you."

"Yeah, well, Abazi took over after we—well, after. . ."

"After what?" Gabe demanded when Kris trailed off. He had a feeling he wasn't going to like the rest of the sentence. "And how long have I been out?"

"We took the Rogues to Wolka Mill last night," Abazi told him, her voice business-like. "Chief Mara will have the dogs out today and we couldn't leave them in the barn to be found. I'm not sure the mill is the best place for them, but that's where you wanted them. And you've only been out for a day."

Gabe watched Abazi's face closely, waiting for her to betray her true feelings for Oswald. "They went with you, Abazi?"

"They went with *you*," she answered sharply. "Kimber and I only joined the fun after you'd dropped the Rogues off. We saw Jer's flashlight going by, and after we got dressed, we followed you."

He frowned. "I thought I was sick in bed."

"You were for a while," Kris said. "But when you knew what Jer and I were going to do, you said they wouldn't go without you leading them. I'm not sure if that was true, but they did come without question when you asked."

"And afterwards?"

"Jer put the cloak on you and you got better."

"The cloak? But it's missing. ." He felt a brief pang at the thought.

"Jer got it back from the dark ones," Kimber explained. "But he didn't want to give it to you because he thought it might make you harm yourself. It seemed our only choice, though. You were pretty sick."

Gabe watched Jer as Kimber spoke, but his brother refused to meet his eyes. Something was being held back, but he wasn't sure what. Something to do with Jer. Jer and the cloak.

"I have a hard time believing a cloak could cure me." But as he spoke, he remembered its powers over him, how it had made him feel invincible. "And I still feel pretty crappy."

Abazi strode over to him. "That's because it's not tied on right." She sat on the bed next to him, and he took in her scent, a strange, but alluring combination of lemons and roses. He pushed himself so that he was sitting up, and Abazi pulled the cloak around his shoulders, then tied the top strings that held it together.

He took a deep breath. Ah. There it was. He could feel the cloak's power and energy flowing through him like a life force, like a jolt of electricity. "That's better," he breathed. His mind cleared and his muscles grew strong. As his senses sharpened, he took in Jer's worried expression. "I can control it," he assured him, then looked away when Jer didn't appear the least bit assured. He would simply have to show Jer that the cloak did not affect him, at least not as strongly.

He took in the time. One o'clock. *One o'clock?* "Why aren't you guys in school?"

"Canceled," Kris answered. "You sound a lot better. Even your eye looks better."

Gabe stretched his arms. "I feel a lot better. In fact, I feel amazing." And Kris was right, he could see out of his eye again.

"Maybe your cloak would work for the Rogues," Abazi suggested.

Gabe's euphoria plummeted. "I don't think so," he managed to reply in a calm voice. "You saw what it did to Jer."

"We should take our chances," she insisted. "I think they're dying."

Gabe shook his head, feeling panicky. Oswald had her under his spell. He must, for her to want to protect him like this! Thank goodness he was out of the way at the mill. He couldn't do any harm there. *But if he really is dying…* a little voice inside his head whispered. *Then I'll call in Filidh*, Gabe told himself. *I will.*

"If only we could make tannin," Jer spoke up. "I think it might help them."

Abazi gazed at Gabe. "Well?"

"I don't even know what that is."

Jer opened his mouth to explain, then stopped, tilting his head. "Do you hear that?"

The excited yips and howls were hard to miss. "They must have brought in Blaine Johnson and his dogs. They'll be searching the woods."

"I like Blaine, and his dogs are awesome," Abazi said. "I think we'd better tag along and make sure they stay safe, especially after what the Ko-goks did in town."

This was new. "What did the Ko-goks do in town?"

"Went after animals," Abazi told him. "Stole a ton of fish and ten pigs have gone missing."

Gabe's stomach turned. "Missing?"

"Yeah, but I'm pretty sure we all know what happened to them."

The image of Straif ripping off the pig's heads and devouring them was not pleasant. "They're getting reckless," he surmised. "Which is bad news for Chief Mara and whoever else joins the search."

"I'm surprised they've held off from searching this long," Kris said. "If it were my kid, I'd have had those dogs out there on day one."

"Like I said before, it seemed to me that Mrs. Morrigan thought Jake was safe somewhere and didn't push the issue."

"She must have realized he isn't." Abazi stood up. "Which would explain why she looked like hell at the store last night. Word around town is that pretty much everyone thinks he's doing this to get back at you, Gabe."

"That's encouraging."

"They also aren't supportive of clearing the woods. They think it's best left alone."

"Then how does Mrs. Morrigan think she can get away with this?"

"Money talks." Abazi grimaced. "Ranger isn't exactly a booming town. If Candi throws enough money at people, along with a few threats, she'll get her way."

Gabe pushed himself to his feet. "You know, if I didn't like Officer White and if Chief Mara had been more of a jerk, I'd say we just let the Ko-goks take them."

"I know what you mean. Old Carl isn't my favorite person, but he's not completely evil like his sister." Abazi looked disappointed. "So what should we do?"

"I don't want to, but I think we'd better go after them. The Rogues are gone, so they can't offer protection."

"What are you going to tell Mom?" Jer asked. "And you can't wear that cloak everywhere. You should take it off."

"I'll just tell her it was something I ate...and now I'm better. As for the cloak, I can handle it, Jer. I told you that."

Jer's face transformed into angry mode—compressed lips, glaring eyes. "And I told you that it's not safe. Not even for you, Gabe."

Gabe turned away. "I'm getting dressed, then we're going out to the woods."

"Do you even care about the Rogues?" Jer demanded. "Or about Jake? Or Hollie? Or do you just care about your precious cloak?"

"You're starting to sound like Gollum," Gabe accused. "It's not like the ring, okay? It's not turning me into some kind of monster. It doesn't rule me." Even as Gabe spoke the words, he wondered if that was true. Then he brushed away his worries. These were dangerous times and if he had to sacrifice himself for a little while, he would. Besides, he felt good in his cloak. It had saved his life. What was wrong with that? "Listen," he said in a conciliatory tone, "I also want to see if we can find Jake. Now that we know he's definitely in the woods, maybe we can track him. Kimber's great at tracking people." He didn't wait for her to respond. "I saw something taking him from the Ko-goks, and it was glowing, which means it's probably good."

"Unless it was using magic to disguise its badness," Jer mumbled.

"Yes, well, unless it was using magic," Gabe conceded. "If that's the case, then it's even more pressing that we go after him."

"And Hollie?" Kris asked. "We need to find Hollie."

"I would love to find Hollie," Gabe said truthfully. He felt anxious about her, about her continued absence. When the Freeze came, she'd been worried she wouldn't make it through the winter. Had she been right? How would they ever know? What does a lifeless Dryad leave behind? A dead tree? A body? Or did it depend on what form they were in when they died? If she'd been a tree, they likely wouldn't find her. But he didn't share these thoughts with the others. He had to stay focused. He had to think positive. Wearing the cloak made that easy. "I believe we'll find her, alive and well. I don't blame her for hiding out. Her friends are acting crazy, the Ko-goks have grown even more demented, the other trees are struggling. She's playing it smart by laying low. If she sees us, she'll let us know. That's why going into the woods is our best option right now."

"Then let's go!" Kris said impatiently. He placed the book he'd been holding back on the shelf and stood up.

"I'm not going with you," Jer said quietly, his expression stubborn. "I have other things to do."

Kimber, who Gabe noticed had avoided looking at or talking to Jer the entire conversation, focused her attention on him. "And what's more important than helping our friend?" she asked coldly.

He didn't look at her. "It's just something I have to do."

Gabe was pretty sure there wasn't anything Jer had to do. He was sulking and when he sulked, he would pretty much cut off his nose to spite his face. If that meant missing out on this latest outing and a chance to be with Kimber, he would do it. Right now he was mad at the world, and he was not going to get over it any time soon.

"All right. Then maybe you can help Mom," Gabe said.

"I told you I have something to do," Jer repeated obstinately. "Something important. You can believe me or not, but it's the truth."

"Fine. Stay here." He turned to the others. "Anyone else staying?" No one said anything, but Kimber looked pensive. "All right. Let's get something to eat, gather our weapons, and head out."

Jer gave him one last, speculative look, then scurried out of the room. Everyone waited a few seconds in silence, then slowly followed after him down the stairs.

Gabe held back for a moment as he pulled the cloak tighter around his shoulders. A musky apple scent filled his senses and he inhaled deeply. *Life…life.* No way was Jer taking this from him. No way.

Chapter Twenty-Two

The Scheme

Mom was surprisingly accepting of his reason for being ill. After Dad had gotten so sick, she'd gone all paranoid on them. She'd been paranoid before, but now if they so much as sniffled, she was all over them. Liquids! Sleep! Decongestants! Vitamin C! It was like living with a mad doctor.

"Your color is much better," she assessed as she turned from shoving wood into the woodstove. "And your cuts and your eye don't look nearly as bad as they did. No fever, either?"

"Nope. I feel great. Starving, in fact."

"I can't believe I'm saying this, but that's a good sign." Truth be told, she was likely just relieved he was okay and didn't have to worry about him anymore. "You girls want anything?"

"No, thank you, Mrs. Hawthorne," Kimber said politely. "We ate lunch before we came."

"Any plans for today? Jer went by a few seconds earlier and said he'd help me with the muffins."

Gabe nodded, as though this was normal, though it went to show that Jer didn't really have anything important to do. He just wanted to avoid them. "I thought I'd get some fresh air. Maybe go outside, check out the stream."

She frowned. "So soon?"

"I'll take it easy, go slow."

"We'll make sure he does," Abazi said. "He can be a bit pigheaded." She gave Gabe a meaningful look, though he wasn't sure what he was supposed to get out of it, other than remembering the image of half-eaten pig heads. "But we'll keep him in check."

Mom laughed. "Yes, he can. All right. But be careful. That stream may not have looked like much this fall, but it can get pretty high in the spring. And this spring has been a doozy, so it's probably flowing faster and deeper than usual."

An image of Shishiqua River, flowing swift and dark, crept into Gabe's mind. He frowned. Where had that come from? He shook his head and the memory of what had happened last night returned to him all at once, like a right hook to the jaw. The sickly Rogues, the smell of rot that pervaded the air inside Wolka Mill, the suffocating darkness. He'd led them there and left them. Some might say, abandoned them.

He shook his head once more and headed for the fridge. He couldn't think about that, about any of it. He'd done the right thing. The Rogues were safer at the mill. He had to remember that.

"Well, it's probably just as well you're going out," Mom went on. "Grandpa and his friend, Vernon, are coming over. Luck was on our side for once. Vernon has a shop dealing in an assortment of things, and he had a furnace he can give us for a few hundred bucks. It's old, but it works, and he'll put it in for free, bless him. Then maybe we can look for something newer this summer."

Normally Mom didn't like talking about their finances, or lack thereof, in front of other people, but she was probably so used to having Kimber and Abazi around that she thought of them as family. Either that, or she was just too tired to care anymore. On the plus side, she seemed optimistic that they'd still be here this summer. Or maybe she'd blocked out the thought of the property taxes, due *tomorrow*. Like Gabe, she was good at simply pushing anything that displeased her out of her mind.

He took out the fixings for a turkey sandwich and quickly assembled it. As he ate, Kris and the girls fetched the muffins to bring along and filled thermoses with water. Mom left to add more wood to the fireplaces, then to do some writing while she waited for Grandpa Hawthorne and Vernon to arrive.

Jer stayed out of the kitchen and they didn't see him as they headed for the barn. They quickly gathered their weapons, then made a beeline for the woods. In the distance, the dogs barked off and on. Gabe was glad for them, since it made their job of finding the search party much easier. Though what they would do when they found them was something Gabe had not thought through. He'd just have to wing it, and why not? He had the cloak to protect him. He was...*invincible.*

The group was silent as they trudged through the woods toward the baying dogs. With each step, Gabe grew more confident, more exhilarated at the thought of the battle to come.

Battle?

He blinked as the word repeated in his mind. Was this it? Had the time come to end all this? Maybe.

With a smile, he picked up his pace, soon leaving the others behind. "Gabe!" Abazi called after him, but he ignored her calls. He was going to do what should have been done years ago. He was going to rid the forest of its blight and he was going to, well, he was going to *do* something. What that something was, he hadn't quite figured out, but it occurred to him it might involve having to remove certain individuals from this life *permanently*.

It should worry him that he didn't care that others might die at his hand. But it didn't. Overhead, the sound of whispers followed him. "It's all right," he assured the voices. "We're goin' to end this. The time has come!"

The whispers grew louder and the wind picked up, chasing after him as he strode toward the search party, determined to find Jake and send them all away from this place. *His* place. The barking was almost deafening now and he realized he was dangerously close to the dogs. He sped up.

~~~~~~

"Are you kidding me?" Candi Morrigan cried out when the dogs started baying again. She was growing tired of this nonsense, feeling quite sure they'd been going in circles for the past hour and were probably chasing a rabid raccoon. Carl was such an idiot, he'd think they were making good progress. If only they'd let her take over. Blaine Johnson wasn't the brightest bulb. Sure people claimed he was some sort of dog whisperer, but that didn't mean he knew the first thing about tracking. Or dressing, for that matter. Who in their right mind still wore those stupid Elmer Fudd caps?

"Calm down, Candi," Carl drawled in his fat, irritating voice. He might be her half-brother, but that didn't mean she had to like him. He'd inherited his dim-witted mother's brains, that was for sure, along with her big gut, two big strikes against him. "I told you that you didn't have to come. This can take a while, and might produce nothing."

"It might produce *something* if you two knew your job." That half-wit Blaine ignored her jab, as he'd been doing since they'd started. Just once she'd like to see him get mad. It was rather infuriating to insult someone who hadn't the brains to know they were being insulted. "We've been going in circles for the past hour, you know."

"That's because whatever the dogs are chasing shares the same scent as that jacket of your boy's. They don't get it wrong."

"So you're saying my Jakie is running in circles like some sort of mad idiot?" Though if he was, at least it meant he was still alive.

"I'm not saying nothing," Blaine replied blandly. "It could be Jake and he could be disoriented. Or it could be someone who's got Jake, or something of his," he added, "and is trying to throw us off track."

"Someone? Who?"

He shook his head ruefully. "Now that I don't know."

She groaned. "Seriously, Carl?" She indicated Blaine, who was busy picking something out of his ear with his free hand. "This is the best you can do?"

"Blaine Johnson is the best tracker north of Boston. Heck, he's probably the best in all New England."

"Well, I beg to differ."

"Do you want to do this on your own, Candi?" Sometimes Carl found himself a backbone and it was quite annoying.

"I could probably do a better job," she replied grumpily.

The two dogs, a bloodhound and a German Shepherd, suddenly pulled on their leads, growing more excited with each jerk forward. "Something's changed," Carl pointed out, needlessly.

Despite herself, Candi grew hopeful. Things had not been going well lately. From the start her development project had been undermined, under-supported, and underappreciated. And now Jakie had seemingly disappeared off the face of the earth, which was not how she'd planned it.

The scheme was to have him pretend to have been drinking and 'wander' over to the Hawthornes to start a fight with Gabe Hawthorne. Jakie hated Gabe with a passion (and rightfully so), so he hadn't needed any convincing. The first part had gone smoothly, with Jakie managing to 'accidentally' leave his jacket behind as evidence and to also give Gabe a black eye, making it look like they'd been fighting. Afterwards, he was to head to the family hunting shack on the north side of town and hole up there for a few days.

Her plan was meant to achieve multiple outcomes. First, Jakie's disappearance would place the spotlight firmly on the Hawthornes, making it difficult for them to concentrate on paying, or even questioning, their impending tax bill. She had made Dick pull some strings down at Town Hall so that the bill was quite a bit higher than it should be, ensuring the Hawthornes couldn't pay it off. The bank would then foreclose on the house and Candi would swoop it up. It was prime real estate, after all, and necessary to her development project.

The second outcome was to gain support of the townspeople, who were annoyingly and irrationally attached to this hideous forest. Despite people going missing in the woods over the years, Rangerites were strangely reluctant to have someone cut them down. And while she could blackmail a lot of them to get her way, she couldn't influence all of them. There was always some stubborn holdout, and typically one with the biggest mouth…like Eleanor May.

Of course, it didn't help that someone owned the woods, which everyone knew, but who it was, nobody had a clue. Candi, with Dick's help, was working on changing that. Soon they'd be able to do what they wanted with the forest. But in the meantime, it was important to have the town behind them, especially after Agnes had abandoned her to go stay with her sick sister. What awful timing!

So Candi was forced to get creative. Having Jakie go missing in the woods, returning with horror stories about what lay within, would be just the necessary shove to get these backwoods yokels to do as she wanted. It was genius.

And necessary. While she liked being married to a lawyer and living in a small town where she could be the big fish in the pond, she didn't like that Ranger was so out of touch with the 21st century. They didn't even have a tanning salon, for Pete's sake! For six months of the year, she resembled a fish's underbelly. She didn't want to move back to Boston, where she'd lived for several years before marrying Dick, because as she knew, she was important here in Ranger and was clever enough to realize she wouldn't wield nearly as much power in a bigger town, where lawyers and real estate agents were a dime a dozen. But she sure missed everything the city had to offer—from gyms and jewelry shops to cafes and bars.

Now, thanks to her, all of that would be coming to Ranger. At last!

The only problem was that Jakie wasn't anywhere to be found. He'd never made it to the hunting shack, she was sure of that, since she'd checked. And after finding several empty beer bottles in the garbage can in their kitchen, she was also quite sure he'd drunk a lot more than necessary. She'd found his cell phone in his jacket, so he didn't even have that, but she'd told him not to call anyway. Phone calls could be traced.

So it was very possible he really had gotten himself lost in the woods that day. She'd hoped he'd holed up at a friend's house, but had ruled out the last of them yesterday, along with any other place he might be hiding. He'd been missing for several days now and Candi was worried, rightly so, that her little Jakie, such a sensitive boy, but rather stupid, too, would not be able to survive in these woods.

The bloodhound howled, bringing Candi back to the present. "Can't you shut them up?" Their constant barking was giving her a headache. She could really use a boost right now. She fumbled in the pocket of her Burberry coat and pulled out a flask and a bottle of pills. Shaking two into her hand, she swallowed them with a swig of gin. She didn't particularly care for gin, but it didn't have any odor, and there was no way she was going to be accused of smelling like a brewery. Alcohol had gotten her into trouble before and since then she'd learned to be more careful.

"I told you, something's changed," Carl snapped back. "Now will you just shut it for a moment and let Blaine do his job?"

Candi was about to tell Carl that he could shove it up his big backside, but decided that maybe he was right about something changing. They were heading in a different direction now. "What's that?" Someone was standing in the woods in front of them, about twenty yards away. Blaine pulled on the leads and stopped the dogs with a sharp command. "I think that's Gabe Hawthorne!"

Carl looked surprised as he squinted into the woods. "I think you're right. But what's he doing out here?"

"I told you he's the one who did something to Jakie!" At some point, Candi would have to recant this accusation, but not until the Hawthornes were driven out of Ranger and she had her shopping mall and condos and a decent bar that didn't have peanut shells on the floor.

"But if he's guilty, then why isn't he running?"

Candi pulled out her snub-nosed pistol. "That's what I'm going to find out."

Chapter Twenty-Three

Like Cannibals

Jer knew the others thought the worst of him. *Well, let them*, he thought as he packed up the muffins for Mom as quickly as he could. He had to be careful with them, because they were for the store and had to look presentable, not all smooshed, and the whole process took longer than he thought it would.

Mom was working on the computer and barely looked up when he told her he was done and was heading out. He knew she would assume he was joining the others and didn't disabuse her of her mistake.

"Remind them not to get too close to the stream."

"Hm," he responded vaguely. He didn't like lying to his mother, and this was the best way to get around her. If she weren't typing, she'd see through his ruse, but she was caught up in her story and didn't catch him this time. "See you later."

"Hm? Oh, yeah. See you." She flipped him a sort of goodbye salute.

The rain had stopped, the sun was out, and it was a glorious day, but Jer didn't see any of it as he hurried down the steps. Depending on the answers he got, there could be a lot to do today, and it was almost two o'clock already. He'd checked on the Internet for sunset times and found the sun set around half past six. So little time!

Already a lot of snow had melted, leaving only small patches, even in the woods. The moss was flattened from the heavy snows and Jer was glad for it. He had to hurry. Last night the Rogues had looked on the verge of death and the longer Gabe wore that cloak, the more likely he was going to become dependent on it. Jer was mad at his brother for treating him like a kid, but he knew what that cloak could do. Wearing it had instilled the delusion that he was all-powerful and infallible. Only a very strong person could handle that well, someone older and with a load of wisdom. Gabe wasn't that person. Not yet.

Jer called out her name as he ran, being sure to avoid heading the direction the barking was coming from. "Aurelia!" he shouted every fifteen steps. He didn't want to call too loudly, knowing there were plenty of listeners.

Winded, he stopped and grasped his knees, panting. Where was she? Was he even close? He knew he couldn't trust the trees to stay put, or the rocks, or Shambolic Stream, even. So he could only go on instinct and instinct had sent him toward the mountain, near Straif's Dark Domain.

When he'd caught his breath, he called again, softly, "Aurelia? Are you there? It's me, Jerome. I need your help." She didn't answer, but was that a stirring in the treetops? He looked up, but could see nothing. "I put aside my childish thoughts and deeds, just like you said. I'm taking action, even though Gabe is being a butthead right now."

There was a swirl of air around Jer, like a wind devil, then absolute stillness. He spun around. "Aurelia?" His eyes widened. "Aurelia!"

She had transformed to her human form, and she looked both eerie and absolutely stunning. Her skin was a silvery gray and her long hair was soft yellow and pale green, the colors woven together like braids. Her fingers were long and delicate, as were her features. Her dress was made from leaves the same color as her hair and had dark nuts for buttons.

"I am…glad…ye came, Jerome," she breathed, each word a labor. "My change has weakened me, but…I need ye to see…me this way."

"You shouldn't have changed!" Jer cried. "Not for me."

"It will help ye…to hear me."

"I heard you when you were a tree. I wish you would've stayed that way. Here, sit down." He gently guided her to a large rock, awed at the feeling of her skin, like marble.

She smiled and sat down. "That does feel…better." And in fact, she sounded better, less breathless. "What I meant was that I can…no longer speak while a tree." She stopped and inhaled deeply, as though breathing itself was hard for her. "What brings ye here, Jerome?"

He crouched down beside her, loath to release her arm, but figuring he probably should. "I was reading about tannin, what it can do for trees. It's like a miracle drug! All you have to do is produce it and you'll be all right. You can be well again, Aurelia. All of you!"

"Tannin?" Her brow crinkled. "Ah, yes, tanneen. But not all of us produce…tanneen."

"I know. That threw me for a while, but then I thought, what if you could share it with each other. Can you?" He watched her eagerly, hoping for an affirmative answer. Everything depended on her saying yes.

"We can. But ye see, the trees...of the Forest Immortal are sick. We cannot...produce the very medicine necessary to save us. We lack the strength."

Jer hoped he hadn't heard right. "*None* of you can do it?"

She tilted her head to one side, considering. After several seconds, she brightened and said, "Ah, yes. There it is. The oaks, they are...great producers. Perhaps...they can do it?"

The oaks. The Rogues were oaks. Crap. "They're sick, too. Really sick."

Her beautiful shoulders slumped. "That's bad news, indeed. I thought the Rogues looked a little off, but I didn't...quite realize the extent of their illness."

"There's no one else?"

She shook her head sadly. "It was a hard freeze. No one...made it through untouched."

A thought occurred to Jer. "What about Gabe? Could he do it?"

She sat still, her mind working to remember what it had once so easily produced. "I suppose that...he could. He is...our Yggdrasil, after all. Our beginning."

Jer grew excited. "Then he's the answer!"

"Ye're right!" She smiled, then her countenance darkened and she sighed. "I remember now. I had forgotten, as I have...with so many things. It's an ancient remedy, not one...to be used lightly. He cannot do it."

"But why?" Jer protested. "It solves everything, Aurelia."

"It takes...a lot from a creature, doin' this."

Gabe's tough, Jer thought. He could handle it. "What does he have to do?"

"He has to go...through a full cycle," she explained, watching him with her steady gray eyes.

"Okaaay. What does that mean?"

She paused. "It's like goin'...from the Freeze, at its beginning, to the melting, all...in one day."

"Oh." Jer still wasn't clear on what this meant.

She saw his expression. "He has...to go through buddin', flowerin', and berryin' at a speed that...is typically not possible."

Jer swallowed. "He could die from doing it?"

She looked grave. "Most likely he will. And if...he dies, so shall we all. Only our King...can save us now."

"How does he do it?" Jer persisted.

"He will know," she replied. Jer was doubtful about this and it showed on his face. "He will, Jerome. If he does...not know, then he is not...our true King."

That didn't sound good. "So if he doesn't do it, the forest dies. But if he does, he'll likely die and still not save the forest."

"I'm afraid that is the way of things, my friend."

Jer felt sick. He had the answer, but it wasn't a viable solution. "Is there any other way?"

She glanced up at the sky. "If there is, I do not...know it. And if I do not know it, it does not...exist. I'm the only remaining Curator."

"Curator?"

"Isis of the Sycamores...once was a Curator. She's dead now."

"I know. We saw her." They were silent for a moment. "What's a Curator?"

"A keeper of information, of history. She knew...far more than me. We had not...expected her death, though we should have."

"I can't believe that stupid Straif killed her," Jer growled.

She blinked. "Oh, no. Straif did not kill Isis. No, that was Dame Hazel."

Jer pulled back, stunned. "Dame Hazel? But why?"

"I'm sure she had...her reasons."

"Are you serious? What reason could she have to kill that beautiful tree?"

Aurelia sighed. "I wish that...I knew. I think I once did, but now, well, it's...so hard to think, to concentrate."

Jer stood up. "I need to find Gabe and the others." He had no idea what he was going to say when he found them, since he couldn't ask Gabe to sacrifice himself to save a forest. Though if Jer could do it himself, he would. These weren't just trees, they were living creatures, not all that different from himself. He finally understood this through his time, though brief, spent with Aurelia.

"Ye've grown, Jerome." She smiled at him.

"I don't feel like I have. I'm still mad at Gabe, and everything I've done to make things better has failed."

"Ye've looked...beyond yer anger to help another. That is part of coming-of-age."

"Yeah, well, me coming-of-age won't help you guys."

"As long...as there's good in the world, we are all better for it."

Jer frowned. "I'm not giving up, Aurelia."

She gave him a luminous smile, which made him think of the sun coming out from behind the clouds. "I did not think...ye would, Jerome. Now go. The dark ones stir."

Jer took a few steps away from her and searched the woods. He didn't see or hear anything unusual out there, but he knew Aurelia was right. Something wicked this way was coming. "Ye will find...the way, Jerome," she whispered. "Just stay strong...and stay safe." He turned back to face her, but she was gone. In her place stood a magnificent gray tree.

"You, too, Aurelia," he whispered back, wishing he shared her faith in him. Because right now the only thing he wanted to do was run far away from the madness his life had become, leaving it all behind for someone else to deal with.

~~~~~~

Kris couldn't believe they'd lost Gabe. But he'd run on ahead so quickly, not even bothering to wait for Kimber, who was struggling with a glitch in her brace. She'd tripped over a rock and dinged it, causing one of the joints to lock up. By the time Kris had swung her onto his back, the forest had swallowed Gabe up. Kris didn't dare yell for him, not in these woods. He had a feeling that it wouldn't take much to set the whole place into motion. The air was thick with tension and it made him feel sweaty and uncomfortable, which was unlike him. Usually he was the one stirring things up, meeting things head on. But now that Hollie was missing, possibly dead, he didn't feel so brave or sure of himself, and this felt less and less like an adventure with every passing hour.

"Do you see him?" Abazi asked worriedly. "Maybe Jer was right about that cloak."

"Maybe he was," Kris acknowledged. "And won't he be glad to hear that."

"He was right about more than that," Kimber said over his shoulder.

"What do you mean?"

"He didn't want me coming with you guys. He said he was worried about me, but what he really meant is that I tend to make things harder for everyone."

"Jer didn't mean that at all," Abazi snapped. "Geez, Kimber. You're so smart, except when it comes to relationships. Jer's worried about you because he likes you a lot."

"Oh, like you're all accepting of the fact that Gabe likes you?"

"After he hears what I did to my mom," Abazi replied breezily, as if she didn't care one way or the other, "I'm sure he'll just love me to pieces."

"Gabe won't hear it from any of us," Kimber said quietly. "It will have to be you who tells him."

"I'm not telling him anything," Abazi said grumpily.

"And I don't believe Jer has feelings for me. So we're even."

Kris sighed. "You girls make things so complicated. Gabe likes you, Abazi, and he'll keep on liking you after you tell him the story about your mom."

"Yeah, right," Abazi grunted, but her tone held hope in it. Tainted hope, but hope all the same.

"And Jer likes you, Kimber," Kris went on, needing to make his point, "and he wants to keep you safe. That's called chivalry. Maybe it comes across that he's treating you like a child, but he can work on that. After all, he knows what it feels like. Me and Gabe do it to him all the time."

"So you're saying I'm acting like a child?" was Kimber's rather infuriating response.

He bit down on his tongue to keep from saying yes. "We're all allowed to behave that way once in a while, aren't we?"

"But I can't behave that way. I always have to act strong and adultlike or my mom will have me back in diapers, and you guys won't let me come with you anymore."

Kris was about to tell Kimber how wrong she was about that, but he didn't get the chance. There was someone coming toward them, making no effort to be quiet. The search party? No. He'd have heard the dogs barking. So who was it?

When a small crowd of people emerged from the trees, Kris couldn't quite take in what he was seeing. Dame Hazel? It sure looked like her. Behind her was a strange, ratty-haired lady with crazy eyes, followed by...no way! It was Jake Morrigan, hobbling, one shoe on, one shoe off, and he was carrying Hollie.

Kris lowered Kimber to the ground and rushed forward. "Why are *you* carrying her? What did you do to her?" Hollie, so full of life and color, was now limp and pale as snow; she looked like she'd already been dead and buried for a few days.

Jake looked both scared and defiant. "They made me do it." He pointed at Dame Hazel and the crazy lady. "I only agreed because this one saved me from those freaks." His face was streaked with mud and scratches and he looked like he'd lost a few pounds. There were bits of moss and a multitude of sticks in his normally perfectly coiffed hair. Jake was a mess, but he was alive. Kris felt some gratitude for that, if only because it proved Gabe's innocence. "And I didn't do anything to her. After she saved me, she collapsed." So Hollie had been the one at the field—the blur that had rescued Jake. Kris should've known it was her. It was exactly the sort of thing she'd do—brave and crazy as all get out.

Kris held out his arms. "Give her to me."

"Gladly," Jake snarled and passed Hollie's seemingly lifeless form over to Kris. Her body was still warm and he noted gratefully that her chest beneath her green shift rose and fell every few seconds.

"What's wrong with her?" he appealed to Dame Hazel. She looked more haggard than usual, her dried apple skin like cracked ice. Her corkscrew hair was in disarray and her purple cloak, which had once made her look like royalty, was torn in several places.

"She tried to get around the Freeze," she said wearily, "and now she's payin' the price."

He knew she must have tried to defy the laws. But what if she had done it for him—so she could come see him? He'd never forgive himself if she didn't survive. "Is she going to die?" he whispered, peering down at Hollie's delicate features, usually so lively and now so still.

"I do not know," Dame Hazel answered shortly. "That depends on the next few hours. The whole forest is dyin' as we speak. Our lives depend on Gabriel and Oswald."

Abazi stepped around Kris, and Jake's eyes widened to see her there. Up to that point, he'd been staring off into the woods, as though calculating making a run for it. "But Oswald's sick, Dame Hazel. Really sick. We put him somewhere safe, but he needs help."

The old woman's eyelids drooped worriedly. "And where's Gabriel?"

"We don't know. He ran ahead of us. He was trying to keep the search party safe from the dark ones."

"They were searching for me?" Jake asked excitedly.

"They had the dogs. Didn't you hear them?"

"I thought they were those stupid Kogs."

"Ko-goks," Abazi corrected him. "You're lucky to be alive, you idiot. You owe your life to Hollie, don't you?"

Despite his worry, Kris had to smile. That was the second nice thing Abazi had said about Hollie. He had to remember to tell Hollie that when she woke up. *If* she woke up. *Don't think that way!* He refused to believe anything bad was going to happen to her. It was how he got himself through Dad's illness, and Dad had lived. Maybe it would work with Hollie, too.

Or maybe he was being a delusional idiot.

"We must find Gabriel," Dame Hazel repeated in a distant voice. She looked and sounded as though the connection between body and soul was growing weaker by the second. Her knees buckled and she nearly fell. The strange woman rushed to her and helped support her, and Kimber hurried to her other side. Normally quite short compared to everyone else, Kimber's stature served her well for helping the equally diminutive Dame Hazel.

"Who's that?" Kris nodded at the crazy lady.

"This is Faeth," Dame Hazel answered. "She's Oswald's mother."

"Wait a minute," Abazi spoke up. "I thought she was Gabe's mom."

"No." Dame Hazel shook her head, and Faeth gazed down at her in bewilderment. "No."

"I think she's losing her mind," Abazi whispered in Kris's ear. "Like they all are."

"Gabriel's mine," Faeth announced through trembling lips speckled with bits of dead leaves and dirt. "Oswald's mine. They're all mine."

Abazi's eyes widened and she made a subtle circling gesture with her finger, indicating what she thought of Faeth's state of mind. "Of course," Abazi soothed, facing Faeth. "And we're off to find them both. All right?"

"Yes," Dame Hazel acknowledged. "It's time."

"Time for the funny farm," Abazi muttered. "Why are we always stuck with the loonies?"

Whenever Abazi was feeling nervous, she got snippy, and it was best to just ignore her or she'd really kick it into gear. So he gazed down at Hollie, so helpless in his arms, and promised himself to do whatever it took to save her. "Maybe we should head back to the house and wait for Gabe there."

But it wasn't going to be that easy. In the distance a chant arose, racing towards them like a wild horse. "Blackthorn! Blackthorn! Spill the blood, return to life! Blackthorn, Blackthorn! Take the power, end the strife!"

"Now what?" Abazi groaned, turning toward the sound.

"It's Straif and the Ko-goks!" Kris cried. "They're coming."

"Then I'm outta here!" Jake yelled, and started running in the direction he'd been scouting.

"You know your way out, Morrigan?" Kris called after him. He didn't like the guy, but right now he was committing suicide.

Jake slid to a stop. "No one can find their way out of this place! I tried. I fought with that crazy lady," he pointed at Faeth, "after she took me, and got away from her, then *she* found me," he pointed at Hollie, "and took me to her cave, but I got away then, too. And then *they* found me." His voice took on a dead tone. "They were going to eat me, like cannibals!"

"We know our way out," Kris told him, though he wasn't confident that they did. Kimber was a tracker, but she had Dame Hazel to look after, and besides, she couldn't move fast enough to outrun the Kogoks.

Jake swallowed, looking uncertain. "I just want to go home."

Kris wasn't sure any of them were going to get home, but that wasn't going to stop him from trying. He'd outrun all the dark ones to save Hollie. He'd fight them with his bare hands, if need be. But one thing he wouldn't do is give up. "I'll find a way out of here."

"Yer way is this a-way!" a little voice shouted behind Kris.

He spun around. "Wildrr!"

The little fairy bowed and his oversized pink hat, covered in black berries, slid over his large, round eyes. He pushed it back up. "In the flesh." There wasn't much flesh to see, hidden as it was by his twiggy, green topcoat and blue and green striped leggings.

"You found Gabe, didn't you? Please say you found Gabe."

"I did. And at this very moment he's about to be shot at." As predicted, several short, sharp blasts rang out. "Follow me, dobbers!" Wildrr ordered. "We've got work to do!" He spun around and charged through the trees, brandishing what looked suspiciously like his panpipes. "And keep yer fool heads down!"

Chapter Twenty-Four

The Sick and Dying

"**S**on of a—! Candi, put that gun away!" Chief Mara shouted at his sister. "You're going to kill someone!"

Gabe smiled. Now *here* was a challenge. He turned and plunged back into the woods, mentally urging them to follow him. He'd gone only a few strides when the dogs started barking. The chase was on.

The thought briefly occurred to Gabe that his brother and Kimber and Abazi hadn't caught up with him. He wondered what had happened to them, but figured they'd be fine. Everyone would be fine. Well, most everyone.

It was time to lead them all away, some to safety, some to their deaths. It was the way of things now. To save his kind, some would have to die. *Die?* Was that really necessary? *Yes, yes, yes...* "No, no, no," he groaned. "*Not* necessary."

Yet the idea stuck with him. To achieve what he wanted, someone would have to die. Surely he was thinking of Straif and the Ko-goks? Not anyone else? Like Mrs. Morrigan or Carl Mara? If they tried to stop him, then yes, maybe they would have to die. It was for the greater good, after all.

Gabe shivered. He didn't like the way this mental conversation was going.

Thankfully, a movement up ahead distracted him from his macabre notions, and he searched the spot, trying to determine what he'd seen. Two figures, he soon discerned. Running fast. Kris and Abazi? Maybe. But then, where was Kimber? He slowed. He wasn't sure he wanted to follow them. He had to go somewhere now, and couldn't risk being detoured.

Where do you have to go? a niggling little voice questioned.

None of yer business!

Bang! The sharp retort of gunfire shook the air, followed by another. The second shot whistled by Gabe's right ear, after which several more rang out in quick succession. He ran faster until he heard shouting, then, "Hey!" followed by silence, then a scream.

He stopped and swung around, chest heaving, and his eyes widened, not sure he was seeing right. Candi's gun dangled from a tree limb's grip, while other trees swung their branches through the air, low to the ground, as though a hockey game was on, with her fleeing figure serving as the puck. The trees left Blaine and Chief Mara, both farther back, alone, apparently deciding they weren't threats. Occasionally a branch would hit Candi's butt with a satisfying smack and she'd leap into the air with an angry yelp. It was sort of funny to watch until one tree reached down and grabbed her by the ankle, swinging her into the air, then turning her upside down to dangle like a lure.

Chief Mara reached the spot where she was hanging and pulled out his gun, aiming it at the tree. "P-put her down!"

When Blaine arrived, he looked up to see Mrs. Morrigan swinging upside down and an amused smile warmed his face. The dogs were straining at their leashes, urging him onward. They had caught sight of Gabe.

It was time to show himself. He strode forward, his hands in the air. "I must thank ye once again, Ailem, for helpin' me out. But ye really must put her down now."

"She was tryin' to destroy ye, Yggdrasil," moaned the giant Wych Elm, "and if'n ye die, we all die."

"I know," he soothed, feeling strangely powerful and in command. So different from their last meeting when he'd had no idea what he was doing. "But I'm not goin' to die, and neither are ye. The time has come to end this."

"You!" Mrs. Morrigan screeched, her face red from being upside down. "Where's my son?"

"I've no idea," Gabe answered calmly.

"She's bad," Ailem bellowed. "We must rid our forest of her putrid presence. We've been watchin' and waitin' for ye, bidin' our time." So they had been the ones shadowing him, back when he'd come to the woods with the chief and Mrs. Morrigan to search for Jake, and just moments ago, when he'd seen the two running figures.

"Now Ailem, don't do anything stupid. If she's hurt, then ye'll give the town good reason to take down this forest." It was funny advice coming from him…the guy who'd been content to kill whoever got in his way.

"You tell this monster to let me go!" Mrs. Morrigan shouted.

"If I did that, ye'd break yer neck."

She scowled, then reached inside her jacket. "Maybe this will stop your smart-aleck remarks." She pointed a pistol at him, surprisingly calm even though she was dangling in the grip of a talking tree. "Lucky for me I carry a spare."

"Look out, Gabe!" There was a rush from behind and Gabe was tackled, falling to the ground as a shot rang out.

He sat up. "Kris!" Abazi and Kimber were not far away, their expressions horrified. There were other people with them, familiar people, though one of them was lying on the ground, unconscious, possibly dead.

"Agh!" Mrs. Morrigan shouted as the tree branch swung her through the air like a pendulum and her gun went flying. Another tree grabbed hold of her, then passed her along to another one.

Kris jumped up and pulled Gabe to his feet. "Are you okay?" Gabe nodded. "Good, cause Straif's coming. He's not far behind us. And Hollie's sick. I have to carry her, so I can't fight. I don't know what to do." Kris wrung his hands, looking back over his shoulder at the figure on the ground. It was Hollie, Gabe realized, and she wasn't moving. He felt a growing pressure inside him. "What should we do, Gabe?"

For the first time since he'd donned the cloak, Gabe wasn't sure. Kris sounded scared, which wasn't like him, and the trees kept playing hot potato with Mrs. Morrigan, who was hollering and threatening to sue.

It was too loud! There was too much going on! He could handle Mrs. Morrigan; he could handle the trees. He felt so strong, he thought he could handle Straif, too. But all of them at once? It was too much. *Too much!*

The resounding smack of flesh hitting flesh echoed through the woods and Gabe blinked back tears. "Focus, Gabe!" Abazi stood directly in front of him, holding her hand and looking mad. "You brought us out here, now figure out what we should do!"

"I don't know," he mumbled, rubbing at his cheek. "I don't know everything!"

"Finally," she replied, triumphantly. "Now we can get somewhere."

Gabe's hand dropped. "What's that supposed to mean?"

"It means you get that we're all in this together. Right?"

But *he* was the King, not her. Their fate, the fate of the Forest Immortal, it all rode on his shoulders. "But I'm the King," he whispered. "I'm supposed to be the one who makes the hard decisions." *I'm the one who might have to kill.*

"Seriously, Gabe? You think you're that great? The rest of us have brains, too." She glanced over at Jake, who was mumbling to himself. "Well, most of us."

"So I take it you have an idea?"

"I do. You and I are going to distract the Dryads and the Ko-goks, while Kris and the others head to your house. They can hole up in the turret. It should be safe there."

"And where are we going?"

"To the mill, duh. Where else?"

"Put me down!" Mrs. Morrigan screeched from above them.

"I think they're taking her away." Kris pointed upward.

Gabe watched the trees pass Mrs. Morrigan down the line, away from them. "It looks that way. Okay, I'm going to do something to get the Dryads to follow me and Abazi." Gabe looked around, then found who he was searching for. "Wildrr!" he called. The little fairy left Hollie's side and ran toward Gabe.

"Sirruh! Yes, Sirruh!" Wildrr saluted mockingly. "What pleases ye?"

"Can you lead everyone to the house with your panpipes? Because Mrs. Morrigan won't go willingly."

Wildrr pushed back his oversized cap. "That I can do. Yes, indeedy!"

"Good. Everyone get ready to go." Gabe waved to them to get moving.

Kris ran over and picked up Hollie. "We're ready."

From the shadows, Kimber and Faeth helped Dame Hazel along. He'd seen them earlier, but hadn't had time to process what it meant that they were here. Dame Hazel looked ill, and Hollie appeared to be unconscious. "She didn't turn when she was supposed to," Kris answered his questioning expression. "Because of me, I think. I have to save her."

"Keep her safe in the turret, and we'll see what we can do."

"What's happening to my mom?" Gabe turned to see Jake standing behind a tree, only his head showing. For some reason, he wasn't all that surprised to see him. Faeth was watching him avidly, and Gabe suddenly understood what had happened. Faeth had taken him, possibly because she thought all boys Gabe and Oswald's age were her sons. Jake, being drunk, likely hadn't put up that much of a fight, and Gabe knew through experience that Faeth was stronger than she looked. Then, with the help of the trees, she'd managed to take him far into the woods, out of sight. Gabe wasn't sure how Hollie had become involved with Jake, but again, it didn't surprise him that she had. He would have to ask her later...if she revived. *When* she revived.

"Nothing I can't handle," he answered Jake's question.

"You stay away from her, Freak!" Jake pointed an accusing finger at him. "You're one of those *things!* I heard you talking weird. You're evil. This whole place is evil!"

"Then you'd better make sure you stay with Kris while he heads back to the house." The 'evil' word didn't bother Gabe as much as the look of disgust on Jake's face. He shouldn't care what Jake thought about him, but, stupidly, he did.

Feeling far from invincible now, he lifted his arms to speak. "Put the human down!" he bellowed with all the force his tree persona could muster, and his deepened voice reverberated throughout the forest. "You must leave her be and follow me. There are more important things to attend to now." The whole forest went quiet, disturbed only by the dying echoes of Gabe's voice.

At last there was a stirring amongst the trees, dismayed hisses and muddled whispers that filled Gabe's head and ears. They didn't know what to do. They were sick and confused. He had to make them believe him, trust him, or they would turn to Straif, who was coming, and Straif would make them his.

I need ye to be with me, trees, he spoke to them in his mind. *I need ye to follow me. I'll end yer suffering. I'll make ye whole again.* It was a promise he wasn't sure he could keep. Or how. But he had to say something to convince them he was the one to follow, not Straif. Never Straif.

He waited. Nothing changed. *Please,* he beseeched. *I'll make ye whole again!*

With a holler, Mrs. Morrigan was plopped down in front of him, her face bright red and her eyes stained from mascara. She wasn't crying, though. She was furious. "This is why these trees need to be chopped down!" she shrieked, shaking a finger and advancing on Gabe.

"Your son is here," was all he said, and stepped aside.

Her eyes widened. "Jakie!" She pushed past Gabe and ran toward Jake. Gabe didn't care for her, but she seemed to care for her son. She wrapped him in an embrace and they both buried their heads in each other's shoulders.

Gabe walked over to two birch trees. "Can ye help us?" The birches shivered, then spun up in the air like tornadoes, to land as humans. Gabe blinked, in awe of their human form. One had mostly white skin, with a few black stripes, while the other was mostly black, with white stripes. The white Dryad had coal black hair and black eyes and the black one had white hair and white eyes. The effect was stunning.

"This is an honor," they both spoke at the same time. "What can we do for ye, Yggdrasil?"

Gabe was happy to hear that they still spoke rationally. They were not yet sick. "The honor's mine, Birches. I've a favor to ask. Will ye take the sick ones to me home?"

They nodded in unison. "We're here to help."

He pointed to Dame Hazel and Hollie and the Birches walked swiftly toward Kris. One took Hollie from Kris's reluctant hands. "I need you to be able to fight, if need be," Gabe explained. Kris nodded, though he didn't look happy about it. The other birch took Dame Hazel from Kimber and Faeth. Before walking away, the Birch leaned low and spoke something into Kimber's ear. Her eyes widened, and she nodded.

"We're ready, Yggdrasil."

Catching Wildrr's eyes, Gabe lifted his hand. "Play, Wildrr. Take them to safety."

Wildrr winked and placed his pipes to his lips. Immediately Mrs. Morrigan let go of Jake and turned about, clueless as to what had taken place only yards away from where she was standing. Together, the two of them followed after Wildrr like zombie sheep. The birch tree Dryads went next, followed by Faeth. She was mumbling and staring down at her hands, and had not attempted to speak to Gabe once, which pained him. Kris gave one last glance backward, gave Gabe a salute, then headed into the woods after Wildrr, his staff at the ready.

When they were gone, Gabe turned to Abazi. "Are you ready?"

"Ready as I'll ever be, Immortal. I'm not calling you that other name. It's too hard to say."

Gabe turned around in a circle. "Those of ye who can still change, do so. Ye're to follow me. I'm takin' ye somewhere safe, away from Straif."

"Liar!" a voice from up high accused.

"Be still!" another one bellowed. "We'll go and see which way the wind blows."

"He made me give up the Pale Witch!"

"Ailem?" Gabe called out. "Is that ye?"

There was a whir of movement from the big trees nearby and two Dryads appeared before Gabe. Unlike the birches, these two creatures were less than stunning, more like scruffy and deranged. Both had long, wiry arms and legs and cracked, gray skin. One was bald as a baby, and the other had wild, twiggy hair.

The wild-haired one stepped forward. "I be Ailem."

"And I be Weachu!" the other leaped in front of Ailem.

"Thank ye for appearin' to me," Gabe said with a little bow. Weachu eyed him skeptically, but seemed to like the bow. "And thank ye for savin' me from the Pale Witch. Ye know Straif and his dark ones, of course."

"We do," Ailem answered. "He's an evil blight."

"He gave me an acorn once," Weachu mused, nodding to himself. "I like acorns. Rare these days."

"I'm goin' to need yer help. Both of ye. I know ye aren't sure which side to take, and I respect that. Sometimes it's not clear-cut who's in the right and who's in the wrong. I can only promise that if ye and yer kind follow me, I'll do me best to save this forest from the Pale Witch and from Straif."

"Acorns," Weachu repeated, looking around. "Got any acorns?"

"Nope, sorry."

Abazi reached into her pocket. "Here." She handed over several smooth nuts, and Weachu snatched them greedily from her hand. Gabe had to wonder why she had them in her pocket. "A thanks might be in order," she said dryly.

"Thanks," Weachu said grudgingly.

"So ye'll follow me?" Gabe asked.

"Best to see which way the wind blows first," Ailem answered. "Best."

"Can ye do that while walkin' with me?"

Ailem and Weachu glanced at each other, then shrugged and nodded. "Don't see why not," Ailem said.

"Don't see why not," Weachu echoed.

Gabe was glad, but could only hope they wouldn't turn on him at the worst possible moment. "Can ye ask all the ones that can change over to change?"

Weachu puffed himself up. "Course we can. Do it, Ailem."

Ailem stepped forward importantly and clapped his hands together twice, loudly. The sound echoed through the woods. There was a tremendous roar and within the blink of an eye over half the trees around them were no longer trees. Thousands of Dryads surrounded Gabe and Abazi, but instead of feeling good, Gabe's stomach curdled.

Most of the Dryads sported the same sign of illness that the Rogues had...vague eyes, strange twitches, and marks on their skin.

Gabe's army was full of the sick and dying.

Chapter Twenty-Five

Until We're All Dead

"Hold up, Wildrr!" Kris yelled ahead to the little fairy. He'd heard something on the path near Grandma May's house. Footsteps. Someone was following them. "Stay here and keep playing your pipes. I'll be right back." He tightened his grip on his staff and spun around, searching the woods for signs of their stalker. "Come out now!" he shouted as he advanced. "And I'll let you live."

There was a snort from behind a nearby tree and Grandma May stepped out. "Is that the best threat you've got, whippersnapper?"

Kris lowered his staff, stunned. "Grandma! What are you doing here?"

"Taking a little stroll. How about you?" She glanced back behind her, as though checking on someone. "Don't you have homework?"

"Do you have someone with you?" Kris parried. He couldn't let her see the others, and he wouldn't let her distract him with questions.

Her witchy blue eyes shifted. "Why would you think that?"

"Because I can see his arm."

"Oh, Bruce," Grandma sighed, turning around, then she frowned. "You can't see anything— Oh. Well-played, Kristofer."

A wild and distracted looking man stepped out from behind the tree. He didn't say a word to Kris, not even a greeting. Even though his silver gray hair and beard were neatly trimmed, it was obvious he was sick. Healthy people didn't have dark spots all over their face and didn't jitter like they'd just downed a handful of caffeine pills. "Did you just call him Bruce? As in Bruce *Holt?*"

Her eyes shifted again. "I don't know what you're talking about."

"The jig is up, Grandma. We know he's alive."

Her shoulders slumped. "He's very sick, and I was going to bring him to the house, see if Ayla can do anything for him."

"Mom? But how would she know how to treat a—" Kris stopped himself from saying Dryad just in time. "A heart ailment," he finished.

Grandma May studied him, quite aware he'd meant to say something else. "I ran out of that tea I gave your father, thought maybe she'd have some left."

Kris didn't know what to say. If he said Dad drank it all and Mr. Holt really needed it, then his lie could kill the guy. But he couldn't let Grandma see Wildrr and Faeth and the Birch Dryads, or, for that matter, Mrs. Morrigan. At the very least, there'd be a fight between the two women, and Kris didn't have that kind of time.

"I can run on ahead and check for you. That way you can go back to your cottage and keep Mr. Holt safe."

"What's going on?" Grandma demanded. "You're hiding something."

"No, I'm not!" Kris protested, feebly. He'd never been a very good liar.

Grandma pressed her hand to her heart, her eyes focused on something over his shoulder. "It's true! It's all true!"

Kris spun around with the bad feeling that she wasn't talking about what he'd just said. Behind him stood the whole gang, looking no less strange than he remembered. He couldn't see Kimber anywhere. She was either keeping back to remain unseen, or had stayed with Gabe and Abazi. Luckily Mrs. Morrigan and Jake were still in a trance, thanks to Wildrr's panpipes. "I thought I told you to stay back."

Wildrr shrugged. "Not all are susceptible to the power of me music," he said quickly, before placing the pipes to his lips again.

Kris had a feeling Wildrr had done this on purpose. But why? "Grandma, I can explain—" he began, but Bruce started toward Wildrr, his eyes on the fairy's panpipes.

"Ah, so lovely," he breathed.

Kris took in Grandma May's dismayed expression. "This is all a dream, Grandma May," he tried to convince her.

She shook her head. "I've heard the stories and half believed them and half didn't. I knew there was something odd about Bruce, surviving well beyond what he should have, but I didn't want to push. I was just glad to have him back in my life after all those years he'd gone missing. So what is he, exactly?"

"How much do you know?" Kris asked, reluctant to spill the whole pot of beans.

"I know there's something powerful in these woods, something strange. The whole town knows that. But I never knew what. Not exactly." She stared at Kris, regaining some of her composure. "So what is this? What is he?" She pointed at Wildrr. "And those two?" She indicated the Birch Dryads, who stood patiently holding their human cargo.

Kris really didn't know how much to tell, so he kept it simple. "Wildrr is a fairy." Wildrr touched his cap to Grandma and she dazedly acknowledged him with a nod. "The rest of them are Dryads. Tree spirits."

"Ahhh," she sighed. "That explains so much."

"Bruce Holt is a tree spirit, too. He must have somehow managed to turn himself into one."

Grandma blinked. "He's a *tree* spirit?"

"The tree spirits are sick. There's this bad guy Straif, and his dark ones, and they ate blood and it's changed them." He didn't add that the Dryads believed Gabe could save them. He wasn't about to spill that much.

"I've felt them," she said. "Bruce has tried to warn me, but he isn't himself. He used to be so articulate, so learned. But now..." She looked back at him. "Well, now he drools."

"It's the sickness. Jer was looking into finding a cure. He's back at the house. Maybe he's found something."

"Then we'll go there."

"There's something else," Kris went on. "Straif and his dark ones might be following us, so we'll have to move fast. Dead wood works well on them." He pulled out his bata and handed it to her. "Take this."

Grandma accepted the short baton, pulling her shoulders back like a warrior. "Lead the way."

"Just be ready to run."

"I will be."

Fortunately, the journey to the house was uneventful. Unfortunately, now they had to deal with confronting Mom and Dad. Mom had enough trouble in her life, and the shock of seeing fairies and Dryads might send her over the edge. And Dad, well, stress was not his friend right now. The doctors had warned them to make sure that he didn't worry too much. With the impending tax bill looming over them, he was already on the brink.

At the barn, Kris stopped the strange little menagerie. "We should go to the turret," he suggested. "It's a safe place."

"I always thought that," Grandma said. "Being as how it was able to keep us out for decades."

"You make it sound alive."

"Something about it *is* alive. It didn't want us in there and it kept us out, until you guys moved in. The key really was lost, and all our attempts to get in via other ways were unsuccessful. Your mother and I are both stubborn women, but even we couldn't fight the turret. Yet it welcomed Gabe like he was meant to be there." She paused and eyed Kris steadily. "I don't suppose you know why that might be?"

Kris only shrugged, though of course he knew, and he also knew what had kept them out. The cloak. It was the only answer. For all those years, it had protected the turret and its secrets, keeping them safe until needed. When Hollie had taken the cloak, the protection had been dropped, long enough for the key to appear and for Gabe to take residence. The cloak had made its way back to Gabe, but had accepted his presence in the turret. The timing of it all was remarkable, almost too good to be true.

"Can you watch everyone while I go inside and open the little door?"

"Little door?"

"The one outside the turret." He pointed.

He thought she was going to get mad that they'd kept it a secret, but she only chuckled. "Well, I'll be! All this time and I never noticed it. Now that's some powerful magic."

He was surprised at how well she was taking this. But, after all, she'd grown up here, close to the strange woods, spent her life hearing the eerie stories. So maybe she'd been expecting this all along.

"I'll be right back." To the sound of Wildrr's pipes, Kris dashed across the yard and up the porch stairs. He stole into the kitchen on tiptoe and started down the hallway. Mom was reading something in her office and didn't look up as he creeped past. And then he tripped. Over Little Joe.

"Gabe?" Mom called. "Is that you?"

"It's me," Kris answered, assuring himself Little Joe was all right. He was just fine, purring and knocking his head against Kris's hand in an attempt to get Kris to pet him. Kris scratched him behind the ears, then pushed himself to his feet. "Just getting something for Gabe."

"Oh." She sounded a little out of it. "Well, um, don't be late for supper."

"I won't. Where's Jer? Up in his room?"

"I thought he was with you."

Ice filled Kris's veins. "He told us he had things to do. He had the sulks," he added for good measure.

"Ah. I thought there was something going on."

"I'll see you later," he called, then hurried upstairs. Luckily Gabe had left the doors unlocked, which he never did. Being sick had made him careless. Or had it? There was that timing thing again, as if something bigger was behind all this. Something like fate, or destiny. Kris wasn't sure he liked that. He'd rather make his own destiny.

He unlocked the little door, hurried out to the barn, and slowly escorted the group across the yard, praying all the while that no one glanced out a window. Mom's office didn't have one, but Dad's did…and it looked out over the front yard. Kris could only hope for the best and carry on. Hollie wasn't looking too good. In fact, none of them were. Even Wildrr seemed droopy, though he had been playing his pipes non-stop for over half an hour.

Kris had no idea how he was going to get everyone up the pole. Luckily the Birches politely reminded him of their ability to transform and they took turns lifting people up with their tree arms. Judging by the color in Grandma May's cheeks, the sparkle in her eyes, and the whoops of delight, she actually seemed to enjoy the ride. Still in a trance, neither Jake nor Mrs. Morrigan responded to much of anything, and settled together on a couple chairs by Gabe's worktable.

Hollie was the last up, and he set her still form on Gabe's unmade bed. He pulled a quilt over her and stood for a moment staring down at her quiet features. Even so sick, she really was something to look at.

"Does she have what Bruce has?" Grandma asked softly from behind him.

Kris blinked back tears. "I'm not sure. I think maybe she didn't go to sleep when she was supposed to and it did something to her."

"Maybe that's why she's unconscious and Bruce isn't."

"Maybe."

"Did you find Jer?"

"I'm going to go look for him now." He was probably up in his room, sulking.

"You'd better hurry. I sense something. Something strange."

"What do you mean?"

"I need to see. I feel something coming." Her eyes flicked up toward the half-moon window.

Kris dashed over to the little stairs that led up to the platform. When he reached the top, he stared out at the woods, stunned. Half the trees were gone and the other half were thrashing about as though in the midst of a seizure. But that wasn't the worst of it. A swarm of dark ones chased after two lone figures, racing through the woods toward the road that led to the mill. The Ko-goks had found Abazi and Gabe. But there was no Kimber to be seen. Crap…where was she?

That was bad enough, but it got worse. While a number of Ko-goks were chasing after Gabe, a large-sized group had broken off from the rest and was heading directly toward the house. *They're coming for us*, Kris realized. *And they won't rest until we're dead.*

Just as he thought this, the door to the turret swung open. There was no time to hide the others, not Jake, not Wildrr, not the Dryads. The jig was up.

~~~~~~

Kimber stayed very still while the Dryads followed Gabe and Abazi through the woods. When they were gone, she glanced up into a tree. "You heard everything?"

There was a pause. "Pretty much. I've been following you guys for some time."

"You'd better come down, so I don't have to keep looking up at you."

Jer jumped to the ground. "Hey," he said softly, looking shy and unsure of himself.

"I'm still very mad at you, you know," she said, pushing the words out before they stuck inside her and never got spoken. She'd never really confronted anyone before and the experience made her feel like she both wanted to throw up and sing hallelujah.

He ducked his head sheepishly. "I know." She thought that was all he was going to say, and her anger grew. If she could summon up the courage to speak about hard things, well, then, he should be able to, too. But then Jer surprised her. "I know your CP can make you feel like you're weak or not as good as others, Kimber," he said, picking his words carefully, "but it doesn't make *me* feel that way about you. You're the strongest person I know, and the bravest. Of all of us, you're the one who has entered this forest, time and again, even though it's a struggle for you. It must be so scary knowing you can't outrun these monsters and yet you come anyway, to fight a battle that isn't yours to fight. You could just walk away, Kimber." He paused, then added casually, "Or hobble, as in your case."

Kimber blinked. Had Jer just made a joke about her CP? Maybe there was hope for him yet. "That's nice of you to say, Jer," she replied, stifling a desire to forgive him right away, "but your actions don't back up your words. You still treat me like a little kid."

"I don't try to!" he argued heatedly, his hands held out to her, wanting her to understand. "I just want to keep you safe. I like you so much, Kimber!" Here, he blushed heavily. "And I hate that you're mad at me and don't want to be my friend any longer."

"Oh, Jer," she sighed, to cover up her amazement. He liked her *so much*! "We're just having a disagreement. I wouldn't be a very good friend if I bailed out on our friendship at the first sign of trouble."

"So we're still friends?" he said hopefully.

"Of course we are. But you have to stop treating me like my mom does. It's hard enough when she does it."

Jer nodded. "I know how it feels, being treated like you're six. My brothers do it to me all the time, so you'd think I'd be supersensitive about doing it to others. Guess not." He looked away for a moment, then back at her. "But I promise you I won't ever do it again. I'll treat you with dignity and respect and let you do everything on your own."

Kimber thought about that. "That sounds good. But maybe I wouldn't mind a little help once in a while. I just don't want to be left out of things, because when you tell me to stay behind, I start believing I'm a burden to you."

Jer's eyes teared up. "You're not a burden, Kimber! You're so strong and brave and wise. I mean all that, and I won't ever ask you to stay behind again. Ever!"

"All right, all right!" She laughed. "I get it. Maybe I'm not as strong and brave or as wise as you think, but I'm also maybe stronger and braver and wiser than I think."

"That's better," Jer said with a smile. "We're a team, Kimber. Maybe you can't do it all, but neither can I. Maybe we have to stop trying so hard to prove we're just as good as everyone else."

Kimber wasn't so certain. "I suppose I could go along with that."

Jer studied her for a moment, guessing she wasn't quite there. "I'll take that…for the moment. Because right now we're going to have to run, which means I'm going to have to carry you."

Kimber beamed. "It's what I've been waiting for all along. You're not my knight charging in on a steed. You're the steed itself!"

Jer ducked low. "Hang on, my lady. The Ko-goks are coming and we're going to have to move fast."

Kimber pulled herself onto Jer's back and hoped for the best. She couldn't help noticing he'd gotten bigger over the winter, and looked stronger, too, but she wasn't easy to carry. What if they fell and he got hurt? What if her braces dug into his back? What if she was too heavy? Oh, dear. She shouldn't let him do this!

"There they are!" a guttural voice howled and she looked back over her shoulder.

"Go, Jer!" she cried. "The fiends are upon us!" Despite the serious-ness of the situation, Kimber couldn't help smiling. She'd always wanted to say that. Needing no further prompting, Jer tightened his grip on her legs and took off, racing through the woods at an impres-sive speed. It was almost as good as riding a real horse.

They whipped through the remaining trees, working to stay out in the open, possible now since so many trees had cleared out. The sun was shining brightly, forcing the dark ones to run from tree to tree to avoid getting burnt. It wasn't easy for them to find shelter. None of the trees had leaves and couldn't offer much protection. For the moment, this was the only thing saving Jer and Kimber from becoming dinner. But Kimber knew Jer was going to tire soon. He couldn't keep going at this pace. It would be hard even for Kris and Gabe.

"Are you okay?" she shouted.

"Fine," he panted. "I've been practicing…with a flour sack full of sand."

She stifled a giggle. "Did you at least give me a face?"

"Of course. Hair, too. No more talking now. I need my breath to run!"

Jer accelerated, pushing his way through the thick moss and bits of remaining snow. They were close to the road now. Surely the Ko-goks wouldn't follow them there? Kimber glanced back, and immediately wished she hadn't. They were gaining, with Straif at the lead. He looked more insane than usual, his arms flailing strangely about as he ran. The flailing didn't seem to be slowing him down, though, and with his hood up, he seemed willing to risk the sun.

She and Jer were going to get caught and it was all her fault. If only she hadn't gotten so huffy over such a small thing and wasted time dis-cussing it in the middle of the Forest Immortal. Well, it wasn't a *small* thing, but it wasn't nearly as big as what they were facing now.

She opened her mouth to warn Jer about the dark ones when some-thing hit her in the back and she flew through the air. Kimber closed her eyes and waited to smash into the ground, where she and Jer, help-less to escape, would be overrun by dark ones and eaten alive.

And the only thing her mind could conjure up was that if Jer died, it would be all her fault.

Chapter Twenty-Six

Outrun a Tsunami

"Are the Dryads following us?" Gabe shouted to Abazi as they raced through the woods. They ran shoulder to shoulder, keeping pace with one another. With any luck they wouldn't meet anyone on the way to the mill—their situation would be hard to explain away. Hopefully people were staying at home because of the flooding and wouldn't see a thing. And if anyone saw something, well, maybe they'd put it down to some sort of hallucination. It's what he would have done a year ago.

"Yes," she yelled back. "So are the Ko-goks."

"Then Kris and the others should be safe," he pushed out between pants.

"Maybe, but you and I are going to get our butts kicked."

As they hit the main road, Gabe glanced back to see the horde of Dryads still pelting after them, not exactly at top speed, but fast enough, with Ailem and Weachu pushing them onward, obviously enjoying being in command. Behind them surged a dark wave of Ko-goks.

"Not if I can help it," he said. "I think we can outrun them. They look like they're on drugs."

A trickle of sweat ran down Abazi's cheek. "What's the plan after that?"

There was no plan. Not really. This had all been Abazi's idea. His main goal had been to keep the Dryads from killing Mrs. Morrigan, and to stop the dark ones from going after Kris and the others. Now they were heading to the one place that was probably the worst place they could end up. First of all, Oswald was there, and Abazi would probably go right to his side, and if Gabe saw that he might self-combust in a shower of thorns and white petals. Second, the bridge was the only safe way to get to the mill. The mudflats were like snares waiting to be sprung, and with all the flooding, were likely covered in water anyway. Once they crossed the bridge, they'd be trapped.

"We're heading to the mill, aren't we?" she answered her own question.

"Unless you can think of someplace better." *Please think of someplace better.* "If we go there, we'll end up trapped, you know."

"So you're saying we'll be treed." She laughed in gasps. "Oh, I've been waiting *forever* to use that one!" She glanced at him. "You're not laughing. To tree someone can also mean to force them into a difficult situation."

"You know it's not funny when you have to explain your jokes."

"I have to explain my jokes because they're so brilliant and go over everyone's heads."

Gabe looked back again and wished he hadn't. The dark ones were gaining on them. The sensation that they were trying to outrun a tsunami washed over him. He might be invincible, but the others weren't. "Just keep running."

Abazi glanced over at him. "I know they're gaining on us. We have to move faster."

"It's the Dryads. They're struggling." He saw the stoplights ahead. "We've got about a mile to go. I'm going back there, to help keep them on track. You lead the way."

"Be careful, Gabe."

"You, too."

He peeled off and started running the opposite direction. The Dryads watched him confusedly. "Just follow Abazi!" he told them, pointing. "Follow that girl." Thankfully they seemed to understand. Soon he was level with Weachu and Ailem. "We have to go faster."

"We have to go faster," Weachu mimicked. "We ain't deer, maddy. This is as quick as it gets with this lot."

Gabe glanced over his shoulder. The gap was narrowing. "So ye're okay with bein' meat for Straif and his goons?"

"They won't catch me," Weachu boasted.

"They'll catch ye first," Ailem yelled. "Ye're the one holdin' us back with yer wobbly legs."

Weachu put on a burst of speed. "I've been holdin' back for ye, dobberhead! Clunk for brains!"

"No need to be callin' names," Gabe cautioned.

"I can outrun all of ye," Weachu cried, sprinting past several of the Dryads.

Ailem watched him go. "What a bampot. Always were one, since he were a seedling."

"Can ye make them go faster?" Gabe asked. "The dark ones are gettin' really close."

"Where ye takin' us again?" Ailem wondered. "Ye sure it's better than where we were?"

"I have an idea, something that should keep us safe." He did, actually, but he wasn't sure he could make it work.

A howl sounded from behind Gabe, not that far from him. Only thirty feet, give or take. Straif was right on their heels.

"Go, go, go!" Gabe yelled at Ailem, and the Dryad surged forward, using his hands to push the others onward. "Run like yer life depends on it!"

Because it does.

Abazi had reached the turn that led to the mill. She veered right, but several Dryads kept running straight. "Abazi!" She stopped and looked back. Gabe pointed. She rolled her eyes, then pelted after the others, corralling them like a sheep dog and herding them toward the turn. At last they were on the right course, but it had cost them precious seconds.

Fifteen feet separated the dark ones from Gabe. He pulled out his willow whip and cracked it in the air behind him. He didn't take time to see what damage he'd inflicted, but the screams told him he'd done some. He could see why Jer liked the whip so much. Too bad he wasn't here to use it. But he could help Kris, so that was something, if he could get over his grumps.

Without looking back, Gabe cracked the whip several more times, hoping to slow the dark ones. Abazi had reached the bridge now. "Cross it!" he yelled. "Hurry!"

She pushed the Dryads across and they ran like lemmings toward the mill. Weachu had sprinted to the front, and they followed him inside. Gabe hoped the Wych Elms would do the right thing, pick the right path, and keep the others safe, and he hoped he could rely on them.

The dark ones roared behind him, furious to see their prey escape to safety, and sped up. He cracked the whip over and over, until he reached the bridge himself. "Go, Abazi! I'll hold them off."

But the stubborn girl wouldn't leave him, and together, they stood facing the dark mass racing toward them, determined to kill whatever was in their path. In a few moments, the Ko-goks would overrun them, and all would be lost.

Gabe looked over at Abazi. "I love you," he breathed, knowing she wouldn't hear his words, knowing she wouldn't return them. Then he turned to face death.

~~~~~~

"Dad?" Kris called out, barely able to breathe. "What are you doing up here?" Kris's dad stepped into the turret, cautiously, his eyes taking in the scene before him. It had to be fantastical, unbelievable. "I can explain—" Kris began, but Dad held up his hand.

"We already know."

"We?"

Mom stepped into the room. She was holding something in her hand, something familiar. Kris couldn't believe his stupidity. He'd left his notebook—the one chronicling their adventures—out in the open for anyone to find. Dad saw him looking at it. "I was taking a break and found that on your bed. I didn't mean to pry, but the pictures you drew are so amazing, I just had to see more. Then I realized you'd written a story, as well. Again, I couldn't help myself, and I started reading. What you wrote was so good that I kept going. At first I thought that you'd made it all up." His voice trembled a little. "But then, well, it seemed to parallel too much with our lives. When I remembered the stories I'd heard growing up about the forest, I started thinking, what if?"

"So you believe what I wrote?"

Dad nodded. "I gave it to your mom. I wanted to see if she had the same thought...that it was real."

Kris looked at her. "And?"

Mom waved her arm around the room. "I'd be a fool not to believe. Here's proof right in front of me." She looked up at Grandma May, standing perfectly still on the platform. "I suppose you've known all along." She was trying not to sound hurt, and not succeeding.

"Of course I didn't, Ayla! I would've told you, if only to protect your kids. But I wouldn't keep something like that from you anyway."

"So why are they here? Why are you all up here? And where are Gabe and Jer?" Mom was starting to look frightened.

"Jer's not in his room?" Kris questioned.

Dad shook his head. "No one's upstairs."

"He did say he was going out," Mom added. "I heard him close the front door."

"He could be anywhere," Kris whispered. He swallowed and looked at Mom and Dad, making a decision. "I think I know where he's gone. Gabe, too." Actually, he really only knew for sure where Gabe was going. But maybe, just maybe, if Jer had gone out into the woods, he'd followed Gabe.

"Then we'd better go after them."

Kris held up his hands to stop his parents. "No offense, Mom, but I think you should stay here. You'll need to keep the place safe. The dark ones I wrote about? Well, they're coming here. Right now. They're going to try to get in, but you'll have to keep them out." He said this part slowly and seriously. "You'll have to protect everyone here."

Her eyes widened. "But what about you?"

"I'll be okay. I know how to fight them. They don't like the touch of wood. Gather everything you can that's wood, and then lock the turret doors behind you. I locked the door to the secret entrance already—"

"Secret *entrance?*" Mom exclaimed, looking dazed. "Are you kidding me?"

"I'll explain it later, Ayla," Grandma May interjected. "As much as I can, anyway. Right now we'd better do what the boy says. You read his book. He's been at this for a while. They all have."

"I brought them here," Mom moaned.

"If we're throwing blame around," Dad said, "then I'm the one who's at fault. If it weren't for me, we wouldn't be here."

"Oh, Keith!" Mom looked ready to cry. "It's not *your* fault you got sick!"

He straightened his shoulders. "Then it's no one's fault and we might as well just accept that now. Kris, you go, and we'll hold down the fort. Find your brothers and bring them back."

Kris was relieved his parents were staying, but also felt a bit worried at the prospect of going out amongst all those dark ones alone. There were so many, and they looked insane. That last battle with them had been intense, and a little more painful than he'd bargained for. But he had little choice. He had to find his brothers and bring them back here, for their sakes, and for Hollie's. Kris's own selfishness had doomed her to this fate. It was up to him to do everything he could to help her.

He had an idea that maybe he knew how to save her—Gabe's cloak. He had to get it and bring it back, and the only way he was going to make that happen was to have Gabe in it. No way was Gabe going to part with his precious cloak now. Jer was right. There was something about it that perhaps wasn't the healthiest for anyone who wore it too long.

"Follow me, and we'll get you some weapons, then you go up to the turret and don't let anyone in. Grandma May, you be lookout."

She gave him a mocking salute, but her eyes were proud. "You boys are a credit to your ancestry. Good solid Mainers." Kris wondered if she'd still think that when she found out that Gabe was a tree spirit and that Kris had the hots for one.

Mom and Dad followed him downstairs and took all the baseball bats, except one, which Kris took for himself, and any staffs that had been left behind. They didn't speak as they worked, and Kris worried that they were reconsidering letting him go alone. But as he prepared to go outside his mom only gave him a hug. "Be careful," she murmured in his ear.

"You, too." He hugged his dad. "Get upstairs, lock everything. I don't want to open this door until you're secure."

With a few last worried glances backward, they disappeared down the hall to the turret. When Kris heard the first lock click shut, he reached toward the hooks near the door and lifted the car keys, careful not to let them jingle. He'd seen them while reaching for the bats, and that's when the thought occurred to him. He could drive to the mill.

Well, he couldn't actually drive, but he'd seen Gabe do it and Gabe had let him try it once in the yard. He'd started the truck on his second attempt, no problem. How hard could it be?

As it turned out, very hard.

Dashing out to the truck, he could hear the Ko-goks' footsteps barreling toward him. He jumped inside the cab, taking in the smell of rust and oil and old leather, and jerked on his seatbelt. It wasn't a very good one, but it would have to do. He hadn't realized his hands were shaking until he tried to shove the key into the ignition. He couldn't make it fit. He closed his eyes and tried to make himself calm down, but it was hard knowing the dark ones were coming.

The dark ones are coming!

His eyes sprung open and he tried the key again. This time it went in and he cranked it to the right. Nothing happened. Crap. Something was wrong with the car. What was it? No gas? Dead battery? Blown engine?

He looked up. A dark one was loping around the side of the barn, not even bothering to be sneaky. Not thinking, Kris stomped down on the clutch and brake, and cranked the key. The truck started and he eased up on the clutch, vowing never to let himself think too much on anything again.

Stomping on the gas, the truck lurched forward, sputtered, and threatened to die. Kris pushed down harder on the gas and the truck's engine mellowed out. Remembering at the last second to steer, Kris yanked on the wheel, just missing the corner of the barn. In front of him, hundreds of dark ones filled the driveway. He honked the horn, but they didn't move. He knew they were the enemy and they'd eat him if they could, but he didn't like the idea of running them over. It didn't seem like good sportsmanship.

He cranked down the window. "Get out of the way!" They didn't move, just continued surging toward him like mindless zombies. "Move, move, *move!*"

The first one he hit made a sickening thud against the hood of the truck. Kris winced and glanced in the rearview mirror, stupidly relieved to see the dark one pushing itself to its feet. Apparently, getting hit by a truck wasn't enough to kill the creeps. Even so, as if by telepathy, the other Ko-goks seemed to get the message that being hit by a truck, while not lethal, wasn't going to feel good, and they ambled out of his way. Seeing the opening, Kris pushed down on the gas and the truck sped forward.

The engine was making a weird noise now and Kris remembered that he had to shift. But how? Oh, yeah. Gabe had told him he needed to push in the clutch, then crank on the stick. He did this, causing a horrible shrieking sound, but it soon died away. Mission accomplished. But he still had to make the turn onto the main road. He just wouldn't stop, that's all. Typically no one was coming from the left anyway since it was a dead end.

When he whipped out onto the road, with no harm done, Kris gave himself a mental pat on the back. He was awesome at this! He couldn't wait to get his license. Maybe he could even be a racecar driver.

Then he saw the stoplights, the ones Gabe had dreaded when he'd first started driving the truck. "Be green," Kris repeated over and over. But they were green now and a pick-up truck was approaching from town. Oh, no. The truck was going to trigger the light. Green switched to yellow, bright with warning.

"Slow down!" the light screamed.

"I can't!" he screamed back. There was no way he was going to be able to get the truck going again, uphill, with a tricky clutch. He had to take his chances.

The light turned red. Kris was only about twenty feet away when the truck coming from town started to make its left turn, right in front of Kris. Within feet of each other, he saw the other driver's eyes widen. Grandpa Hawthorne! Kris roared past him, within inches of hitting his back bumper, then slowed to a stop a hundred yards down the road, where it flattened out.

Letting the truck idle, he peered out the window. Grandpa was coming his way, fast. He roared past Kris, did a cookie, and headed back, stopping to face him. "What in the name of Sam Hill are you doing, boy?"

"I can't stop, Grandpa! You have to go to the house. They're under attack." He cringed a little, dreading saying this next part. "Tree spirits have gone bad and they're after Mom and Dad and Grandma May."

Grandpa Hawthorne eyed him warily and Kris was sure he was going to get out of his truck and drag Kris from his. But he surprised Kris, his mouth curving up into a happy grin. "So they're real, huh?" He slapped the steering wheel. "Dangnabbit, I knew it! Hee, hee! Vernon owes me twenty buckeroos!"

"You know about them?"

"I've heard a thing or two." He couldn't stop grinning.

"I'm off to save Gabe and Jer. I can't stay."

"Then I'll head to the house." Kris had never seen Grandpa looking so thrilled in his life.

"They hate the touch of dead wood."

Grandpa nodded. "Good thing I always carry this with me." He reached up to the truck's ceiling and pulled down a well-polished, somewhat nicked-up, cricket bat. "Never much cared for the game, but I always loved their bats."

"Whoa, Grandpa!" Kris whistled. "That'll work perfectly!"

Grandpa touched his hat. "Give 'em hell, son." He turned straight and punched the gas, tearing away from Kris like a speed demon.

"Right back at ya, G-pa!" Kris stepped on the gas and within a short time was approaching the entrance to the mill. He hardly slowed down and the truck skidded sideways, just barely making the turn. Then he punched it again, praying the truck would hold out, that he wouldn't forget to shift.

The moment he cleared the woods, he saw them. The dark ones. They had Gabe and Abazi trapped by the bridge, closing in like a swarm of wasps, stingers out, ready to deliver the kiss of death. Kris clung tight to the steering wheel and mumbled under his breath, "Come on, baby. Just a little farther," as he hit pothole after pothole, each one threatening to throw a wheel, break an axle, send him flying into the river. Fifty yards from the bridge, the engine started making an ominous knocking sound and smoke billowed from under the hood.

The swarm descended on Gabe and Abazi. He was too late! Kris slammed the palm of his hand on the horn and it blared loudly. The dark ones spun in unison, and Gabe and Abazi took the opportunity to start climbing up the bridge. Kris kept blasting the horn and speeding toward the Ko-goks. This time there was no way he could avoid hitting them.

They seemed to sense this and leaped aside as he closed in. As he whizzed past they were so close he could see the saliva dripping from their rotting teeth. He was almost at the bridge now, heading straight toward Straif and Feltry, both were pushing other Ko-goks aside as they struggled to get out of the path of the truck. And then he was past them.

He stomped on the brake, remembering at the last second to push in the clutch at the same time. "Jump!" he screamed at Gabe and Abazi. "Hurry!" His rearview mirror showed the Ko-goks regrouping, spurred by anger. They'd nearly had their prey and Kris had thwarted them. A few long seconds later, there were two thumps, followed by a knock on the window. Kris turned to see Gabe give him a thumbs-up, and he stomped on the gas, a thought nagging at his mind. Where were Jer and Kimber?

Halfway across the bridge, the knocking grew scarily loud and more smoke rolled out. Then, just like that, the engine quit and the truck rolled to a stop. "Crap!" He jumped out. "Something's wrong!" he yelled to Gabe. "It just quit on me." He reached up to Abazi. "Come on!" She grabbed his hand and jumped onto the bridge. Gabe followed after her.

The three of them tore down the bridge and Kris could only hope the truck would slow the dark ones down enough to allow him and Gabe and Abazi time to get into the mill.

When they reached the end of the bridge, Gabe grabbed Kris's arm. "I've got an idea. We have to raise the bridge."

"I think the lever's stuck," Kris told him. On their first trip out to the mill he'd noticed it and wanted to try it out. It didn't budge, and the others had gotten too far ahead so he wasn't able to see what was wrong. Maybe it just needed a little more persuasion. He ran over to the lever and yanked hard on it. It didn't move, just like last time.

Gabe and Abazi joined in, groaning as they pulled, but nothing happened. The Ko-goks were coming, though more cautiously than necessary, as though even in their addled state, they knew this place was cursed. In the past, it was where the Dryads sent troublemakers. It was the 'Other Side,' their place of exile, where outcasts were sent to die. Despite what they felt about it, however, they came on, slowly at first, but once past the truck, more quickly.

"Step aside," Gabe told Kris and Abazi. "I have to do this alone."

"You and whose army?" Kris laughed. "It's rusted. It won't move."

"It will for me," Gabe said, sounding more than a bit arrogant.

Abazi pulled Kris away. "Just let him." He didn't want to go, but now was not the time to let his ego get in the way. This was the wisest course to take, he knew, though a perverse part of him wanted Gabe to fail.

"Fine." He moved farther back, getting ready to run, if need be.

Kris thought Gabe would simply transform his arm into a tree branch and muscle the lever into moving, but his brother surprised him when he crouched down next to two tiny trees growing by the bridge and touched them. Within a few seconds, the scrubby little seedlings began to get bigger. Their trunks widened and their branches lengthened. Within a minute, they were nearly full-grown. Gabe leaned closer and seemed to be talking to them, his lips moving slowly, his eyes dreamy. The two trees reached under the bridge and grabbed hold. There was a horrendous snap, and Kris watched in amazement as their side of the bridge, creaking and groaning, rose into the air. The dark ones howled in fear as they started to slide backward. There was no way to hang on and they tumbled and catapulted down the bridge, back to the other side. Luckily for them, they'd been past the truck, which slid before them, coming to a stop thirty yards from the bridge.

Kris couldn't believe it. Those trees had lifted a bridge into the air. He glanced over at Abazi, wanting to share his awe, but she was staring at Gabe with a strange look in her eyes. He wondered what she was thinking, then shook his head. It didn't matter. They had to get moving. Who knew how long the trees would be able to hold the bridge.

"Come on, Gabe!" Kris yelled to his transfixed brother. "We need to get to the mill."

Gabe patted the trees on their trunks, spoke a few last words, then rose to face Kris and Abazi. "The power of a tree—it cannot be denied. It takes hold of ye, shapes ye, it's who ye are. Ye and the tree. One and the same. Sap and blood. Wood and bone. Intertwined."

Kris frowned. It was a strange thing to say. "Right. Sure. Now come on."

Abazi grabbed Kris's arm and pointed. "What's that?"

Kris shaded his eyes and peered across the river. Lurching down the road was a giant tree, its roots lifting up and down as it walked. In its boughs sat two figures…Jer and Kimber. Kris's elation at seeing them soon turned to fear. The dark ones had spotted the loping tree, clumsy and slow, and were now amassing to overtake it. The tree, seeing them, veered toward the river.

Just as it reached the bank, the dark ones swarmed it and began crawling up its pale gray tree trunk, threatening to topple the whole tree, along with Jer and Kimber, into the roaring black water.

Chapter Twenty-Seven

This Place of Ghosts

Something smacked against Jer's back and the weight of Kimber was gone as though it had never been there. He felt himself flying through the air, dark shadows whizzing by. "Kimber!" he screamed, terrified for her safety. She didn't stand a chance against the frenzied dark ones.

He readied himself for impact, preparing to jump up and fight to defend Kimber, but he never landed. He just kept flying through the air. It was the strangest thing. He glanced back to see Kimber flying alongside him, and was thrilled to see she was all right, though her eyes were closed tight and she seemed to be mumbling something to herself.

Jer looked down and saw a tree branch wrapped around his waist. They weren't flying; someone was carrying them. Had Gabe come back to save them? No, the bark was different than Gabe's. This bark was smooth and gray and...he recognized it.

"Aurelia! Is that you?" There was no answering voice, but the branch around his waist squeezed lightly. It *was* Aurelia, and she was heading toward the road, following after the others.

Seeing their prey fly up and out of reach, Straif directed his minions to forge ahead. Soon the dark ones left them behind as they chased after Gabe and the other Dryads. They turned onto the main road, and Aurelia stuck to the ditch, where she could freeze if someone drove by. Hopefully they wouldn't notice the two humans floating in the air.

Jer was beyond relieved that Aurelia had rescued them, but he was worried about her. She'd been so weak before; this couldn't be good for her. He checked on Kimber again. She had opened her eyes at last and was looking about in wonder and relief. "We're alive, and we're *flying*! What's going on?"

"It's my friend, Aurelia. She's carrying us."

"I should've known. Hello, Aurelia!" Kimber giggled. "She just squeezed me!"

Jer stared at her in surprise as she bobbed up and down and swung back and forth with each step Aurelia took. "You know Aurelia?"

"Oh, yes. For quite a while now. She and her kind have been watching over us since that first time we entered the woods."

"Why didn't you tell me?"

Kimber looked contrite. "I really wanted to, Jer, but she thought it better that the fewer who knew about her and her League of Trees, the better."

Jer felt hurt at being left out. Why was he *always* being left out? His cheeks flushed and his breathing grew labored and he only wanted to strike out, to hurt others as they hurt him. Not only did his brothers treat him like a kid, so did the Dryads. Kimber, too!

It'll be hard. It always is, coming-of-age.

Aurelia's voice echoed in his mind and Jer swallowed hard. He wanted to stay mad, but how could he? He demanded to be treated like an adult, yet when the first hard thing came along, he went straight to anger, just like a kid.

He took a deep breath. Even though he didn't want to, he tried very hard to consider what Kimber had told him from an adult perspective. The League of Trees sounded like a spy network, he determined, and the first rule of spying is to tell only who and what needs to be told.

"She was probably right about that," he acknowledged, and felt a little better, but likely only because Aurelia had trusted him enough to include him in the league's work when she'd asked him to help. That must count for something. Perhaps all that spy work he'd done when he was nine was finally paying off!

"Why isn't she talking?" Kimber asked, her blue eyes worried.

"She's too weak," Jer explained, feeling even better since he knew something Kimber didn't. "I went to her today, looking for answers. I met her near the Dark Domain, you see, after I hit my head. She knew how to fix it, so I thought maybe she'd know something about how to help the Dryads get better. Sorry I didn't tell you, but you were mad at me."

"Oh, I already know you met her. I brought you to her."

"You?"

"It wasn't easy. You're very heavy." Kimber smiled at him. "But I couldn't just leave you on that nasty old field to be eaten."

"So you *saved* my life?"

She eyed him uncertainly. "That's one way to look at it."

Jer had finally found what he was looking for and he was ecstatic. "That's the only way to look at it, Kimber! Now you know for certain that you're hugely important to us, to *me*." He thumped his chest. "You're not only needed, you're my *savior*. And if that's not enough for you, the fact that you were the first of us that Aurelia trusted has to count for something."

"Well—"

"There's no doubt, Kimber," Jer interrupted. She was going to hear this whether she wanted to or not. "So just accept that you're awesome, and…and I love you for it." Jer couldn't believe the L word had just come out of his mouth, but if now, when their lives were at stake, wasn't the time to use it, when was there a good time?

Her eyes were suddenly bright. "All right. I will accept it. I will." She didn't look away from him, but she also didn't say, "I love you, too, Jer," which was a little worrisome, but he was determined not to focus on the negatives like he always did.

"Aurelia told me something about Gabe," he said, filling the awkward silence, "about how he can save the trees, but I'm not sure it's the answer."

"Why not?"

"Because it's dangerous!" Jer had to shout as a pickup truck roared by them. Strangely, Aurelia didn't stop walking.

"Gabe is used to danger," she yelled back, looking around.

"Not this kind," Jer answered, but Kimber didn't hear him. She was watching the road. He followed her gaze in time to see the truck that had passed them, and which looked just like theirs, nearly sideswipe another one. Seconds later, the second truck peeled around and pulled up next to their old beater truck. The two talked for a minute, then parted ways, both heading in opposite directions. Luckily the driver didn't seem to see Jer and Kimber up in the tree, though this time Aurelia froze in place while the truck sped past.

"I think that was my Grandpa Hawthorne!" Jer cried. But who was driving their truck out to the mill? "We have to hurry!" he shouted and Aurelia gave up on the ditch, taking to the road. Before long she was turning down the mill road. When they saw the bridge, Jer was stunned to see it covered by dark cloaks, thick as an oil spill. Aurelia saw it, too, and did her best to move faster. Then something strange happened. The bridge tilted, spilling the dark ones to the ground. The Ko-goks howled angrily, until one of them noticed Aurelia.

"To the river!" Jer shouted. It was their only hope, but not much of one. With its swiftly flowing water and massive chunks of ice, it would be hard for Aurelia to cross.

She clomped to the river's bank and stopped, uncertain what to do next. There was a loud thumping noise, several, in fact, and Jer glanced down to see a swarm of dark ones covering Aurelia's trunk. He looked around, desperate for an idea on how to get them out of this. He spotted Gabe and Kris—he must have been driving the truck—and Abazi on the other side of the river and waved frantically to them. They raced to the water's edge, but it was obvious there wasn't much they could do to help.

Kimber seemed to be listening to something, then she looked at Jer. "Get ready to climb."

"What?"

"Aurelia is going to make a bridge for us. We have to cross her."

There was no time for discussion. Aurelia swung Jer and Kimber over onto her trunk and they both grabbed hold. As Aurelia began to bend, Jer hung on tightly while keeping his eye on Kimber, who was below him. She was strong on the inside, but her body didn't always cooperate with her spirit.

Aurelia's limbs touched the riverbank on the other side, then she burrowed her branch tips into the ground, to create a stable arch. "Come on!" Jer called to Kimber. She scrambled after him, her fumbly fingers struggling to grab hold. Behind her crawled the voracious dark ones, on the hunt, desperate and angry and half out of their minds. Jer could hear their snapping teeth; see spittle flying in all directions. The metallic smell of blood and rusted iron and cracked ice overwhelmed his senses. It was the smell of death.

They were halfway across the river when Kimber cried out, "Jer! My brace! It's stuck."

He scooted back to her, trying to ignore the dark ones clambering toward them. When he reached her side, he tried to wiggle the brace free from Aurelia's branch, but it was hard to use force without one of them falling off the tree. Making it worse, whenever he moved, Kimber seemed to move in the opposite direction.

"Don't let them get away!" screamed Straif, still on the ground.

Jer looked back to see Feltry advancing on him. He wouldn't be able to free Kimber in time. Swallowing hard, he straightened and turned about, balancing precariously on two branches. Surreptitiously, he pulled his bandalore from his pocket and attempted to slip the small loop in the string over his middle finger. But his hands were shaking and the tiny opening didn't want to fit and he was trying not to let Feltry see what he was doing. "Come on," he whispered to himself. "Come on!" Finally the loop slipped over his knuckle and he held the bandalore loosely in his hand, at his side, out of sight. Feltry was close, but not close enough, and it was torture waiting for him. What if he missed his throw? What if it had no effect?

Don't think about it, idiot, he told himself harshly. *Just focus on what you're doing.* It wasn't easy with the roar of the water, the frantic shrieks from the dark ones, the yelling from his brothers and Abazi.

"We're a team, Jer!" Kimber shouted. He glanced back at her, surprised to see tears in her lovely blue eyes. "And I love you, too."

Jer felt a surge of joy leap up inside him. She *loved* him! Feeling invincible, he turned about, just as Feltry was about to leap, and let loose with the most solid, most awesome throw of his life. The wooden disc flew out and smacked Feltry right on the forehead—a perfect shot— then whizzed back into Jer's outstretched hand. Feltry spewed a curse and fell sideways into the river.

Jer didn't wait to see what happened to him. More dark ones would be coming and he needed to focus. "Stay absolutely still," he told Kimber. She nodded, her eyes wide and frightened. He studied the situation briefly, then reached down and carefully maneuvered her brace out of the tree branch as though he'd done it many times before. When she was free, he shouted, "Go! I'll be right behind you." Kimber began to crawl forward, struggling to get past all the branches. The tree limbs made a sort of ladder, but a very challenging one. Kimber would need more time than the Ko-goks were willing to give her.

Jer turned around, readying his bandalore. Dark one after dark one came after him and he let his bandalore fly, knocking them into the water. Some were lucky like Feltry, sweeping toward the low part of the bridge, and able to grab on. Some weren't. When there was a lull in the attack, Jer turned and started after Kimber. She was close to the shore and Gabe was meeting her halfway, his tree hands outstretched to grab her.

Jer wobbled and swayed as he made his way along Aurelia's trunk, which was growing increasingly narrow. She quivered beneath his feet and he tried to speed up. She couldn't stay this way much longer; she was going to fall into the river!

And then, just when he thought he was going to tumble into the water, Jer was across, Kris helping him make the last few steps safely. Solid ground had never been so welcomed, but there was no time to celebrate. Aurelia was in trouble. She groaned and tried to pull her branches from the ground, but she was too weak, and the weight of the dark ones was pulling her down, into the river.

Gabe reached out and touched Aurelia's boughs, but instead of coming loose, something else happened. He was getting her to do a sort of gymnastic move, a back flip like what Abazi did. Straif, halfway along the trunk, bellowed angrily as he struggled to hang on. Aurelia did a sort of buck, like a wild bronco, and Straif and the remaining dark ones flew through the air, landing on the shore, back where they'd started

With one last burst, her roots were on the far side of the river, along with the rest of her, and as soon as she hit the ground, she began to shrink. In seconds she was in human form, crumpled and still. Gabe scooped her up and began to run. "To the mill!"

Jer knew it wouldn't take long for the dark ones to figure out that they could simply climb over the bridge. It wouldn't be easy, but with their tree arms, they'd be able to do it. Luckily, they weren't thinking as clearly as they normally would, and their movements were spastic, giving Jer and the others time to get away.

The trip to the mill seemed to take forever and he couldn't shake the feeling that at any moment someone's hand would clamp down on his shoulder and they would be overrun and he'd lose Kimber. He couldn't lose her now. Not when she'd told him she loved him. Not now. Not ever.

Once inside the old, echoing building, Gabe led them to the place where they'd left the Rogues. Jer knew something was wrong before they even entered the dimly lit room—a strange odor was emanating from it. He tried to place it, then realized it smelled like decaying leaves and earth, a smell he normally liked, but in this context, it meant bad things.

The Rogues, along with the new Dryads, were packed into the room, and all were still as statues. "Are they dead?" Kris cried. "Tell me they're not dead!"

One of the bodies stirred, then sat up. It was Oswald, and he looked terrible. His eyes were red-rimmed, his skin covered in dark welts, and his bones stuck out like twigs under a sheet. "Who comes to this place?" he wheezed. "This terrible place. This place of ghosts."

"That's what my people call it," Abazi said softly. "A place of ghosts, and that's what they are. Gabe, do something!"

Standing in the middle of the room, still holding Aurelia, Gabe studied Abazi, a strange look in his eyes. Moments passed, then he carried Aurelia over to Oswald and gently set her on the ground. He touched her arm and nodded, as if finishing up some sort of conversation between them. For some reason, the gesture made Jer uncomfortable, like something had happened that he didn't want to happen.

Oswald regarded Gabe rather unsteadily, his head swaying on his neck. "How did ye find her?"

"Let's just say she found me." Gabe stood up. "The dark ones are comin'. We have to figure out what to do next. We can't stay here. It'll only be a matter of time before they break in."

"You know her?" Abazi pointed at Aurelia. She didn't seem to have heard a word Gabe had said. "How do you know her, Gabe?"

"She saved me life once," he told her calmly. "When I fell from the trees. She caught me, and she saved me." He gazed at Abazi triumphantly.

She returned his gaze with a stormy scowl. "She should have let you fall," she muttered, but not loud enough for Gabe to hear. But Jer heard it and his insides went icy. Gabe was the only hope for the Rogues, for all the Dryads, and if he knew Abazi hated him in that moment, he wouldn't be in his right mind to make the decision of his life.

And Jer needed his brother to be thinking clearly when he chose whether or not to die.

Chapter Twenty-Eight

Death Welcomed Him

"I need to talk to you," Jer whispered in Gabe's ear.

"Go ahead," Gabe said, feeling a little winded from what Aurelia had told him.

Jer looked around the room. "Not here."

"All right." Gabe already knew what Jer wanted to tell him. Aurelia had explained everything. She was the leader of the League of Trees, a group of Dryads whose aim was to save the Forest Immortal, and they'd been helping him as much as they could whenever he'd entered the woods. She was the one who'd caught him when he'd fallen from the treetops, the one who had helped them escape from the Dark Domain, the one who'd told him to read Mary Webb's book. With Isis gone, she was the only one who knew what he had to do.

He turned to the others. "We'll be back." Kris frowned, but stayed where he was, watching them go with suspicious eyes. He'd been strangely quiet since the bridge. Gabe didn't like it. A quiet Kris was an unpredictable Kris.

"I learned something," Jer said as soon as they were in the cathedral-like space near the entrance. "It was the day I got your cloak back."

"The day ye stole it, ye mean?"

Jer bit down on his lip, obviously fighting to keep his temper. "I got it back from the Ko-goks, who stole it from you."

"Whatever. I already know what ye're goin' to tell me."

"You do?" Jer looked worried. "Aurelia told you, didn't she?"

"I can read her mind, and she can read mine. She told me on the way to the mill."

"She told you *everything*?"

"She said that I have magic in me, something called tanneen. I can cure others with a touch," as he had with the Lady, "but only if they're in tree form. It's more painful for the Dryad that way, though, plus it would be hard to keep up because of the energy it requires. The alternative is for me to produce berries, which have tanneen in them, and the tanneen will cure the Rogues. Then they can use their acorns to help the other trees. I just have to pass through the cycle to make them. I can do that."

Jer put a shaking hand on Gabe's arm. "That's not all." He paused and pulled in a deep breath. "Did Aurelia tell you that going through the cycle will kill you? It takes a lot of strength and you likely won't survive, especially since you were sick. You can't do it, Gabe. You'll die."

Aurelia hadn't mentioned the dying part, though now Gabe understood what his inner voice had been telling him back in the woods. Now he knew whose death was necessary. His own. It didn't seem possible, and yet all too real. "But goin' through the cycle, it'll save everyone's lives? Hollie and the Rogues? The entire Forest Immortal?"

Jer nodded, his face pale. "But you'll die from it." He seemed determined to emphasize that part.

"I'm okay with that," Gabe boasted confidently. "It'll be a good death. A warrior's death."

Jer looked at him funny. "No, it won't! Remember how you said there's no good reason to get yourself killed? Especially if you're meant for better things?"

"I was wrong."

"No, you weren't. Don't do it, Gabe," Jer pleaded.

Gabe puffed himself up. "Ye can't stop me."

"I know I'm small," Jer growled, his change of tone abrupt. "And I get it that I'm younger than you and not as strong, but I'm smart, Gabe, and I know that you can't make a decision like that while you're wearing that cloak. You have to take it off."

Gabe recoiled, feeling strangely frightened. "Ye just want me cloak! Ye've taken it from me twice now. Ye understand its power and ye want it for yerself!" Gabe looked frantically about. He should have known this was coming, should have known Jer was up to no good. "Oswald wants to be King, and he wants Abazi, but she's mine! Everyone wants something from me." Gabe pointed accusingly at Jer. "Even ye. Especially ye."

Jer held up his hands. "You're wrong, Gabe. All I'm asking is that you take it off. You can hold on to it, just don't have it on your shoulders when you make your decision. Besides," Jer hesitated. "I really don't want your cloak, not after what happened to me. I'm scared it will try to make me do something I can't do, like before."

Gabe regarded his brother with distrust. "I don't believe ye. This cloak has made me braver than I've ever been and hasn't once led me astray." The memory of the night when he'd run down the road, when he'd thrown flower petals everywhere, came back to him. He quickly brushed it aside. What was a little flowering? Certainly nothing dangerous, and besides, he'd already flowered twice now and survived. "I feel like the King everyone wants me to be. I'm not even afraid of death anymore!"

"But a little fear is good for a person," Jer said, his voice stronger. "It keeps you from doing foolish things. Look, I'll go stand over there." He pointed to the door. "You take off the cape and consider what Aurelia is asking you to do. If you still want to do it, that's your choice, but you need to make it without the cape influencing you."

Gabe really didn't want to take off the cloak, but if it would convince Jer that he was serious, he'd have to do it. Jer did not give up on things easily. "Fine." He waved his brother away. "But if ye get anywhere near me, I'll toss ye out for the Ko-goks to eat."

"Got it," Jer replied and moved away.

When his brother was standing by the door, Gabe reached up and started to untie the cape. His fingers didn't want to work and he had to force them to do the job. His whole body rejected the idea of parting with his cloak, but it was necessary to show Jer that his big brother could function without it, that he'd feel exactly the same, cloak or not.

Finally, the tie was undone and he slowly slid the cloak off his shoulders. At first, nothing spectacular happened. He inhaled deeply, and he felt the same.

"Are you still willing to die?" Jer called from where he stood, twenty feet away.

Gabe looked at his brother, then down at the clump of wool clutched tightly in his hands. His heart started pumping hard and blood rushed to his head. *Die?* He would really *die* if he did what Aurelia had asked him to do? For some reason, he hadn't quite understood that part. How could he not have understood that? Jer was right. While wearing the cloak Gabe hadn't believed he could die.

Fear was the most powerful emotion Gabe knew, and the cloak took that fear away. Without it, Gabe felt frightened of life and all its sticky moments, and that fear made him tentative and indecisive. The reason he didn't ever want to make decisions was because he didn't want to be responsible for their consequences. If he made the wrong choice, the results could be devastating. Depending on what he decided now, he could die, or thousands could die.

But what if he'd been wrong about there being no good reason to die? What if the 'better thing' he was meant for was this moment in time? He couldn't save Dad's life when he'd gotten sick, could only stand by helplessly and hope for the best, but now he could save an entire species, an entire world.

Fingering the fine material, he remembered with a strange clarity what he'd read in one of Mary Webb's essays, *Roots*. "Therein is locked the very heart of spring." He repeated the words in his mind, and in that moment, it all came clear to him. The answer was inside him, deep in his roots.

"In the root, when April comes," she'd continued writing. "Someone awakes, rubs drowsy eyes, stretches drowsy hands, remembers a dream of light that troubled its sleep, and begins, with infinite precautions, finesse and courage, to work the miracle of which it has knowledge; 'eagerly watching for its flower and fruit, anxious its little soul looks out.'"

He'd told Abazi she couldn't forget her roots, but neither could he. He was a tree spirit, and he had to have faith that whatever happened, this was a necessary act that he must not forego. Besides, this would prove that being a tree didn't make him a ruthless killer. He needed to know that, more than he realized.

"You're not willing?" Jer called hopefully, and Gabe realized he was shaking his head. He wasn't saying no, just having a hard time believing that his death could save so many. It seemed such a small, simple thing, his sacrifice, and yet so big.

"I am," Gabe rasped, then louder. "I am willin'." He said it, and he meant it, though he wasn't sure who was more surprised, him or Jer. He'd always been so afraid of death, but not anymore.

Jer came running back to his side and flung his arms around Gabe. "I don't want you to die!"

"I know that." Gabe reached out and patted Jer on the shoulder. "But this makes up for some things I've done, things I've wanted to do. I wanted to kill Oswald that time in the ravine. I wanted to kill Straif, too. But doing this will absolve me. It will make things better."

"Your death doesn't make *my* life better!" Jer sobbed.

"Sure it does. Now you and Kris will have the turret." He smiled at his brother. "We'll meet again someday, Jer. Somewhere, somehow…"

Jer sniffed. "You won't change your mind?" Gabe shook his head. "Then you can't do it with the cape on." His blue eyes were stubborn. "In case you want to back out, and you can back out at any time…"

"No, I can't, Jer," Gabe said determinedly. "I have to do this. I can't let all these people die because I don't want to die myself. We all die someday. I'm just going a little earlier, is all." He held out the cloak. "Here. Take it. Someone else might need it."

Jer reluctantly reached out to take the cloak from Gabe's hands. "I'll hold on to it for you. Just in case."

There would be no 'just in case' because soon Gabe would be dead, and all his worries over. He should feel happy about that, but for some strange reason, his worries being over just made him sad. He shook the feeling off. This was no time to be sentimental. He had a job to do, and quickly. The Rogues were on the verge of death and the dark ones would likely find a way across the river soon. Every second counted.

"You'd better stay back," he told Jer. "I'm not sure exactly what's going to happen."

"Don't do it!" Jer exclaimed, twisting the cape in his hands. "Please, Gabe!"

But it was too late. Gabe had already let his tree-ness begin its work, consuming his human form until there was nothing but wood and sap and roots. He inhaled deeply and thought about budding leaves. It wasn't long before it felt as though his veins were slithering from his fingertips, and leaves unfurled as they hit the air. The sweet green smell of spring filled his senses and a surge of exhilaration buoyed his spirits. Step two was completed and he was fine, his mind still sharp and rational. Perhaps the flowering part would be harder, though he'd done it easily enough before.

He set about producing flowers, urging the buds to emerge, forcing them to unfold like a bird spreading its wings. By the time the apple scent of his white blossoms pervaded the air he only felt a little tired. This was going well.

One more step—transforming his flowers into berries—and he was done. He had a sudden flash of memory, something he'd forgotten until now. His meeting with the Lady, the quick transformation he'd written off as an illusion, all came back to him. He'd done this before, all of it, and he'd survived just fine.

Or had he? The sensation of pain, of pure agony, plagued his thoughts. Now he remembered. It had been the last step that had caused such torture, and it had only been his hand, turning for a mere second or two. He'd also been sharing the pain with the Lady; this time he'd have to take it all. So what would it feel like to turn his entire body and hold it until Jer could gather the necessary berries? Sheer torture, he guessed.

Surprisingly, knowing this did not change his mind. He was only worried about whether or not he could sustain the change long enough. He didn't think he could. "The cloak..." he slurred through his awkward tree mouth. "For the pain."

"Are you sure?" Jer asked. "You won't stop doing this once you have it on. You won't be able to back out."

"I know, but I won't be able to keep going without the cloak's help. Too painful."

Jer didn't offer any more argument. "It's on," he said when he was done. Gabe couldn't feel it, but he knew it was on him somewhere. His feeling of invincibility, like a drug, had returned. He could do anything! He opened his trees eyes and peered proudly at his outstretched branches, crooked and wild and covered with thorns and leaves and flowers.

It was time.

He closed his eyes again and imagined his flowers turning into berries, full and round, deep red, blood red. *So red that all the blood of men could never make it so again.* The flowers turned in on themselves, crushing all their being into a ball the size of a blueberry. That's when the pain hit. Gabe just managed to clamp his mouth shut in time, trapping the scream of agony bellowing up inside him. Holy hell, this was *awful.* He felt like his fingertips were being split open, his guts pulled out through his mouth, his brain frying in flames. He couldn't take it, even with the cloak. He couldn't go on.

He felt himself losing consciousness and jerked his tree body hard. He had to keep going. He had to! But he couldn't stop his cries of pain any longer. His mouth flew open and his shrieks shattered the still air around him and shook the walls, bursting any remaining windows.

"You have to stop, Gabe!" Jer's voice was horrified. "It's too much!"

"Can't," Gabe groaned as thousands more bursts of torture shot through him. "Pick the berries, Jer," he choked out. "Save the others."

"Kimber, help!" Jer shouted. "Help us!"

The sound of running footsteps echoed through the room. He didn't dare open his eyes to look at whoever had come. If he did, he'd lose his concentration and transform back into a human, and he couldn't do that. Not yet. But soon. He couldn't die as a tree.

The pain was subsiding a little now, but he felt horrible, like death. He understood what Aurelia had meant, that no one could survive this process. Slowly, bit by bit, it could be done. But not all at once. It was like giving birth to a million babies, at the same time.

"What's going on?" Abazi cried. Her voice echoed in the giant chamber, making his limbs shake. "Oh, Gabe, what have you done?" The despair corroding her words told Gabe he was right not to open his eyes. He must look terrible.

"He's saving the others with his berries," Jer pushed out thickly. "Do what you can to make him feel better, Kimber. Abazi and Kris, help me pick."

"Oh, Gabe," Kris moaned. "You didn't have to do this."

"Give the Dryads the berries," Gabe directed. "That will save them. Hollie, too."

"I can't believe you did this for them," Kris said, his voice full of tears. "You sounded like you were dying. Thank goodness you're still okay." Gabe didn't bother correcting Kris. He'd find out soon enough. For now Gabe needed his brother to stay focused and get the berries to the Rogues.

There was a lot of running back and forth and eventually a different sound penetrated the hazy pain engulfing Gabe's mind and body. It was singing. Kimber was singing to him. He tried to focus on that sound, worked with all his might, and slowly, slowly, the pain diminished. But with the pain went his focus. Before he knew it he was shrinking, and then he was human again, his head in Kimber's lap. She stroked his forehead and continued to sing.

"I couldn't help it," he croaked. "I couldn't keep the form." He opened his eyes and squinted up at her. She looked like an angel, the late afternoon sun shooting through the windows and catching her blond hair in a halo.

"It's all right," she soothed. "You did well."

"Are the others okay now?"

"I don't know. Just rest. Get yourself better."

"I'm going to die."

"No, Gabe," Kimber said assuredly. "You're going to be fine."

Someone came running up, then crouched down next to them. "Put this on him. I should've done what he said," Jer gasped, "but I wanted him to change his mind! And then he started screaming and thrashing about and I couldn't reach him."

"What are you talking about?" Kimber demanded. A spasm grabbed hold of Gabe and shook him like a ragdoll, and Kimber struggled to hold him down. "What's happening to him, Jer?"

"The transformation. It's killing him!" Jer cried. "Aurelia said it might and she was right. I should've stopped him. It's my fault!"

Gabe's seizure subsided and he reached out to place his hand on Jer's arm. "You did the right thing," he rasped. "Not...your...fault."

"Gabe!" Kimber shifted aside and soon different arms were holding him tight. Abazi. He could smell her unique scent, so lovely and enticing. He wished he could hold her back, but he couldn't move his arms. "Don't you die on me! Don't you dare!"

If he could smile, he would have. "Oh, Abazi," he murmured. "Bossy to the end."

"There's no end, Gabriel Hawthorne. You're staying here so I can boss you forever."

"Nothing is forever. It's okay, though. I can't feel anything, Abazi. I'm not in pain anymore."

"What do you mean? You can't feel your body? Oh, *God!*"

He shook his head. "It's okay. Really. It worked, right?" If he had saved the others, then he wouldn't be forgotten, wouldn't be left behind. Death made him think of being alone and lonely, and he didn't want to be forsaken. He could die now, because he had Abazi with him. "The others are okay?" he tried again.

Her only answer was to burst into sobs.

Gabe knew what that meant, and it was too much for his heart to handle. He let go, and his mind swirled into darkness. He did not welcome death, but it welcomed him.

Chapter Twenty-Nine

Go Down Fighting

"Hold him still," Kris panted, grabbing the cloak from Jer. "I'm putting it on him."

"It's too late," Jer despaired. "If I'd done it when he asked me to, he might still be alive."

"He's not dead yet." Kris wrapped the cloak around Gabe's still body, not letting himself dwell on the fact that if his brother wasn't dead, he soon would be. His skin was gray and cracked; blood trickled from his ears and nose. Kris didn't know what else to do. They'd given the berries to the Rogues and to the other Dryads, but nothing had changed. They were still sick. Gabe's sacrifice had been for nothing.

No, wait. There would be no sacrifice, because Kris wasn't going to let his brother die. They needed Gabe to lead them. He could be arrogant, especially with that cloak on, he could be a snot when he was feeling grumpy, and he could be a real pain in the butt when they played basketball, never letting any of Kris's shots go uncontested. But he made Kris a better person, plain and simple. He made them all better.

He might not be their real brother, biologically speaking, but he was the only brother Kris wanted. No one else would do. *Ever*.

His shaking fingers tied the strings, securing the cloak around Gabe's stiff shoulders. Abazi wasn't helping in the least, staring down at Gabe's bloody face as though in a trance. Kris took his shirtsleeve and tried to wipe away the blood, but he only made it worse, smearing it all over Gabe's face and neck.

"We need to get him to a doctor," Kimber insisted.

"We could try," Kris agreed. It was something, because there was nothing they could do for him here. "But we'd have to get past the Ko-goks." A loud boom sounded on the wall by the door, followed in quick succession by several more. "What's that?"

The bangs continued, growing louder and more numerous with every passing second. Soon the whole warehouse reverberated with the pounding and Kris could barely hear himself think.

Jer sat down heavily. "The dark ones must have found a way across the river. I locked the door, but they'll probably just knock it down."

Kris felt sick, crouched by his dying brother, the smell of blood like rusted iron mingling in the air with the damp. Dust motes sparkled in the sunbeams passing from window to floor, and Kris watched them drift upward, feeling surreal. "We can't fight them, just us."

"It won't be long before they get inside," Abazi said in a flat tone. "They'll go straight for Gabe. If he isn't dead yet, he will be. They'll tear him apart and drink his blood like it was a frappe. Then they'll go after us."

"Stop it, Abazi!" Kimber scolded. "We can't think that way."

"But I never got to tell him that I love him back!" she gasped, one hand clawing at her chest as though her heart was on fire. "He said it to me earlier. He said it, and I didn't say it back!"

"Don't give up on him," Kimber said, her tone softer. "Please, Abazi!"

Abazi stared at her friend. "Why? He's as good as dead. He's got blood coming out of his ears!"

"We can put him in the gear room. He'll be safer there if the Kogoks break in."

"I'm not leaving him," Abazi ground out. "I won't."

"Then we're all going to die. If you don't help us fight, Abazi, we'll all die," Kris repeated, obstinately. "And then Gabe's sacrifice will truly have been for nothing." He was saying anything he could think of to bring her back to them, to keep her from sinking into despair.

"I don't care."

Something big smashed against the small entry door and it dented inward like a tin can. "We've got less than a minute, tops," Kris calculated. He stood up. "Jer, take that board," he pointed at one lying on the ground close by, "and shove it under the doorknob. That should buy us a little more time." Jer stood and ran off. "I'm moving Gabe." He leaned down to pick him up.

Abazi clung to Gabe's limp body. "No!"

Kris sighed wearily. "You can go with him, Abazi."

She eyed him warily. "No tricks?"

Kris wished he had a trick up his sleeve, but he had nothing. "No tricks."

She let go of Gabe and Kris lifted him into the air. Gabe had a good twenty pounds on Kris, but he felt strangely light, as though all his solidness had abandoned him. Jer finished inserting the board under the door's knob and sprinted back to them. It was an old board and wouldn't hold long. "Come on." Kris started toward the gear room. A noise from the back of the mill spun him around, making Gabe's arms swing. Crap. The Ko-goks were trying to get in back there, too. They were surrounded by darkness.

Things were getting too serious for Kris. He couldn't do this on his own, not with Gabe half-dead, not with Abazi checking out on them. Kimber was great, but she was small and couldn't run fast. Jer was becoming a formidable opponent, but right now he looked shaken from fear and the guilt he was feeling about Gabe. He hadn't done anything wrong, but he wasn't seeing it that way.

Which left Kris on his own, with his own worries to deal with. Hollie was dying, and Kris had been counting on Gabe to somehow know the answer to how to save her. Feeling on the verge of falling apart himself, he bit his lip hard, then drew in a deep breath. Someone had to keep it together. Someone had to be the leader.

It turned out to be Jer.

"Get your weapons out *now*, Abazi!" Jer shouted at her, his expression furious.

She looked stunned. "But I-I…"

"Stop feeling sorry for yourself," he growled, "and do something. We aren't dead yet, and neither is Gabe! So we fight. If we die, we go down fighting!"

Her lower lip trembled and Kris was afraid she was going to break down right then. "You little snot!"

"I might be a snot," he shot back, "but at least I'm not a quitter!"

Abazi's eyes widened with fury. "I'm *not* a quitter!"

"Then what are you?"

"I-I'm a fighter. A warrior! That's what Abenakis do when things get hard! We fight!" It was the first time she'd ever said anything positive about her people and Kris could only stare at her in surprise. She glared at him. "What are you looking at?"

"A warrior?"

She grinned through her tears. "Damn right." She pulled out her bata and a willow whip.

"I'm going to check out the situation in the back," Jer said.

"We'll be in the gear room," Kris replied.

"I'm coming with you," Kimber said to Jer.

He paused, then nodded. "Of course you are." Together they hurried toward the room where the Dryads lay dying. Kris watched them go, wishing Hollie was here, wishing he had her wisdom and cleverness and sense of humor to get him through this.

"Get the door for me, Abazi," Kris ordered, staggering toward it. Gabe might be lighter than Kris had expected, but he still felt like deadweight. Kris grimaced. What an awful choice of words. Then he allowed himself a small smile. Gabe would love that, so he said it out loud. "You're deadweight, brother of mine."

Abazi gave him a strange look. "What are you doing?"

"I don't know. Just talking to him. Making a joke. Maybe it will help. It makes me feel better, anyway."

She swung open the door and it creaked in protest. "Then tell him he's got a lot of junk in his 'tree' trunk. That's funnier."

Kris laughed out loud. "That's terrible."

She grinned. "You wouldn't know a good pun if it bit you in the butt, Hawthorne."

He was careful not to hit Gabe's head on the doorframe as he maneuvered his brother into the gear room. It looked exactly as it had the last time they'd visited it, full of giant gears and smelling of oil and river muck. Kris gently set his brother on the ground, close to the gears, then pulled the cloak tighter around him. After checking to be sure he was still breathing, Kris left the room. "Are you staying with him?"

Abazi shook her head. "I want to, but that won't do him or us any good. You guys need me." Kris nodded and was about to shut the door behind them when he saw something across the room that made his skin crawl. The board holding the entry door snapped in two, sending the pieces flying, and the door swung open.

A mass of dark ones poured through the opening, screeching and hissing. Kris pulled out his willow whip, glad to finally get to use it, and grabbed the baseball bat from his back sling. He hefted it in his left hand. One of the many good things about being ambidextrous was that he could fight equally well with both hands, at the same time. It was why defenders from other basketball teams hated him.

Abazi already had her weapons out and they exchanged a worried look. "We're cut off from Jer and Kimber!" she yelled over the growing noise.

"We'll have to make our way toward them."

"But we can't leave Gabe alone."

The dark ones spotted them and raced toward them. "You watch him. I'll get the other two."

But it was too late. The dark ones filled the space quickly, blocking the way. "Get in the gear room, Abazi, and protect Gabe. I'll figure something out."

She hesitated, then nodded. "I have an idea—" she began, but before she could tell him what it was, the Ko-goks were upon them.

Kris cracked his willow whip, knocking the first wave back. Swinging her bata back and forth, Abazi dove into the gear room and slammed the door shut. Cracking the whip with one hand and swinging the bat with the other, Kris managed to knock a number of dark ones to the ground. Back by the door, arms folded, hoods pulled back to reveal cruel, pitted countenances, Straif and Feltry waited for Kris to tire before they went in for the final kill. Their cold surveillance only strengthened his resolve to fight.

A dark one, black thorn in hand, leaped at Kris and he kicked out, knocking its legs out from under it. Within seconds, it was back up, jumping again. It had obviously gone mad, foam dripping from its gaping mouth, eyes red and rolling in dark sockets like loose marbles. Kris hit it in the stomach with his bat, winding it.

"Back off!" he roared, but the Ko-goks paid him no heed. They were aware enough to know they were dying, and this made them desperate.

Snapping the whip with an increasingly weary arm, Kris knew he couldn't keep this up. He was in good shape from all their training and from basketball, but there were hundreds of dark ones packed into the mill, limiting his ability to maneuver. If they didn't kill him with a thorn, they'd likely crush him. He could only hope Jer and Kimber had found a way to escape.

Kris was seriously considering retreating to the gear room when there was a disturbance off to his right. Something was cutting through the crowd of dark ones like a thresher in a wheat field. Moments later, a path opened up and Jer ran through it, heading toward Kris. His blue eyes were determined as he spun his staff in one hand and threw his bandalore with the other. In a few seconds he was at Kris's side. They stood back to back, swinging their weapons to keep the dark ones at bay.

"What happened to Kimber?" Kris shouted frantically.

"I don't know!" Jer cried. "She went ahead to check on the Dryads while I looked through the back rooms. Then the dark ones came, and we got separated. I made my way to the room with the Dryads, but the door was stuck tight and I wasn't strong enough to get it open." His voice was wild with fear. "I tried so hard, Kris! But I couldn't get it open!"

Kris couldn't help imagining the dying Dryads falling in front of the door, trapping Kimber inside. "I'll head over there and see what I can do. I'm heavier than you; maybe I can put my weight into it. In the meantime, I want you to get to Abazi in the gear room. She said she had an idea. I don't know what it is, but maybe she'll get us out of here. I've got nothing."

"I don't want to leave Kimber," Jer said reluctantly.

"I'll get her, Jer," Kris promised. "I'm not letting anyone die. Not on my watch. You can join me if Abazi's plan doesn't work."

"All right," Jer finally agreed. He fought his way back to the gear room and made it inside, slamming the door behind him. Then it opened again, and Jer pushed a dark one, who'd gotten his arm in the crack, away. The door banged shut.

The crack of wood on bone, the ear-numbing hollers and shrieks echoing off the walls, the shouts of command by Straif and Feltry, all filled the room, making Kris's head throb. Blinking, he continued swinging and attempted to make his way toward the back room, toward Kimber, but he couldn't seem to make much progress.

And then something bad happened. A dark one, crawling low and unseen, rose up and shoved a thorn into Kris's thigh. He stared down in surprise, then roared in agony...the pain was sheer torture. He swung the bat and took out the dark one, then stared at the black spear protruding from his leg. Blood soaked the pale denim around the wound, spreading like spilled cranberry juice.

He sunk to his knees. "Jer!" he cried, but through all the noise and chaos there was no way his brother could hear him. As Kris struggled to stand back up, a groan filled the air, as though the entire mill was protesting, followed by a metallic screech loud enough to pierce the sounds of battle.

The room went silent as the mill began to shake. Another shriek rose up, so loud that the air vibrated and Kris's eardrums, already overwhelmed, felt ready to burst. He thought the entire building was on the verge of collapse, and when a deafening boom rang out, he was pretty sure he was right.

He ducked low, covered his head with his arms, and waited for the worst.

Chapter Thirty

They're Hungry

"I can't believe we did it!" Jer breathed in awe. He hadn't realized he had it in him—the strength to break the lock holding the water-wheel in place. All he'd used was a rusted sledgehammer left behind decades ago and his sheer will to make Abazi's plan work. Before striking down on the lock, he thought about Kimber and that he had to save her, and with one swing, he'd snapped it in two.

In a short time, the wheel began to churn in the ice-filled water. Then Jer had climbed outside and broken off a series of bolts holding the waterwheel in place. It was scary work, being so close to the turning wheel. Judging by the screeching sounds it was making, it was not too happy to be turning. When the groaning began, he jumped back inside, shut the door, and covered Abazi and Gabe as best he could as the water did its work.

Within a surprisingly short time, the river's power pulled the wheel into the water, making the most horrible noise Jer had ever heard. For a moment he thought they were all going to end up flattened when the mill collapsed on them, but it held up. He wasn't sure how much longer it would stand, though. The ancient building was like a centuries old corpse, ready to turn to dust at a touch. Luckily, the platform had remained intact when the wheel toppled into the water and caught against it. The other end of the wheel had snagged a part of the bank sticking out on the other side of the river. It was a precarious set-up, and likely wouldn't last.

Abazi peered out the small doorway at their handiwork. "I didn't think the wheel was going to reach the other side, but it did. Barely. We'd better get Kris and Kimber. It's not going to stay in place for long."

"I'll get them," Jer said. "You stay with Gabe. I think together Kris and I can break down the door where Kimber is."

"Good luck," Abazi told him. "And hurry."

With a nod, he swung open the gear room door and stepped outside to find a sea of bodies covering the floor. The dark ones must have thought the whole building was going to go. He spotted Kris immediately and his body went cold. He hadn't made it to Kimber. She was still trapped. Jer had to save her. *Now.*

He sprinted into the room, then stopped dead. Next to Kris lay Oswald. *Oswald?* How had he made it out here? He was supposed to be dead. Besides that, the door had been jammed shut; there was no way he could have opened it. The Dryads had barely been able to open their mouths, much less stand, when Jer had handed out the berries, and for most of them he'd ended up pushing the berries through their lips.

Jer headed for Kris and Oswald, moving quick and light. Kris stirred and sat up, clutching his leg, and that's when Jer saw the thorn sticking out of his thigh. He felt a little light-headed and had to shake his head to clear it. When Oswald, still lying down, reached over and plucked out the thorn, blood oozed from the wound like a giant leech. Jer nearly lost his lunch, but luckily he was able to hold it in. He had to know what was going on with Oswald and where Kimber had ended up.

He kneeled down by Kris, who was still holding his leg and grimacing. "What are you doing here, Oswald?" Jer asked. "How are you alive?" He looked the Dryad up and down and could find no sign of illness; the dark marks had disappeared.

Oswald shook his head, looking a little dazed. "I don't know. I don't even know where I am, or why I'm here."

"You're at the old mill. Gabe brought you here to protect you from Straif. You and the Rogues were really sick, and you nearly died. We thought you had, actually." Jer almost couldn't believe that Gabe's berries had worked on the Dryads, but they had, amazingly well. His sacrifice hadn't been in vain. Jer knew that should make him feel better, but it didn't.

"I'm most definitely alive," Oswald replied. "But not just me." He threw his arm backward and Jer saw the Rogues, tall and fine in their dark green cloaks, advancing into the main part of the mill, a variety of exotic Dryads following after them. They looked, at worst, a little tired and unsure of themselves. Was it a miracle that had saved them? Or had it all been a trick?

And where was Kimber? Jer couldn't see her anywhere. He had to go after her. "Get everyone into the gear room," he told Oswald. "And hurry. We have a way to get across the river, but I don't know how long it will hold up."

Oswald pushed to his feet and reached down to pull Kris up, at the same time kicking back a stirring Ko-gok. "Yer brother's hurt, but he should be all right now."

"Easy for you to say," Kris said through gritted teeth. "You didn't have a thorn through your leg."

"It didn't go *all* the way through, so ye'll be fine." Oswald placed two fingers in his mouth and let loose a piercing whistle. "This way!" he motioned, and the Rogues began to herd the Dryads toward them. "Ye're to cross the river," he told the first of them.

Jer got out of the way as they scurried past him. "Be careful," he warned. "The wheel's likely to go at any time. You'll have to move fast." He wasn't sure if any of them heard him, but he hoped so.

"I ain't crossin' no wheel," a bald, scruffy looking Dryad proclaimed. His arms were crossed and his lower lip jutted out mulishly. *He* had heard what Jer had said.

"I'm with Weachu," another, equally scruffy Dryad said. They stepped into the path of the fleeing Dryads and stood their ground. "Ye're headin' toward certain death, mates."

Judging by their confused expressions, the Dryads weren't sure who to listen to. Jer thought about yelling at the idiots to get moving, but changed his mind. Whenever his brothers yelled at him, he just got more stubborn and dug his heels in, even if it meant he could get hurt in the process.

"Okay, fine. You two can stay with me and fight the dark ones." He indicated the roomful. The Ko-goks were looking about, dazed and uncertain, unable to function fully without their leader's commands. Neither Straif nor Feltry were anywhere to be seen, but likely they were lurking close by, waiting for the perfect moment to strike. Jer shuddered and tried not to think about it.

Weachu glanced over at his companion. "I can't stay here. These jokers need me leadership abilities. Right, Ailem?"

Ailem nodded vigorously. "Right ye are, Weachu. We're needed." The two strange Dryads turned around and began pushing the crowd forward. "Keep her movin'," they shouted. "We're in charge here, so let us take the lead!" Jer was glad to see the backs of the two troublemakers.

"We need to get Kris out of here," Oswald said to Jer over the heads of the crowd, his expression less than comforting. "The Ko-goks'll figure things out soon enough. They're hungry, we're meat. They don't need anyone to tell them that. I'll take him, then return. Ye keep everyone movin'."

"Have you seen Kimber?" Jer asked, scanning the crowd. "I can't see her."

"One of me Rogues has her. They should be along soon."

Jer hoped so. The dark ones were growing increasingly restless, grabbing at Dryads as they raced past, snapping at each other. At any moment, total chaos was going to break out. "Go, then. I'll watch things out here."

Oswald slung Kris's arm over his shoulder and took the brunt of his weight. Kris didn't look so good. He was sweating and his face was pale. Was that why Oswald had looked so worried? Perhaps he had only said Kris would be all right to keep Jer from panicking, but maybe he wouldn't be.

Jer's insides turned icy. Two of his brothers were down now, leaving him to take charge. It was what he'd always wanted, and yet now he didn't.

The Dryads stopped moving forward. "Go, go, go!" Jer yelled. "Keep moving!" But they couldn't go any farther. There wasn't enough space in the gear room and a mass was gathering around the doorway.

Jer still couldn't see Kimber anywhere, and the dark ones, sensing a predicament, began to turn their attention to the Dryads. Jer had to do something.

He pushed his way into the crowd of dark ones, struggling to make headway. "Follow me!" he cried when he finally reached the center of the room. He could only hope the Ko-goks were so out of it that they'd follow anyone who gave commands. "This way!"

Jer pelted toward the room where the Dryads had lain dying. If he could get the dark ones in there and wedge the door shut, it would give the others time to escape. He glanced back, glad to see the Ko-goks following him. He wasn't glad, however, to see their identical expressions, like he was a roast beef dinner and they were starving. Come to think of it, that description wasn't far off base.

He darted into the foul smelling room, turned right and followed the wall in a circular fashion. The dark ones did exactly as he did, filing into the room, one after the other. By the time Jer was back at the door, the room was nearly full of Ko-goks. He was about to slip through the doorway when the door slammed shut in his face. He tried the knob, but the door wouldn't budge. He banged on it and hollered, "Let me out!" but the door remained shut fast.

Jer slowly turned around. The Ko-goks, seemingly more alert now, advanced on him, one ponderous step at a time, and there was no Aurelia to stop them from crucifying him. Not this time.

~~~~~~

When Abazi had seen the Dryads filing into the gear room, she'd thought she was hallucinating. But there they were, alive and well. She wished she could ask them what had happened, if it had been Gabe's berries that had saved them, but there was no time. She left Gabe safely tucked out of the way and led the line outside.

"You can do it," she told the first Dryads, encouraging them to climb on the wobbly waterwheel and make the perilous journey across the river. "It's our only hope of escape." They had listened to her, had believed her, and one by one, were making it safely across.

But with each passing second, the chances of the wheel coming loose and heading downstream grew. Or it might simply fall apart. The water banged at it relentlessly, threatening to tear it to pieces.

She was exhausted, trying to maintain her balance on the shaking platform and watching to be sure the Dryads got across. There were so many of them, some strange looking, some, like the Rogues, no different from the kids at school. One young Dryad—a female—shivered in fright. "I do not like water," she whispered to Abazi.

"Just pretend you have something great waiting for you on the other side. It will help. Stay focused. You're going to make it."

The Dryad gave Abazi a little smile. "It's the only way?"

Abazi nodded. "I'm afraid so."

"And what about ye?"

"I'll only cross when everyone else has."

The little Dryad drew up her shoulders. "Then I shall get movin'!"

It was a small victory and Abazi reveled in it, because right now, she needed to feel hope. Hope that Gabe would be all right. Hope that everyone crossed safely. Hope that this madness would finally end.

Oswald emerged from the gear room, supporting Kris, and Abazi stared at him. "You're alive, too!" She couldn't believe how well he looked.

"I am," he replied shortly, avoiding her eyes. "I'll have to carry him across."

"No way!" Kris argued, his speech slurring a little. "I'll be all right. I can make it on my own."

Abazi was doubtful. Kris looked really ill. "What happened to you?" she shouted over the roar of water, while directing the next Dryad to the wheel.

"Poisoned thorn," Oswald explained briefly. "He's young and strong and can fight the poison, but he's compromised. He cannot cross alone."

"Poisoned?" Kris echoed. "I didn't know that!"

"We're running out of time," Abazi yelled.

"Get the others across," Kris groaned, going to lean against the wall of the mill. "I'll wait, maybe find another way."

For the moment, Abazi wasn't going to argue with him. The Dryads just kept coming and it was all she could do to keep them moving. A few minutes ago, things had slowed down for several precious seconds when Ailem and Weachu had started arguing about who got to go first. She finally pushed Ailem ahead, onto the wheel, prompting Weachu to scurry after him.

They'd better hope they didn't cross her path again, she thought to herself, or she'd be tempted to beat some sense into them, or at least take her acorns back. Ever since she'd given them to Weachu, her luck had soured. After discovering that Gabe was a Dryad, she'd read up on trees and learned that acorns were symbolic of strength and power and good luck. Knowing that, she'd taken a handful of the acorns the oaks had thrown at Gabe and carried them around with her from then on. But the moment she'd given them away, her luck had run out, and now Gabe was dying.

"Where's Gabriel?" Oswald asked, coming to stand next to Abazi and helping her direct the frightened Dryads. "Decided to keep himself safe?"

She stared up at him. "Didn't you know?"

Oswald's eyes darkened, as though he sensed he wouldn't like what she was about to tell him. "Know what?"

"He's really sick. He did the change...to give you berries, so that you could live, and you did." There was no question in her mind now. The berries had saved the Dryads.

"He did what?" Oswald stepped back and grabbed both her arms. "Where is he?"

"He's in the gear room." She pointed. "He's unconscious."

"He sacrificed himself for us?" Oswald looked as though he simply couldn't believe it, or didn't want to.

"I guess he did," she said wonderingly. "He knew it could kill him and he did it anyway. It was horrible, Oswald. He's bleeding from his ears. That's never good. He's going to die, isn't he?"

Oswald didn't answer her question. "I must go to him."

"The wheel is going to give at any minute."

He paused, then grabbed the arm of the next Rogue coming through. "How many more?"

"Fifty or so," the Rogue told him. "I tried to stay behind, but I couldn't fight the crowd. It's like tryin' to swim upstream. Like that." He pointed at the fast flowing river, relentless in its speed. "I can try again."

"No." Oswald leaned in close to the Dryad and seemed to be communicating with him, though his lips didn't move. When he was done, he gave the Dryad an encouraging slap on the back.

"What's he going to do?" Abazi asked as she watched the Dryad leap agilely across the wheel. There was a groan as the wheel shifted and moved a little. When Oswald didn't answer, she asked another question, one more pressing. "Can you get Gabe across safely? I don't want him to die in there."

"I'll do me best, Abazi Wanibagw."

He turned to go and she grabbed his arm. It was solid, like the oak tree he became, and she could feel the muscles in his arm rippling under her fingers. "It's good to see you back to your old self, Oswald. We were all worried about you."

"It's good to be back to me old self." He grinned, then the grin faded away. "I'm not sure I can do for Gabriel what he did for us."

She nodded. "I understand." She didn't, really, or maybe she didn't want to. Here Oswald was, alive and thriving, when Gabe was dying in this stinking, wet, horrid place and his ghost would linger here and he'd never escape. She pressed a hand to her lips to keep from sobbing out loud, and pushed Oswald toward the door. "Go. Help him however you can." *If only just to be with him as he lies dying*, she didn't say aloud, but Oswald seemed to understand.

"I won't let him be alone." Then he turned and pushed his way through the Dryads still making their way out. They seemed to hold back for him, as though he'd told them to step aside. When he was gone, they continued on their way out.

Abazi was able to get twenty or so more across when a strange noise caught her attention. She grabbed the arm of the Dryad about to step onto the wheel and jerked him back. The sound grew louder and louder, a sort of wrenching sound, like pulling a nail out of a board, and then the wheel gave in to the power of the water, one end flipping up into the air, then completely over. Loose boards flew out as the wheel hit the water. Within seconds, it was under the surface, sinking fast. Their escape route was gone.

~~~~~~

Oswald didn't know what to think, or how to feel, as he kneeled down next to the human who had been his nemesis for so many years. This boy, this man, had saved Oswald and his kind, knowing he could die doing so. It was absolutely confounding.

Oswald didn't remember much of anything that had happened since the Freeze set in, though he did have the sense that they hadn't been well. In fact, a part of him had known for some time that something was wrong with his band. But they hadn't been *that* sick. Had they? He couldn't be sure now. So much was a mystery, so much of the past few months was a blank to him.

When he'd found himself awake in a reeking room in what turned out to be the last place he or any Dryad would ever want to go, he had no idea how they'd gotten there. When the little one, Jer, had told him that Gabriel had brought them to the mill to protect them from Straif, Oswald hadn't quite believed him. He thought it more likely that Gabriel had drugged Oswald and his Rogues and lured them to the Other Side, as payback for the acorn attack, and for not telling him about the Freeze.

Oswald could not believe his enemy would give his life to save the person who had taunted and cursed him from the moment they'd met. But he had. Gabriel had willingly sacrificed himself to save the Forest Immortal, to save Oswald, and Oswald wasn't sure he would have done the same.

His joy at being alive, at being given the chance to recover and carry on to fight another day, shriveled within him like fruit in the hot sun. He'd as good as killed the King of the Forest Immortal. It hurt deeply bestowing that title upon Gabriel, but Oswald deserved to hurt, and Gabriel deserved to be known as the true King.

Inside the dark room, Oswald felt his way toward the lump of clothes that had to be Gabriel. He kneeled down and pulled his enemy, weak and dying, onto his lap. Gabriel was losing his battle against death, wheezing and struggling for each breath. Oswald rocked his King in his arms and cursed the world and what it had done to bring about this unjustifiable state of affairs.

He pushed back the bloody locks of hair sticking to Gabriel's forehead and the memory of their father's death returned to Oswald. This time, instead of running from it, he relived it. He had to see it for what it truly was—a sacrifice from a man who abhorred violence, who had loved Oswald like his own, who knew the truth about what had happened and never once blamed Oswald for his part in his own father's death and for nearly getting Gabriel killed.

For it was Oswald who had lured Gabriel into the forest that day, years ago. He knew about the human, knew there was something concerning him that Dame Hazel kept hidden, that Oswald's own parents kept hidden. So he took Gabriel into the woods to find out what it was. He wanted to know what was so special about this child. Why did his parents speak about protecting him when they thought Oswald slept the sleep of the trees?

It wasn't until years later that Oswald figured it out. They had wanted to protect Gabriel because he was their real child, and because he was the *true* King, not the child whom they pretended was theirs. It was Dame Hazel who must have switched them at birth, placing Gabriel safely into the hands of a family that would take him far away from Straif and his growing anger and discontent. Oswald was raised as the patsy, the pretend King, a mere figurehead. It was the only answer to explain everyone's reverent attitude toward Gabriel, and a hard one to swallow.

But before Oswald knew all this, he simply was aware that Gabriel was someone his parents paid altogether too much attention to when he came to the farm as a four-year-old. So Oswald took him, and somehow Straif had found out that Gabriel was in the forest. Straif must have known things, too, known that Gabriel was special, and he'd gone after him like a wolf. He'd nearly had him, until Father had stepped in and saved Gabriel, sending him into the treetops with a toss, where they whisked him away to Dame Hazel.

For his trouble, Father was killed. Oswald, hiding in the trees, had seen it all.

He'd never forgotten what he'd done, and it ate away at him like canker rot. After that, growing up, he'd done everything he could to make amends, to make his father proud of him. But when he'd found out from Dame Hazel that the man he'd thought was his father was actually Gabriel's, he'd taken his anger out on Gabriel. He'd blamed him for all that was wrong with his life. It was easier, and much more palatable than continuing to beat himself up about what he had done to their father. He'd even led Straif straight to Gabriel, just before the Freeze, in the hopes of being the hero and having the Forest acknowledge him as the true King.

And this is what all his lies and anger had led to. Father's sacrifice had been for nothing.

Well, not entirely for nothing, since the Rogues and the other Dryads were alive because of Gabriel. They were still quite weak, but they were alive. It was bittersweet knowledge, and the most Oswald could do for the boy who'd saved his life was make sure he didn't die in this place...this terrible place.

It seemed so very little to do for his King.

Chapter Thirty-One

Darkened the Doorway

Kris watched the wheel sink under the water with a sort of fatalistic detachment. *Of course the wheel self-destructed before we all got across. Why not? Might as well send along a tornado, too, maybe throw in some hail?*

Now how was he going to save Hollie? There was no way he'd reach her in time.

He pulled himself to his feet, feeling woozy. "What are we going to do?" he asked Abazi, who looked shell-shocked.

"I don't know!" She stared at the waiting Dryads. "Can you transform? Use your tree branches to get across?"

The one at the front shook her head. "We're still too weak from the sickness, and besides, many of us are still too small to span the river."

"But we can't go back through the mill," Abazi said despairingly. "Too many Ko-goks."

Kris looked around, wondering if they could go around the mill. But the building sat at the edge of the river, with little room to maneuver. One false step and a person would be swept out to sea. The light rain coming down didn't help matters, either. "Where did Oswald go?" he asked.

"He's in the gear room with Gabe."

"And Jer and Kimber?" He sort of remembered seeing Jer in the mill, right before Oswald brought him here.

Abazi's eyes filled with dread. "I don't know. I haven't seen them come through yet."

"So they're still stuck inside…with the Ko-goks?" Kris didn't like the sound of that. He also didn't like the look of the sky overhead. The sun was on its way down, but there would still be light for another hour or two. But light wasn't the problem. The wind was picking up and dark clouds were forming over Mount Vidar. Ominous rumbles sounded off in the distance. A storm was coming, and he had a foreboding feeling they had to get out of here before it hit.

"They're going to be killed!" Abazi cried, her voice raw with fear. "I'm going back inside."

"You're not going anywhere like that. I'll go. You keep the Dryads from panicking and try to find another way across. If we could get to the bridge, that would be our best option."

Kris didn't bother telling her that the only way for them to get to the bridge was to either follow the 'no wider than a balance beam' bit of rock between the river and the building, or go back through the mill. "Sure. Be careful. The place is full of Ko-goks and they're acting really weird."

She nodded, then pushed her way back into the mill, past the mass of remaining Dryads. "I don't suppose you can swim?" he asked the dark-skinned Dryad standing on the platform. The Dryad didn't answer, only stood looking at the river with a strange expression on his face. Kris shrugged. *Not the friendliest chap, is he?*

He really needed to keep looking for another way to get them out of here, but all he wanted to do was lie down. He felt so tired, so hopeless. Hollie was surely dying, and Gabe was probably already dead. Kris clenched his fists and pushed that thought out of his mind. Gabe was *not* dead. Hollie would *not* die!

Oh, crap. We're all going to die.

He leaned against the building and closed his eyes. The sound of thunder was growing louder with each passing second, and a few drops tapped on his eyelids. So tired. A loud thunk sounded by his ear, and Kris's eyes flew open. Another clunk rang out as a hand clamped down on Kris's arm and yanked him away. He looked at the place where he'd been standing to see three branch arms, twigs like fingers, grasping hold of the protruding spoke where the waterwheel had once turned. He looked back at the Dryad who had pulled him out of the way, the same one who hadn't responded earlier, then let out a startled snort of laughter. The Dryad joined in, chuckling at the near miss. Two massive oaks spanned the river, their roots anchoring them on one side, their branches holding on for dear life on the other.

"Thanks!"

The Dryad nodded, grinning. "My pleasure!" He pointed. "Look."

A Dryad was racing across the river on the oaks, waving to them. "We must hurry," he cried. "The oaks cannot hold for long. They're still weak from the sickness."

"Then let's get moving!" Kris pushed his new Dryad friend ahead of him. "Go. I'll get the others."

The Dryad nodded and stepped onto the oaks as Kris yelled into the doorway, "Keep 'em coming! We've got a new way across."

Before long, a line of Dryads was crossing the oaks, their steps hesitant and unsure. It was raining harder now, making the oaks slippery, slowing down progress. Finally, the line seemed to end. Kris ducked his head into the gear room. "Oswald? Are you in there?"

"We're here," Oswald called. He was sitting with Gabe across his lap, like a child. The scene reminded Kris of a statue he'd seen in an art book.

"Where are the others? Abazi and Kimber and Jer?"

"Abazi went after the other two. She's been gone for a while."

Kris felt suddenly dizzy and caught himself on a gear. "We have to go. The oaks have spanned the river, but they're weak. Are you, too?"

"I'm fine," Oswald said shortly, but Kris sensed the Dryad wasn't at his best, either.

"Can you get Gabe across?"

"I can."

"I'll tell them there are only a few of us left."

Kris ducked back out and hurried over to the Dryad directing the others. "We only have about six left to cross. I'm going to get the others now."

"We'll try to hold on, but I can feel them trembling. They're in trouble."

"We'll hurry," Kris said, then headed back into the gear room. "Take Gabe. I'll fetch the others."

Oswald didn't respond, and Kris hoped he was up to getting Gabe across the makeshift bridge. He pushed open the door to the gear room and peered out. The room was empty, not a single creature was stirring. Where were the Ko-goks? Where were Abazi and Kimber and Jer?

He stepped out and scanned the area once more, making sure it wasn't a trap. But no one was there. Not even a mouse. Wait. What was that? A sound like a series of ringing bells spilled from the room where the Rogues had holed up. Kris pulled out his willow whip and approached the closed door. What was going on in there?

He pushed the door open and peeked inside. In the middle of the room, two people stood side by side...Kimber and the Dryad, Aurelia, and they were singing, a duet that made his heart swell with emotion. Hundreds of Ko-goks sat on the floor, though a few were lying down, seemingly in a stupor. One by one, Jer was giving them something. A berry. Jer was feeding the *enemy*!

He was about to charge in and stop this madness, when someone grabbed his arm. He swung around, ready to fight. "Put that down, Slick."

"Abazi! What's he doing?" He pointed at Jer.

"Aurelia told him that the dark ones are sick, that they're not at fault. They were turned by Straif and Feltry and have lost their way. They don't deserve to die. 'We, each of us, have good in us,' she said. 'And bad, too.'" Here, Abazi's lips quivered. "So we're saving them. She said it was our moral imperative, and she's right. Even what we think is beyond redemption can be saved. Jer's almost done, and look at them. Really *look* at them, Kris."

Kris turned to study the dark ones and was surprised by what he saw. No more gaping holes for mouths and eyes, no more spikes piercing their skin. No more anger.

"Gabe did this," she said in a whisper.

Kris nodded, feeling awed by what his brother had done, and saddened, too, knowing what it had taken from him. "So what do we do with them?"

"We take them with us," Abazi said simply, and he supposed it was the only right thing to do.

At last Jer straightened up and Kris remembered why he'd come. "The way across…the oaks have made a bridge, but they can't hold on much longer. We could try the lift bridge, but I have a bad feeling Straif and Feltry are waiting for us to do just that."

Jer tucked away the last of the berries and joined them, looking wary. "You're okay with this?"

Kris shrugged. "I guess it's not their fault Straif made them this way." He watched in awe as Kimber lifted her arms into the air and the Kogoks stood, still a little wobbly, and went to her. "But how'd you figure it out?"

"I thought they were going to eat me," Jer explained, heading for the door, "and I was looking for my bandalore and I found a berry and threw it and one ate it and the effect was almost instant. Much faster for them than for the other Dryads, though I'm not sure why. Then Aurelia and Kimber broke down the door—they were together all this time—and they started singing to the dark ones, which calmed them enough for me to keep doing what I was doing. Aurelia told me it was the right thing to do."

Earlier, Kris hadn't wanted to run over the dark ones with the truck; something about it didn't seem right. He clapped his brother on the back and the movement made his head swim. "You're a hero, Jer."

Jer blushed, then grinned. "I thought I was going to pee my pants when I couldn't get the door open."

Kris stepped out of the room, holding the door for the rest to file through. "So how'd you end up in here with all of them in the first place?"

Jer shrugged. "Bad luck, I guess."

"Oh, Jer," Kimber tutted as she passed by. Aurelia continued to sing, but it no longer seemed necessary as the Ko-goks calmly followed her out the door. Abazi led them toward the gear room and Kris was amazed at the change in the dark ones. They seemed so normal now, if a bit dazed and out of it. "Jer led them all into this room to give the others time to get out of the mill."

"What?" Kris yelled, and his head spun again. "You crazy idiot, Jer. You could've died!" He caught himself on the door. "I can't lose two brothers," he almost sobbed. He didn't even want to lose one.

"Gabe's dead?" Jer cried.

"No. *No!* Not yet. Oswald's with him."

"Then maybe there's still time," Jer said cryptically and grabbed Kimber's hand. "Come on. Let's get out of this awful place."

She smiled up at him and Kris was reminded once again of Hollie. He pushed away from the door. He had to get to her. He had to save her.

The Ko-goks filed through the gear room, disappearing one by one, with Abazi making sure they stayed on track. They were back to 'normal' in appearance, but it would likely be some time before they were themselves again.

When the last of them was gone, Kris ushered Abazi and Kimber and Jer in front of him. Once inside the gear room, he searched it to be sure Oswald and Gabe were gone, but was surprised to see them still there, still in the same position.

Abazi knelt by their side. "Come on, Oswald. The Ko-goks are across now. We have to go!"

"I did this to him," Oswald moaned. "I must be punished."

"Fine. Punish yourself after we get him out of here."

"I'll stay here. Ye must take him yerself."

"And who's going to carry him?"

Oswald indicated Kris, and Kris shook his head. "I can barely walk, and Jer can't do it. He has Kimber."

A figure darkened the doorway. It was Aurelia. She made her way to Oswald. "It's time to go, me friend. The oaks are nearly done in."

"I'll stay," Oswald said calmly.

"And leave the Forest without a leader?"

His head snapped up. "I'm not good enough to lead, Aurelia. I've done wrong, and now I must pay the price."

"Do ye think ye're the only one who has made mistakes?"

"No, of course not!" He looked flustered and completely unlike himself. "But I killed me father. I killed Gabriel."

"Straif killed yer father, Oswald, and Gabriel chose this way. He knew that he might die, and yet he still chose this way."

Aurelia rose and reached down to grab hold of Oswald's arm. "Come, Oswald. We must cross now or more lives will be lost."

Kris reached down and grabbed Oswald's other arm and together he and Aurelia heaved the Dryad to his feet, with Gabe still clutched tightly in his arms.

"This way," Jer urged. Kris let go of Oswald and followed Jer out onto the empty platform. The last of the dark ones jumped off the oaks, to the safety of the other side. It was raining harder now and the rumbles had grown to sharp cracks every few seconds. His leg wound stung fiercely now and he felt more nauseous with each step. Staring at the trees spanning the river, he had a bad feeling about this. There was no way he was going to keep his balance on the slippery tree trunks.

"Go," he urged his brother. "Take Kimber and go."

Jer gave his brother a doubtful glance, then pulled Kimber along with him. He was about to step on one of the trees when the Dryad waiting for them opened his mouth in surprise. The trees groaned and their grip on the mill loosened. "Run!" Kris shouted as he jerked Kimber and Jer backward, out of the way of the whipping branches.

The Dryad turned and dashed across the oaks, just barely keeping ahead of their shrinking trunks. With a mighty leap, he launched himself toward the shore, where a host of Dryads caught him. The two oaks whiplashed upward, changed to their human forms, and landed in the water. The river pulled them along and the depleted tree spirits began to sink.

Working together, several Dryads on the shore whipped out their branch arms, snagged the two helpless Dryads, and plucked them out of the water. They were safe. But Kris and the others were not. They were stuck on this side of the river, and if Kris wasn't seeing things, the water was rising. They would have to try the bridge. It was their only hope.

Since all the dark ones were now out of the way, Kris was tempted to think it would be safe to cross. And yet the question still remained...

Where were Straif and Feltry?

Chapter Thirty-Two

Choose Between Them

When Kristofer told Oswald that the makeshift bridge the Dryads had created was no longer in place, Oswald felt a growing agitation. No one else seemed capable or even able to take command, so that left him, alone, to carry the burden. The problem was, he wasn't sure he could do it, not when he was still weak from the effects of the disease that had slowly been taking their lives for a long time now.

Do not let their deaths be in vain, a voice whispered in his ear. He glanced around, but he already sensed it wouldn't be any of the others speaking to him. He knew that voice, and it came from a dead man.

Father?

It is I, the voice answered.

But how can that be? You're dead. I watched ye die.

Ye watched me body die, not me soul. I'm a part of ye, Oswald, and always will be. I'll always be here for ye when ye're in great need. We are connected through our minds, our roots, our shared past. It's a bond that cannot be broken.

It didn't seem possible, and yet here his father was, speaking to Oswald as though he were still alive. *Are ye all right, Father? Are ye well?*

There was a low chuckle. *As all right as a dead tree can be.* Oswald couldn't bring himself to laugh with his father, considering he was the one who'd gotten him killed. *But ye're not all right, me son. That's why I've come to ye.*

I don't think I can do this, Father. I'm not meself, and as ye know, and I'm not King. I have no right.

There was a moment's silence. *Ye don't have to be a king to be a leader, me son.*

Oswald bit back a sob. *But I'm so weak, Father! I'm spiteful, and I do foolish things.*

We're all weak, Oswald, and we all do foolish things. But weaknesses can be overcome, as can foolish things. Ye shall overcome, me son. Ye shall overcome. The voice faded away, leaving Oswald alone.

He strained to hear more wisdom, but none came. It didn't matter. Father was right. He might not be King, but that didn't mean he could simply give up. He needed to stay alive for the Forest Immortal, for Gabriel's family and friends, for himself, and for Aurelia. He needed to take charge and do what he could. If need be, he'd go down fighting, like his father had. Like Gabriel had.

He turned toward the doorway, Gabriel still in his arms, and made his command. "We'll go through the mill, out to the bridge."

"I haven't seen Feltry or Straif for a while now," Kristofer said, his voice weak. "I think they're waiting to ambush us."

"I'm quite sure ye're right. Are ye able to do something for me?"

"As long as I can still swing a bat, I'm your man."

Oswald couldn't help but smile. He would like this Kristofer for a brother. "I need ye to scout ahead."

Kristofer gave him a salute. "Aye, aye, Captain." He stepped in front of Oswald, and as he did, his eyes landed briefly on Gabriel. The sight of his dying brother seemed to strengthen his resolve to persevere and Kristofer straightened his shoulders. "I'll be back," he announced in a strange accent, then limped out the door.

He returned within two minutes. "All clear. No one's in the mill."

With great caution, they filed out of the gear room. Just being outside its oppressive atmosphere gave Oswald hope that they could escape. "Ye'll have to check out the main door," he advised Kristofer.

"Already on it," he answered, and hobbled off.

Their motley crew, injured and distressed, followed after him. Oswald hoped no one was in the building, since none of them was ready to fight. That would have to change as soon as they went outside. Who knew what dark ones remained alive and unchanged? Abazi had explained what Jerome had done, and though Oswald would never have done it himself, he'd sent the message to his Rogues that the Blackthorns had been cured and were no longer the enemy. He could only hope his band would accept his word. Perhaps they would. They'd never once spoken ill of Gabriel, and in fact, had seemed reluctant to carry out the acorn attack on him. In fact, they seemed to accept Gabriel more easily than Oswald ever had, so maybe they'd welcome the Blackthorns back into the fold. He could only hope so. Enough lives had been lost in this foolish battle.

Even though most of the dark ones had been cured, Straif would not have been so stupid as to allow himself to remain unprotected. So it was likely there were several Ko-goks that remained unchanged. It was best to be cautious. Hopefully Straif had managed to find a way back across the river, and was now returning to the forest to regroup.

Kristofer popped his head through the doorway and motioned for them to come. When Oswald caught up to him, he said, "I didn't see anyone, but that doesn't mean they aren't out there. I say we form a circle around you and Gabe, to keep you safe." Oswald wasn't sure that was for the best, but Kristofer was probably right. Carrying Gabriel made Oswald useless in battle. He nodded his agreement and they cautiously headed outside.

The moment they left the building, Oswald took in the heavy rain, the darkening sky, and a strange noise coming from the river. Something dangerous was heading their way. "To the bridge," he ordered. "And hurry!"

On Kristofer's instructions, the small group gathered around Oswald, and together they raced toward the bridge. Nearing it, Oswald took in the two trees holding up the one side.

"Gabe did that to a couple saplings," Kristofer explained when they stopped. "I'm not sure how we can get them to let go."

"I can do it," Oswald said. Closing his eyes, he spoke to the trees, telling them that their job was now over. They could lower the bridge. The two trees, still very young, seemed not to understand him. Why weren't they listening to him?

Because they're not mine to command.

It was a bitter realization and Oswald forced himself to acknowledge it. "Gabriel says to release yer burden!" he tried again. It was the right thing to say. Like slithering snakes, their branches withdrew and the bridge lowered bit by bit. As it came down, Oswald looked about, assessing the situation. The water was very high now, and there was a menacing rumble coming from up river. Once the bridge was down, the river would flow right over it, and crossing would be extremely treacherous. But it was the only way.

"Look out!" Kristofer shouted, pointing.

The bridge was nearly level now. Oswald watched in alarm as numerous dark forms rose up from where they'd been hiding on the bridge's beams. There were certainly more than ten dark ones, more like twenty, and they'd been lying in wait for Oswald and the others, for Gabriel and his blood. From amidst their numbers strode Straif and

Feltry, leering in triumph. Oswald and the others backed up, but there was nowhere to go.

"Talk about killin' two birds with one stone," Feltry crowed triumphantly. He looked mad as a March hare, his teeth bared and his sunken eyes red to the point of glowing. "Or should I say thorn?" He raised and lowered a long, sharp spike in a continuous stabbing motion as he advanced on them.

"Destroy them!" Straif screamed and charged.

Oswald broke from the group, shouting to the trees, "Take Gabriel!" and the closest one reached a slender branch arm down and gathered Gabriel up. Kristofer and the others retreated, pulling out their weapons as they ran. They didn't go far before turning and facing their enemy.

With a whoop, Abazi threw her tomahawk at the dark one about to pounce on her and the Ko-gok went down, writhing and screaming. She yanked the blade from his torso and turned on the next. Kristofer cracked his willow whip, taking out several in one swing while Jer held his own with a strange piece of weaponry Oswald had never seen before. Kimber used her bata to fight off the attacking dark ones, cracking them on the head when they got too close. They were fighting well, but how long could they keep it up?

Several Ko-goks headed straight for Oswald, but before they could reach him, he pulled out his short staff and went on the offensive, knocking down three as they leaped through the air at him. Behind them marched Feltry, while Straif peered up at the tree that had taken Gabriel. His lips were moving, though no words came out, and Oswald felt a chill go through him. Straif was spelling the tree, and it wouldn't be long before the young sapling gave in, handing Gabriel over to Straif like a sacrificial lamb.

But there was nothing Oswald could do about that; soon Feltry would be upon him. A branch arm whipped out and knocked Oswald's staff out of his hands, and he gaped at Feltry, not expecting such power. How could he be so sick and yet strong enough to change over? There was no time to ponder this, for in the next moment, Feltry leaped at Oswald and knocked him to the ground.

Oswald flipped Feltry onto his back, his hands groping for the dark one's bony wrists. He had to stop that deadly thorn. He might be better now, but he was not yet fully recovered; he wouldn't survive the poisoning. "Ye should just give in." Feltry grinned like a demon, revealing cracked and yellowed teeth. "Just give in. Ye're not King, ye're nothing. So why bother fightin'?"

"I'll never give in to ye!" Oswald cried, clamping his hands down on Feltry's wrists and twisting with all his strength. Feltry screamed like a wounded eagle as he dropped his thorn, and it was all Oswald could do not to let go and clap his hands to his ears.

Feltry grimaced, then flipped his legs up and clamped them around Oswald's torso. With a violent twist, he threw Oswald off and leaped to his feet. Oswald rolled and hopped up to a defensive stance, ready to fight. They circled each other, Feltry snarling, Oswald calculating what to do next.

But before he could figure out his next move, Feltry was on him, taking him to the ground and rolling. They kept on rolling, and Oswald realized with a sickening jolt that Feltry planned to pull him into the river. He didn't seem to care that he'd go, too, or maybe he was too far gone to remember he was mortal.

They hit an incline and picked up speed, rolling over and over on the wet grass like a boulder down a mountainside. Oswald looked around for help, spotting only a mass of dark ones surrounding the others. He tried to free himself from Feltry's grip, but the Ko-gok clung to him fiercely, his jagged nails biting into Oswald's flesh.

The palm of Oswald's left hand hit a fist-sized rock and he grabbed hold. They were only a few feet from the river's edge and the roar of the water was deafening. On their next flip, he smashed the stone against Feltry's head and the Ko-gok's grip on him broke.

But the momentum was too much for Oswald to stop himself in time and they both tumbled into the frigid river. Feltry whipped out a branch arm and grabbed hold of the bridge, saving himself. Oswald tried to turn, but he couldn't raise his arms out of the water. He was too weak and the ice chunks made it nearly impossible anyway, slamming into him like giant fists. He raced helplessly toward the bridge, doomed to be crushed by it or sucked under to drown.

Just as he was about to crash, a branch arm shot toward him, wrapped around his waist, and yanked him out of the water. As he flew through the air, Oswald realized it was one of the young saplings. And then he saw something else, off in the distance and coming fast, something much more frightening than Straif and Feltry and all the Ko-goks combined.

The river.

Like a tsunami it roiled toward them, muddy and littered with dead trees and ice chunks, and it would drown them all. *Run!* he shouted in his mind to the Dryads across the river. *To the mountain!* One of his Rogues stood up and looked around, trying to assess where the danger was coming from. *The river*, Oswald tried again, nearly too weak with fear for his band to get the words out. *It's flooding!*

Just as he began to despair that they couldn't understand him, there was a flurry of movement, and his band members started herding the Dryads toward the road. They just might make it. Those on this side of the river didn't stand a chance.

Unless...

"Can ye save the humans?" he asked the sapling and pointed at the fighting group. The young tree didn't answer and Oswald tried again. "Gabriel needs ye to get rid of the dark ones."

Oswald waited with bated breath, hoping for a miracle. The tree gave a little shudder, then sent out its tree arms and began flicking away the dark ones like bothersome black flies. When the Ko-goks were dispatched, the sapling lifted Kimber, then Jerome into its branches. Abazi was next, with Kristofer coming last. The humans were safe now, but someone was missing. Where was Aurelia?

He frantically searched the area and with each passing second of not seeing her, his chest tightened with fear. When he finally spotted her, his stomach sank nearly to his toes. Straif had her, one of his deadly thorns pressed to her throat.

"Set me down!" he commanded the tree. It hesitated for a moment and Oswald thought it still was not taking orders from him. But then, with a sort of bow, it obeyed, lowering him to the ground.

The moment Oswald's feet hit grass, he raced toward Aurelia, knocking over any remaining Ko-goks in his way. "Let her go, ye fiend!" he ordered Straif, his heart knocking in his chest. "Take me instead!"

Straif threw back his head and laughed, sputum dripping from his hideous black mouth. "Ye always were a mad one, Oswald Eik. Just like yer mother and father. Thick and demented as nutters, they are. Well, *were*."

"Ye murderer!" Oswald cried, ready to jump.

Straif pushed the thorn in harder and the blood trickling down Aurelia's gray skin looked black. "Stop where ye are, or she dies before ye get a chance to say goodbye."

Oswald froze, his eyes meeting Aurelia's. She looked frightened, but was trying very hard not to show it. "Save yerself," she told him, her lips trembling. "And save yer brother."

He didn't need to ask who his brother was. "Gabriel's dyin', Aurelia. He can't be saved."

"Remember yer father," she said. "Remember what he gave ye."

Oswald frowned. "What did he give me?"

Straif jerked Aurelia backward. "Enough! Just get Gabriel down here, Eik. *Now.*"

"He's of no use to ye, Straif. I told ye. He's dyin'."

Straif blinked slowly at him. "I want his berries. There be more, I'm certain of that."

"He gave them all to yer Ko-goks. Ye abandoned them to die, but yer cowardice gave them life."

Straif didn't move, nor did his expression change, but Oswald sensed something growing inside the Ko-gok, something dangerous. "Then I'll drink his blood, as I've always planned. Make them deliver him, or she dies an agonizing death." He pressed the thorn deeper and Aurelia's gray skin went nearly white.

Oswald held up his hands. "I'll do it. Just give me a moment. These trees only listen to Gabriel. They don't listen to me."

"Start cuttin'," Straif commanded, and Oswald spun around. Behind him stood Feltry, dripping wet and furious. In his hand was Abazi's tomahawk. He pulled it back and swung, sinking it into the trunk of the tree holding Gabriel. The tree quivered and shook in pain. Feltry struck again, and again, and the tree shrieked in agony.

"Stop!" Aurelia screamed. "Make him stop!" she implored Oswald.

"Don't move a muscle," Straif warned, shouting to be heard. The river had grown louder, and thunder echoed across the sky like war drums. The storm was directly overhead now. If Oswald didn't figure out something soon, they'd all be dead. But he was trapped between saving the love of his life and the person who'd saved his life, and if he didn't choose between them, they'd both die.

Chapter Thirty-Three

Good Riddance

Gabe struggled to open his eyes, which were crusted shut with blood. With a shaking hand, he rubbed away the dried gore and at last managed to open his eyes and look around. He was still alive. Barely.

It took a moment for him to realize he was up in the air, in a tree, with no idea how he'd gotten there. He peered around and saw his brothers and Abazi and Kimber in another tree close by. Down below, Feltry was swinging a tomahawk at the tree holding Gabe, striking swiftly and with seeming delight. The tree cried out and Gabe's skull vibrated with sympathetic pain. Not far away, Straif held Aurelia captive, a sharp thorn to her throat, while Oswald could only look on in horror as a snake of blood ran down her neck.

Gabe struggled to sit up. He had to do something. He felt awful, his lungs full of gunk and his heart sluggish, yet amidst all the pain he couldn't quite believe he was done. He must keep fighting. He *would* keep fighting, until he drew his last breath.

A distant part of his mind protested his insane thinking. The voice actually sounded a lot like Jer, telling Gabe it was the cloak making him think this way. He hazily pushed Jer away. He didn't need that kind of negativity right now. He had work to do.

Pulling his cloak tighter around him, Gabe willed his arm to transform. It refused. He tried again. *Just this once more*, he told himself, and after a few seconds, his limb did what he asked, though it didn't seem happy about it, the effort sending searing throbs through his entire body. With what little strength he had, he threw down his arm and knocked Feltry to the ground. But a few seconds later, he was on his feet and attacking again.

Before Feltry could strike the tree, Gabe flicked the end of his branch and knocked the tomahawk away, into the water. *Sorry, Abazi,* he thought distantly.

"Gabe, no!" someone shouted, distant and hazy. "You're too weak!"

"I'm dyin' anyway," he shouted back. "So let me do this."

Before anyone could protest further, he sent his tree arm whipping toward Straif. The Ko-gok leader's eyes widened and the muscles in his hand tightened as he prepared to plunge the thorn into Aurelia's neck.

"No!" Oswald leaped at Aurelia, knocking her from Straif's grip and sending them both sprawling. Oswald barely hit the ground before he was back on his feet, dragging Aurelia up with him. Gabe wanted to help them as they raced toward his tree, but his transformed arm was shrinking, returning to flesh and bone. He'd done all he could. His head fell backward and cold rain spattered his upturned face.

Straif's angry roar revived Gabe and he looked up to see Oswald and Aurelia perched nearby, tree branches wrapped firmly around their waists. His eyes closed again. They were safe.

"Gabriel!" Oswald shouted in his ear. "Hang on!"

But he couldn't. He was dying. He could actually hear the roar of death approaching, keen to snatch him and bear him away to the other side. He coughed weakly and waited to die, but his lungs labored on. Then the whole tree began to shake and Gabe peered down to see the river, big as a tidal wave, racing toward them. He understood now what Oswald was telling him. *Hang on.* With arms like cooked noodles, he grabbed hold of the tree trunk and squeezed with all his strength.

Below him, the wall of water smashed into his tree. Screaming, the dark ones were swept away, disappearing beneath the black, ice-filled water. The sound of metal rending apart—like a soda can in a garbage disposal—made the air shake, and the entire bridge gave way, the voracious water swallowing it whole. Next went the mill, the water undercutting its foundation as easily as a knife through cake. The sound of breaking glass and metal rent the air and the building toppled. The river washed over it, bearing massive pieces of metal away, while the rest of the mill sank beneath the roiling surface like a ship breaking deep.

His tree shook hard, then began to bend as the weight of the water pushed against it. *Hang on, little one. Ye can do it. I believe in ye. Just a little longer!* Both trees were struggling now. They moaned and cried out, arching more and more as the weight of the water pushed against them, relentless as a steamroller. It wouldn't be long and they'd be submersed. Gabe tightened his grip and closed his eyes, praying the trees would be able to hang on.

Seconds passed, then minutes, and slowly, slowly the trees straightened back up, reaching for the sky with all their might. Gabe opened his eyes and looked around in wonder. His trees had won their battle to stay upright, and Gabe felt as proud of them as if he'd been their father.

Ye're heroes, he told them.

His mind went black for a moment; his body was telling him it was time to let go.

Don't die, Yggdrasil, they pleaded, their voices sounding so young and innocent. *We need ye. We all need ye.*

Ye have Oswald, he told them. *He'll lead ye, and protect ye. He's yer true King. Follow him and he'll see ye safe.*

"Gabriel!" Oswald pulled himself over to Gabe's side. "Ye're not goin' to die. Not if I can help it!"

"Too late," he muttered, his eyelids fluttering. He felt light, as though if he were to let go, he would float up in the air like a balloon. It felt rather nice. His eyes closed and his fingers began to unfurl, loosening his grip. Death wasn't so bad. He didn't know why he'd been so scared of it. His head dropped forward as he gasped for air. It wouldn't be long now.

Oswald grabbed hold of him and held him tight. "Eat this." He pushed something through Gabe's lips.

"What is it?" he slurred. Then, remembering the last time Oswald had given him something to eat, he tried to push it out with his tongue. He wanted to die with dignity.

A soft hand clamped over his mouth. "It'll cure ye, Gabriel," Aurelia told him. "Eat it. No trick this time. Oswald's through with all that, aren't ye, Oswald?"

"It's from our father," Oswald said, paying no mind to Aurelia. "He gave it to me in case I'd ever need it. And I do need it, because I need *ye*, Gabriel. I need ye to live. We aren't blood, but I feel we're brothers. We share the same roots, don't we? We're Dryads."

"Brothers?" Gabe mumbled around the hard, bitter tasting chunks in his mouth. He really wanted to spit them out.

"Just eat," Aurelia commanded.

Unable to do anything but chew the bits that were threatening to choke him, Gabe finally swallowed the horrid stuff. "What was that?" he pushed through thick lips.

"An acorn," Oswald answered proudly.

"An acorn?" Had he heard wrong? "But they're poisonous to humans!"

"If ye eat a bunch of them, sure," Oswald snorted. "One, and ye'll be fine. More than fine. Our father was a strong and magical tree spirit, Gabriel, and the acorns he produced are full of good medicine. This'll cure ye, just like yer berries cured us."

"Then why didn't ye take it when ye were getting sick?" Gabe wondered aloud. It didn't make sense.

"And watch me fellow Rogues suffer? Not a chance. Besides, I forgot about it." Oswald grinned. "The sickness, ye see."

For the first time in a while, Gabe felt like laughing. "'Tis me good luck, then." He pushed himself up on the branch holding him like a child. "Are the others okay?"

Oswald pointed. Kris and Jer, Abazi and Kimber, all waved, their faces questioning. He gave them a thumbs-up and their worried expressions turned to delight. In the midst of their celebration, their tree gave a lurch and they quickly wrapped their arms around its trunk, holding tight.

"What's happenin'?" Gabe demanded, looking around.

"The trees cannot hold their roots," Oswald explained, his brow furrowed. "They're too young and the dirt is soft and loose from the flooding."

"Are they goin' down?"

"If we don't do something quick, they will."

"Can we get across to the other side? The road is still somewhat intact, I see. We have to get over there if we want to save ourselves and the trees."

"Can ye transform?" Oswald asked, looking chagrined. "I seem to be—" he looked away, "unable to, at the moment."

"I don't know." Gabe wasn't feeling as awful as before, but he was still very weak. Even so, he gave it a try, but when nothing happened, he shook his head regretfully. "I've nothing left." Then he remembered something he did still have, and with reluctant fingers, made himself untie the damp cloak clinging to him and pull it off. Once the material left his shoulders, he felt his energy diminishing, but he didn't care. The cloak wasn't meant for him. He knew that now. Much as it pained him, he had to give it up. "Here. Take this." He held it out, but Oswald recoiled as though it were a snake. "Take it!"

Oswald shook his head stubbornly. "I cannot! It's the King's cloak!"

"Well, I'm abdicating. I gift this cloak to you and pass along the mantle of authority."

Oswald blinked unbelievingly. "Ye'd really just give it to me?"

"I'm not giving it to you, you earned it, Oswald. You saved my life twice now, and besides, I told you I never wanted to be King. That hasn't changed, and it never will. Now take the stupid thing before I change my mind."

Oswald reached out to touch the cloak, then pulled his hand back. "Ye're sure?" Gabe nodded heartily and pushed the cloak into Oswald's hand. He wasn't sure at all—already he wanted it back—but if they were to live, the cloak had to hang around Oswald's shoulders.

Oswald took it and pulled it around him. His fingers trembled as he tied the strings, but when the cloak was fastened, he grinned. "I guess I can no longer call ye Usurper."

"Nope. Just brother."

Oswald's eyes darkened and he swallowed hard. "That I can do...*Brother.*" Gabe reached out to him and they clasped hands together, then did a guy's version of a hug, shoulder to shoulder. Gabe wouldn't have minded the other way, but it was kind of hard to hug up in a tree.

Their tree shook again and Oswald straightened up. "Right." Taking a deep breath, he flung out his arms. As they flew outward, skin turned to bark and bone to wood, swift as a flying bird. It was a magnificent thing to watch, and for the first time, Gabe felt lucky he could do it himself.

In a short time, Oswald managed to transfer everyone in the other tree over to the dirt road, with only one minor incident when he nearly dropped Kris, who kept twisting about trying to see everything. When he went to reach for Gabe, Gabe stopped him. "Aurelia next."

Oswald paused, then gave a sharp nod. "Thank ye."

Aurelia smiled at Gabe. "I knew I saved yer life for a reason!" She patted him on the cheek, then she was gone, whisked across the water to safety.

"Ye're next," Oswald said, "and don't argue."

"Oh, I won't argue." Gabe found that he wanted to live now, very much so, even a life filled with Ko-goks and bullies and threats of foreclosure.

When his feet touched the ground, he collapsed in a heap. Abazi raced over to him and gathered him in her arms. "I thought you were dead!" she cried. "I thought you were dead!"

He pulled her to him and buried his face in her hair. "Not just yet. Got a few years left in me, I think."

"What happened to you? How did you get better?"

"Oswald gave me something. It was one of my father's acorns, and eating it saved my life." Already he was starting to feel better; his lungs weren't so gunky, his head didn't feel as stuffed full of cotton.

She tousled Gabe's hair. "See? Oswald's not all bad, is he?"

"No, he's not," Gabe said quietly.

"So how's he going to get himself across?"

It was a good question. Oswald's branch arm was now wrapped around the other young tree. In a blink, the tree transformed itself, becoming a little boy. Gabe was stunned. A child had saved their lives! What a brave young thing! Soon the little one was on their side and he ran to Aurelia and threw himself into the Dryad's arms, sobbing. Aurelia soothed him, murmuring soft words and stroking his head softly.

Oswald let go of the tree he was in and stood up on one of its branches. He took a deep breath and pushed off from the swaying tree, jumping feet first. A heartbeat before he hit the flooded ground, he transformed into a tree. A split second later, the other tree toppled, transforming into a child as it fell. Oswald whipped out a branch, catching the girl just before she hit the shallow water. Then his branch extended, carrying the girl to the other side where he set her on the ground. The girl collapsed, and Kimber and Jer hurried over to her. Jer pulled off his jacket and kneeled down to wrap it around the shivering child. Then he picked her up and held her close. In a few moments, the girl lifted her head a bit and looked around. Seeing the boy was okay, she relaxed and leaned back into Jer. She looked like she was going to be all right, despite her wounds, which were fortunately not as horrific looking as what they could have been considering what Feltry had done to her tree form with the tomahawk.

The two trees were going to be okay, but Oswald was in great trouble. Stranded, he had no way of getting across the river. But he didn't seem to understand that. Still in his tree form, he headed for the raging torrent, seemingly determined to cross. *Oh, that cloak!* Gabe cursed it. What Oswald was about to do was suicide. But Gabe remembered how the cloak had made him feel—as though he could do anything. And he was the one who'd given the stupid thing to Oswald, thinking he was doing him a favor.

"Let me up," he wheezed to Abazi.

"You're not going anywhere." She tightened her hold on him. "You might be better, idiot, but you're not out of the woods yet. I'm not losing you," she added in a soft voice.

"Oswald's not going to make it across that river. Not alone."

"But you're sick!" she protested. "You can't help him." She pushed Gabe off her. "I'll do it."

"You? What are you going to do?"

"I don't know! Call up the spirit of my ancestors or something." She marched toward the water's edge as Oswald took his first step into the river. The water caught him right away and its strength threatened to pull him down. A chunk of ice crashed into his trunk, knocking him sideways, but he kept his balance and continued forward, step after agonizing step.

He was ten feet from the bark when a black branch shot out of the water and grabbed hold of his trunk. He tried to shake it off, but the branch clung to him like a squid. Another branch grabbed hold, and a few seconds later, two heads emerged from the river. Straif and Feltry.

They were still alive.

As Oswald continued to push his way across the raging river, he struck at the two Ko-goks with his branches, but they just took the blows, one after the other, their eyes intent on one target.

Gabe.

Gabe pushed himself to his feet, swayed and nearly fell, then joined Abazi. She saw him and gave him a shove. "You stay back!"

"I have to end this," he croaked, and he meant it. The other dark ones might have been salvageable, but Feltry and Straif were not. It was likely they'd been evil before the illness, and wouldn't stop being so once saved. No. Straif and Feltry had to go, and Gabe was the one to do it.

Oswald was close to shore now, and seizing their opportunity, Feltry and Straif pushed off him, leaping onto the bank. The grass was wet and slippery, but they grabbed hold and managed to scrabble up to drier land. Gabe's brothers staggered to their feet, and Abazi and Kimber raced toward Straif, ready to fight, but he ignored them, marching straight toward Gabe. He was determined to get his blood, and now. Time was running out for the Ko-gok leader. His skin looked like it was melting and the holes for his eyes and mouth had stretched wide.

Feltry joined his side, resembling a bloated corpse more than a human now, and together they faced off with Gabe. "Give me what ye gave the Dryads and I'll let them live." Straif threw a dripping arm back at the others.

Gabe straightened his shoulders. "I'm not sure why you think you can beat us when time and again we're the ones who've beaten you."

"But now ye're weak," Straif sneered. "Like a pig to slaughter." He gave a sneering laugh, then his branch arm whipped out, heading straight for Gabe's head.

Gabe lifted his arm and blocked the blow. It hurt, but not nearly as much as if Straif had connected with his head. "Not as weak as you think."

Straif scowled, then threw out a branch arm and wrapped it around Jer's neck, lifting him in the air. Jer dangled helplessly, slowly choking. "Give it to me, or he dies. Ye've got five seconds."

Gabe's heart seized. Jer's eyes were wide with fear as he struggled to free himself, kicking and jerking as though being hung. Kris hobbled over and tried to help him, but Straif just lifted Jer higher, out of reach. Jer's only hope now was for Gabe to transform, but he was so weak, so tired. He didn't think he had it in him.

Remember your roots, he told himself. *Remember who you are. You are a Dryad, and no one can take that away from you.*

At that moment, the sky opened up and a beam of light fell upon his head like a benediction from the heavens. The warmth from the sun's heat spread through his body and Gabe knew the time had come. Closing his eyes, he imagined his arm transforming, and when he opened them back up, he saw his arm becoming dark with hawthorn bark. Feeling the power of the tree surging through him, he whipped out his branch arm and seized Feltry around the neck.

"Let me go, ye scurfy stang!" Feltry screeched angrily as he flew into the air. Gabe only squeezed harder, shutting him up.

Straif retaliated by tightening his grip, and Jer's face went purple. "Do ye think I care about him?" His eyes touched on Feltry's struggling form, then flicked away in disgust. "Him and his brother are scurfy blights, always screwin' up, always bringin' us down. I'm tired of him. Tired of them both."

Gabe almost felt sorry for Feltry at that moment. But not quite. It was too late for him; he was already rotted to the core.

"Yer time's up, Usurper," Straif went on, his voice rising. "Ye thought ye could come to *my* forest and run it? Ye and yer kind have been causin' me trouble since we crossed over, and I'm done with the lot of ye. Ye're the worst Dryad I've ever seen and I've seen a lot of poor excuses. Ye'll never step foot in my forest again."

Gabe blinked. "Did you just say I was the worst Dryad you've ever seen?"

"Ye're even worse than Dorn's mate, Barb," Straif spit out. "The worst of the worst."

Gabe was surprised at how angry he felt. Months ago, he'd have been happy to hear that he wasn't a good Dryad—it made it less real that he actually was one. Now this jerk was saying that Gabe was a *bad* Dryad? He was getting pretty damn good at being a Dryad! And the forest was not Straif's; it belonged to all the Dryads!

Gabe let fly another branch and brought it down on Straif's arm with a terrible force. The impact was so strong that he snapped the limb in two. The Ko-gok roared angrily and dropped Jer. Jer hit the ground hard and his body went still. Gabe couldn't tell if he was alive or dead.

With a growing fury, he advanced on Straif. "I'm a good Dryad!" he bellowed. "Say it!" He pulled back his branch arm and struck again, taking off Straif's other arm, which was attempting to change over.

"Never!" Straif shrieked. As he worked to re-grow his arms, Gabe struck him again, marking his cheek. Then again, slashing the other. Black blood oozed from his wounds, and Straif fell to his knees. Gabe was about to end him once and for all when Feltry lashed out and struck Gabe's forehead hard. His grip loosened and Feltry dropped to the ground.

Gabe staggered forward, determined not to be derailed from his mission.

Straif…must…die.

"Watch out, Gabriel." Abazi cried.

Gabe spun in time to block another blow from Feltry. Oswald, out of the river now and back to his old form, stumbled toward them. His strength was nearly depleted, yet still he came, his cloak flapping in the wind and rain.

The others rallied behind him, and as one, they raced toward Feltry and swarmed him, raining blows on his body. In a short time, he lay still on the ground, Oswald's foot on his neck. Together, they lifted him and tossed him into the river. The deadly current caught him and bore his still form away. If he wasn't dead, he soon would be.

One down, and good riddance. One to go.

"Gabe!"

Gabe turned just as Straif leaped. He raised his arm to block the blow, but it never came. Straif stopped short, clutching at his chest. His hands encircled a black thorn piercing his heart, and he dropped to his knees, staring at the thorn in disbelief.

Jer came running up, stopping in front of Straif, his hand clutching his raw looking throat. He looked him in the eye. "I promised myself I'd get you back." He turned to Gabe. "He was going to kill you. I-I had to do it."

"Ye can't even make yer own kills," Straif taunted, thick black blood spilling from his lips.

Gabe peered down at him. "Oh, yeah?" With the last of his strength, he lifted the Ko-gok into the air and threw him in the water. The dark one fought against the raging river, but it was stronger than him, hungrier, too, and it sucked him down. He slammed into the bridge, then was pulled under, disappearing into the deep.

Gabe met Jer's eyes. "There. We both did it."

"Yes," Jer whispered. "We killed him, but we saved the other Ko-goks, right? That makes up for what we did to Straif, doesn't it?"

"We saved the other Ko-goks?" Gabe said uncertainly. "How?"

"I gave them your berries. I thought you would want that—to give them a second chance."

Gabe remembered the accusation Straif had made—that a crime had been done to the Ko-goks. If that was true, Jer's act of kindness should make up for whatever it had been. "You did the right thing, Jer, though I'm not sure it gets us off the hook entirely. It's something we'll just have to live with."

"I think I can do that," Jer replied shakily.

Gabe slipped his arm around his brother's exhausted shoulders. "Today you are a man, Jer." Jer's mouth pursed and Gabe thought he was going to start crying, but instead he burst out laughing. Gabe stared at him, wondering if he'd gone mad. Then he started laughing himself. "Okay, yeah, maybe that was a bit much…"

"And today I am a *woman*," Abazi sang out, nearly doubled over in laughter.

"Me, too!" Kimber proclaimed with a giggle.

"Hey, I'm a man, too," Kris joined in.

"As am I," Oswald grinned.

Gabe slapped him on the back. "And I'm a good Dryad, right?"

Oswald nodded. "Almost as good as I am."

"I'll take that." Gabe looked around at the bedraggled group. The storm had passed, the sky was clearing, and they were all still alive. "Shall we go home?"

Kris's eyes suddenly widened. "Hollie! And Mom and Dad! They're in trouble!"

Despite their exhaustion, despite their pain, the group gathered up the little ones and Aurelia and raced toward the truck, hoping against hope that they wouldn't be too late.

Chapter Thirty-Four

A Blizzard of Seeds

When they tore into the yard, Kris, sitting in the back of the pickup, was surprised to find it empty. Fortunately, the truck had started right up for Gabe—apparently it had overheated, as it liked to do.

He looked around, waiting for the sneak attack, but none came. Was it too late already? Were the Ko-goks in the turret, killing his family at this very moment?

He leaped out of the truck and hobbled up the front steps, bat gripped in his hand, ready to take out some Ko-goks. As he neared the door, it swung open.

"There you are!" Mom greeted, looking pale and frazzled. "Is everyone okay?" Her eyes swept the yard, quickly doing a head count on the others approaching the house.

"They're fine," he said quickly. "Where are the Ko-goks?"

She grinned, looking ten years younger. "We sent them packing. Grandpa Hawthorne ran off most of them in his truck. He just drove in circles and swung his cricket bat. After a few of them got smacked on the head, they retreated. We really didn't even have to do much fighting." She looked a little disappointed at that, then perked up. "But I have something unbelievable to tell you. It's about Bruce Holt…"

"Yeah, I know. He's alive."

She frowned. "Am I the last one to know anything in this house?"

"Probably. Where is he now?"

"He's up in our bedroom resting. He isn't well. Grandma May went to fetch him something, I think."

Kris reached into his pocket and pulled out two precious berries from the store he'd pocketed at the mill. "Give him these. They'll help."

She took the red berries, eyeing them suspiciously. "I suppose I shouldn't bother asking." Kris shook his head and she sighed. "Well, anyway, Grandpa Hawthorne is with Dad in the parlor and—"

"So you're all okay?" Kris interrupted, growing anxious. "Hollie's okay?" Mom looked confused. "The one who's really sick... She's a, well, one of those tree spirits I wrote about in my book. With the crazy red hair?"

Mom looked chagrined. "I'm sorry, hon. She's still unconscious. The other one, the little round one, is with her, but she doesn't look too good either. I was just going up to check on them, maybe call a doctor? Dad's got low blood sugar, so he's eating something."

Kris pushed past her and into the house. "I'll check on them. You get those berries to Mr. Holt."

Mom nodded and held the door for him. "Is there anything I can do?"

"No doctor. Just send Gabe up."

She gave him a funny look, but didn't ask what Gabe could do for a Dryad. Kris hurried inside and up the stairs to the turret. There he found Faeth pacing the floor, mumbling to herself. Over in one corner Wildrr sat cleaning his pipes. He looked up. "If'n ye're lookin' for the troublemakers, I got rid of them."

Kris froze. "You killed Jake and Mrs. Morrigan?"

Wildrr's eyes sparkled. "I certainly wanted to, seein' as the trouble they were up to. But no, they're alive and well. I led them out to the road to where the burly one and the one with those snarlin' brutes were waitin'. Then I spelled the lot of them and sent them on their way. They won't remember a thing about today."

Kris released a pent-up breath and turned to face the bed where Hollie lay. On the other side of the bed sat Dame Hazel, eyes closed, shoulders slumped. "What's wrong with them?"

The fairy shrugged. "Whatever it be, I canna cure it. Tried a few things, of course, but no change, as ye can see with yer own eyes."

Kris could see it, and wished he couldn't. Hollie looked so small lying in Gabe's bed. He wanted to gather her in his arms and protect her forever. He settled for kneeling down next to her and taking her cold little hand in his. "Hollie? Are you awake?"

She stirred a little and he called her name again, louder this time. Her eyelids fluttered, then opened and she turned her head to look at Kris. Seeing him, her green eyes lit up like sunlight through emeralds. "Kristofer," she pushed out, her voice weak. "Ye came for me."

"I brought you something." He pulled the berries from his pocket and held them out to her. "Eat these. They helped the other Dryads."

She eyed them doubtfully. "I'm not sure these will cure what ails me, Kristofer." But she took the berries anyway and struggled to chew them. After she swallowed, she lay back against her pillow, the simple act exhausting her.

"Anything?" he asked hopefully. She shook her head. "It will probably take some time. It did with the other Dryads."

She gave him a tired smile. "Probably." But she didn't look convinced.

"What happened, Hollie? Why are you like this? Is it the sickness?"

She shook her head. "Worse."

He squeezed her hand. "Tell me."

But before she could start, the sound of pounding feet came from the stairs, and the others filed into the room. Oswald spotted Hollie and strode over to her side. He kneeled beside Kris, his eyes questioning. "I already gave her the berries," he explained mournfully. "But she doesn't seem better."

Oswald shook his head. "She needs stronger magic than that."

"Try the cloak!" Gabe said from behind them.

"It's worth a try." Oswald untied the strings and yanked off the cloak. Kris helped Hollie sit up, pained by the thinness of her shoulders and arms, and Oswald wrapped the cloak around her like a blanket. Kris laid her back down, then watched her like a hawk. Nothing changed, but again, the cloak's magic might take time to do its work.

"Tell us what caused this," he begged Hollie. "It might help us figure out what to do for you."

She sighed as he took her hand once more. "When I got back to our hideout, I met with ye, Oswald," she nodded at him, "to be sure everyone was returned and in their places for the change. But I noticed something strange about yer behavior. Ye wouldn't look me in the eye, and there was a dark spot on yer left cheek that hadn't been there when I'd last seen ye. So I knew right then…the sickness had struck ye and the oaks."

She paused for a moment as a bout of coughing seized her. When it passed, she went on. "I really wasn't goin' to stay awake. I knew the risk was great with our growing weakness, and I wasn't about to push me luck. I wanted to be here come springtime." She looked away, at the wall behind Kris. "I-I wanted to see ye again, Kristofer. But I couldn't let them go unwatched. Many of the Rogues kept wakin' up and tryin' to run, or didn't want to go to sleep in the first place. Dame Hazel and I took turns keepin' watch and makin' sure they stayed safe."

"Well, it paid off," Oswald told her, his voice husky. "Thanks to ye and Gabe, we're alive. Our illness is past and we'll be strong again soon."

She smiled at him. "I'm glad that our sacrifice was not in vain, then."

"Sacrifice?" Kris echoed. That terrible word again. "What are you talking about?"

"I'm dyin', Kristofer. What I did…it comes with a price."

Kris turned to his brother. "Save her, Gabe!"

Gabe grabbed his brother's arm and pulled him away from Hollie, forcing Kris to let go of her hand. "I don't know what else to do, Kris!" he hissed when they were by the door. "We tried the berries. We tried the cloak. Nothing worked."

Kris couldn't accept this. He *wouldn't*. "Isn't there anyone in the forest who knows something?"

Gabe was about to shake his head, then went still. "There is someone."

"Who?" Kris demanded.

"Filidh. Remember what he said? That he could cure the Dryads. Well, maybe he can cure Hollie. He likes her, too. He'd do it, if he could."

"Call him, then. He said you only had to think of him and he'd appear."

Gabe turned to Oswald. "You okay with losing the ravine?"

Oswald gave him a funny look. "Of course we are! We no longer need it, now that Straif is gone. And it seems a small price to pay if Filidh can save Hollie's life, galling as it is to give that gaffer what he wants."

"Right," Gabe replied. "Just making sure." Then he closed his eyes in concentration.

A strange rumbling sound billowed up around them, followed by a loud bang and lots of smoke. When it cleared, Filidh appeared, looking as wild and foresty as usual. "Ye called?" he asked, a gloating smile on his lips.

"Hollie and Dame Hazel are sick." Gabe pointed at them. "They stayed awake to help the Rogues, and now they're dying."

Filidh's hand clapped against his chest and he staggered a little as he strode over to the bed. He kneeled down by Hollie, his face full of fret and fear. "What were ye thinkin', child?"

She took his knobby hand in hers. "I had to do something, Filidh. We cannot lose our oaks."

"We caint lose *ye!*" Tormented, he glanced up at Wildrr, who gave him a grave salute in acknowledgement. "Ye tried yer spells?"

"I did. She didna respond."

Filidh's shoulders shook. "Oh, wee one! Why didn't ye call Filidh to help ye?"

"Ye know how ye fight with Oswald."

He looked aghast. "Why, wee one, that were just for fun. Right, Oswald?"

Oswald's expression spoke otherwise, but he said, "Right, Filidh. Of course."

Filidh's shoulders slumped. "Oh, if only Filidh hadn't been such an ornery old cuss."

"But can you fix her?" Kris demanded. He slipped around to the side of the bed opposite Filidh and took Hollie's other hand. It felt as cold as it had been before the berries, before the cloak. She was no better, but for the moment, she was no worse.

"Filidh don't rightly ken. There is something…"

"What is it?" Kris demanded.

"It goes way back. To yer beginnin'." He nodded at Oswald, then at Gabe. "To the beginnin' of the Forest Immortal." He took a moment to clear his throat. "Long ago, a Dryad of great charm and darin', Liabreg of the Hawthorns, fell in love with a beautiful human named Huath. Such was their love and desire for each other that Liabreg decided to violate all the laws of the Dryad world and turn her into a tree spirit.

"But there were a problem. A human man, Yakob, loved Huath as well, and when she began to act strangely, secretive-like, he followed her into the woods. There he saw Liabreg turn into a tree. When he tried to warn Huath about Liabreg, tellin' her he were the devil, she wouldn't listen and Yakob, being scorned, began to plot against Liabreg.

"Liabreg and Huath were able to keep their secret until Huath began to flower. She couldn't let her family, or any human, see her this way, and so she went with Liabreg to hide in the woods. When she didn't come back, Yakob accused Liabreg of murderin' her. Liabreg confessed to his fellow Dryads about what he'd done. Many were upset with him, rightfully so, but agreed to help him hide her. He was their King, after all, and they loved him.

"When days passed and Huath couldn't be found, Yakob roused the townsfolk with his hateful tales and accusations of black magic and they began the hunt for Liabreg. The Dryads of the forest were forced to flee, takin' Huath with them, as she couldn't return to her family with flowers comin' out her ears. Chased by Yakob and the villagers, the Dryads ran to the end of the earth, where the big water stood. Unable to go any further, they were trapped there.

"Yakob was determined to get his love back, believin' she was under Liabreg's spell. He thought he had them trapped, and was gloatin' something fierce, when Liabreg and Huath and all the hawthorns disappeared in a flurry of petals. The rest of the Dryads, though disinclined to leave their homeland, turned into seeds and flew away, across the ocean, to follow their King. T'were masses and masses of them, a blizzard of seeds and petals, and it must've been a sight to behold.

"On t'other side of the great water, the natives saw them comin'. They saw the seeds and petals transform into trees, right on the spot. This, of course, scared them something awful. But time passed, as it do, and the Dryads laid low, until eventually they began to venture into the villages, pretendin' to be humans from across the waters. They tried to fit in, live like humans, but there were an aura of peculiarity about them. So most took to the forest, preferrin' to live the life they've always lead. Over time the natives came to accept them, but most white folk never were comfortable around the Dryads. If they were to come across one, they'd ignore them, or try to run them off."

"That sounds familiar," Abazi said snidely.

"But what does all that have to do with saving Hollie?" Kris asked. She was looking more and more shrunken with each passing second.

"I'm gettin' to that part. Ye see, Huath wrote it all down. That's how Filidh ken all this. There were troubles with her changin' over. She didn't want to sleep the winter through. Caint say I blame her. Sleepin' that long baint right. So Liabreg found a way to keep her awake, and he stayed awake with her. And even though Liabreg wanted to be in the forest, he built this place." He looked around. "This turret."

"What?" Gabe stepped forward. "You mean, Liabreg and Huath are my ancestors?" He looked at Oswald. "Or yours." Oswald shook his head, just as stunned and confused as Gabe.

"Ye're all related, is what I'm sayin'. One way or t'other. But what I'm also sayin' is that it's written down. How to survive the Freeze."

"Where?" Kris cried.

"In the diary."

"Diary? Where is it?"

"That human's gots it. The smartypants with the riddles. It fell out of me pocket one day and he snatched it up."

"So that's how Bruce Holt was able to turn into a Dryad!" Jer exclaimed. He was holding Kimber's hand tightly, his eyes bright. "The secret must be in the diary."

"But that doesn't help us," Kris persisted, growing impatient. "We don't have the diary." He looked helplessly at Filidh. Then he remembered. "But wait. Bruce Holt is here! In Mom and Dad's room. I'll go get him."

"There's no need for that," came a voice from the stairs.

Kris spun around. "Grandma May!"

"I fetched the diary," she said, sounding winded. "Never rode my bike so fast. Bruce had been asking for it, but when I got back, he was all right." She looked around for a moment, as though searching for the right words. Then her eyes settled on Gabe. "He was there that day, last fall, when I was so mean to you at the cottage. It wasn't fair to you, but I panicked." It was as close as Grandma was going to get to an apology and Gabe accepted it with a nod. "He was sick and doing strange things, and I was afraid you'd see him. But now he's better! Better than he has been for months. I can't fathom why."

"About that..." Kris said. "I had Mom give Mr. Holt some berries."

"Berries? But it's spring. Where on earth did you get them?"

"From me," Oswald spoke up. Gabe glanced at him sharply, but Oswald's expression remained bland. "I'm the tree spirit, Mrs. May. They're mine." Kris couldn't believe it. Oswald was covering for Gabe.

"All right, then," she acknowledged. "So you're the one who can save your friends." She nodded at Hollie and Dame Hazel. "You have to make them go through the change. The only berry that will save them from not hibernating is their own."

Oswald's calm demeanor disappeared. "But I can't do that!"

"There's no other way," Grandma stated flatly.

Gabe stood up and faced her, his shoulders pulled back and his head held high. Only those who knew him well would detect the slight trembling in his hands. "Oswald can't do it." He blinked a few times. "But I can."

Chapter Thirty-Five

Through Pain Comes Life

Gabe waited for the disgust that was sure to distort his grandma's features, but it never came. "All right, then do it. There's little time left for them. Anyone can see that."

"You're okay with this? That I'm a, I'm a—" He couldn't say the word.

"That you're a Dryad? Of course I am. Besides, it finally makes sense why the turret welcomed you. This place was made to protect Dryads from harm, and from the sounds of this Straif I've been hearing about, you needed protecting."

Gabe remembered the voices he'd heard when he'd first donned the cloak, and he remembered his dreams of fleeing from a pack of angry townspeople. Liabreg, brash and bold, had not built this place to protect himself, Gabe suddenly realized, but to protect his human love. Gabe wasn't much of a romantic, but he thought Liabreg's sacrifice— first leaving his homeland, then his kind in the forest—was pretty amazing.

"There's only one problem," he said to his grandma. "I don't know how. I mean, I made the berries, but I don't know how to make someone else do it."

"Ye grew those trees," Oswald reminded him. "It can't be all that different from that."

It could be, but Gabe decided not to say that aloud. "I can try, but I'm not sure I have enough strength to do that again. I feel like I've been gutted."

"Yeah, I get that," Oswald said sympathetically. "I feel pretty much the same."

Abazi stepped forward. "Hollie said something to me once. She said that Oswald will do what needs to be done, and he'll do it *with* Gabe. So maybe you guys can do it together."

Gabe looked at Oswald. "I'm game."

Oswald nodded solemnly. "As am I."

On the bed, Hollie started twitching, her whole body seizing up in pain. "Hurry!" Kris cried.

"Take the cloak off," Gabe ordered Kris. Kris did as he was told and handed the cloak to Oswald, who donned it quickly. Then Gabe kneeled down beside Oswald. "Take her hand." Oswald took one hand and Gabe took the other, then he clasped Oswald's free hand in his own. He could feel the strength in Oswald's grip, and was glad for it. "Imagine her producing leaves, then flowers, then berries. In that order. But we have to do the producing for her. She won't survive if she tries to do it all herself."

Oswald squeezed Gabe's hand in response and their work began. Gabe felt the blood roaring in his ears as he commanded Hollie to transform herself, to create, to bud and berry, all within seconds, and wished there was some other way. He knew the pain she would soon be feeling, and he knew it could kill her. Hollie's hand jerked in his as groans escaped from her slack mouth, then a violent scream erupted.

"You're killing her!" Kris shouted, knocking into Gabe.

Gabe's eyes flew open, and Hollie stilled, as did the process. "Stay on task, Brother," Oswald whispered. "Through pain comes life. Remember that."

Gabe closed his eyes to the agony in Kris's. *Through pain comes life*, he chanted in his head. *Through pain comes life.*

Hollie screeched again as the glorious scent of her flowers filled the room. "Make it stop!" Kris begged, but this time, Gabe ignored him. He focused on telling Hollie's body what it needed to do. *Produce berries. Make them burst forth. The pain will be worth it.* He hoped.

"I can see berries!" Jer exclaimed.

Gabe opened his eyes to a wondrous site…Hollie, half in tree form, was covered with waxy, dark green leaves, tiny white-green flowers, and blood red berries. "Pick them and feed them to her," he told Jer. "Quickly."

Jer stepped between them and plucked the berries from the tiny twigs sprouting all over Hollie's body. He pushed a handful between her quivering lips. "Chew, Hollie!" he commanded. "Your life depends on it."

She tried, but she was too weak. "Sit her up," Gabe ordered. Kris propped her against the pillows, keeping her steady. Gabe drew in a breath and made himself do what Oswald had done for him. Turning his arm into a branch, he sent one slender twig into her mouth and pushed the mass of berries down her throat. She gagged, but managed to keep everything down. Gabe withdrew his branch and watched, waiting to see what would happen next.

Hollie convulsed and Kris held her tight, his eyes wide with worry. "You can do it, Hollie," he encouraged. "You can do it."

She spasmed once more, then everything began to withdraw—her twigs, the leaves, and all the flowers and berries, until she was in her human form once more. She lay still, her eyes closed and shadowed. Kris looked around at them. "Did it work? She's still so cold!"

Gabe wasn't sure it had, and her icy skin worried him. He sent a burst of warmth through his fingertips. Oswald turned a startled look on Gabe. "That's like sunlight."

"You can feel it, too?"

Oswald nodded, a relaxed expression settling over his features. "Send more."

Gabe willed himself to transmit more warmth into Hollie, hoping to bring her back to life.

"It's not working," Kris said disbelievingly, and tears flowed down his dusty cheeks. "It's not working. She's going to die."

Hollie coughed and her eyes flew open. "Who's goin' to die?"

"You're okay!" Kris laughed, hugging her to him while everyone clapped and cheered. "I can't believe it. You're alive!" Hollie let go of Gabe and Oswald's hands and returned the hug so tightly, Gabe thought they'd meld together.

He pulled his hand from Oswald, who was strangely reluctant to release it. "It's like nectar to bees," he said with a sheepish smile, before finally letting go. "Ye'll have to teach me that trick."

Gabe smiled and reached out to pat Hollie on the leg. She looked fantastic. Her skin was back to its normal woodsy brown color and her hair was a vivid red again. "Good to see you're back."

She pulled away from Kris and scowled at Oswald and Gabe. "What took ye so long?" Then she laughed at their wide eyes. "Just messin' with ye." She raised her arms above her head and stretched. "Now that was a nice awakenin', I tell ye. How do ye feel, Dame Hazel?" She looked to her left and froze. "Dame Hazel?"

Gabe pushed himself to his feet and rushed around to the little old woman, still slumped in her chair. He grabbed hold of her icy hand and Oswald, right behind him, took her other one. At their touch, her eyes flickered open. "No, no, no," she rasped. "That's not for me."

"Let us save ye, Dame Hazel!" Oswald cried. "Just give us a chance."

"It be me time to go," she sighed wearily. "But don't ye worry, young ones, I'm ready for it."

Oswald's eyes teared up. "But ye can't go. What'll we do without ye? I've no one to guide me. No family now. Just ye!"

"You have us," Gabe said quickly. "You can stay with us, Oswald."

Oswald blinked back tears. "I appreciate the offer, Gabriel. I do. But me home's in the Forest Immortal. I know yer parents are me real ones, but in reality, they're not, are they? They're yers."

"In all ways," Dame Hazel said, her voice cracking.

Gabe frowned. "In all ways? What does that mean?"

She pushed out a smile. "I didn't switch ye. I only made ye think I did. It weren't right, but it was all I could think of to do. I had to make Straif think Oswald weren't the true King. I had to make him think it were someone else, to keep Oswald safe. And when Oswald took ye from yer yard, it helped start the tale."

Gabe remembered being in the gear room, and through their tree spirit mind connection, 'hearing' Oswald confessing what he'd done. So Gabe knew the whole story, and he understood now why Oswald had hated him. He didn't blame him. He'd had a hard life and Gabe had come along and taken the one role he'd thought was his, and had worked toward for years, without doing anything to earn it. It's why he'd given back the cloak.

Dame Hazel seemed to already know what had passed between them, but Oswald looked stunned. "I knew ye took Gabriel, Oswald, but I couldn't let ye know that I knew. I needed ye to fret a little, and I needed ye two to be friends. That's why I kept sendin' ye to him, findin' ways to bring ye together. To me greatest sorrow, each time seemed to make things worse. But I see that ye two succeeded on yer own where I failed."

She chuckled weakly before continuing. "Once Oswald's father gave his life to save ye, Gabriel, well, after that, it didn't take much convincin' to make Straif think ye were the true King. I let Faeth believe ye were hers because it helped with the subterfuge, and I let Oswald believe he was King because he needed that with a father dead and a mother losin' her mind to the rot and grief. Ye," she looked up at Gabe, "were goin' away anyway. Ye were safe, or so I thought. When yer family came this last time and didn't leave, I had to act."

"So you manipulated Hollie into spying on us," Jer deduced, "making her think it was her idea when it was yours all along. You had to know what was happening here, if we were staying permanently. Right?"

She winked at him. "Ye're a smart one, Jerome Hawthorne."

"Ye set me up?" Hollie questioned, her eyes wide with disbelief.

"I figured ye'd like a little adventure. Why do ye think I taught ye how to turn?"

Hollie looked a little hurt. "I thought ye were passin' along yer magical wisdoms to me."

"Oh, I were. But this time, I had a job for ye, and I couldn't have ye knowin' everything and sayin' something to either Oswald or Gabriel, lettin' on what I knew, or didn't know."

"I wouldn't have said a thing!" Hollie cried, her green eyes flashing.

Dame Hazel patted her hand. "Just like ye didn't say anything to Oswald about the cloak?"

Hollie looked a little sheepish. "That was an exception?"

Dame Hazel laughed. "More like the rule, Chatterbox."

"Oh, all right. So why did Gabriel see me as an ugly baby and the rest did not?"

"That were yer own fault. Ye forgot he'd already seen ye when he came into the forest as a wee one. He had an imprint of yer true self in his mind, and that sort of knowledge makes the magic go bad. A sort of alarm bell to keep ye from trickin' yer friends."

Hollie made a face. "I wasn't tryin' to trick a friend. I was tryin' to get information."

"And the cloak."

"I couldn't help that. It called to me. And besides, I gave it back."

"But what made you pick me, Dame Hazel?" Gabe interrupted. "How did you know I could do this stuff? Or did you make me do all of it with your magic?" He didn't quite believe it had been her magic, didn't want to believe, actually, but he had to know the truth.

"Ye did it yerself, Gabriel. I saw what ye could do when Oswald took ye. He transformed, and ye did it, too. Just copyin' him. Ye liked it, what ye could do. It didn't scare ye in the least."

So he truly was a Dryad. "So why was I scared of the forest?"

"I made ye scared so ye wouldn't wander inside. Ye weren't the King, but Straif thought ye were. And I knew there were something special about ye that would be needed later. I could sense it. And I were right."

"So Oswald truly is the King?" Gabe asked warily, still trying to make sense of all that he'd heard.

"I'm sorry, Gabriel," she said softly. "Liabreg started all this when he changed over a human. Introducin' her blood weakened all those who came after, allowing the sickness to creep in. When Bruce Holt changed over, his transformation was the trigger that set off the worst of our illness, and made Straif into what he became, though he wasn't a good spirit before." She shook her head. "I brought ye into this, Gabriel, and I'm sorry for that. This was not yer battle."

"He was my ancestor, too," Gabe answered. "So I'm glad I could help. And it all turned out in the end, right?"

"But ye should be King!" Oswald cried, his brow furrowed with guilt and worry. "I did ye wrong, and I don't deserve the title. *I* brought ye into this, not Dame Hazel. I'm so sorry, Gabriel! I've ruined yer life."

Gabe laughed out loud. "Don't be sorry, Oswald! I'm *glad* I'm not the King! Truly." He clapped the stunned Oswald on the back, then noticed something. "The tree has changed!" Instead of a hawthorn, it was now a mighty oak.

"Really?" Oswald tried to see. "Are ye sure?"

"As sure as I can be, and I'm happy for you." Gabe had never felt so free in his life. "It means you're the one true King, which is the best thing for everyone, including me. Don't you get it? My family is still my family! Though I'll share them with you, of course," he rushed to add. "After hearing Filidh's story, I imagine we're all related anyway." He paused. "There's one thing I still don't get. Why can I eat meat and not turn like the Ko-goks did?"

"Because ye're part human, that's why," Dame Hazel answered shortly, as though she didn't want him to pursue that line of thought. Because it was likely that if he were part human, so were many of the other Dryads in the Forest Immortal. Being part human had come from a violation of the Dryad laws, and few could forget the weakness it had introduced. Straif had likely come from the line of Dryads not happy about having to cross the ocean, and didn't support bringing in human blood. So he would not have allowed his trees to mingle with the 'tainted' Dryads.

Jer's blue eyes widened suddenly. "Wait a minute. If you're part Dryad, Gabe, and you're our real brother, then that means—" He broke off.

"Holy crap!" Kris whooped. "I'm one of you!"

Gabe remembered what Grandma May had told them about their ancestors—that they had come over from Europe under mysterious circumstances. He guessed now he knew what those circumstances were...

But could this be the crime Straif had spoken of? Being forced to leave their homes and their way of life, all because Liabreg had done something he wasn't supposed to do? Being King, he'd gotten away with it, but that didn't make it right.

If all this were true, Gabe felt even more glad that they'd saved the dark ones. It went a small ways toward making things right again.

"How come ye didn't react that way when *ye* found out ye were a Dryad, Gabriel?" Oswald asked dryly, though his brown eyes were sparkling.

Gabe laughed. "I reacted the same way you did when you found out I was King."

"Fair enough." Oswald smiled, then it dimmed as he focused on Dame Hazel. "Tell us what we can do for ye," he pleaded over the sound of her labored breathing.

"Watch over the forest, help Isis along, save the others."

"Isis is no more," he told her, his voice gentle. "Straif burned her, remember?"

"Dame Hazel did that!" Jer yelled, then clapped a hand over his mouth. "I was talking to Aurelia," he went on in a strangled voice. "That's the important thing I had to do earlier—find out how to save the Dryads. She told me that Dame Hazel had done it, but that she must have had a good reason." He glanced back at Aurelia for help and she gave him an encouraging nod. He turned to the old woman. "I'm sorry, Dame Hazel. I didn't mean to blurt that out."

"It's all right, Jerome. It had to be done."

"You really did it?" Gabe exclaimed, horrified. "But why?"

"She asked me to. She knew about what ye needed to do, Gabriel, to save the others. But she was old and sick, and she couldn't risk Straif findin' out and takin' steps to stop ye. She couldn't tell me the specifics, for fear I'd be compromised. It's happened before," she added darkly.

"So we just let ye die?" Oswald cried out.

She nodded, then winced. "Like Isis, I will return. Plant this." She held out her hand; in it was a smooth brown nut. "Through pain comes life," she rasped, struggling to draw breath. "Isis will come back through her remains, as will I, but watch her, help her to forge strong roots. Plant me nearby, and we shall keep an eye on each other, until we're ready to return to human form."

Oswald took the nut from her. "I will," he promised, gripping it tightly in one fist and her hand in the other.

Dame Hazel closed her eyes, shuddered, and went still.

"Through pain comes life," Gabe whispered sadly, and understood. "Take her now," he said to Oswald, whose hands covered his face. "Go to your people and begin again." Oswald nodded, his shoulders still shaking.

"I'll go with you," Kris volunteered. "My leg's feeling better."

Oswald looked up, surprised. "Already?"

Kris smiled sheepishly. "Well, I kinda ate one of those berries, thinking maybe it would help a little. Well, it helped a lot, and now I know why!" He looked so excited.

"We'll go, too," Jer volunteered, his arm firmly around Kimber. "We can help distribute the berries."

Oswald straightened up. "And ye, Aurelia? Will ye join us? Now that I'm King?"

She came to him with a smile. "Oh, Oswald. Did ye think I'd make me choice based on something so silly?"

He stared at her, dumbfounded. "But ye saved Gabriel."

"I couldn't just let him die. Besides, I knew what he was meant for, just as I always knew what ye were meant for."

"And what's that?" he asked, shyly. Oswald shy? Gabe wouldn't have believed it if he hadn't seen it with his own eyes.

"Ye're meant to be with me," she said firmly.

"Ye really choose *me*?"

"It's always been ye, Oswald. Just didn't want to make it too easy on ye."

He threw back his head and laughed, a mixture of joy and relief. "Oh, Aurelia. Ye're definitely the one for me." He stepped forward and hugged her tightly.

"We'll do it together, Oswald," she whispered to him. "Ye won't be alone."

Gabe looked up and saw Faeth staring at the three of them, her eyes wet with tears. He nudged Oswald. "Can you help her?"

Oswald looked up, then parted from Aurelia. Together they turned to face Faeth. "I'll do me best. One of yer berries, one of me acorns? Maybe that'll do it." He beckoned to Faeth. "Come, Mother. We shall not part ways again."

She gasped, a mix of joy and pain. "My wee one," she sobbed, coming to him. Aurelia and Oswald wrapped her up in a hug, enveloping her with love. Her eyes caught on Gabe and she frowned for a moment, then shook her head and returned her attention to Oswald and Aurelia. For whatever reason, she no longer saw Gabe as hers. He just hoped it would stay that way.

Kris picked Hollie up from the bed and carried her to the stairs. "We need to get going, before the sun gets too low." Everyone filed after him, from the young Dryads to Grandma May to Kimber and Jer, arms about each other, and Fiidh chatting to Wildrr about his grand plans for the ravine. Gabe watched them go, then caught Abazi's arm. She stared at his hand in surprise, but didn't pull away.

"We'll be down in a minute," he called. "Maybe you should get something to eat before heading out?"

"Good idea," Kris seconded, his voice echoing up the stairs.

When they were gone, Gabe turned Abazi about to face him. She didn't meet his eyes. "I must look awful," she said.

Gabe studied her. "I don't think I've ever seen you looking more beautiful." He hadn't, especially now that he knew for sure she didn't like Oswald. When the Rogue leader and Aurelia had hugged, Abazi hadn't even flinched. In fact, she looked happy for them. That's when Gabe knew he'd been a fool not to trust her, and that he still had a chance to win her.

She actually blushed. "Geez, Hawthorne! Did something happen to your vision when you nearly died?"

"My eyes are perfectly fine. But I don't want to talk about that. I want to talk about what happened with your mom. I heard you telling the others about her death."

"You heard...*everything*?" She sounded ill.

"I heard you blaming yourself for your mom dying."

She shook her head back and forth. "You don't get it. Remember how I told you I'm not good for people? Well, I'm not. I'm just like my mom. I do bad things, and I disappoint people, and I'm probably going to end up like her. So you need to stay out of my life, Gabe, before I end up hurting you beyond repair." With a sob, she pulled away from him and took off down the stairs.

He watched her go, his heart sinking in his chest. He'd blown it. He should've just died back at the mill, because right now, his reason for living wanted nothing to do with him.

Chapter Thirty-Six

The Rest of Eternity

When Gabe reached the kitchen, he found it full of people, including a couple newcomers. Grandma May had her arm around an older gentleman, who must be Bruce Holt. Though he looked tired, he didn't look ill. The berries had worked on him, and Gabe was glad Kris had shared them with him, even though he'd probably wanted to give them all to Hollie.

Abazi's dad, Mr. Wanibagw, was there, too, and he was hugging Abazi tightly. Mrs. Wistman was doing the same to Kimber. "We were so worried!" she cried, stroking Kimber's hair. Kimber just smiled and hugged her harder.

"We were fine," Abazi insisted, pulling away from her dad. "I'm not going to die like Mom. I'm not that irresponsible."

Mozi looked confused. "What are you talking about, Abazi?"

She sighed. "Mom did something stupid, and I have to deal with the aftermath, that's what I'm talking about. You're so protective of me, Dad. I feel like I'm suffocating!"

The room went quiet, everyone uncomfortable and wishing they were somewhere else. Mozi looked around, not sure what to do. One by one, people looked away, not wanting to add to his distress. Finally, he took a step toward his daughter, his hands out. "Abazi, it's not being overprotective when I don't know where you are and I hear stories that the river has flooded and taken out the old mill." He wiped a hand over his brow. "And really, what does your mother have to do with that?"

Abazi's mouth screwed up. "She has *everything* to do with my whole rotten life! I hate her for leaving me, for doing what she did! I *hate* her!" Her fingers curled up into fists. "And now Gabe is going to think I'm the same as her!"

Gabe stared at her. Where had she gotten that idea? He was shaking his head, about to step forward and straighten her out, but Mozi was talking again. "But the accident wasn't her fault, Abazi. Or yours."

Her eyes teared up. "How could it not be my fault? I was a spoiled brat! I wanted ice cream and she died fetching it for me!" She wiped away the tears dripping off her chin, looking both miserably guilty and furious at the same time. "Why did she drink on my birthday, Dad? Couldn't she have held off for one day?"

"Drink? What nonsense is this?" Mozi demanded angrily, which was kind of shocking. Gabe had never seen Mr. Wanibagw angry.

Abazi gave a startled sniff. "She was a drunk, Dad. You don't have to pretend otherwise. She was a stupid stereotype...a drunk Indian!"

Mozi's dark eyes welled up. "No, Abazi! Where did you hear that?"

She gulped. "It's common knowledge. Jake Morrigan teased me about it, years ago. He said my mom was a drunk and had been drinking and hit a tree."

Mr. Wanibagw shook his head, stunned. "Your mother was *not* a drunk, Abazi. In fact, she rarely drank, and certainly not on that day. She was driving to the market to get your ice cream while I tended the grill. I should've gone, but she said I was the only one who knew how to grill the kabobs just right." He wiped away a tear. "Anyway, she was hit by a car on the way home. She died instantly."

Abazi gaped at him. "W-who hit her?"

"Candi Morrigan." He spit out the two names, like poisoned pills. "She was the one who'd been drinking, not your mother. Her husband's firm got her off," he added bitterly.

Gabe felt a fury build up inside him. That horrible woman! She had caused so much trouble for everyone, but worst of all, she'd killed Abazi's mother and gotten away with it. She was a criminal, and she needed to pay the price for what she'd done.

"It's true, Abazi," Mom spoke up, her voice gentle. "Your mother loved you so much and she was not a drinker. She said even a glass of wine made her sleepy and she didn't like not being alert when around you."

Abazi looked around, her eyes wide and scared as though she were trapped. "Really? You're not just saying that?"

"That tart, Morrigan!" Grandma May put in her two cents, her voice disgusted. "She drinks like a fish and thinks no one can tell. The only reason she got off was because the trial was held in Augusta, not here. No one there knew what a lush she was."

"She started drinking in high school and never stopped," Dad explained. "*She's* got the problem, not your mom, never your mom, Abazi."

Abazi gulped. "I-I can't believe it. All these years…"

Mozi swiftly went to her and put his arm around her shoulders. "It's my fault, Abazi. I should've told you, but I was worried what you would do to Mrs. Morrigan. You always were so headstrong…"

"Were?" Kris said loudly. "Still is, you mean."

Abazi glared at him, then she sniffed and laughed. Gabe gave his brother a grateful look. Kris had just sacrificed himself to help Abazi. He really had to remember that about his brother…that he was pretty unselfish. Kris winked at Gabe and Gabe gave him a nod.

"All right," Abazi sighed. "So I might have messed with her brakes if I'd known. I was tempted to do that even before I knew she'd killed my mom. So yeah, I would've done something bad to her, and I wouldn't have regretted it."

The whole room relaxed, like a release of pent-up breath. "So what do we do now?" Jer asked. "Everyone knows Mrs. Morrigan did something wrong, and we can't just forget that. And we're still going to lose our house because we can't pay our taxes, and she'll still try to get the forest taken down."

"I didn't steal all her memory about the forest," Wildrr piped up. He was sitting on the counter, munching on a blueberry muffin. Mom stared at him like he was the most fascinating thing she'd ever seen, which he probably was. "She'll be rememberin' enough to think twice before messin' with us again."

"But the taxes…" Jer persisted.

Abazi smiled. "I was going to tell you guys earlier, but then, well, things started happening." Mozi beamed, obviously in on what she was about to say. "I asked the tribe to donate some of our powwow funds to help you keep your house."

"What?" Mom exclaimed. "Seriously?" She looked absolutely thrilled. "How'd you manage *that*?"

Abazi laughed. "Believe me, it wasn't easy. You can imagine how my people reacted to the idea of giving money to white folk so they can keep their land. Ironic, huh? But anyway, when I explained that your keeping your land was essential to saving the woods, they agreed to do it. Plus, they like your family, so that helped your cause."

"And it gave them a good story to tell," Mozi added with a wink, "an opportunity no good Indian can pass up."

Mom looked a little flustered. "But it's too much! I'm not sure we can take it…"

"Sure you can," Abazi said simply. "It's my revenge against Candi the Killer."

Mom smiled. "Well, in that case, thank you. We'll pay you back...*someday*," she added glancing over at Dad.

"Actually," Dad said, a big grin warming his tired face. "It will be sooner rather than later. I have a job!"

"What?" Gabe exclaimed and Mom stared at Dad in surprise. "When? How?"

He laughed. "I've been working like crazy lately, staying up late, pushing it to the limit. I know I must have looked like hell, and I'm sorry I worried you about that, but it was for a good cause. I didn't want to get your hopes up, so I couldn't say anything. But anyway, the company liked what I did and agreed to hire me for a one-year contract. I can work from home, too."

The whole room exploded into cheers and clapping. "You can stay!" Kimber cried, hugging Jer tight. He hugged her back and lifted her off the floor. She squealed happily.

"I say we celebrate with food!" Kris shouted.

"I agree," Mozi said as everyone mobilized, heading for the refrigerator and cupboards, talking and laughing. Even the Dryads joined in, happy for their friends, happy to be alive. "But first, can someone explain who, or should I say, *what*, all these, um, creatures are?"

Jer stepped forward importantly. "Mr. Wanibagw, Mrs. Wistman, what I'm about to tell you cannot leave this room..."

Seeing his chance, Gabe grabbed Abazi's hand and pulled her down the hall, into Mom's office. Before she could protest, he placed a finger on her lips, then turned and shut the door. "You're not leaving until we work this out."

She crossed her arms, a frown marring her brow. "Work what out?"

"First of all, I'm really sorry about what happened to your mom, and for what you've gone through all these years. It must have been torture for you." She sniffed a little, and nodded. "And if I could get away with it, I'd choke the life out of Mrs. Morrigan. But I don't want to go to jail; I want to be with you. And since I want to be with you, you can't go to jail, either. I know you're still mad at Mrs. Morrigan, and I totally get that because she wasn't even my mom and I want revenge, but I need your promise you won't do anything foolish."

She rolled her eyes. "You're such a buzz-kill, Hawthorne."

"*Promise.*"

She sighed. "Fine. I promise I won't murder her. But I will make sure she's driven out of this town. She will pay for what she's done. Her and her whole skanky family."

"Jen's not a bad kid."

Abazi's eyes went fiery. "I promised not to kill Candi, but I said nothing about her daughter."

"All right, all right." Gabe held up his hands, laughing. "I just had to be sure."

"About what?"

"That you really do like me."

"I do like you, Gabe. More than that," she muttered under her breath.

"I love you, too, Abazi," Gabe said, feeling as though his heart was going to burst through his chest.

"But I'm ornery and bullheaded and I make really bad puns. You'll get to know the real me and stop liking me." She stood perfectly still and tense, as though preparing herself for a blow she knew she couldn't avoid. "Right?" She peered up at him.

"I don't think that's even possible," he breathed, meaning every word.

Her shoulders slumped in relief. "Really?"

"Really."

Tears filled her eyes. "You're such a sap!"

He smiled. "Good one." He wiped away a tear slipping down her perfect cheek. "Remember that song you taught us to use as a signal last fall? About the man who loses his love and searches for her forevermore?" She nodded warily. "Well, I don't want to be that guy. I don't want to lose you and then have to search for you for the rest of eternity. I want to keep you right here, with me, right now."

Then he did something he'd wanted to do for a while. He took her in his arms and he leaned low to kiss her lovely lips. And the kiss was perfect. And the one after that was perfect, too.

The door flung open. "Ewww, get a room, you two!" Kris yelled.

"I thought we had one," Gabe replied dryly.

"Come on. You're going to have to drive the truck. Mom won't let me, even though I did an awesome job driving it to the mill. It only quit on me because it overheated, and that doesn't count as bad driving." He beckoned. "Hurry!" Then he disappeared.

Gabe peered down into Abazi's gorgeous brown eyes. "More kisses later?"

She gave him a mischievous smile. "Definitely."

Together, hand in hand, they strode down the hall, into a better future. Not perfect, just better.

And that was enough...for now.

Epilogue

Mom and Dad accepted the news that their son was a Dryad much better than Gabe thought they would. They had a lot of questions and even asked for a quick demonstration. When he turned his finger into a twig, they actually clapped in delight. Mom warned him she'd probably be looking at him funny once in a while, but it was only in observation, not disgust. Dad asked if Gabe could use his powers for sports, then laughed, claiming he was only kidding. Kind of.

After their celebration meal, Grandpa Hawthorne happily ferried them about the woods in his truck, with Oswald directing the trees to clear a path for him and Gabe. He said it made him feel young and useful again, and who could resist an adventure like this?

They buried Dame Hazel and held a moonlit planting ceremony, where they said their lighthearted goodbyes to her. They knew she'd be back again and Gabe was looking forward to seeing a young Dame Hazel leaping and bounding about the woods. Or whatever it was hazel trees do. After the planting, Grandpa used his flashlight to help them find Isis's new shoots. Amidst her burned remains, they looked like little green emeralds on black velvet. Isis was being re-born and Gabe felt like he was witnessing a miracle.

Afterwards, they drove around, tracking down stray Ko-goks and force-feeding them berries or the tannin-laden acorns the oaks could now produce in mass. They even saved Dorn, who was still annoying after his transformation, but not evil like his dad and brother. When he finally realized *he* was in charge of the blackthorns, just like he'd always wanted, with no Feltry to knock him down, he actually rose to the challenge, going on to build a great legacy for himself and his kind as protectors of the forest. And after Jer threatened to chop him down while he was hibernating during the Freeze, he gave up on his pursuit of Kimber, eventually finding a blackthorn to adore. After a few years, and his love's influence, he even stopped being so annoying, which was great cause for celebration by the citizens of the Forest Immortal.

The Morrigans picked up and left not long after that day, known afterwards by those involved as the time of the Meltdown. Abazi spent her birthday ensuring the Morrigans were no longer welcome in Ranger. She said it was the best birthday present she'd ever gotten, and she even agreed to let Gabe take her out to eat afterwards to celebrate. In the days to follow, she became a lighter person, less weighed down by her guilt and anger. But she kept her sarcastic wit fully sharpened, and Gabe was glad. He didn't want to be with someone who was too sweet; he wanted to be with Abazi. He'd never tell her that, though, at least not in those words. Once Abazi learned the truth about her mother, she got more involved in tribal affairs, eventually becoming a great advocate for her people and a proponent of preserving Aberaki traditions. Like Gabe, she not only accepted her roots, she embraced them, and the both of them were the better for it.

At about the same time the Morrigans disappeared, so did the Briar Borders. One day they were there, the next they were gone. Apparently they weren't needed anymore. Gabe would probably never know who'd put the protective hedge there—Dame Hazel, maybe, to keep him out, or Faeth, to keep him in. Or had it been his own mother? He'd seen her looking up at the great border the day before it had disappeared and her lips were moving, as though she was talking to it, telling it that its job was done. But that couldn't be possible, could it? Well, why not? She knew a lot about trees, easily accepted that Shambolic Stream moved, and besides, he had to get his Dryad-ness from somewhere. Why not her? Or maybe he'd gotten it from both sides of the family. It would explain his last name—Hawthorne. And weren't there May trees, too? The question was, did she know she had Dryad in her? Maybe she'd always sensed it, in him, in herself, in Dad. Maybe. He'd probably never know, but he was okay with that. A little mystery in life is good for a person.

Bruce Holt produced the deed to the forestland, which he'd hidden in Huath's diary. He'd changed over, he explained, because of his bad heart, as Kimber had guessed. The riddles had come from him, of course, written in hopes of getting them to do what he, in his sickness could not...fetch the deed he'd left at the May house just before he'd changed over.

He and Grandma were dating now, and Grandma seemed really happy. Apparently Bruce Holt had always loved her, and when the woods began to go bad, he'd created the protective area around the cottage, to keep her safe. Bruce's return to Ranger, as you can imagine, caused quite a stir, but people got over it soon enough. There was a lot to do, cleaning up the mess from the flood and reclaiming the old road that ran through the forest. Oswald was able to direct the trees to make way, so that none were lost. The townsfolk didn't question how this happened, which made Gabe wonder just how many of them were descendants of the Dryads who'd sailed on the wind across the sea.

Grandpa Hawthorne made good money directing the operations, and so did Grandma May, who set up a stand near the clean-up and road building to sell food, along with her jams and herbal concoctions. In the coming years, the new road brought an influx of tourists, just enough to boost the economy, but not so many as to spoil the town. Agnes Deacon, upon her return, unapologetically seized the reins and tackled this new project with as much enthusiasm as she had the old one. When Gabe and Abazi went off to college two years later to study forestry management, upon their return old Aggie welcomed them with open arms.

Chief Mara, eager to prove he wasn't his sister, became the forerunner for protecting the forest. He grew more relaxed and content, too, which showed in his new demeanor and wardrobe (Kimber's mom helped him with that). Gabe was glad for him, and so was Kris, who was able to avoid two tickets for speeding when he first started driving, legally, that is. The chief felt so bad about Gabe being accused of kidnapping Jake, and for the tax bill scandal (he returned the amount they overpaid, with interest), that he was always lenient on them. For their part, the boys tried not to take too much advantage of his guilty conscience.

Wildrr stopped by the house on occasion and was always good for stirring up some sort of celebration. Sometimes he brought the Lady in human form and she would sing while Wildrr played his panpipes. He seemed to come whenever things were growing a little too hectic, too detached from the important things in life, and he calmed them all down, relishing his role as a strange sort of uncle to the family.

Filidh also came and went whenever the mood struck him. He'd taken over the ravine, which lasted about a week, then decided it was too boring being all alone and not having anyone to fight with, so he invited the Rogues back. Oswald reported that there was some big blow-up at least once a month, which he considered good training for handling crises, a common occurrence for a king. He'd learned it wasn't smart to get complacent, as the Dryads once had, allowing Straif to gain too much power.

"Not on my watch," he'd taken to quoting with great relish after hearing Kris say it. He liked human sayings and often visited with Gabe at night, after the others had gone to bed, to brush up on the latest lingo, or just to talk over any difficulties he was having. Mom and Dad sort of adopted him as a fourth 'son' and spoiled him whenever they could. Gabe was no longer jealous or worried they'd pick Oswald over him. Oswald liked the attention, but was always glad to return to the forest. He said it was where he belonged.

He and Aurelia ruled the forest together, and the difference in it was immediately apparent. The birds and small animals returned, the moss lost its grip and flattened out to a reasonable height, the Bittersweet was wiped out, and there were saplings everywhere. Sometimes when Gabe went out to the Forest Immortal, just to reconnect, he'd close his eyes and he could hear the laughter all around him, like little children playing tag and he was home base. It was a comforting sound.

Faeth never quite fully recovered her wits, but enough of them to no longer be afraid, and to take joy from seeing Oswald and Aurelia create a new family of Dryads.

Determined to learn the secret of how to become a Dryad, Kris had gotten hold of Huath's diary from Bruce Holt and was slowly translating it. Apparently Dryads aren't the best record keepers, especially those who weren't terribly literate as humans. Bruce Holt wasn't any help. After being sick, he couldn't remember what he'd done or how he'd cracked the code, so to speak. But if anyone could figure it out, it would be Kris. Besides, he had Hollie to encourage him…or poke at him, depending on her mood. After all, she still had the note he'd left in her cave, telling her she was the 'sweatest' girl in the world. Yes, he'd misspelled, sweetest, and Hollie vowed she'd never let him hear the end of it. They spent a lot of time together, and when Kris went off to college, Hollie cried for three days straight. It's said that her tears started several new seedlings.

But like Gabe, Kris knew he'd be back. He was determined to make a living in Ranger so Hollie wouldn't have to leave the forest. He planned to market the Shaker, his blueberry- picking machine, and he also wanted to be a famous writer and illustrator. He already had one great idea for a 'fantasy' graphic novel…

Jer wasn't as interested in becoming a tree. He was more interested in hanging out with Kimber and going for long horse rides through the woods. When they weren't riding, they were cooking up something. Literally. Their plan was to attend a culinary school and return to Ranger and open its first high-end restaurant. Gabe wasn't sure how successful it would be, being that most people in Ranger weren't exactly gourmets, but he wished them luck. Jer was a very determined person, and Kimber matched him in determination, though she had a calming influence that kept him from losing his mind when he reached too high.

Mom finally published her first book, a memoir about Dad's illness and having to start over again on an old farm in Maine, and it actually sold reasonably well. She, of course, had to leave out the part about the

Dryads, but there were hints if you knew where to look. She also took over Ronald Pruspin's position at *The Ranger Rag*, and at first, subscriptions dropped by twenty percent because she refused to gossip. But then people started to hear about themselves and their children doing good things in the community, and that, along with Mom's sense of humor, increased subscriptions by forty percent.

Dad continued getting work from the company that had first hired him, and his recovery from transplant surgery progressed quickly after that. He began lifting weights again, and put on weight, too, and he and Mom started going out on dates. He'd never be the way he was before the surgery, but he was getting along, and sometimes that's all a person can hope for.

Mozi finally proposed to Kimber's mom, Mrs. Wistman (a.k.a. Beth), and they got married the following spring. The ceremony took place in the forest, amid a storm of flower blossoms provided by Gabe. It was a great celebration, though Wildrr and Filidh got tipsy on too much dandelion wine and ended up nearly drowning in Shambolic Stream. Gabe plucked them out and left them to sleep it off up in a tree. He wished he could have seen their faces when they awoke, a hundred feet up in the air.

This wasn't the end of their troubles, but all in all, knock on wood, things were much better for the Hawthorne family. Gabe had even come to fully accept his tree-ness. Reading Mary Webb's poems had helped him immensely and he owed her a debt of gratitude. He wasn't sure which of his ancestors had left her book on the shelf, likely one of Grandpa May's parents, but it was a great comfort and went a long way toward helping him accept his 'other' side.

It also helped knowing that his family, and likely most of Ranger, was just as nutty as he was.

Ha!

As Abazi would say, "What a-corny joke. You're barking up the wrong tree if you think I'm going to laugh at that."

And then she would laugh at that. Because she loved Gabe, and Gabe loved her back.

Or loved her *bark*. Oh, they were getting really bad now. Time to make like a tree and leave...

But I'll be back, Gabe thought happily. *I'll be back*.

Mary Webb

Mary Webb (1881 – 1927) was both a poet and romantic novelist. Born in England, she set the majority of her work in the wild and beautiful Shropshire countryside. She apparently developed Graves' disease when she was twenty years of age, a thyroid disorder which gave her considerable discomfort and likely shortened her life. From her disease, she developed great empathy for those who had any sort of difficulty that made them different, and which made them suffer as a result. In 1912, she married Henry Webb, but it was not a happy marriage. Eventually, Mary left Henry and moved to their country home, Spring Cottage, to live alone. Not long after her move, she died at the young age of 46.

The poems and essays used in this novel were derived from Mary Webb's book, *Poems and The Spring of Joy* (1929), published by E.P. Dutton & Company, Inc. Mrs. Webb also published several novels, two of her better-known works are *Gone to Earth* and *Precious Bane*, both made into movies.

When I started writing *The Forest Immortal Saga* trilogy (or treelogy, as my sister suggested calling it), I didn't know about Mary Webb's works. When I came across them while writing book three, I was amazed at how much her words connected to the books' themes…the beauty and power of nature, the wonder of trees, the preciousness of spring and rebirth. I was also surprised to find so many references to hawthorns, the starring tree in the trilogy. Sometimes I'm amazed at how connected we are in this world. I can easily imagine that if each individual put down roots, over time, all our roots would weave together, forming one big web (or should I say Webb?), as though the whole world was holding hands.

I feel privileged to have read Mary Webb's works. You can find them on the Internet, or do like I did, and track down a paper copy of her works. She is a talented poet, and I feel grateful and privileged to have discovered her.

I'll leave you with one last poem...

Green Rain

Into the scented woods we'll go
And see the blackthorn swim in snow.
High above, in the budding leaves,
A brooding dove awakes and grieves;
The glades with mingled music stir,
And wildly laughs the woodpecker.
When blackthorn petals pearl the breeze,
There are the twisted hawthorn trees
Thick-set with buds, clear and pale
As golden water or green hail –
As if a storm of rain had stood
Enchanted in the thorny wood,
And, hearing fairy voices call,
Hung poised, forgetting how to fall.

~Mary Webb

About the Author

When author, Kristina Schram, was growing up she wanted to be a star. When that didn't turn out quite like she expected, she turned her mind to achieving other goals: Earning her Ph.D. in Counseling Psychology, working as an Artist-in-Residence at local schools, being a free-lance editor and reader, coaching parks & rec basketball, protecting the earth through recycling and using green products, and publishing her first novel, a YA fantasy called The Chronicles of Anaecor: The Prophecies.

Knowing what it's like to struggle with self-doubt and lack of confidence, her biggest dream (in addition to owning a castle) is to stamp out low self-esteem for everyone, especially young people. She lives in beautiful, wooded New Hampshire with her husband, three boys, and various pets, and can also throw a tomahawk, if need be. One of her favorite things to do is walk with her dog in the woods, where she searches for the impossible around every corner. Sometimes she finds it.

For more information on Kristina Schram, feel free to make a trip to her website: www.kristinaschram.com. She's also on Facebook, Twitter, and Pinterest.

Other Books by Kristina Schram

The Chronicles of Anaedor: The Prophecies (Book One)

 Strange things happen to fifteen-year-old Lavida Mors. Maybe that's why her father sends her to Portal Manor, a mysterious family estate she never knew existed. Lavida quickly discovers that not everything at Portal Manor is as it seems when she stumbles across a secret passage to a hidden world—Anaedor. Long ago, humans drove the Anaedorians, a civilization of magical and strange beings, into the dark world of huge caverns, frigid rivers, and bottomless pits deep within the earth. Malevolent forces, led by the evil Malvado, seek to control all of Anaedor, but an ancient prophecy tells of a hero who will save them from destruction. While trying to escape the dark realm, Lavida must battle overgrown leeches, survive a poisoned arrow, and outwit a giant, all while trying to convince the hopeful populace of Anaedor that she is not the savior they believe her to be.

The Chronicles of Anaedor: The Return to Anaedor (Book Two)

 After escaping from Anaedor, fifteen-year-old Lavida Mors starts a training course with her guardian, Mrs. Keeper, in hopes of improving her magic skills before the dreaded Malvado returns. But while trying out a new spell, something awful happens, and she vows never to do magic again. When an unexpected discovery forces her to return to Anaedor, she is faced with her most terrifying challenges yet. Strife reigns in the hidden underground world as lootings and burnings break out, and numerous enemies conspire to capture Lavida, fight her, even kill her. Without magic, how can she possibly flee from dragons, escape the Goblins, outwit the ruthless Frio, and fight a duel with a young rebel intent on proving she's not the One? Time is running out. If Lavida doesn't learn to trust herself and her skills, a series of catastrophic events will ensure that she and her friends never make it out of Anaedor again.

The Chronicles of Anaedor: The Lost Ones (Book Three)

Sixteen-year-old Lavida Mors is in for a long, hot summer. With no way into Anaedor, the Lost Ones seeking refuge at Portal Manor are taking over the house, creating havoc and misery. Lavida is overwhelmed trying to keep up with her chores, learning magic, and fighting off the Pixies— tiny creatures who have made it their mission to harass Lavida at every turn. Meanwhile, unbeknownst to the residents of Portal Manor, the AAK is hard at work opening a Portal to the Upland. They are successful at last, and the twins, Loria and Darian, on the run from Malvado, and the AAK leader, Trey, manage to make it through the opening only to have it collapse behind them. With no way back into Anaedor, they are forced to take refuge at Portal Manor. As they try to settle into this strange new life, tensions between the humans and the Anaedorians grow, creating rifts between Lavida and her friends. To make matters worse, Frio, Amoral Hunter Leader, is hiding out in the Upland, and when he goes after Lavida, he starts in motion a series of events that could end up costing Lavida her life.

The Chronicles of Anaedor: The Uprising (Book Four)

In this final book of the Anaedor series, sixteen-year-old Lavida Mors is placed in grave danger when a group of young Anaedorians infiltrates the Upland. Their orders are to eliminate the evil one, whom they believe is Lavida, and then launch an Uprising to take over the Upland. Disguising themselves as humans, they befriend the unwitting Lavida and her friends, allowing them easy access to Portal Manor. Darian and Loria, Blendar twins and Lavida's friends, and Trey, ex-AAK rebel leader, have come to the Upland to warn Lavida about the intruders. But before they can, Darian learns something about Lavida's past that turns him against her. Surrounded by betrayal and danger, and faced with an astonishing revelation that makes her question everything about her existence, Lavida feels increasingly alone and afraid. If she cannot convince Darian and the others that she is not the evil being they think she is, she will lose everything to the Uprising.

Mayhem at Nepenthe Manor: A Pandora Belfry Adventure (Book One)

Precocious and morbidly obsessed with death, Pandora Belfry has spent her entire life at Nepenthe Manor, a dark, Gothic mansion also known as the local loony bin. Recently turned fourteen and growing exasperated with her stifling life, Pandora wants two things more than anything else in the world—to make her escape from the asylum, and to get her mom to finally act like a real mom. Until these wishes are granted, she acts as self-imposed ringleader to a wayward posse of inmates. Known amongst themselves as the Secret Six, Pandora and her friends spend their time at Nepenthe Manor stirring up trouble—holding weekly Midnight Meetings to concoct schemes, sneaking into places like the Nepenthe family cemetery and the forbidden attic, and generally doing everything they can to avoid the curse of living a mundane life. But when a mysterious new inmate arrives at the manor, things change for Pandora, and not for the better. In retaliation for a trick she plays on him, the charming and handsome Xavier connives to take over the posse, threatens to divulge one of Pandora's biggest secrets, and refuses to tell her what he did to get himself locked up. This boy is obviously hiding something, and it's up to Pandora to use whatever nefarious means necessary to find out what it is, before he destroys the only world she's ever known.

The Labyrinth of Lunacy: A Pandora Belfry Adventure (Book Two)

Pandora Belfry, along with the eccentric members of her posse, is back, and looking for trouble. The posse's first order of business is to break into the off-limits labyrinth, even though they can't find its door. Against her mother's wishes, Pandora also works to solve the mystery of her father's identity. Perhaps he's a staff member, or maybe he's the stranger haunting the beach late at night. Topping the list of possible dad candidates is the new therapist, Dr. Steele, who keeps popping up in Pandora's life like an annoying, but handsome, nanny. To add to her problems, Pandora's date with the slimy, but oddly fascinating, Dougie Daft, is fast approaching. She isn't sure how to get out of it, or even if she dares to. Her new acquaintance, Giganticus, certainly doesn't want her to go, but if she doesn't, she'll be obligated to Dougie Daft, and that's the last thing any sane person would want... Come join the posse on their latest, a-maze-ing adventure. Just one warning: Watch out for snakes!

I Shall Return: A Paranormal Gothic Romance

Journalist, Lily MacKenzie, is off to the Highlands of Scotland on a newspaper assignment. But in reality, she has another mission in mind, one she desperately needs to keep secret. Her arrival starts off unexpectedly when she encounters Greg Huntington, a stranger who seems to know her even though they've never met. Things grow more peculiar as she gets to know the Derings of Dundeid Castle, the lodging where she's staying. Andrew Dering, the god-like laird, is welcoming enough, but appears to be hiding something. His cousin, Vivian, seems intent on sabotaging Lily's efforts, while another relation, Ophelia, sees Lily as her savior from a mysterious illness. As Lily works to unravel the mystery that set her on her journey, events grow increasingly complicated and dangerous, and she finds herself caught between two very different men. The reason behind her mission makes it difficult to trust either one, but when she finally ends up choosing, things go very wrong, and Lily ends up fighting for her sanity and her very life.

The Wrath: A Paranormal Gothic Romance

When a cryptic letter arrives from Evalina Filmore's two aunts, she travels to England to find out what they want, figuring this will be the chance to experience the romantic adventure she has so often read about in her beloved gothic novels. When she arrives, she finds the eerie mansion, the strange atmosphere, and the adventure, as hoped. But there are troubles. On the train, she meets a man who, upon learning her name, walks away without a word of explanation. Not long after, she passes unharmed through a wood called the Wrath, even though, as she later learns, no one ever has. While in the Wrath, she meets a tantalizing and seductive stranger, one who just might be her gothic hero. But he has a secret. It seems everyone in the village does, including her aunts, and it's up to Evie to figure out what is going on before the Wrath lures her in and never lets her go.

The Battle to Become an Author:
When Great Expectations Go Awry

Are you looking to find an agent and/or get published? Are you a published author frustrated with the whole process? Or have you simply heard the horror stories and are looking for a ray of light before plunging into the fray? In this short booklet, author Kristina Schram discusses how one's unrealistic expectations about becoming an author can contribute to feelings of negativity and isolation. Dr. Schram offers a real-world discussion of this growing issue, humorously incorporating her own experiences throughout. She also offers insights and ways to cope with the increasingly difficult battle to become a published author. Come prepared to challenge your own expectations, to laugh and to cry, and to battle against the forces conspiring to keep you from reaching your writing potential!